The
Burning Woman

Also by Margaret Ritter

Simon Says
The Lady in the Tower
Caroline, Caroline

The Burning Woman

by
Margaret Ritter

G.P. Putnam's Sons
New York

SBN: 399-12310-5

Library of Congress Cataloging in Publication Data

Ritter, Margaret.
    The burning woman.

    I. Title.
PZ4.R615Bu 1979   [PS3568.1827]   813'.5'4   78-23850

PRINTED IN THE UNITED STATES OF AMERICA

For the Teds, Pat, and Ellen.

The
Burning Woman

Chapter One

He came to me from the sea and for many days it was all I knew of him or thought that I might ever know, he was so near to death when I found him. Yet from the first I knew that in some mysterious, magical way I had willed him there. I was sure this nameless stranger was the companion I had waited for, the lover I had longed for in my lonely solitude, that it had been his voice I had heard so often in my mind's imagining.

Even now, all this time afterward, when I awake crying out to him from the shadows of a dark and haunted dream, it is bitter anguish to know I am alone once more. And when sleep will not come, cannot be coaxed, I light a candle against the night, take pen and paper and begin to write of all that was and will never be again. As I write I cannot help but weep, remembering all the golden days of joy and wonder, and I would gladly give as ransom all the diamonds and rubies, emeralds and pearls that he later gave me for one agate that then was mine.

I recall so vividly how it began with the sudden hysterical, piercing scream of a solitary white sea bird who wheeled and circled, crying havoc above the tall, twin

9

rocks at the far end of the beach; the ones the Spanish call the little pillars of Hercules.

The cry shattered the perfect stillness of the clear, rare April morning and as I write these words I can almost see a mirrored image of myself standing by the shore, a wild, free, fearless girl who once was me.

The Mediterranean had stretched out before me like a pane of smooth, sparkling, polished glass that narrowed, diminished, and disappeared beneath the horizon. Above me the sky was a benediction of cloudless blue. The wide white sand beach that margined the water's edge was as immaculate and unmarked by human foot or folly as it must have been on the first day of all creation.

Gone were the fishing boats that yesterday had put into our cove to repair and retar their hulls. Beside them had bubbled a cauldron of pitch and at a distance the women and old men had laid out their nets for mending.

In the afternoon clouds had begun to gather. They had come swiftly, colliding in the sky, then congealed and turned to a sickly black and green.

The fisherfolk, looking up at the dark, threatening sky, had grumbled at the interruption, but fearful for their boats, they had hauled to and sailed away north to the safety of the great sea wall at Málaga.

I had hurried up the cliff to the terrace of our house to find our servants, Maria Luz and her husband, Paco, scurrying about carrying the more vulnerable clay pots of geraniums and nasturtiums to the shelter of the kitchen. Within the courtyard Paco had tethered the donkeys, Sancho Panza and Don Quixote, who strained and pulled against their ropes, their eyes rolling outward with fear.

The chickens had gone early to their roosts, from which no brave cock could crow them out again. Maria Luz, her round cheeks quivering, went to and fro, muttering stark imprecations against unruly, unreliable nature. Here in southern Spain storms were far from ordinary events. They must be met with fear and respect.

For the most part the seasons came and went and my father and I lived a life of even, unbroken tranquility. We, not the weather, were the oddities at variance with our environment. A retired Major from His Majesty's army, a relict of the Peninsular Campaign and his motherless eighteen-year-old daughter.

When my father and I had come here nine years ago we had been the object of much speculation and suspicion. The villagers of Los Molinos had been fearful that we meant them some diabolical harm. It had been difficult to find servants. Maria Luz and Paco had been warned that they would put themselves in mortal peril by going to live in the same house with the one-armed Englishman and his child.

But they had come, at first for the generous wages, and in time they had remained out of love and friendship. Maria Luz had never pretended to be a mother to me, but as that most pitiable of Spanish creatures, a barren woman, she had hungrily and literally taken me to her ample bosom and Paco endeavored to walk in my father's footsteps.

In time my father had earned the trust and affection of all his neighbors. As an amateur herbalist he made up medicines for the villagers from plants he gathered in the hills above the sea. They had no physician of their own and were grateful for his care. But for all his persuasion he could not separate them from their superstitions.

I knew that Maria Luz, who believed herself to be enlightened by her contact with an educated man, had in her apron pocket at this very moment three pebbles that had been blessed by the priest on Good Friday. If the coming storm grew violent, she would fling the stones at turbulent heaven in the sign of the cross and thereby save us all from disaster.

At dusk, just as the rains began, my father came in from the hills. We dined early so that Maria could spend her evening in prayer and Paco with his pipe. In the little parlor, after we had drunk our Turkish coffee, we drew our work tables close to the hearth. A fire of olive wood burned brightly and the tendrils of wild thyme and rosemary that clung to the wood gave out a pungent, pleasant aroma.

Outside the tempest raged out of Africa with such fury

11

it seemed as if Tarik ibn Saud had come again to lay new siege to Spain. All along the coast from Gibraltar up to Malaga the wind shrieked and howled like wailing Berber women. In the sharp streaks of lightning I fancied I saw flashing scimitars cut and rend the sky.

I sat attempting to color in some sketches of herbs and wild flowers, but my mind was not concentrated upon the task. Above the tumult I heard the scratching of my father's quill pen. He was on this, as on every evening, engaged in the writing of a history of the Peninsular Campaign and his memoirs of his long friendship with Arthur Wellesley, now the great Duke of Wellington. He wrote, paused to find the word he wanted, and then wrote on.

Here in our little house by the sea we led a good life. Happily I had been spared the dictates of a nervous spinster governess. My father himself taught me the disciplines of music, mathematics, Greek, and Latin, and then had left me free to learn my other lessons from nature.

The world beyond the schoolroom was my greatest joy. No two days were alike, each was a different adventure. In the mornings I would run down to the sea. I never knew whether I might choose to wander south towards Gibralter or, if the wind was at my back, to walk north towards Malaga.

Beside the sea there was always something to occupy me. I was as busy as a housewife, tidying up the sand and gathering shells. There was always the possibility that I might find an injured sea bird whose wing might be mended before he could fly again. If my father was physician to our neighbors, I was nurse to all dumb things.

My father might know a place in the hills where the wild thyme grew, but I had discovered the caves that honeycombed the cliff in which some ancient man had left a wall painting like a legacy in stone.

I loved to climb the steep rocks above the caves where the lichen and moss formed patterns more rich and intricate than any tapestry hung in a royal palace.

When I came home at dusk Maria Luz often scolded me. She said I ran wild as a mountain goat and that my bare,

12

brown arms and legs would disgrace a gypsy. I knew that she was afraid that I might be lost in the caves or fall on the sharp rocks, yet I laughed at her fears. Not to be heartless or rude, but in those days I was as reckless and headstrong and blind to danger as all young things who have never known fear.

In the long evenings while my father was busy with his writing, when I had tired of sketching I would sometimes turn the pages of the illustrated magazines that he had sent out to him from England. I saw in them pictures of English girls of my own age. Their hair was tortured into painful curls. Their heads were covered in absurdly shaped bonnets tied with silken ribbons. My own hair hung loose to my waist and I had only a kerchief for my head.

Their gowns were so gathered and puffed that their arms and bosoms looked swollen, and I counted myself lucky to wear only the simplest and most comfortable of dresses.

Even less to my taste were the illustrations of peacock-proud London dandies and their ladies tripping out a quadrille at an exclusive club called Almack's. The men's necks were grotesquely stretched by starched cravats and the ladies looked as silly as simpering sheep mindlessly skipping down a shambles.

No, London was not for me, nor England, where my father said it rained all the time. Here when it rained I could hold up my face to heaven and stand until I was drenched to the skin. In England I would surely be sent to Bedlam for such behavior.

And yet for all I would not have exchanged my life for any other, there were times when I wandered along by the sea or climbed the cliff that I had wished for a companion, a friend with whom I could have shared my world of beauty.

And at last one day, out of my heart's necessity, I had begun to speak my thoughts aloud. It was a drowsy afternoon when I had swum far out to sea and back again to lie beneath the sheltering thatch of the beach hut. The world was all still and warm and silent save for the pull of the sand and water and I had heard myself say aloud, "Listen, do you hear? The sands are singing in the shallows." And from the air, because I willed it, I imagined that I had heard his voice answering me.

"It is not the sands you hear, Catherine, but mermaids singing in the sea."

That is how our first conversation began and I did not then, nor do I now, think of it as odd or unnatural that I should talk to him whenever we were alone or that he should answer me, for I was sure that one day he would come to me and that my dream would be made reality.

And so on that stormy night, as I sat in the parlor by the fire musing, dreaming on my own, my true love, I was startled when suddenly the storm invaded the room; the wind, howling louder than before, had gusted down the chimney, and sent grey ash swirling out thick upon the hearth.

My father glanced up as if to reassure me there was no danger when he was near and I could not help thinking once again that we were for all the world like Prospero and Miranda on their island. We had often made a joke of our likeness to those two isolated characters and hoping it would amuse my father, I spoke Miranda's opening lines of dialogue.

"If by your art, my dearest father, you have put the wild waters in this roar, allay them. The sky, it seems, would pour down stinking pitch. . . ."

He smiled in recognition of our old game. And when I had finished Miranda's speech he replied, "I have done nothing but in care of thee, my dear one, thee my daughter, who are ignorant of what thou art." Then, stopping short, he frowned and sighed. "I wonder, Cat, if that is true?"

He never called me Cat unless he was serious, but always Catherine, after my mother.

"I wonder if it is true that I have done all I could for you? It might be better for you if we had stayed in England, despite everything." He paused and then continued. "There you would have grown up with girls your own age and taken your place in society. Perhaps I've cheated you."

"No," I protested, "I should hate to be dressed like a sheep, mewed up in hot, stuffy rooms. I'd miss the sea and being free to go where I like. I'd die of boredom if I were in England sitting on the edge of little gilt chairs simpering over tea cups." My father looked away into the fire.

"England is your true home, Cat, your rightful inheritance." He did not turn again to meet my eyes. It was as if he meant to evade or deny some statement he had not yet made. Once again I felt the strange hesitation that always came when he mentioned England, and perhaps because in that moment we were especially close, drawn together against the storm, I might have been bold enough to ask him some further questions, but I did not want to make him unhappy. I knew that if the mystery had to do with my mother it would sadden him to speak of her. He had loved her with all his being, loved her as he had never loved another, not even me.

So rather than tax him I rose, and saying I was tired, gently kissed him on the forehead and said goodnight. His hand reached up and touched my shoulder with a kind of caress, but he did not look up at me again.

That night I lay in my lonely, narrow bed listening to the howl of the wind and the hard raindrops pelting like pebbles flung against my window. I lay waiting for someone, something for which I had no name.

In the morning when I woke it was late. The sun was well up and shining. My father had already gone out.

When I had made my breakfast I took my cloak and walked down the cliff path towards the sea. The air was so still, in contrast to the tempest of last night, that when a stone dislodged beneath my sandal it fell thundering down the cliff face as if it were an avalanche.

At the edge of the sea I stood for a long time, unwilling to step upon the sand for fear I would destroy the crystal perfection of its surface.

And so I stood until the scream of the sea bird broke the spell with a cry that was to change all that I had ever been. With that cry I knew, as one knows in a dream, that the storm had only been a portent of things to come, that the bird was a harbinger who bore tidings, a messenger who summoned me, and I began to run, my cloak swirling out behind me. I ran swiftly and surely, for I knew that I was running toward my destiny.

As I drew near the twin rocks at the end of the beach I thought I saw a shape between them. Then, as the shape blurred and altered within my line of vision, I became fearful that it might be some half-formed creature from the depths of the sea, or more terrible still, a dying dolphin. Here once we had found a poor, beached creature who had been washed up and pinioned on the rocks, unable to return to its own element. It had looked at us with such sad, beseeching eyes that I had wept in pity for its plight.

On and on I ran, more swiftly than before, and then I stopped, transfixed before the jagged rocks. There between them lay the figure of a man. His body was covered with a thin layer of fine white sand. He was so motionless that he might have been mistaken for a marble statue, one of the Greek gods in my schoolbooks dislodged from the halls of Olympus.

One hand was extended towards me, as if in supplication, the other lay palm down, the nails dug deep into the sand, as if his last conscious act of will had been to cling to this wild, inhospitable shore.

As I knelt down beside him I was sure that this was indeed no god but a cruelly wounded mortal man. Beneath the crystal surface of the sand I saw the cuts upon his back, darkened by ugly welts of congealed blood. He had been so savagely thrown between the rocks that he had nearly been flayed alive. Whatever costume he might have worn, all that remained were the tattered remnants of small clothes to cover his nakedness.

Recovering from my first shock of discovery, I perceived that there was some wretched disharmony in the attitude in which he lay, and saw with sickening clarity how one of his legs had been wrenched and dislocated from its socket.

I heard myself cry out in panic to think that he might already be dead and that I had come too late to save him. Death had ever been my enemy. Death had taken my mother and I had been too young and too helpless to forbid him. Now that I was older I did not intend to lose to death again.

Yet I could see no sign of life, no rise and fall of breath. I gathered all my courage and brushed back the curls from his forehead. The wet, gritty powder of the sand fell from the heavy locks and I saw his face. It was bruised and swollen, yet battered as he was I could not but wonder at the traces of such beauty. Never before in my life had I seen such beauty in any man's face.

With trembling fingers I touched his temple. He was cold and clammy. From his chilled and marbled flesh I could feel no answering pulse and then, perhaps because I wished it, I thought I felt a little flickering of life. Even with this small hope to sustain me I did not know what I could do for him. I could not carry him, he was too great a weight for me. I must have help and so I did all that was then possible. I covered him with my cloak and ran back the way that I had come crying out as shrilly and hysterically as the sea bird for someone to help me.

By the time I reached the foot of the cliff Maria Luz and Paco were at the top of the path hurrying down towards me.

I sent Paco back to fetch a blanket from the house so that he and I might make a litter to carry the wounded man up the cliff. I ordered Maria Luz to run up into the hills to find my father and tell him he must come at once and make ready his chest of medicines, for there had been a dreadful accident.

Between us Paco and I, more by our necessity than our strength, managed to carry him up the cliff and into the house. By the time we arrived Maria Luz and my father had already prepared a bed in the small spare room, and beside it, on a little table, was my father's open case of medicines.

Paco and I deposited our burden and opened the blanket to reveal its pitiful contents. Maria Luz drew back and crossed herself at the harrowing sight before her. Paco, exhausted by his labors, muttered that we had done all for nothing, for the man must surely be dead.

"He is not dead," I heard myself say sharply.

17

He could not be dead. I would not have it so. I had waited for him, longed for him to come to me. I would not let him die, not before I had heard his voice, not before we had come to know each other.

My father said nothing. He was as pale as death himself. Upon his face was an expression of consuming pity. I knew that he felt compassion not only for the man who lay before him but for the remembrance of himself as he once had been—a wounded captive dumped out upon a French surgeon's bloody slab. He had been helpless in the hands of a doctor who had neither laudanum enough to keep him from his conscious agony nor skill enough to save his shattered arm. He had been hostage to an enemy who was too inept or indifferent to probe for the musket ball that was still lodged near his heart.

In that moment I knew that I must take command, that I must issue the orders if my patient was not to die. He must be stripped and cleansed. No particle of sand must be left in any wound to inflame and mortify. I must begin the work, and now.

My father did what he was able. He had learned to compensate skillfully for the loss of his arm.

It was painstaking work. Each wretched rag had to be pulled and stripped away. With cotton wool and water we blotted away every grain of sand from the wounds. Then they had to be purified with a tincture of herbs and alcohol, and salved with healing ointment.

Maria Luz scolded all the while. She said that no proper Spanish girl would be permitted to see a naked man. But I ignored her. There was too much to be done to pretend to false modesty.

It was while I was finishing up the salving of his wounds that I noticed the ring on his left hand. It was a crested bloodstone set in gold. As I turned his hand to look at it more closely I saw that the ring was broken and the sharp edges of the band were embedded, cutting into his flesh. And more than this, all along the palm and halfway up his forearm were the scars of recent burns.

"Look," I said. "Look at this."

"The burns have healed," my father said, "but the scars are still tender. They cannot be more than three or four months old. Put some ointment on them and cut away the ring."

When I had done so and handed my father the ring, I noticed that he stared at it while I finished treating the last of the wounds.

"The poor devil," he said. "If it be he, what in God's name was he doing here?" I was so anxious to finish what I was about that although I saw my father put the ring into his waistcoat pocket, I forgot it and his words until long afterward.

When we had done all we could for his wounds, then came the business of setting the leg into its socket. My father was our guide. He felt along the hip, looking with his sensitive fingers for its exact, original location. At his command Paco and I applied the needed pressure, and at last we felt the hip slip back into proper place. Although my father felt sure the ligaments were stretched and perhaps torn, he decided against binding it up for fear the bandages might irritate the wounds. Then all that was left to do was to turn our patient gently onto fresh sheets. At his feet and on either side we placed three bolsters over which we laid a coverlet like a sheltering tent.

When we had finished, Paco and Maria Luz began to clear away the basins and bandages. My father replaced the medicines in their chest.

Paco shrugged his shoulders and made a long face. "If you want to know what I think, I think we have done all this for nothing. We have laid out a corpse, that is all." I was angry beyond all reason.

"He will live," I said sharply. "You will see. In a few days he will be all right again." And I turned to my father. "He will live," I said. "Tell Paco that I am right."

"I am not God, Cat," my father answered gruffly. "I am sorry, I have done all I can. Now we must wait and see. There will be a fever and if he passes the crisis, then . . ." He sighed. "I have done all that I can do."

I knew I should not have pressed him. His hand was

19

shaking with fatigue. He had used himself beyond his meager reserve of strength.

"You must get some rest," I said firmly. "I will stay, and when the fever comes I will call you." He was too drained and tired to argue with me. He looked at his watch.

"Yes, yes. I think I will rest a while, but you are to call me if there is any change," and I agreed.

When they had gone, I drew up a chair to the side of the bed and began my vigil. I too was tired but I would not, could not leave him. When I had been a child I had sat by my mother's bedside. She had been so patient and uncomplaining that I had not suspected how ill she was. She had said I was too young to be her nurse. She had thought the burden too great for me to bear and she had sent me out to play in the garden. When I had come in again she had gone. Death had taken her and I had not been watching. I would not make the same mistake again. I would not yield up my patient. And I was sure that as long as I looked at him he would live. It was a fiction, a childish fantasy, I knew, but it sustained me, and it was an excuse to gaze upon his face.

During that night I looked so intently and so long that his face was to be forever fixed upon my mind. Even bruised and swollen as he was, his face bore proof of pure and perfect beauty, the kind a sculptor might single out. I could not guess his age. Thirty, perhaps older.

His brow was high, ringed by dark curls. At his temples there were strands of white I took at first to be some unnoticed residue of sand. As I brushed at them I found the whiteness was his own, and I wondered what shock or sorrow had been the cause of it.

His eyes were deepset, his lashes long and dark. His cheekbones were molded high on either side of a nose so classically formed that a noble Roman might have envied it. Yet his mouth, to me, was his best feature. It was wide and shaped in a wing. The lower lip was full and the jaw beneath was square and strong. And as I sat gazing upon such beauty I wondered who and what he might be.

20

In the evening my father came again. He had rested, but he still looked tired. He wanted me to come away and dine with him but I refused, so he sent Maria Luz with some broth and bread and wine for which I had no appetite.

At dusk I reluctantly lit the lamp, masking its shade so that the light would not hurt his eyes. In the dim half-shadows weird shapes were projected upon the ceiling. They were so distorted and misshapen that it seemed a cabal of specters now kept watch with me.

Before he retired my father came again to ask if there was any sign of fever. I said that I had promised I would call him if there was any change. But I spoke with a faint heart, for surely by now the fever should have come. There had been time enough and plenty.

On and on I sat, past the midnight hour, and then against my own will, I dozed and slept. I had no idea of how long I had been asleep when I heard, from what seemed a vast distance, a sound that woke me.

It was a low, blood-chilling moan, a sound made by a soul in fearful, dreadful torment.

In an instant I sprang up and bent over him. In the dim light I saw that he lay just as he had before. His eyes were closed, but now his cheek was flushed and burning hot to my touch. While I had slept he had passed from a region of arctic cold to one of tropic heat. His breathing was rapid and shallow. He must struggle for every breath he took. Almost imperceptibly his lips moved and again I heard him moan. I thought he had spoken some words, but they were so low and indistinct I could not make them out. I bent lower, my ear close to his lips, to catch at any sound, but there were still no words.

Then suddenly, without warning, his eyes opened wide and I found that they were staring into mine. His pupils were large and dark and bright, dilated by his fever. He started, transfixed by nameless terror. I could only imagine what he thought he saw, for he stared as if he looked not at me but into the mouth of hell itself.

Swiftly his hands came from beneath the coverlet and

fastened with superhuman strength about my neck. I would not have believed it possible for a man so ill to find such strength. I tried to free myself, to shake him off, but he held me in a throttling vise and brought me even nearer to him, till his mouth pressed close to my ear, and he whispered fiercely, "Which one are you? For the love of God, which one?"

And then his strength was gone. His grip snapped and he sank back into the delirium from which he had come. His hands loosed from about my throat and I could breathe again.

I stood shaking, still gasping for breath. Whoever, whatever phantom he had imagined me to be, I knew that he had meant me murder.

"Which one are you? For the love of God, which one?" I could make nothing of those words. The only fact that I was sure of was that he had spoken in unaccented, perfect English. As I stood, still shaken from what had happened, my father appeared in the door wearing his dressing gown.

"What is it, Cat? I thought I heard you call." I hesitated, and then I let the moment pass when I could have told him what had happened. Instead I said, "It is the fever. It has come." My father crossed quickly to the bed.

"He has thrown off the cover," he said. "That will never do. We must put some quilts on him, keep him in a sweat until the fever breaks."

For the next hours we worked and watched over him together. He was a restless patient. Sometimes he thrashed about and fought against us. Sometimes he spoke; always in English, but the words were mere fragments and made little sense. He was, my father and I agreed, terrified of fire. He moaned and lashed out against it like an animal trapped in the flames. How odd that he should be so afraid of fire when he had been lost at sea and the burns were old enough to have healed.

At last, just before dawn, the crisis came. The fever broke and he lay inert, as still as death, but sleeping the

blessed sleep of nature, not the fathomless unconsciousness of delirium.

"Can't you give him some medicine, water, something to
make him more comfortable?" I pleaded. My father held
me close to him.

"Believe me, Cat, this sleep is better for him than any
medicine I possess. When he wakes he will be thirsty
enough to drink to your satisfaction."

Our patient slept until noon. My father did not leave
him again, nor did I. The next time he opened his eyes
they had lost their bright and hellish glitter. He looked
first at the ceiling and then at my father and at me. He
frowned as if we were strange creatures who had material-
ized unbidden from his imagination.

"Pray do not be alarmed." My father spoke gently to
him. "You are quite safe. There has been an accident, a
wreck at sea, but you are safe. My daughter Catherine
found you on the shore and we have brought you to our
house. Do you understand?"

He did not speak but closed his eyes again, and his face
contorted as he groaned in pain.

"The pain you feel," my father spoke again, "is from
your hip. It was dislocated. If you will trust me to be your
physician, you will drink this potion."

He opened his eyes again. They begged silently for any
release from all-consuming pain.

"It is laudanum," my father said. "Please drink it." As he
spoke the pain struck again.

And so, like a good and biddable child, he allowed my
father to hold up his head while he drank, and then he
slipped away again to easeful oblivion. I was pleased to see
him out of pain, but vexed to think that we knew no more
about him than we had before.

"You should have asked him who he was or where he
came from." My father gave me a reproving glance.

"He has had a severe shock, Cat. When he wakes again I
am sure he will tell you all that you are so anxious to
know."

23

But my father was wrong. When he woke next I was alone with him and he could tell me nothing. In a faint but steady voice he asked, "Where am I?"

"In Spain, near the little fishing village of Los Molinos." He looked puzzled and bewildered. I continued.

"It is below Málaga and above Gibraltar," and he nodded in recognition. I longed to make my manner as soothing as an elixir. "You must have been at sea when the storm struck."

"I don't remember."

"Perhaps there is someone we might notify. Someone who would be concerned for your safety." For a long moment my patient lay still, and then his mouth twisted wryly, not in pain but in helpless dismay.

"I do not know whom to notify nor would I know what to say to them if I did. You see," he paused and then with a great effort, continued, "I have no memory of who I am or how I came to be here." I tried to speak as calmly as if I had just been told the time of day, nothing more.

"You have had a very bad time of it. I am sure that when you have rested you will remember everything."

But he did not remember, not that day nor the next. His deathly pallor left him. He listened and he spoke with comprehension and understanding, but he remembered nothing of who he was or where he had come from and, curious to tell, he did not seem to care. He appeared unconcerned, as if by forgetting the past a great and tiresome burden had been removed from him.

"You must question him," I said to my father. "You will know what to ask until he remembers."

"No," my father answered brusquely, as if I had made some outlandish suggestion. "I have seen this sort of thing before. It happened to the bravest men after the shock of battle. They simply forgot what was too painful to remember. Do not press him, Cat. He will remember in his own good time."

"Are you sure? Sure that he will remember?"

"Does it matter so much to you, Cat, who he is?" My father looked at me carefully.

24

I did not know what to answer him. How could I tell my father that I knew this nameless stranger was my dream come true? How could I say that in some mystical way I knew that I had willed him here. Now that he had come to me I wanted to know everything about him. It seemed cruel that now he was here I must wait before I could ask him all I so longed to know.

Yet I knew my father was right. It would not be wise to force him to answer any more questions until he recovered.

In the days that followed I set myself to make him well and strong again. I was his constant companion and his faithful, tireless nurse. I fed him until he was able to feed himself, tempting his invalid's appetite with rich broths and succulent egg flans from Maria Luz's kitchen. I bathed him, treated his wounds, and dressed him in my father's voluminous old-fashioned nightshirts. No matter what I did he scarcely spoke a word. He seemed to be detached from the present, not caring where he was or what was done for him. He sat propped up against the pillows, docile and uncomplaining as a rag doll. About him was an air of hopeless apathy, as if he had forever overspent his strength and now was totally bankrupt of all vitality.

I had to coax him to stand. I had to urge him to take his first tentative steps. I supported him, my arm around his waist, his about my shoulders. I knew it must be painful for him but he had to walk again. At least he had to try. I kept at him, forcing him to walk a little more each day, but although he made the effort to please me he remained as disinterested in his progress as I was determined that he should succeed.

When he could sit in a chair with some reasonable comfort I brought soap, towels, a basin of hot water, and my father's straight razor to shave away his growth of beard. It was obvious that I was new to the work. My clumsy efforts to lather his face left almost as much soap in his nose and ears as on his cheeks and chin. Still, I might have inspired some confidence had my hand not been trembling so.

Above the seafoam of the soap his eyes grew merry for a

brief moment. He raised one quizzical eyebrow, looking in mock horror at the sharp razor.

"I trust you are my friend, Miss Rainey, and not my enemy." I felt myself flush, the color rising hotly to my neck and face. I was indeed his friend, had been, was now, and would be forever. If only he could remember he must surely know that, first of all.

"Yes, I am your friend."

"Good, then I will have no fear but leave this business up to you." He closed his eyes to possible slaughter and left me to proceed as best I could.

When I had finished I brought a mirror so that he could see the result. He held the glass before him, staring at his reflection. After a time he began slowly to turn his head from side to side. He looked so bewildered that I knew he had no conscious memory of ever having seen his own face before. He was more of a stranger to himself than to me. At last he handed back the glass.

"Whoever that face belongs to," he said in a low, even voice, "the fellow has an excellent barber."

I saw he had become pale. It hurt me to think that he was unhappy and that such a simple thing as sitting for an hour had drained and exhausted him. As I helped him back to bed a plan began to take form in my mind.

I must get him out of this room. He was recovering much too slowly. Sitting all day in that great white cocoon of a bed he had become a prisoner of his pain and despair. The longer he stayed there the harder it would be for him to return to the world outside. Tomorrow I would begin to set him free. I would take him out of doors onto the terrace where warm sun and pure air would restore some of his confidence and put color in his face.

I was sure it would be good for him, but what he was to wear on his first expedition abroad was a puzzle. My father had assured me my patient's leg and hip were healing nicely, but they still pained him too much to allow him to draw on a pair of trousers. He could hardly be expected to go out of doors in his nightshirt. Then I remembered a Moroccan *djellaba* my father kept in a hall cupboard. This

26

long, flowing, hooded robe could be slipped on over his head. The *djellaba* was an inspiration.

Next afternoon my beautiful patient stood before me clad in Arabian garb. He wore the nomad's costume as if he had been used to it all his life. He was as handsome and splendid as a tribal sheik about to embark on a caravan for Samarkand. I was so proud of him and his noble bearing that I could not wait to show him off.

The whole household had been aware of my plan to get him out of doors, but I had cautioned them not to stare or seem overly curious. As we came out of the house, a triumphal procession of two, I could see Maria Luz hovering discreetly at the kitchen door while Paco peeped over the garden wall. My father was seated in his study window pretending to be busy with his accounts. I was sure they must admire him as I did. To me he could have rivaled the first Hidalgo of the Andaluz, the Duque of Alba himself.

He walked slowly, leaning heavily on his cane. I was on his other side. Only I could know what effort it cost him to make that stately walk. His hand clasped my arm with a grip of iron and the knuckles of his other hand were white as they grasped the cane. Step after painful step he took. I counted thirty-two before he reached the waiting welcome of a high-backed wicker chair. As he sat I heard him sigh with relief and saw the perspiration glistening upon his forehead.

I felt that I had been his torturer, his tormentor. He had only come out because I asked him to. He raised his eyes and looked up at me.

"Are you pleased with me now, Miss Rainey?" He might have read my thoughts and I felt another pang of guilt.

"Yes," I said, "I am pleased with you." There was no need to say that tomorrow I intended to ask even more of him. Yet I wanted him to be well and strong. I did not want him to remain an invalid. I wanted him for my friend, my companion, not my patient. I wanted him to be as he had been when I first dreamed of him, not as he was now—sitting, gazing out to sea.

He stared unblinking for so long that I was afraid he

would be blinded by the glare. I wanted to cry out to him, to draw him back from the edge of certain disaster. But at last he lowered his gaze and what followed was worse still, for he looked in horrified wonder at the scars on his hands and arms. He examined them carefully, then the finger where his crested ring had left its imprint, like a brand seared into his flesh. Then at last, with the aspect of one who is both subject and witness to a great tragedy, he clasped both his arms around his body as if to cradle and comfort himself.

"Was there any trace of my boat?" he asked almost in a whisper.

"No."

"Do you know from what port I sailed or to which harbor I was bound?"

"No."

"Was I alone? Was there anyone else burned in the fire aboard the boat?"

"No," I said, choosing my words carefully. "You had been burned before the wreck. The scars were there when I found you. They were recent, only a few months old, but they had already healed."

He turned to me, and his hood dropped back from his head onto his shoulders. "Why would I have come to this place? What reason would I have had to be here?"

"There was a storm," I said lamely. And to cover my confusion I began to read aloud.

"You have learned your Greek well, Miss Rainey. But I would rather that you had studied metaphysics or the arts of the occult, then perhaps you could tell me who I am and how I am to get home again." I shut the book.

"Would you like some tea?' ' I asked.

"No." He shook his head. "Please help me back into the house. I am very tired."

I did as he asked. I led him limping slowly back again to his cell, his prison, in which he felt more safe and secure than in the sun's bright, self-illuminating light. As I pulled up the coverlet and smoothed at his pillows I determined that tomorrow we must go down to the sea. What the sea had taken from him the sea must restore.

It was at breakfast that I told him what I had in mind. When he understood that I meant for the two of us to walk down the cliff path his face became a continent of disbelief. He did not say so but I knew he thought me mad. Perhaps I was.

We were a curious sight, to be sure. I went first, carrying a large basket filled with towels and food and a blanket. I walked at an angle, one hand holding tightly to his. He came after, very slowly planting his cane as carefully as a mountaineer.

Step by step we made our way to the bottom. There he could walk more confidently out onto the sand. When we arrived at the beach hut I knew he believed that we had come to the end of our long, harrowing journey, but I deposited the blanket in the shade and said, "We will leave the basket here while we swim."

"Swim!" He would have turned back toward the cliff had I not led him forcibly on toward the water's edge.

"I know that you can swim. You would not have got to shore unless you could. Swimming will be the best exercise in the world for your leg. In the water you will be nearly weightless. Moving your leg will take hardly any effort."

I felt the tension in his hand as he tried to draw back. But I would not allow him to stop. At the water's edge he dug in his heels, balking like Sancho Panza or Don Quixote when they were afraid of something in the road ahead. If I had had a carrot or a sweeting I would have bribed him with it.

"You must take off your sandals and your *djellaba*." I spoke calmly, as if I did this sort of thing every day. "The cloth would billow around you like a sail to weigh you down." I saw that he was shocked. He must think me shameless, but I did not care. To prove that I meant to have my way, I stepped out of my dress and stood waiting in my shift. And then, like a boy who, despite his own fears accepts a dare, he lay down his stick, took off the *djellaba*, and hand in hand we waded out into the sea.

We walked out until the water was above our waists and then I turned to him and took both his hands in mine. I told him to let himself float free. I promised that I would hold onto him. That I would never let him go. I did not know at first if he would trust me, but in the end he did as I asked, first floating and then kicking his legs. I kept him at it until at last I saw he was tired and could do no more. Then I led him back to shore again and dried him with heavy towels. While he rested I massaged his hip and leg with sweet oil of almond and while he slept I kept watch over him. The sun was warm, the sand was soft, the day almost as silent and still as the one on which I had found him lying between the rocks. That day I had prayed that he would live and now I prayed that he would be truly well again.

That evening we made our slow way up the cliff, which must have seemed as high to him as the Pyrenees. Perhaps it was because I wished it to be true but I thought he seemed better, not worse, for his experience. I knew I must not stop what I had begun.

Again the next morning we went down to the sea. And the next morning and the next. Each day he grew stronger until at last there came the glorious day when he walked without my help, and without a backward glance he hurried confidently on to the water's edge, then ran until he could dive beneath the surface.

I ran after him and we swam together side by side out toward the horizon. On and on we swam, far beyond the point where I usually would have faltered and turned back. Then at last we stopped, and treading water, turned face to face.

The sun shone down on his head, the drops of water glistening in his hair like dew in a crown of laurel. The bright sun dazzled my eyes till I saw his reflection in the water and in the sky as clearly as if it had been etched into both elements. And more dazzling than the sun was his smile.

There were no words needed from him to say that he thanked me, no words from me necessary to tell him how proud I was of him. Then as we swayed out of our depth we saw something so bright, so blinding in each other's eyes that it made us both shy away, and we turned and swam for the safety of the shore.

That day he dried us both, then placed the towel like a mantle about his shoulders. Together we walked hand in hand toward the shelter of the thatched beach hut. We lay resting side by side, so close together that I could feel the outline of his body. We were wrapped in a timeless quiet of the heart and soul.

"Listen," I said slowly. "You can hear the sands singing in the shallows." And I held my breath, waiting for his reply. "It is not the sands you hear, Catherine," he said drowsily, "it is mermaids singing in the sea."

At first I was not sure that he had spoken or if it had been only my imagination. But then I knew that I had heard him. That he was here beside me, the companion I had waited for, the lover I had longed for, and that I would never be lonely again.

And I lay back, never dreaming how soon his past would become a torment, an obsession that would drive us from this present Eden.

Chapter Two

That night, for the first time, he came to dine with my father and me. When he joined us he had changed from the familiar *djellaba* into corduroy trousers and an open-necked Spanish peasant's shirt with long, gathered sleeves. At his waist was wound a wide red cummerbund. He looked as handsome and daring as a corsair, and although he still walked with a slight limp it now seemed a part of him, as if it were a relic from his past.

It was plain fare that Maria served us, but because he sat across the table from me the simple meal became a feast and the evening a festive occasion. Soon he and my father were as easy together as if they had been old friends. They talked of London and of politics, of plays and the new romantic poets. They talked, and I was content to listen to the sound of his voice.

After dinner they drank their brandy in the parlor instead of banishing me from the table as the ladies were in England. When their glasses were filled and they had settled down in comfort, my father handed him a translation of Homer that had come by the last packet and asked him his opinion of it. I saw my father watching intently as he turned the pages, stopping here and there to read a passage.

"Well, what do you think of it?" my father asked.

"An accurate translation but perhaps too literal, for it often misses the meter."

"Did you learn your Greek at Eton?"

Without a moment's hesitation he replied, "No, at Harrow, sir." Then he looked up in astonishment. "How could I remember the name of my school and all that we have spoken of this evening and yet not be able to remember my own name or how I came to be here?"

Only then did I realize how skillfully my father had been drawing him out in conversation.

"You must not worry about it." My father hastened to reassure him. "By the time that I return I'm sure you will be quite yourself again." Now it was my turn to be astonished.

"Return?" I echoed him.

"Yes. I have some urgent business I must attend to. I leave tomorrow for a week or so." Our guest rose abruptly to his feet.

"Then I will go with you. I must not impose upon your hospitality any longer. I already owe you and your daughter a greater debt than I can ever repay." I felt as if my heart had stopped beating. He could not go, not now when I was sure beyond any doubt that he was the one I had been waiting for. As I tried to think of a convincing argument to keep him, my father spoke.

"No," he said firmly. "You are much stronger, but not yet well enough to travel. I'll make the fullest enquiries about you, of course. As for your being in our debt you are welcome to stay as long as you like. We enjoy your company, don't we, Cat? We've been alone here far too long. Catherine says we've grown like old Prospero and Miranda." I held my breath and after a moment's hesitation our guest looked at me and smiled.

"Then I will gladly stay and be your Caliban." I felt he was as glad to remain as I was to have him there.

My father left the next morning, taking Paco with him.

Always when he had gone before I had missed him sorely, but now I scarcely noticed that he was away. I had my heart's companion for company, and each day was so rich and full of our shared adventures that I did not even stop to wonder where my father had gone or why.

Each hour of those days was spun from gold. I was mazed by happiness. I knew that I and my world had changed, that we were not the same as we had been before he came. This year the flowers were all a brighter color, the sky a more piercing blue. I was so free and lighthearted that I felt almost weightless and to prove that I was more spirit than substance one day I ran down to the beach with my arms outstretched as if at any moment I might take wings and fly. He followed after me until he caught me up, held me for a moment, and to my sorrow let me go again.

But never by the light of the moon nor in the noontime glare of the sun did I ever once believe that it would not always be summer forever. I knew as if it were a proven fact that this was a year without winter and that nothing would ever change.

Yet inevitably there was a change. One morning we looked down from the terrace and saw that the fishing fleet had come back again. It seemed a shocking invasion, an act of trespass upon our private domain. I did not want to go down to the beach while they were there. I did not want to share him with anyone, not even for a few days.

"Today," I said, "we'll go up into the hills."

With bread and cheese tied in a kerchief and a wineskin slung over his shoulder we set off north, walking along the edge of the cliff toward the high rocks. We climbed steadily all the morning, stopping now and again for me to show him the lichen and the moss. I watched him trace out their rich patterns with his long, sensitive fingers. As always, I felt especially drawn to him when he was observing something new. His eyes were so wide with wonder he might have been seeing the world for the first time.

On and on we climbed slowly up the last of the crags until we reached the pinnacle by noon. We ate our frugal lunch sitting on a flat shelf of rock. The wine arced from the *bota* into our open mouths, cooling our parched throats. We savored each morsel of bread and cheese. When we had finished eating we threw out the last of the bread to the sea birds who swooped down to catch the crumbs before they could fall into the sea.

Afterward we lay, our arms pillowed behind our heads, our backs against the sun-warmed rocks, watching the white birds wheeling, circling, flying like brave banners in the cloudless sky. But without shade it was too warm for a siesta. We missed the cool shelter of the thatched beach hut.

"I know!" I said. "I know of a place where it is always cool and shady. I don't know why I've never taken you there before." I scrambled up and hurried down the way that we had come, confident that he would follow me. At a cleft in the tall rocks I turned toward the entrance to my secret cave. The opening was so well hidden behind a screen of thorn bushes that no passerby could ever find it.

"Here," I called out to him, "give me your hand. I'll go first, it is dark at the beginning." We went slowly, feeling our way carefully hand over hand along the rock face. Soon we came to a second, wider passage and paused to let our eyes become accustomed to the dark.

"Can you see anything?" I asked him.

"I'm blind as the proverbial bat." He laughed. "I must depend upon you to guide me."

Holding fast to his hand, I led him on step by step up a sloping tunnel to the cave. A slender shaft of light filtered down through a chimney in the rock from the cliffs above. As our vision slowly cleared and focused, there on the wall above our heads we could discern the crude line drawing of a man who appeared to be about to do battle with a huge bull. The bull was a massive creature with long and sharp horns, while the man was slight as a boy and was armed with only a stick to which had been tied a flat stone.

No matter how often I came here I was always filled with awe for the courage of the man and admiration for the unknown artist who had labored so long to leave this legacy.

In the cave it was silent, always cool, the air faintly tinged with the musty odor of antiquity. It was so still that I could hear the timeless shifting of the sea below.

"Do you like it?" I asked, and I felt the pressure of his hand as it gripped mine.

"It is truly spendid," he said in a whisper. "It might be Theseus and the Minotaur."

"My father says that this was here before written history, long before the Phoenicians came, or the Greeks and Romans. The Spanish believe it is a magic cave. A place where lovers' wishes come true." I drew him nearer to the wall and we sat upon two flat stones, spectators in our private gallery.

"The Spanish," he said, "are romantics."

"Do you believe in true love?" I asked, looking at him quickly and then away again.

"I believe," he said after a long pause, "that it is very rare. And you, Cat, do you believe in true love?"

"Oh yes. I have good reason to. My mother and father fell in love at first sight. Because he was only a poor soldier her mother disapproved of the match, but nothing could keep them apart. When they found out my grandmother meant to keep them from marrying, they eloped."

"And they came to Spain?"

"No." I felt the tears start up in my eyes. "My mother never came to Spain. We lived in a little cottage in Kent; lived on love and roses, my mother said. I do not remember the house very well, but I remember the garden full of roses." I wondered if the house were still there and if so who was living in it.

"It was the Duke of Wellington who persuaded my father to come to Spain. The Duke and my father had been boyhood friends in Ireland. Wellington asked my father to serve as his liaison officer between the British and the Spanish generals. My father did not want to leave us, but he felt it his duty to go." I tried to blink back the tears, for if I wept a river of tears it would not alter the past.

"My father was wounded and taken prisoner by the French. It was many months before he heard that my mother was gravely ill in England. He was so wild to get home to her that he broke his parole and escaped." I remembered all too clearly how I had watched her grow weaker with each passing day. Yet she had never complained nor given up hope of seeing him again.

"She died only a few days before he arrived." I remembered too, standing with him in the churchyard looking at her grave. That day, if he had had his way, they would have buried him beside her.

"Afterward he came back to Spain and brought me with him. He felt it was a matter of honor to return to the French and his parole. When we arrived in Spain, Wellington had driven the enemy over the Pyrenees and into France, and for my father the war was over."

"Why didn't you go back to England?"

"I'm not sure." I answered truthfully, for there had always been some mystery about our staying. In part I knew that we had stayed because it seemed all England conspired to remind him of my mother. "Whatever his reasons we stayed and traveled south, then south again until we came here. We have had a good life here, much better for me than if I had grown up in England. I would not want to be prim and proper and always have to think of what was ladylike. Here we are close enough to Málaga that he can have his books and periodicals sent out to him from London and far enough from Gibraltar so he can avoid the British garrison and the remnants of his old army life." I felt a tear fall down my cheek, and it seemed childish to weep for what had been and would never come again.

"I am sure of one thing," I said, wiping my face. "Not a day has gone by in all these years that he has not thought of her. I know that he loves her now as much as he did the day he first set eyes on her." I had never had anyone before with whom to share my feelings and now I had told him all my sorrows. It was a bittersweet sort of joy. I felt him close beside me, felt him reach out and touch my cheek with his hand.

"You have been so lonely," he said softly. I had been

38

lonely but so had he, I was sure of it, and perhaps that was why he had heard me calling out to him and why he had answered.

"Yes," I said, "I have been lonely but I had my dreams, and now that you are here and we are in this magic place all my dreams have come true." He took his hand from my cheek and knelt beside me. He began to speak as if he were reciting words that I should remember and recognize.

"In such a cave did Merlin dwell and with him the Ariel, Amelle." I was puzzled. I did not know what the words meant, or why he had spoken them to me.

"What is it?"

"It is, I think, the beginning of a poem." His eyes were wide, his head to one side as if he were trying to listen to an echo from the past. "I do not know who wrote it or why it came to mind. Perhaps it's because Merlin was the most powerful of magicians." I should have asked him then who Amelle was but I did not. Instead I asked, "Do you believe in magic?"

He smiled. "When I was a boy I believed in Merlin." It was the first time he had consciously remembered even that much from his past.

"If you believe in magic, then surely in this place all your wishes will come true. Make a wish. There must be something that you wish for."

"I wish," he said, "that there was a wise old sibyl living in this cave and that she could tell me who and what I am."

"If there were a sibyl," I replied, "she would tell you that it did not matter who you had been, for here you can be anything you want to be. You can be rich or poor, of high or low degree. What you are is for you to choose." He smiled again, and his eyes began to shine.

"If I wish," he said, "you must promise not to laugh."

"I will not laugh."

"Then I would like to be a Knight of the Round Table, one of King Arthur's men." I tapped him lightly first on one shoulder then the other, as if I held a sword.

"Arise, Sir Caliban." He rose to his feet, then held out his hands to me.

39

"And will you be my Lady Fair?" I put my hands in his and he raised me up, and then he began to circle round and round the cave. He might have been some magus invoking a spell. Despite the streak of grey in his hair he looked young as a boy. And he cried out for all the rocks to hear. "In this cave we will make our Camelot!"

And so it began, our game of magic. A game that became so real to us that we were lost in it. The cave became our Camelot, our castle, our fortress, our refuge from the past and from the future.

We brought in wild flowers by the armsful and coverlets to make a couch. We filled the niches with candles and built our hearth in a little ring of stones. Together we made a home of the heart where I loved him and he loved me, and there the days slipped by, dissolving into one another like raindrops into the ocean.

Once, lying with his head upon my lap, he said, "I wish that I had known you all my life," and then he said his wish had already come true because his life had begun the day that I found him.

Another time he took up a handful of pebbles from the floor of the cave, and as they fell showering through his fingers he said, "I wish that these were diamonds and rubies and emeralds and pearls so that I could give them all as a gift to you."

And I would have sworn that as they fell I saw them glitter green, red, and fiery white, and that they shone more brightly than a treasure trove. One small agate had fallen in my lap and I put it in my pocket to keep forever as my talisman.

Another time in a more somber mood he said, "I wish that when I die there would be no monuments for me, only a simple stone with these words on it: 'Catherine kissed me.'" And I made that wish an instant reality.

I had had no experience of kissing, and I did not know that once begun I could no more have stopped myself than I could have held back the north wind. It was he who stopped, who held me away from him.

"What is it?" I asked, bewildered. "What is the matter?"

"Nothing," he said. "I am happy, that is all. It tempts the gods to be so happy. It will make them jealous."

"Nonsense," I said, and I would have kissed him again but he would not have it so, and I knew that somehow he was half-afraid, as if he had made a prophecy that must be fulfilled.

"Don't be afraid," I said, "there is nothing to be afraid of here. Here we are safe from every harm. We can wish away any hurt." And on that day I believed what I had said, believed it with all my heart.

Outside the world could have disappeared for all I knew. I was in love and I was blind to danger, oblivious even to the rain that fell in torrents and drenched us to the skin as we walked home that evening. By the time we arrived we must both have looked as if we had drowned and risen from the bottom of the sea.

Maria Luz fussed over me like a mother hen.

"Where do you go all day? What do you do?" she muttered as she rubbed my hair with a rough towel. "You act like one bewitched." Perhaps I was. I did not care. I only wanted to remain in this thrall, enchanted by the life we shared together in our kingdom by the sea.

Next day the fisherfolk had gone and we could go down to the beach again. I knew that he had missed the sea and the sun, and because I was green in judgment I believed that everything would be just as it had been before. And for a time it was. We swam, we roamed the shore looking for shells, we built our castles in the sand but now there was a difference, one that, try as I might, I could not ignore.

Now, no matter how content or at ease he seemed to be, suddenly, without warning, a word, a sight, or a sound would affect him so completely that for that moment it would seem the breath had almost left his body. His gaze would slip away from the present and he would look into a realm unknown to me. It was as if a dagger had struck at him and when the pain subsided a haunting fear remained behind, a fear of something so monstrous that he was fixed in terror.

41

"What is it?" I pleaded with him. "What is it that you see?"

"It is nothing."

"If it is nothing, why are you so frightened? What is it you remember? Please tell me."

"There is nothing to tell that makes any sense. Sometimes there is a flash of light. I see someone, I do not know who. I do not see a face; only a hand, a shoulder, or an arm. Never the face. It drives me a little mad. It is like being Tantalus in torture." He had spoken all this so softly that I had to strain to hear. Then he looked down at his hands and stared at them with as much concentration and consuming emotion as he had on that first day on the terrace.

"Sometimes," he said slowly, "I know there is a fire. I almost feel the flames. I cannot tell you any more." He looked at me, begging to be released from this inquisition.

He claimed to remember no more about his own identity than he had before and I believed him. Because I wanted him to have had no other life before this I hoped that it would pass, but when he least expected it the fear, the panic would come in a flash to overtake him.

In an effort to distract him, I challenged him to swim out farther and farther toward the horizon. I drew him into competitions to build the sand castles higher still, and each time we walked we went farther south toward Gibraltar. One day I took him to the little pillars of Hercules and showed him the place where I had found him. I did it, I think, because I wished that we could go back to the beginning and start our life together over once again.

He stood staring at the rocks that lay in little rows as sharp as shark's teeth. He stared so intently that they might have been runes cast into a coded message that only he could decipher. When at last he looked at me there was more pain reflected in his eyes than I had ever seen in them before.

"I hope," he said, "that I will never give you cause to regret having found me."

"Regret!" It was a cruel, senseless thing to say. "Why would I regret it?"

"Because," he said, "I think there is something in me that brings harm to others. I don't know how or what it is, some evil, a curse that puts those who are closest to me in danger." Tears sprang to my eyes; I could not keep them back.

"You see," he said sadly, "I wish you only joy and already I have made you cry." He reached out and touched me on the cheek as he had that first day in the cave, but now his palm left such a burning impression that he might have branded me.

"I am not crying," I said, "it is the sun in my eyes. It is the glare." He was too kind, too polite to point out that the sun was at my back and that I stood enveloped in his shadow.

"It is late," he said, "we must go back, we have already come too far."

As we walked slowly home, for the first time in my life I was stricken by the soul-tempering heat of a Spanish summer. The heat had never affected me before but now suddenly I was tired, drained.

We ate our supper that night in silence. We, who had always chattered away like magpies, might as well have been strangers at an inn. I was sure that Maria Luz noticed the difference and I could not meet her eyes. At last, unable to bear the constraint between us any longer, I excused myself early, saying that I had a headache from the sun, and fled to my room. I sat in the dark, afraid of the shadows on the wall. I tried to sleep but it was useless.

I heard the clock strike ten and then eleven. I heard Caliban go down the passage to his room. I heard the clock strike twelve. It was well past midnight when I must have fallen into a fitful half-sleep. I do not know what hour it was when I awoke again, but I knew at once what it was I heard. It was my love, my stranger from the sea, and he was moaning.

I threw a shawl around my nightdress and ran down the

43

hall to his room. He lay drenched in perspiration, lost in some far-distant private hell. His words when he spoke were low, barely audible. His thoughts were broken and disconnected, but there was a single theme.

"Fire," I heard him say. "The fire. She's burning! Oh, my god, I must save..." For a long moment there was silence and then he cried out, "Amelle!" He had said that name before, in the cave. "In such a cave did Merlin dwell and with him his Ariel, Amelle." Was Amelle a phantom, a figure in a poem, or was she something more? I had no time to wonder on it for he began to turn from side to side, his hands lashing out, beating at the air, which in his nightmare he took for flames.

I shook his shoulder and then I shook him again, calling out to him.

"Wake up! Please wake up. It is only a bad dream." His eyes opened wide. He was between two worlds, this and a hell of unreality. I saw relief sweep over him as if he were twice saved, once from the sea and now from eternal damnation.

"It was a dream," I said once more to reassure him. "Do you remember what you were dreaming?" He did not answer for a moment and then he shook his head.

"No," he said, "I do not remember." But he was lying. He would not tell me what had come to him in his dream. There was a barrier between us for the first time.

Whatever he remembered, it haunted him the next day and the next. It poisoned all his hours and mine. My one hope was that when we were back in our magic kingdom all would be well. I had suggested that we go there but he had put me off.

At last, one morning when I could bear it no longer, I resolutely turned toward the cliff path instead of going down to the shore. Within our cave the air was still cool and dry with the dust of centuries long past. Just to be there made me feel more secure.

"It is all right now," I said to him. "You'll see, now that we're here again everything will be just as it was before. You can wish away whatever threatens you."

I reached out to him and drew him close till we stood with our bodies fitting to each other. Involuntarily my arms went up around his neck and I stood on tiptoe to kiss him. I meant to stop him from denying the magic I knew existed between us, a magic I believed in with all my heart.

The kiss was long and deep, unlike any kiss that I had ever known. I knew that he too must be aware of the tremor that shook the very stones whereon we stood.

My heart began to beat wildly. His mouth on mine was warm as he returned the kiss. Our tongues touched like two flecks of flame and my whole body seemed to ignite. I knew with my last clear thought that my instinct was a more powerful force to bind and hold him to me that any words of reason.

With each kiss a new languor overcame my senses. My body now seemed to have a separate will, a need of its own. I wished him to take, to possess, to support my weakness. I wanted more than kisses. I wished for his hands to caress, to explore, to claim me. It seemed as natural and as right as the air. I had no more thought of shame than a flower unfolding to the sun.

I caught at his hand and drew it to my breast, fumbling to unloose my bodice. As his hand touched me I heard him catch his breath, and I saw in his face for one fleeting second a look of surprise. Then unmistakably it was replaced by one of longing and desire.

I was inexperienced, so innocent in love, but I knew something of coupling. I had seen the mare and the stallion in the fields when they found each other. I had observed them as they stood nuzzling neck to neck in a ritual of mating born of mutual desire and consent. They circled round and round each other before they came together, as it seemed we now were circling in a dizzying spiral of steps toward the couch that might have been prepared for just this purpose.

I knew I wanted to lie with him, for us to be free of the garments that separated us. I wished to feel him near, to be buried beneath his weight, to have him cover and fill me. As I lay reaching up for him to join me, I felt a warm moisture between my legs and I knew that nature had prepared the way for his coming. I marveled at the design of my body that without my will had made me eager to respond to him.

Now, with his hands touching, stroking, caressing me, I could not wait to unfasten the laces and buckles, to loose the last of the garments between us. I was eager, tremulous, caught in a tide of passion, as I felt him rising hard against my thigh. And again I wondered at the fact that while a woman might hide her feelings and desires a man could not.

But as I reached out to loose the belt of his breaches, his hands suddenly held me back. I heard him groan angrily as he pulled himself away from me with as much force as a drowning man might try to free himself from the sea.

"No," he said, "I will not take you here, not like this." I sat up, bewildered.

"Why?" I asked, feeling the aching emptiness, the torment of unfulfillment.

"It's all wrong, Cat."

"What could be wrong between us?" I tried to draw him to me again. I was willing, pliant, his to take, but again he drew away.

"You offer me everything, Cat, I have nothing to give you in return."

"You have yourself."

"But you know nothing about me."

"I know all I need to know. What more could I want to know than this? We are here together in our magic Camelot."

"No, Cat." He pulled me roughly to my feet and did up the fastenings of my bodice, then brushed at my hair to make me neat and tidy, as if the incident had never happened.

"This is no Camelot, Cat," he said soberly, "it is a cave for a Caliban, nothing more. Look, Catherine, the flowers have died and withered on their stems."

"Stop, please stop!" I cried out, putting my hands to my ears so I would not hear the shattering of my illusions or the breaking of my heart. "This has been our refuge, our home, you know there has been a magic here between us." He shook his head sadly.

"It would take more than Merlin's rough magic to make this place a home. I do not believe in fairy tales, Cat, I believe in reality." He picked up a handful of pebbles, letting them fall between his fingers.

"I may wish all I like, but these are not diamonds, nor rubies, nor emeralds and pearls, they are only a handful of worthless stones. I would gladly give you a king's ransom, but I have nothing of value to offer you."

"I want only you." I pleaded with him in vain.

"And I am nothing, no one, a man without a past or the prospect of a future, a man without a name." He looked at me squarely and I saw that he was inflexible.

"Come, Cat," he said, "there is nothing to keep us here." He turned abruptly, starting back the way that we had come. Without any thought of pride I ran after him and put my arms around him to hold him back, wishing to bind him to me forever. I buried my face in his shoulders and spoke, half-whispering, half-sobbing. "This cave would be enough for me. I would live here happily forever if you were here."

I clung to him and tried to kiss him again, but he would not let me. He loosed my hold on him as if he wished nothing more than to break a chain that bound him, to be free forever from some terrible burden.

"Don't, Cat, it hurts too much." But I would not let him go.

"There is a magic between us. You know it is so. I called out to you and you came to me. I have not imagined it." He stared at me, amazed. I did not know if he was shocked by my outburst, but I did not care. I saw once more that expression on his face that I had come to recognize with dread. I knew that he was slipping away from me into another time, another place, a place where I could not follow him.

"I am no Merlin," he said angrily, "and you are no Amelle." I shuddered as if someone had walked across my grave. The hair on my neck rose in icy prickles and I was sick with dread. He had spoken that name on our first day here in this cave, and he had spoken it again in his nightmare and now today.

"Who," I whispered, "who or what is Amelle to you?"

"I do not know," he said. "I cannot remember, but I think that long ago I brought her great harm." He reached out to me then and wiped away the tears that had fallen without my even knowing they were there.

"You can see how it would be with us," he said sadly. "You are so young and I am old. I am weary to the depths of my soul. If I were to stay with you in this kingdom by the sea, I would bring you nothing but unhappiness. I told you once that I hoped you would never regret having found me. I think you already do regret it a little. I know I do, for I have made you cry again."

He turned and walked away. It was as if he meant to exile himself from Eden and banish me from any hope of heaven.

I followed after him and was grateful that he said nothing more and that we could walk home in silence. I had had enough of words. I was numb with pain. Or thought I was until Maria Luz met us on the terrace. I knew by her face that she was waiting there to tell me some news and that the news was bad.

"It is your father," she sobbed. "He has come back. Paco brought him home. He is very ill." Without waiting to hear any more I rushed past her and ran to my father's room. He lay in his great bed propped up against a mass of pillows. His eyes were closed and he was pale, as pale . . . I stopped myself from finishing with the word *death*. The rapid rise and fall of his chest was proof of the struggle he was waging to draw each breath.

I threw myself down beside him. Suddenly he looked so old and fragile to me. I took his hand in mine and he opened his eyes and saw that it was I.

"Don't cry, Cat. I have a great deal to say to you. I want you to listen carefully. I've known for some time that my

48

health was failing. That's why I went down to Gibraltar to settle my affairs. When I am gone you will be provided for. It is not what I would like to leave you, but it will be enough to give you independence." He paused for a moment, struggling for his next breath.

"When I am gone, Cat, I think you should go back to England. This is no place for you alone." Then he motioned Caliban, who was standing in the doorway, to his side.

"When I was in Gibraltar I made some enquiries about you. Please look in the box there on my night table." Caliban took the small box and looked inside.

"Do you recognize the crest on the ring?" my father asked.

He looked at the ring carefully and then shook his head.

"I believe," my father said, "that it will be proof of your identity."

"Do you know who I am?" I saw how much the answer meant to him.

"I think so," my father replied guardedly, "but it would be wrong to give you false hopes. When I am gone I want you to take Cat down to Gibraltar. Give this letter to Sir Humphrey Runcible." He handed Caliban a letter that had been lying on the coverlet. "Sir Humphrey is an old friend. He will be arriving at Gibraltar in a few days' time to serve as Special Commissioner. The letter explains everything. He will know what I wish him to do." My father hesitated and then looked up searchingly at Caliban.

"If you are whom I believe you to be you will, I am sure, be going to England. I ask you to befriend Catherine. In England she will be a stranger and alone."

"I am her friend now and always and I am yours." He looked from my father to me and then back again to the figure on the bed. My father seemed satisfied, as if he had negotiated a treaty and made his peace.

"Then," he said quietly, "you will stay, it will not be for very long."

I protested. I told him he was wrong. I said that in a few

days he would be well again but in this, as in all things, he was a wise man and a man of his word. Caliban did not have to wait for long.

My father died in his sleep without pain. We buried him in the garden near the flowers and herbs that he had tended so carefully.

Caliban read out the service from the Book of Common Prayer and Maria Luz wept, for she could not believe that he was buried in holy ground and Paco looked as bereft as if he, not I, had lost a father.

I had no tears. It was too great a loss. I was too numb to feel or cry, but one thought sustained me. I knew that at last he was where he had so long wished to be—he was with my mother.

And after the service Caliban began at once to make preparations for our journey down to Gibraltar. Whatever the questions that lay like swords between us, they would soon all be answered, or so I thought.

Chapter Three

We had meant to set off for Gibraltar at first light. Caliban stood waiting for me in the courtyard, impatient to be off, while I kept remembering a dozen details I had yet to settle with Maria Luz.

I had agreed to go because I knew that he would never be free to love me until he knew the truth about his past; and because it had been my father's wish that I see Sir Humphrey Runcible about my inheritance. I knew my father had hoped that I would go back to England rather than live alone in Spain, but I did not want to leave. It was my intention to transact our business, Caliban's and mine, and then for both of us to come straight back home again.

Yet that morning, standing with Maria Luz in the safe, familiar kitchen I had an unwelcome presentiment that if I came here again I would be so altered that Maria Luz would take me for a stranger.

I went over my instructions once more. Maria Luz and Paco were to keep the house till my return. Then Caliban touched my arm and said, "It is late, Catherine, we must go."

Maria Luz gave one more long wail and then, resigned

51

to my going, she traced the sign of the cross upon my forehead.

"*Vaya con Dios.*"

She and Paco stood at the gate and watched us go, waving after us until we were out of sight.

We took the road above the sea, the road of Hercules. For the better part of an hour we walked along in silence, each rapt in our private thoughts. I had told him before we left that I did not mean to go to England, and he had said nothing in reply. Surely he must understand I did not wish to become the object of my formidable grandmother's attention. If she had made my mother's life so unhappy, there was every reason to believe she might have the same effect on mine. I was sure now that she must have been the mysterious woman who had come once, long ago, in a huge old-fashioned coach, to call at our little cottage in Kent. My mother had hastily sent me up to the nursery with orders to stay there until she had gone away again. I did not know why my grandmother had been so unkind to my mother, but I meant to keep well away from her. But—of far more importance to me—I meant to stay in Spain because it was in Spain that I was sure I could keep Caliban mine.

The sun was high overhead when we stopped for lunch. We sat beneath a fig tree and ate the bread and cheese and olives Maria Luz had packed for us. I found I had no appetite.

"You know," I said, "whatever happens, whoever you are or were, I will stand by you. I will always be your loving friend." He looked up and our eyes caught and held.

"Even if I am some brigand from the Barbary Coast wanted for piracy or murder?"

"Yes," I said, "even then." He rose abruptly.

"Come Catherine, we must be going." He held out his hand to help me rise, and for a moment he held me close to him, almost as if this were a farewell.

There was no time for a siesta, not if we were to get to Gibraltar by nightfall. I had already made us late. Reluctantly we picked up our knapsacks and started out again. I had brought only a change of clothes, nothing more. It seemed an assurance that we would be going home again the day after tomorrow, but in my pocket I carried the agate that was my talisman. Whenever I touched it I would be always reminded of a time and a place where wishes had come true.

In the afternoon, rather than dwell upon our own sober thoughts we talked of this and that. Of the weather, which was fine and our feet, which were not. Our rope sandals were not sturdy enough for this rough and rocky ground. He had cut us two stout sticks to use as walking staffs and in our wide-brimmed hats we must have looked for all the world like two pilgrims who had lost their way.

By midafternoon we were halfway across the high plateau above Gibraltar. I had to admit to a certain excitement and curiosity. I had never been to Gibraltar before. My father had sometimes taken me with him to Málaga but never to Gibraltar. I knew he had wanted to avoid his old army acquaintances and the British community as much as I wanted to stay away from England. But now I was nearly there I was curious to see the great rock that had only been a shape like a mirage at the end of the horizon. I expected something splendid of the fortress that stood sentinel between two continents.

The way to the place was well traveled. All the tracks and paths and roads converged upon the plateau like little creeks and streams and rivers on their way to the sea.

As we drew closer to the gate at La Linea it seemed we were swimming against the tide, for all the people who had been into the town for a market day were coming out again, homeward bound. There were weary farmers, their tired donkeys pulling empty, wooden carts and children already fast asleep in their mothers' arms.

It was nearly dusk when we arrived. Caliban stopped a passing soldier in a scarlet coat and asked the way to the Special Commissioner's house. After a short walk we were at the end of our journey. It was a square stone house; a plaque proclaimed it to be the property of the British Crown.

Standing there before the large ornate doors, we were such a gypsy-looking pair I half-expected the sentries who stood guard would try to bar our way, but in a very civil fashion they asked us to wait while a page was sent to announce our arrival.

In a few minutes the door was opened by a pale, thin, harried-looking young man. Only by the merest flicker of his eyes did he betray what a distasteful sight we were to him.

"I'm Mortimer Cheevers-ffrench," he said in a voice as thin and pale as himself. "Secretary to Sir Humphrey Runcible. Can I help you?"

"We wish to see him," Caliban replied evenly. "Is he at home?"

"What is your business with him, if I may ask?" His manner conveyed the distinct impression that we two could have no possible business with one so grand as Sir Humphrey.

Caliban silently handed him my father's letter. As he read it his manner changed dramatically. He looked first at me, and then, having read on to the end, he stared at Caliban. His jaw seemed to have come unhinged so that for the moment he stood completely dumb. Then he recovered himself and with an entirely different manner, one I felt sure he reserved for those he believed to be of some significance, he bowed to me, snapped at the page who opened the doors wide, and stood aside so that we might enter.

As we were ushered into a wide marble entry hall, he began to prattle nervously.

"I am sorry to have kept you waiting. Sir Humphrey is not at home, he is dining with the Commandant. Was he expecting you? No, I thought not, although he sometimes forgets to tell me. Now then, let me make you as comfortable as possible until he returns." He gave a sharp pull at a bell rope and I could hear the ring in a distant part of the house.

"If I may suggest, Miss Rainey, I'll have the housekeeper, Mrs. Matcham, show you to your room. I am sure she can find something suitable for you to wear. I can see that you have brought little with you."

Then he looked at Caliban, who had listened to all this with quiet patience. Once again, I observed how stunned Mr. Cheevers-ffrench seemed to be by the very sight of him. "Have you some accommodation for me as well?" Caliban asked.

"Yes, yes, of course. You understand, I'm sure, that in your case, there must be some formalities." He coughed discreetly. "I see by this letter," he held it up as proof, "that you have a ring. Is that correct?"

"Quite correct," Caliban answered, "but I would prefer to wait for Sir Humphrey Runcible himself." Mr. Cheevers-ffrench took this rebuff with what seemed to be relief.

"Of course, just as you wish." He bowed his head to Caliban. "But that may not be for some time. I do not know when Sir Humphrey will return."

"I am prepared to wait," Caliban said. "A few hours do not matter when I have already waited for so long." Then he turned to me. "I will not see you again, Miss Rainey, until I have something definite to say to you." In his eyes I read the message that I too must be prepared to wait, but I hoped that it would not be for very long.

Then Mr. Cheevers-ffrench hastily explained to the housekeeper, Mrs. Matcham, who I was and what I would require. She led me brusquely up the wide staircase and down a series of corridors. Her manner was cool and efficient.

At last we paused before a door that Mrs. Matcham opened to reveal a room much larger than my room at home. It was elegantly furnished. The wide canopied bed was hung with rich brocade topped at the four corners with sequined plumes. The Persian carpets were soft as velvet. Above the mantelpiece was a large mirror whose elaborate frame was gilded with gold leaf. The mahogany chests were almost as high as the ceiling and at the far end of the room double doors gave out onto a balcony that overlooked a formal garden.

"I hope you will be comfortable," Mrs. Matcham said.

"I am sure I will be," I replied, but I was not at all sure. This room was overwhelming. Before I could take my bearings, a bevy of maids appeared carrying a tub, a screen, and canisters of hot and cold water so that I might bathe.

Mrs. Matcham asked if I would like to have my supper served in my room and I readily agreed. I would rather have eaten in a tree than to have found myself in the company of strangers.

"Then I will have something sent up on a tray," she said with polite deference. "And I will find you some of Miss Fanny's clothes. Miss Fanny and Lady Runcible are away sightseeing in Granada, but I am sure she wouldn't mind." And with a little nod she left me.

I gave myself up to the luxury of a much needed tub. I chose some castile soap and bath salts from a liberal assortment on a silver tray. When I had bathed and stepped from behind the screen wrapped in a towel as large as a pony blanket, I discovered that my clothes had been taken away and in their place others laid out on the bed. The undergarments were of such flimsy stuff they would never last a day roaming the seashore or climbing in the hills. The dress was of the finest muslin, so light it weighed scarcely more than a lady's handkerchief. It was cut very low at the neck with puffed sleeves and it fell straight from beneath the bosom, revealing my figure as clearly as if I had nothing on at all underneath. The shoes were satin, too fragile for walking out of doors, or in. And in order not to split the narrow skirt I had to take little, mincing steps.

When I looked at myself in the long pier glass I did not recognize the reflection. If these were the clothes that English girls wore, if this was the sort of room they lived in, I would always be a stranger in England. How could they live mewed up like this with never a moment to themselves, the maids all coming and going like cuckoos from a clock?

At that moment, as if I had known she was at the door,

another maid appeared carrying my supper on a tray. I certainly could find no fault with the cold chicken nor the crisp salad and apple flan. The wine, served in a crystal goblet, was of a much better vintage than I was used to. And yet, although I sat on a little gilt chair before a carved and polished table, I could not help but miss my own shabby room and the plain fare Maria Luz served at our old refectory table.

Still more maids came to take away the tray, another to turn down the bed and lay out my night things. At last, when they were gone, I began to pace up and down the room.

Where was he? Why did he not come? I heard the clock strike midnight and I knew he was not coming, not tonight. I finally prepared for bed and lay in the enveloping darkness.

In the morning I awoke to find a maid hovering over me. She had brought me some coffee, hot crusty rolls, and thick apricot preserve. I drank the coffee, then dressed again in Miss Runcible's fine white dress. I combed my hair and sat down to wait, my mind running as wild and aimless as a frightened rabbit in a field. Why had he not come for me? What had happened to him? Were they holding him prisoner for some crime?

Suddenly I was startled by a knock at the door. Before I could find my voice to answer, Mrs. Matcham stood in the doorway.

"Miss Rainey, Sir Humphrey would like to see you in the library. Will you follow me? I'll show you the way." There were a multitude of questions I would have liked to have asked her, but I had the chilling feeling they would be answered soon enough.

In the library Sir Humphrey sat behind his desk sorting over some official-looking documents. He was a grey-haired man about my father's age. He rose at once and came to me, his hand outstretched.

"Catherine, my dear, I am so sorry to hear of your father's death. We were once great friends, he and I. I knew your mother too, long ago. No finer, gentler soul ever lived." He looked at me closely, his blue eyes clear and penetrating.

"I see in you the best of both of them." He held my hand for a moment longer and then motioned me toward a chair. "Please sit down. I'm in rather a rush this morning but I wanted us to get this sad business over with." He took up my father's letter, which had been lying on his desk, and looked at it to refresh his memory.

"Your father was most anxious to leave you adequately provided for. You will have a few hundred a year from holdings in the six percents to be paid quarterly from Coutt's Bank. The London solicitor who handled your father's affairs and now will act for you is known by me to be a highly reputable man." He took off his eyeglasses and sighed. "Your father regretted that he had no more than this to leave you but when your maternal grandmother dies you can expect something quite substantial from her."

"I think," I said, "that my father would prefer me to remain independent of her." He replaced his glasses and spoke in a sharper tone.

"That may not be an easy thing to do. She is a forceful lady and she has a way of getting what she wants. However, if you should decide against seeing her, you will still be able to live quite comfortably in England if you are a little prudent about expenses."

"I do not wish to go to England," I said. "I want to stay in Spain."

"Well, well. I had not considered that possibility." Sir Humphrey looked quickly at the clock. "We must discuss this further, but at the moment I am afraid I must leave you. There is a review of the troops I cannot put off. It is a pity Lady Runcible and Fanny are not here to entertain you, but we will dine together tonight, you and I, and then I promise to give you my full attention." He rose to go and still nothing, not one word, had been said about Caliban. It began to seem like a conspiracy of silence. I felt that I might soon go mad.

"I know you are in a hurry, but I cannot let you go with-

58

out knowing what has become of the man I brought here last evening."

"Ah yes." Sir Humphrey stood by the desk busily putting some papers into a portfolio. "He wants to see you. He's waiting now in the morning room. An extraordinary story, you finding him like that when the whole garrison had been out looking for him." I could bear it no longer, I must ask.

"Do you know who he is?"

"Oh yes, yes. No doubt of who he is."

"Then tell me, I beg of you. I have been waiting for hours for some news of him." Sir Humphrey shut his case with a snap and turned to me, his blue eyes narrowed and his mouth a straight line.

"He has made it abundantly clear that he prefers to give you all the details himself. In fact, he insisted upon it. It is all a most unusual business, first to last." He shrugged. "But then he is notorious for his eccentric behavior. I suppose we mustn't keep him waiting any longer."

"Is he free?" I stammered.

"Free?"

"I mean, he's not a prisoner, is he?"

"Bless me, my dear, whatever gave you that idea?" Sir Humphrey looked genuinely startled. "What an idea. No, far from it. He's only waiting to thank you. I know he's grateful for all you have done for him. But now I really must be off." I could not let him go, not yet.

"You knew him?"

"Not personally, although I have seen him about London. I know the family, of course, an old, respected name, Halyard. This present Lord Halyard has made something of a reputation for himself as a poet." He stopped. "But there, I've said too much already. Lord Halyard is waiting for you in the morning room."

Sir Humphrey left me before the door of the morning room. Lord Halyard! Suddenly I found that I was afraid, more afraid than I had ever been in my whole life. Finally I squared my shoulders and knocked, then opened the door.

59

At first my eyes were blinded by the bright morning sun that streamed through the open French windows into a brilliant yellow room. Silhouetted in a shaft of sunlight was the figure of a man.

He was the same height as the man whom I had once known better than I knew myself, but there the resemblance ended. As he slowly turned his face was blurred in the shadows, but I could see it was haloed round by hair that had been newly cut and dressed in a current fashion. The dark curls remained, but they had been so artfully arranged that each one rested in its appointed place.

The rough corduroys and peasant's shirt had been replaced by the clothes of a London dandy, a tailor's peacock who might have served as an illustration in one of my father's periodicals.

His blue coat had been so skillfully cut it fit without a wrinkle. His neckcloth was elegantly tied to fall between the stiffly starched points of an immaculate shirt. The waistcoat was a marvel of the needlewoman's art. His breeches were of the palest buckskin. They hugged and held his thighs like a second skin, and below the knee they were caught in Hessian boots polished mirror bright.

He leaned upon a silver-headed cane in an attitude of haughty arrogance. From his neck, hung on a black ribbon, there dangled an odious quizzing glass. For an instant I was terrified to think that this London fop, this pink of sartorial perfection might raise that glass and peer at me.

My friend, my companion, my lover, was gone, and in his place there stood a total stranger. It took all my courage to look up into his face. His features still retained the traces of that beauty I had once admired, but to my dismay I saw that he had powdered over them to mask his deep tan. I was afraid I might burst into tears, and because I did not want to reveal my feelings to a stranger I drew a deep breath, found my voice, and said, "So, my Lord Halyard, you know who you are."

"Let us say," he replied in a cool, distant manner, "that I have been reminded of who I am."

I gasped. "Don't you remember anything more than you did before you came here?"

"Alas no, but I have come into the possession of a multitude of facts, a number of which might prove amusing to you." He spoke in a tone as stilted and affected as his stance.

"It would appear," he drawled as if he were bored by all he said, "that I am not a pirate or a murderer. I'm not wanted for hanging after all. The fact is I am the sixth Baron Halyard, my family seat is a considerable property of great antiquity given to an ancestor by Henry the Eighth for the token sum of fifty-three pounds. Good old Harry, ever generous to his friends if not to his wives." He paused for a moment to see how I had taken his new, swift rise in the world. He raised a supercilious, questioning eyebrow and at that moment I could have hated him for what he had become.

"Then perhaps you would be amused to learn that I am a poet, the author of a trifle in several cantos entitled *The Nomad*. When it was published three years ago it was gobbled up by an adoring public. It seems I found myself famous overnight and the toast of London." He frowned. "I do not remember the poem so I cannot tell you if it is in rhyme, or indeed if it is of any worth at all.

"The rest of my story is perhaps not so amusing." He changed his attitude and stood erect and resolute. "I am informed," he said gravely, "that I had a wife and that she died last winter in a tragic, senseless fire at Longfields Abbey. I am told that I tried to save her, which would, I believe, explain the scars upon my hands and the nightmare in which I imagine myself to be in the flames of hell." He paused and looked away as if he were trying to see into a past that he could not recall.

"They say that my wife, who was my cousin, was very beautiful and that she was universally loved. Because she died so suddenly and tragically there was a great deal of talk. Wild rumors and insinuations; all the sort of thing which I imagine must always befall those who are in the public eye or live too close to the stove of society. I am sure that is why I chose to leave England and travel as far away as possible from any scenes that would remind me of her death." He looked at me. "Can you say nothing, Catherine?"

I shook my head. I did not trust myself to speak. All the rumors and insinuations in the world meant nothing. What mattered to me was that Caliban had loved someone before he met me. She had been a great beauty, a woman of his own rank, and she had been his wife. Although he had forgotten her, she had once existed, and some day he would remember her again. Then how would he compare me to her?

"I think," he said, oblivious to my heartache, "that I must have chosen to come to Gibraltar because I had been here once before on my grand tour after I left Cambridge. I arrived here about three months ago, alone, which caused some stir. When I had been here before it had been with a large retinue. I rented a villa and a boat. I kept to myself. I went out sailing each day alone. On that last day, despite the fact that there were storm warnings posted in the harbor, I went out again alone and this time I did not come back. They turned out the garrison to search for me but no trace was found. I was presumed to be dead. You know the rest."

I knew then that he had come to me only because he had been running away from the memory of one he had loved. I was altogether wretched, and I had brought this misery upon myself. I had agreed that we must come to Gibraltar, believing that when he knew the truth he would sweep me in his arms and tell me that he loved me. I had been a fool.

We stood in a silence that filled the room. Despite the sun reflecting from the yellow walls I was cold with shock. My time with him was all past. All our golden moments lost as if they lay at the bottom of the sea. For one second I saw in his face an expression of the old tenderness, but then it was gone, and the cold returned like a frost upon his features.

"Well," he demanded imperiously, "now that you have found me and restored me to my true identity what do you intend to do with me?"

"I was not aware, my Lord Halyard, that I was obliged to do anything with you."

"Ah." He smiled wryly and made me a mock bow. "But you are wrong. The Chinese have a saying that when you have saved a person's life you are then responsible for that person forever." His mockery was intolerable. How could he make a joke of his salvation or of his life?

"I am not Chinese, therefore I am not responsible for you. You are free to go and do as you please. A man of your rank can surely have no need for my friendship." I had meant to hurt him in return for the pain that he had given me but now I saw something snap. His shoulders sank. It was as if all along he had been a boy who whistles on his way through a graveyard rather than admit he was afraid.

He took a step toward me and it required all the remnants of my pride to make me hold my ground. He looked at me closely.

"Can it be, Catherine Rainey, that you are a snob? I have never noticed that flaw in your character before. When you thought me a nobody with nothing to my name you gave me your hand and you kissed me. Now that I am a lord do you mean to dismiss me like a lackey? Have you forgotten that only yesterday you promised to stand by me and be my loving friend no matter who or what I had been?" He touched my cheek with one finger and brushed aside a tendril of my hair.

"Have you forgotten that we slept together side by side? Do you not remember any of the days that we have spent together?" Tears came to my eyes, sudden and sharp; I could not stop them.

"You are cruel to remind me of such things. It is not fair, you know it is not."

"Are you fair to me, Catherine, now you intend to abandon me?"

63

"I have not said I meant to abandon you."

"Then will you stand by me and be my loving friend as you promised?"

"You know that I will if you need me." He had won me over, talked me round as easily as he had brushed away the lock of my hair.

"And will you come with me to England?" I could not have guessed that that was what he had on his mind. I drew back from him.

"You know very well I had not intended to go to England. I do not want to go to England."

"Yes, I know." He agreed as patiently as one would agree with a child. "But you see, Cat, I must go to England. I have learned that my affairs are in a tangle, my estate in pawn. I cannot leave such business to an agent. I must go and settle things myself and I want you to come with me." I did not know what to say to him. It was the last request I had expected at this moment.

"Catherine," he said gently, "it was your father's wish that you go to England. I promised him that I would protect you as best I could. I have made some enquiries about your grandmother from Sir Humphrey. It is said that she made a torment of your mother's life. As you are a minor she might be able to have herself appointed your guardian until you are of age. She could make you her virtual prisoner."

"All the more reason for me not to go to England. You know I do not think of England as my home."

"But my home is there and I ask you to go with me. I am asking you to marry me, Cat, and go to England with me." At first I thought it was not possible that I had heard him aright.

"Marry you!" He drew back rebuffed, taking my surprise for refusal.

"If the idea offends you then I suggest a marriage in name only, a marriage of convenience. It is the best means I have of protecting you."

"I have not said I was offended," I answered.

"Are you aware," he continued as if he had not heard

me, "that as a minor your grandmother, when she finds out your father is dead, will be able to secure your inheritance and withhold it until you are of age? You could not stay and live in Spain on nothing even if you wanted to. However, if you marry me, by English law your property is mine and you might do as you choose. Your grandmother, Lady Blessing, is a harridan, there is no other word for her. She lost control of your mother when she married your father. She lost once, but I do not think she would let you slip through her hands. She is too wary an old bird for that." He held out his arms to me; it was an invitation.

"You may not need me, Cat, but I need you." He half-whispered the words, they were so freighted with emotion. "You make the difference between life and death to me." There was a note of urgency in his voice, a tone of appeal I had never heard before.

"Without you I am lost in a dark maze. I fear that at the end of the labyrinth there is a monster greater than the Minotaur waiting there to destroy me. If you are not with me, I am alone. I do not care to live without you, Cat."

It took all my will for me to make that first step toward his waiting arms.

"Do you remember nothing about the fire at Longfields, nothing about your wife?" He shook his head.

"I remember nothing, not the fire nor the woman who was my wife. Believe me, Cat, if my affairs were not in such desperate straits I would take you by the hand and we would go back to the house on the coast. We would live together in a cave by the sea and be as happy as if we were king and queen of our own kingdom, but I know you are not such a romantic as to think I can stay. You know I must go and that you must go with me." Again I hesitated, unable to take that final step.

"What would you have me say, Cat? Once I gave you pebbles from the sea. Now I offer you diamonds and rubies and emeralds and pearls. What more would you have me say? You cannot doubt that I love you."

I knew it, had known it all the while, but he had never said the word love before. What was I waiting for when this was all I had wanted? He knew who and what he was, he knew the truth of his nightmare. He was waiting, wanting to take me in his arms. He had already told me at last that he loved me, and yet there was something, something like an echo in a dark passage.

"Listen to me, Cat." He took my hands in his. "The Duke of Calford's yacht, *Persepolis,* is in the harbor. She sails tonight. The Captain, to whom I am known, is willing to take us aboard. It means that we will not have to wait weeks for the packet. The yacht would be ours alone, we the only passengers until we reach Dover." He held my hands in a tight grip. I did not think I could break his hold even if I wanted to.

"Do you mean for the Captain to marry us?"

"No," he said thoughtfully, "these nautical marriages can sometimes be questioned. I would prefer that we be married by the garrison chaplain. Then we will be sure it is legal and binding. The chaplain will agree to waive the banns, there are still some privileges of rank, Cat. I think I can safely say that within the hour I can have a special license, some witnesses, and the chaplain. I can command all but the bride to be. What is your answer?"

We were married late that afternoon in Sir Humphrey Runcible's library. We had for our witnesses Mr. Cheeversffrench and Mrs. Matcham. A bemused Sir Humphrey gave me away and the groom stood alone without a best man.

We exchanged our vows and my husband kissed me before the assembled company. We signed the register, and I, Catherine Elizabeth Rainey had taken Richard George Henry Halyard to be my lawful, wedded husband. I was Lady Halyard for better or for worse in the sight of God and man until death did us part.

Our health was drunk, there were congratulations and best wishes all round. Then just as we were about to depart I remembered the agate Caliban had given me in the cave. I had left it on the dressing table upstairs. I excused myself and ran up to fetch it. The agate was my lodestone, my talisman, it was the only jewel that I would ever really want.

When I came down again Halyard had gone into an anteroom with Sir Humphrey. I heard him asking that word should be sent to Maria Luz and Paco to tell them we would be away for a considerable time. In the library I could see Mr. Cheevers-ffrench and Mrs. Matcham with their heads close together. I would have turned away to wait in the hall rather than interrupt them, but my shawl caught on the handle of the door. They did not see me but I saw them and could not help but hear them as well.

"I find it shocking," Mrs. Matcham was saying, "shocking they should be married in such haste."

"I thought it all went off very well," Mr. Cheevers-ffrench drawled. "You did your best, Mrs. M."

"His wife has only been dead a few months, not even a proper period of mourning; no good will come of it, I tell you that." Mrs. Matcham sniffed in disdain.

"The bride looked quite happy." Mr. Cheevers-ffrench was condescending in his manner. I had not been conscious of looking either happy or unhappy.

"Poor thing, I pity her." Mrs. Matcham's eyes snapped. "He's notorious. His reputation with women is a public scandal."

"It's hardly his fault if women throw themselves at his head. You shouldn't listen to rumor and speculation."

"Indeed." Mrs. Matcham drew herself upright, rising to the challenge. "Well, where there's smoke there's fire. What about Lady Elden? That was more than rumor or speculation. That was a scandal. Dressing herself up like a page and following him everywhere. He could have stopped her if he'd tried. And what about Miss Vane riding on a horse down St. James's naked as Godiva, just to attract his attention." Mr. Cheevers-ffrench smiled.

"Surely that was a laughing matter."

"Not to his wife." Mrs. Matcham had the last word.

"Was he married at the time? I don't remember." Mr. Cheevers-ffrench would not be bested.

It made me sick to hear such gossip. How dare they talk

of him so, a man that they had barely met. They did not know him as I did. I could tell them he was no seducer. It had been he who had drawn back from me when we had been alone, not I from him.

"He'll break the girl's heart, you'll see." Mrs. Matcham looked triumphant. I could not bear to see the look of pleasure on her face.

I shut my eyes as if by doing so I could shut out her face and the words that I had heard. When I opened them I saw my husband standing in the doorway opposite. I knew that he had seen me. What I did not know was how long he had been standing there or how much he had heard of the malicious backstairs gossip. Was this the sort of rumor and innuendo he had run away from? If so, then I did not blame him for leaving England.

In one sharp jerk I got my shawl free and I saw him record the fact. Then at last he spoke.

"Ah, Cat, there you are. We must be going. Goodbye." He spoke to Cheevers-ffrench and Mrs. Matcham as if nothing at all were amiss, but in the carriage driving toward the quay my husband turned to me.

"What happened, Cat? What did those two say to upset you?"

"Nothing, nothing really." I could not tell him that in my mind there had been planted the seeds of jealousy.

"Are you quite sure?" He scrutinized me carefully. "We have enough unknowns to face without keeping secrets from each other." I turned to him, learning guile and how to dissemble out of my heart's pain.

"From this moment on I will keep no secrets from you, you may depend upon it."

"And I will keep no secrets from you, Cat. You may depend upon it."

We had made a pact, a bargain as binding as a marriage vow. But, I thought, you are already used to scandal, to rumor and gossip, to every ill of society, and I am a novice, a reluctant and unwilling newcomer to the game.

Once aboard the yacht we stood on deck by the rail

watching as the crew cast off. We stood until the lights of Gibraltar receded into the distance.

"Shall we go to our cabin, Cat?" he asked. I hesitated and then I nodded.

"Yes, but first answer me one question. Was your wife's name Amelle?"

"No, whatever put that into your head? My wife's name was Arabella."

Chapter Four

The *Persepolis* found her first wind and it caught and held, billowing out the canvas overhead. We were outward bound for England, embarked upon our *lune de miel*; that moon of honey, which the Spanish say is a gift to all newly wed.

I still could not believe it was real. It had all happened so quickly. In the space of one day both he and I had become different people, he a lord and I his lady. Both of us must now answer to different names and both wear different clothes. I was not sure I would ever become completely reconciled to the change in his appearance any more than I would become used to hearing cruel gossip and slander about him.

Yet aside from that one unfortunate incident all my dreams and wishes had come true. My love had come to me and when he had known who and what he was and the reason for his nightmare he had declared his love for me. Amelle, whoever she was, belonged to his past. I had always known that he had had a life before he came to me. I must forget it as he had forgotten and remember that this day, this hour, was the beginning of our new life together.

71

At that moment, with the moonlit sea all round us, it easy to forget everything as he took my hand in his and said again, "Well, Cat, shall we go to our cabin?"

Our cabin was, in fact, a richly appointed suite. There was a large sitting room and a bedroom beyond. It had been lavishly furnished to suit the whims of its owner, the Duke. Piled by the entrance was a stack of Lord Halyard's trunks and my own small knapsack. Two old dresses and a shift were not much of a trousseau for a fine lady.

He took my cloak from my shoulders and put it on a nearby chair. Then he led me toward a table covered with a snowy white cloth and set with an array of cold meats, cheeses, fresh fruit, cakes, and wine. It was a splendid wedding feast.

"The Captain asked us to dine with him, but I made our excuses."

"What did you say to him?" I asked, the color rising in my cheeks.

"I said that as you had nothing suitable to wear, we would prefer to have all our meals alone." I looked at him in dismay only to find that he was smiling.

"Never mind, Cat, when we get to London I'll buy you enough dresses to last you a lifetime." He had been teasing me, trying to set me at my ease, but I was suddenly painfully aware of my lack of experience in his world. I found that I was trembling.

"Are you cold, Cat?" he asked kindly.

"No."

"Are you hungry?"

"No."

"A glass of wine then?" I took it gratefully. Although I was not thirsty it gave me something to do with my hands. He raised his glass and drank my health; this tall, handsome, distinguished stranger who was now my husband.

"To my dear wife." He set down his glass and took mine from me and then he bent down and kissed me. It was not like any kiss I had ever known. In the cave it had been I who had kissed him. Now it was he who took the lead. His

72

lips on mine were warm and soft, the kisses gentle and lingering, but they were soon followed by others more demanding and insistent.

"If you are not hungry or thirsty or cold, Cat, then let us go to bed. It is, I think, what we both desire." I could not find the words to answer him, and taking my silence for consent, he picked me up in his arms and carried me across the threshold to the waiting bed.

He stood above me, looking down for a moment. His dark eyes held mine like a caress, and then he blew out the light and I heard him say, "I do not think a marriage in name only would suit either of us, Cat." And it was true.

That night our bed became a second ship in which we embarked upon a voyage of discovery. In his lovemaking, as in all things, he was sensitive, aware of my unasked questions and fears. It was as if he could read my mind. Sometimes I was not sure I had not actually spoken aloud. That night he more than fulfilled the promise he had made during the marriage ceremony when he had sworn that, "With my body I will thee worship."

Slowly, deliberately, he began to undress me until I lay naked, trembling upon the bed. Then, rising, he took off his shirt and his trousers and as the undergarments fell away there, in the half-light, I could see how erect he was and I could not doubt his longing for me was as great as mine for him.

Yet knowing how unused and untried I was he did not take me at once, but gently caressed my breasts, held the nipples hardening against his fingers, teased at them with his tongue till they grew taut and throbbed to the touch. And then, with his hands, he stroked at my back and thighs, parting, separating till at last he drew himself over me and, kneeling between my legs, he whispered, "I will try not to hurt you, Cat, I would not want to cause you pain."

He raised me slowly up toward him, holding my buttocks and tenderly penetrated, withdrew, and entered again, thrusting past the barrier of my maidenhood, then drove within me, filling me, joining, covering me, possessing me and hesitating for a moment, waiting for a signal that I was willing for him to renew his advance.

For the little pain that he had caused me the rest was unforeseen joy. I could not have imagined such pleasure, as I opened to him, arched to meet him, and found a wild hunger within me, as if I were a parched land long without rain.

Toward the end of our coupling I felt I was lost in some far country where my senses were dulled and yet more acute than they had ever been in all my life. Suddenly I felt him tense and heard him cry out at the instant of our release.

Afterward, lying still and calm beside him, I knew with a sense of wonder that I would never be lonely again. I had a companion, a lover who would be with me for a lifetime. The wildness that had always been a part of my nature had found its mate. With him I had been set free.

"Do you think me shameless?" I asked him. Maria Luz had said that bold women displeased their husbands.

"No." Was he laughing at my question? I could not tell.

"Bold?" I asked, wanting to be sure of his approval.

"You are a companion worthy of the gods." He turned my face up to his so that I could see his eyes in the shadowed darkness. "I love you, Cat, but then you know that already, don't you?"

"Yes." I knew that he loved me but always, like a cold splinter in my mind, there was the thought that he had loved another before me and that he had told her so, while I had never loved anyone but him.

"You know that I love you," he repeated and now he was smiling, "but do you have any idea of how hungry I am? We have gone to bed without our supper." The idea of going off to bed without our supper like two naughty children made me laugh.

"I'm hungry too," I said, sitting up and drawing the bed clothes around me. "In fact, I'm famished."

"Then stay where you are and I will bring you something to eat. I don't want you out of my sight, not even for

74

a minute." He had put on his dressing gown and turned back at the doorway tying up the sash. There was something in the look he gave me that I could not fathom.

"Oh Cat," he said, "there is no one like you. I couldn't bear to have you change." When he came back he brought a tray laden with food and drink. Together we made a sweet feast of food and love. There was not a particle nor a crumb that we did not sample for our pleasure. We took our fill and when we slept there were no nightmares, only rest and tranquil dreams. Later when we woke I remember saying to him, because I still could not believe the miracle that had come to me, "Why do you?"

"Why do I what?"

"Why do you love me?"

"Because you make me happy. Because you amuse me. I have never known anyone like you. You care for me as I am. Not for some lord or poet but for me. You are fierce as a tiger with a cub when you think I may be in danger and because," he was suddenly serious and his hand gripped at my arm so tightly I almost cried out, "because I know that you would never betray me."

We lay for a long time looking into each other's eyes. Only yesterday, or had it been the day before, I had loved him enough to give my life for him. Now I knew that I loved him enough to kill to keep him mine and the thought was frightening. Passion such as mine was a force that I had not dreamed possible.

And that passion grew and magnified. Each day with him I was astonished by a new and more intense joy. If he was an able teacher in the ways of love, I was a more than willing pupil. I never wanted the nights to end or the days that followed. With the power of love we seemed to have reversed night for day. At night we walked alone around the deck, by day we slept and made love grow. We seldom saw a living soul. The ship was ours and the sea. The weather was warm and fine; a brisk running wind carried us before it. If he had asked me then I would have said that I wanted no more than the present, it would have been enough for all eternity.

75

Yet when it suited us to change our pattern I was just as happy and content. One day he ordered an awning hung in the bow beneath which we could sit in shaded comfort to read and talk. It seemed in those days that we never stopped talking. We said all the words that lovers the world over had always said to each other, but they were new to me.

We spent an hour on how small my hand was in comparison to his and another hour on the color of his eyes, a third on the true color of mine. And always every hour we were together he told me how happy he was. How happy he said I had made him. He had not dared to dream such happiness was possible.

Sometimes in the afternoons we drank mint tea and played at chess. And then for hours on end we sat silently lying against a bank of pillows watching the clouds skimming by overhead.

He had found me a pair of old nankeen trousers and one of his open-necked shirts. In a sailor's stocking cap to keep my hair from blowing in the wind I must have looked for all the world like a cabin boy who had wandered into a sheik's tent. What the crew or Captain thought I neither knew nor cared. They stayed well away from us and we from them. For this time was ours and ours alone and in the clear, tranquil light of day the remembrance of our lovemaking clung like a sensual fragrance.

In the beginning I had been so eager, so hungry for his embraces that I thought we would always come together quickly, like wildfire sprung from lightning, but in time he taught me to take pleasure slowly, to savor and abandon myself to prolonged delight. He opened to me a world of ecstasy as opulent, as richly exotic as if I had been born some Far Eastern queen.

The first time I awakened from a siesta to find him watching me I was shy of his gaze. I felt vulnerable in my nakedness. I would have drawn the sheet up about me but he took it from my hand and let his eyes sweep over me.

"There is no need for false modesty, Cat. I like to look at you. There is nothing wrong in that. You must know how beautiful you are."

76

Slowly, almost lazily, he began to touch, to caress me, moving his fingers lightly over my throat and my shoulders, down to my breasts. Then, the pressure increasing, his hand slid along the flat surface of my belly to part my legs and to stroke within my thighs with such a sure and gentle touch that it made me feel I was made of silk and velvet.

It seemed he always knew where I longed for him to touch me. He always anticipated what I was too unpracticed, too unsure to ask or even to know that I wanted.

His hands were so expert at kindling desire that I would have been ready for him to enter me at once. He too was aroused, his manhood erect, but instead of coming into me he drew me toward him and I felt him lift me up, holding me above him as he slowly set me astride him, fitting himself to me, filling me to what seemed the center of my being.

It was a new, intense, unimagined pleasure. I felt as weak as if I were melting around the fire within me. I would have moved against him but he held me pinioned in what seemed a sweet, unbearable, scalding flame.

"Be still, Cat," he whispered, "we have time to taste all that love has to offer."

I obeyed his command as he kissed my breasts, while tremors of delight broke in wave after wave within me. Still he would not allow me to move until with his hands on my buttocks he guided me so that I rose and fell at his pace. Now all was sensation so intense that I felt I must surely faint from pleasure. I was weak, without a will of my own. I heard myself cry out or was it some other voice that I heard, for I was aware that I was being transformed into a new being who did not care who heard her cry or guessed the reason why.

I was drugged by the intensity of our passion, mesmerized by the pressure of his hands, the urgency of his commands.

Yet never once did he join me in surrender or allow himself release. He stayed hard within me, guiding me on until at last he saw that I could bear no more. Then he let me rest. We lay side by side still joined in love's embrace while he dried me with a scented towel and fed me with sweetmeats.

I was sure that I was so spent by pleasure that no further passion was possible. I knew that he had taken the last that I had to give of love, but I could not have guessed the swift reawakening of desire that I was capable of as he began to move again, to draw above me, thrusting deep within me. From a calm valley I rose again, higher and higher, to a new plateau and on toward a summit where I lost all control. I clung to him, my nails against his back, arching up to him, embracing him, demanding now that he move against me in an almost violent rhythm until together we reached the final peak and fell, plummeting down into the valley of total surrender and sleep.

In the days that followed it seemed that from practicing the arts of love my flesh had become a different texture, that my shape had altered to fit in harmony with every contour of his hard, lean, masculine body. Our scent had mingled and been bonded into one perfume.

I could not believe that any woman had ever had a husband, a lover as tender, as perceptive, as sensitive to a wife's longings and desires as he.

I took a fierce pride in his care and concern for me. He always considered my happiness before his own. I knew that it was this tenderness, this gentle consideration that kindled a desire within me so deep and constant that it was like a rich and unexpected treasure.

I could not have enough of him nor he of me. It was the right, the natural exploration of a new continent of the senses, but I think, too, we desired each other so because we knew, without speaking of it, that our golden weather, our moon of honey, would soon be coming to an end.

Still, I was startled when one day not long afterward I saw a trunk had been set beneath the awning. It was only an ordinary trunk but it seemed as threatening and ominous as Pandora's box. I tried to pretend it was not there. I refused to look at it. I saw a vein throbbing at his temple and I knew that he was as anxious as I was. We were both afraid of the shadowed past that yet might rise and blight our future.

"I must open it," he said apologetically. "I must know something of my past so I won't look a complete fool before the world. It would be tedious to have to be forever explaining I am a man without a memory." He turned to me, his eyes wide and troubled.

"I do remember some things each day about places and people and trivial incidents, but I remember nothing of Arabella or the fire and perhaps," he looked away again, "it is just as well not to remember her or that night."

For my part I was grateful that he did not remember Arabella, beautiful, enchanting Arabella, or the night that had brought him such grief and sorrow. It seemed another bond between us that he was as reluctant as I about her memory.

After a long moment's hesitation he reached into his pocket and handed me a scrolled brass key. "You open it." His hand was shaking.

As the lid of the trunk swung back I half-expected bats and toads to come flying out, but instead there was only the usual fitted tray in which were piled packets of letters that had been forwarded out to him at Gibraltar, some books, and then I saw, half-buried in the untidy pile, a purple velvet box of the sort in which ivory miniatures were kept. On it were the initials *A.H.* embossed in gold.

I had a chill of dread to think that the first thing I might see would be the face of Arabella, but then I had to see her portrait sometime. It was inevitable that one day I would have to confront her beauty and come to terms with it. I hastily handed him the packets of letters, thinking they would divert him until I became more calm and resigned, but he sat staring, his gaze fixed upon the velvet box.

"First that box," he said, and I think he too both feared and was compelled to confront her, to have it be done and over with.

"Will you open it?"

Inside the box, nested in satin and cotton wool, lay an ivory miniature of a woman's face. Her eyes, the singular feature in her face, were a startling green. They were wide and clear and her gaze direct. Her brow was wide and firm, like Halyard's. Her hair was curled in an old-fashioned cluster of ringlets, as if she had lived in a different century. Yet her clothes were of a present fashion. He looked at her face, staring down at it, trying to remember her, and then he shook his head.

"I do not think that it is Arabella." I had already guessed as much. This woman could not have been considered a great beauty by any standards, yet I was drawn to her. I felt sure that she had always been loving and kind, a woman of generous sentiments.

He turned the miniature over and there on the back I saw engraved two dates, one for birth and one for death. As his fingers touched the ivory I saw the past return to him.

"Oh," he sighed, a long, sad sigh as heartfelt as if he were a mourner at a funeral. "It is—it was—my sister Amelia. Of all the people in the world how could I have forgot Amelia?"

"She is dead then?" I asked. I could not imagine him with a sister. Had he other brothers and sisters, I wondered? He had always seemed to me to be so alone.

"Yes, she died the year I was away from England on my grand tour. I did not know she had died until I got home. The news was a great shock to me. I had loved Amelia deeply. We were lonely children, she and I, always in each other's company. I remember once . . ." He turned to me, excited by his sudden rushing return of memory. "I remember I was away at school and she sent me a plum pudding stuffed full of sixpences. I had run out of pocket money. It had been stolen or I had overspent, I don't remember which, but I was forbidden to have any more for the rest of the term. Amelia's solution was to send me that marvelous, fantastical present. There was a note in the package. It said only, 'Eat with care.' I knew it was a code and that I must beware." He paused. "Amelia, like you, was always loyal and true."

His face was transformed. He was surprised and overjoyed by the recollection and the telling.

"I remember too," he went on excitedly, "Amelia and me hiding away from our mother in the west wing of the house at Longfields."

"Hiding from your mother, but why?" He frowned, his brow furrowed.

"Life with my mother was not always easy for Amelia or me. I used to make up fairy stories for her about a princess named Amelle and a handsome prince who rescued her. But that is enough about Amelia," he said.

The floodgates of memory had closed as abruptly as they had opened. In the days that followed I was to see the same sort of thing recur again and again. A look, an object, a change of weather would set him to remembering and then, as swiftly as the stream of recollections had come, they would be gone again.

"I wish," I said gently, "that I had known Amelia."

"Yes," he said, "you would have loved her as I did." He put the velvet box back into the trunk and began sorting over the packets of letters. I would have liked to ask him more about Amelia but I saw I could not expect to share all his life at once. He would tell me more about her in his own good time.

"Here," he said, handing me a sheaf of letters. "I'll take the ones from my publisher and you deal with the rest."

The letters that he handed me were addressed in different hands but all were flowery and some were scented. As I opened the first and began to read I gasped in shock. It was from a woman and her demands upon my husband were as explicit as they were incredible. Especially as she claimed to be a stranger to him. After the first I was more prepared for the rest and we both read on in rapt silence until he exploded with a great oath.

"Can you believe it? My publisher, a fool by the name of Fanner, wants my permission to abridge *The Nomad* so that he can bring out a cheap edition. He says, and listen to this, '. . . owing to the temper of the times it would be desirable to cut some of the more controversial passages.' And in the same letter the pompous ass has the gall to ask when I will be sending him the next canto as there is a great demand for it."

He set down the letter, his eyes flashing.

"When I get to London I'll soon tell Mr. Fanner what he can do with his controversial cuts and cheap editions. No

81

author likes to be chopped and changed merely for publishers' profit." I had never seen him in such a temper before. It was a revelation to learn that he was capable of so deep a rage. It was also frightening, and seeing that he had upset me, he threw off his mood.

"I'm sorry, but it makes me angry, it really does. Now tell me, what was in your lot?"

"Your female admirers," I said drily, "would disagree with your publisher. They want you just as you are, nothing expurgated or cut, not even a syllable. One says if she cannot have you she will throw herself into the Thames. Another claims your souls are twins and sends a lock of her hair and some poems of her own composing for which you were the inspiration. She says they are for your eyes only, which is just as well for they have made me blush. And here is a handkerchief that was once wet with this next lady's tears. Tell me, is this the sort of thing I must expect in England, to have you constantly besieged by unknown ladies?" I had asked it lightly enough and in truth I felt light of heart, almost gay, for if these unsolicited protestations of love and admiration were all that gave rise to gossip I would bear with such foolish women gladly. He flushed and scowled.

"Never mind, Cat, you have the real man, not the counterfeit. All those silly women do not write to me but to some phantom of their imaginations." He took the letters from me, put them back into the tray of the trunk, and drew out two copies of The Nomad.

"We might as well read it now, Cat, and find out what all the hullabaloo is about. It would be curious for an author not to know his own work. I would like to know what Fanner considers controversial."

We began to read silently; I with mixed feelings of reluctance and curiosity. I was aware I was no critic, I was not competent to judge the merits of the work, and I was half-afraid of what The Nomad might reveal of Halyard's past, but soon I forgot all my doubts and qualms as I became drawn and absorbed in the tale of a young man who is so completely possessed by an unholy, forbidden love that he is compelled to flee from it, to roam the earth like a no-

82

mad. As he wanders, doomed, damned, always before him is her image, she who by turns is the siren, the Circe, the eternal enchantress. She will not let him rest but leads him ever on until at last in a great storm he is dashed upon the rocks of some far distant shore. There, finding refuge in an ocean cave, he still calls out for some magic that will transport him back to her and the last canto ended in suspense with the words, "In such a cave did Merlin dwell, and with him his Ariel, Amelle."

I laid down the book, quietly fixed in thought. The story was so like his and mine, and yet it had been written long before we met. I was numbed by the shock of recognition, overwhelmed with gratitude to find that the mysterious Amelle was not real but only a creature of his imagination. I felt a burden had been taken from me and I was weak with relief.

"You're crying," he said sternly. "Are they tears of laughter?" I shook my head.

"No, why would you think that?"

"Well, it's an adolescent poem," he said severely. "A young man's howling, all self-pity and self-indulgence. No wonder I did not write another canto."

"Little wonder," I answered him tartly, "that you became famous overnight. Half the women in England must have wanted to save you from yourself."

"And the other half," he said, "to save themselves from me." He was laughing at me and at himself. "Don't moon for some imaginary romantic poet, Cat." He kissed me. "Real kisses are much better than dreams or young girls' fancies."

I knew that he was right. To have him mine in reality was sweeter than to have only some spirit lover, but still I had had my own sweet dreams and fancies and he had come to me from air and wind and water. There had been power in that old dream and now sitting with him, his wife, his lady, I determined that I must give up such foolishness and come of age.

I had been jealous of Arabella who was dead, of Amelle who was no more than his imagining. I promised myself that I would never again dwell upon those he had known before me. I watched him fondly as he carelessly tossed the copies of *The Nomad* into the tray alongside the letters and the miniature of Amelia. I thought it strange that he was not more pleased by the poem that had brought him such great fame, but he seemed not to regard it one way or another and, as if eager for new discoveries, he lifted out the tray and set it aside. We peered at the contents of the trunk.

There was a jumble of old clothes, a spy glass, a pair of sturdy climbing boots, and a sheaf of invitations long out of date. There was one for a ball at Lady Jersey's and another from the famous actor Edmund Kean asking Halyard to join him at Hummuns's Hotel for supper after the play.

There were bills, lots of them, one from his tailor, several quite large ones from his wine merchant, and messages from his clubs. It was like solving a puzzle to piece together the bits of information about his habits and preferences. He said it was like making a dossier on oneself. In the end he had a list of facts, which he set himself to memorize.

His tailor was Weston, his wine merchant Berry Brothers, his clubs Wattier's and Whites, his solicitors were Chubb and Dickson, his banker Coutts, the same firm as mine, and his favorite hotel in London was Grillon's in Piccadilly.

"You see," he said, elated, "how much we already know about the man that was once me. We'd have made splendid archeologists unearthing old ruins, discovering lost cities and civilizations. Oh Cat, what a good time we are going to have! You'll love London. There's always so much to do. The theatre—I hope Kean is still playing Richard at the Drury Lane and I'll want to show you off at Almack's. We'll see all the sights and dine with friends and we'll spend whole afternoons in galleries looking at paintings. We'll have a wonderful time in London."

I was not so sure. I had no longing for London or society. But I could not bear to spoil his mood by saying so. It was obvious that he was as eager for London as a child for Christmas. He was going home to England, while I was going to an unknown country I had sought to avoid.

At the bottom of the trunk I saw a large roll of what I took to be drawings and, thinking that I would divert him from further talk of London, I asked him what they were.

He took out the roll, undid the cord, and spread them out so that they lay flat. From the moment I saw what they were I was seized by cold revulsion. They were a series of drawings, each similar in theme to the one before: scene after scene of stone fortresses and castles that had fallen into irretrievable decay. The battlements had crumbled, the castellated walks were in ruins. The dungeon's yawning pit was obscured by a clinging overgrowth of vines, yet one saw the broken chains that still hung from rusted rings.

The prisoners who had once been held there had long since died but one knew that, when in some dim and horrible past their flesh had rotted, their bones had been carried away to a dark forest lair by the jackel and the fox. The maze of ruined horror and splendor made me sick with dread.

"They are terrible," I said. "What are they and why do you keep them?"

"They are the *Carceri* by Piranesi. He is a very great artist, Cat, and these must have cost me a handsome price. I was lucky to get them."

"Lucky!" I gasped.

"Piranesi called them 'the prisons of the mind.' He means to suggest that those irrational fears we hold deep in the prisons of our mind are the ones that are most real and terrifying. You see, there is nothing really terrible or frightening in the pictures. There is nothing out of the ordinary. What do you really see? Stones and vines, a broken arch, and yet there is the feeling of the bizarre, of the hopeless. There is seemingly no escape. There are no human figures. There are no real prisoners, no bodies, yet one imagines one can hear their tortured cries. There are no real rats but one hears the faint scurrying of feet.

"Piranesi believed that we all hold fears deep within us in a perpetual, eternal nightmare only waiting for too many mince pies to bring them to the surface."

If Halyard meant to make light of my fears or to diminish my distaste for Piranesi's work, he did not succeed.

"Put them away," I said. "I don't want ever to see them again."

"As you like, but they will be even more valuable one day."

He rolled them up and went on sorting over the contents of the trunk, ignoring my Philistine views, until at last he drew from the bottom of the trunk a leather case, the contents of which seemed for him to be the prize of the day. Inside there was a brace of pistols. I hated guns most heartily but after my outburst over the drawings I did not like to say so. Besides, his pleasure was too great to be diminished by a thoughtless word.

"Don't worry, " he said, taking aim at the air. "I feel sure I've never fought a duel. I won't shoot at people, only at targets." I could tell by the manner in which he handled the pistols that he had had experience of guns. "I remember I used to go to a shooting gallery in London called Manton's. I often used to go there for an hour or two. See these wafers, they serve as targets. I have wisely made a reputation as a good shot. It prevents rash men from calling me out so that their names will be linked with mine.

"Tomorrow I'll begin to practice again. I wonder if I still retain some of my old skill." He closed the trunk but kept out the box of pistols and took them with him to the cabin.

He set them gently, almost lovingly, on the table beside the bed and although I was sure they were not loaded, sure that he must know how to handle them, I did not like them being there.

That night, for the first time since the voyage began, he did not take me in his arms. He merely gave me a kiss goodnight, a chaste kiss upon the forehead, a kiss that one might give a friend but not a lover or a wife.

I slept badly, tossing and turning, and behind a thin curtain in my mind I knew that there lay ruins of broken castles and a figure who fled like a nameless wanderer; someone for whom there was no rest. Was that figure Halyard or was it me? Later in that same dream I heard, or thought I heard, the crack of a pistol being fired.

I woke in the dark and reached out for him, but he was gone. I saw him standing by the porthole. I had no idea of how long he had been there or what thoughts or dreams kept him sleepless in the night. What was he thinking of?

Was it of Arabella, or Amelia, or Amelle? I wished I had the courage to say to him, "A penny for your thoughts." I was sure that he would tell me because he had promised not to keep secrets from me. He had given me his word, but then when I might have asked him I did not because I was afraid of what the answer might be.

Next morning I woke to find him dressed and waiting for me so that I could join him on deck and watch him shoot. He seemed to feel that the sight would prove entertaining. But I was far from enthusiastic.

That morning the weather had turned colder. It seemed that overnight we had passed from one climate to another. Days full of sun and warmth were no longer a surety. By afternoon he still stood, loading, aiming, firing almost compulsively at the wafers held up for him on a long pole by an apprehensive, reluctant sailor.

Above me the clouds had begun to spread across the sky like a thick curtain that shuts away the light. A stronger, more insistent wind began to blow, turning the sea rough and contrary.

That evening when at last we went back to our cabin a little mizzling rain had begun to fall. I watched as he cleaned and carefully put the pistols away into their case, then set them gently on the table by the bed.

"Why do you keep them with you?" I asked. He seemed to find the question curious, as if I should by instinct already know the answer.

"For protection."

"Protection from what, from whom?" He shrugged.

"Perhaps from the evil that lies waiting in the prisons of the mind." It was more another question than an answer. He seemed to hope I would accept it like a bribe to ask no others. And as he saw or thought he saw that I was satisfied, he began to talk through dinner and into the evening of all that we would do in England, of what unique

87

delights lay in store for us in London. He was like a restless passenger on a tedious cruise who looks ahead to help pass the time more quickly.

The next day we passed another ship. It was our first sighting. Signal flags were hoisted and the crew pressed to the rail giving a great huzzah. We had entered English sea lanes. Halyard's face was shining with anticipation.

"Think of it," he said, "soon the Channel, then Dover and then home."

We had sailed irrevocably over invisible lines drawn upon an arbitrary nautical chart; sailed away from Spain and summer toward England and the autumn.

Yet he seemed happy, exuberant, exultant; full of himself and the future. It was as if damp and fog were the true elements to enliven him, not the sun or dry, cloudless skies. And he continued shooting at the small white wafers even when the visibility was almost nil.

The fog, as we came up on Dover, was unremitting. We stood off at anchor in the Channel. The Captain said he would not risk docking until the morning and not then if the fog did not lift in time. Halyard was so impatient to set foot on English soil that he insisted we be put ashore in a longboat.

As we came across that short stretch of water I listened to the dip of oars in the water and it seemed to me that we were being rowed across the River Styx with Charon at the helm. I was being ferried to oblivion whilst he was peering into the mists, straining for the first sight of land like a boy coming home from school.

As we climbed up the damp stone stairs cut into the side of the sea wall the fog misted and swirled about us, clinging to our skin like cloying oil. It penetrated into the folds of my cloak and sunk into the marrow of my bones. We were enveloped by the foul stuff which was as suffocating as if we had been trapped in grey smoke.

At the top of the landing I saw a man. He stood muffled in a greatcoat, his face pale and luminous. He was shorter than Halyard and of a stocky build. He lacked Halyard's easy grace and elegance but there was, in the one brief moment when our eyes met, the impression of great vulnerability; as if he stood there in the mists completely defenseless and open to attack. When he saw Halyard his mouth opened as if he were about to scream and then the fog closed, sealing us off from him. As we passed him by, from somewhere in the gloomy mass I heard him cry out in a muted, strangled voice, "My God, Halyard, is it really you?"

I felt Halyard stop short and stiffen. He stood looking, waiting, but he could see or hear nothing.

"Who's there?" he called out. "Who called me?"

"It's Tom Grace," came the answer, and a man stepped forward out of the fog. He stood level with Halyard, pale as if he had seen a ghost. Neither of them spoke a word. I could not tell whether it was because Halyard knew the man or whether he did not and was afraid of giving himself away. It seemed a millenium that they stood looking at each other. At last it was Tom Grace who said, "Do you not mean to speak to me, Hal? Did you mean to pass me by without a word, your oldest friend?"

"Tom Grace," Halyard said slowly. Was it recognition or a question? He extended his hand but Grace ignored it, choosing instead to embrace Halyard as if he were his long-lost brother.

"My God," he said, standing back again. "I still cannot believe it is really you. It is like a miracle. But why did you not let me know that you were coming? I've not had so much as a word from you in all these months. And why did you not speak to me? Are you angry with me? Have I done something to offend you? Do you imagine that I have done you some wrong?"

"No," Halyard answered hastily. "I did not see you for the fog. You took me by surprise. I had not expected anyone to meet me."

This mild enough reply seemed to upset Tom Grace even more.

"I was with you, Hal, the day that you left England. You might have known I would be here to see you return."

"How did you know that I was coming?"

"There was a report at the Admiralty of Calford's yacht being sighted. There was a rumor that you were aboard. When I heard that the *Persepolis* was to dock at Dover I came at once." Tom Grace looked again at Halyard with dismayed bewilderment.

"Have you any idea of what it has been like for me not knowing how or where you were? There have been all sorts of rumors, each more terrible than the last. Some that you were lost at sea, others that there was no trace of you, and the worst was that you were dead."

I felt myself trembling uncontrollably. It was more than the fog, it was the coldness of the words I had just heard.

"I regret not writing you," Halyard said drily. "How inconvenient for the gossips that I must prove them wrong."

"Don't make a joke of my anxiety," Tom Grace burst out with feeling.

"Sorry." Halyard made him a bow of contrition. "But now we mustn't stand here in this raw weather debating my manners or my mortality while Cat catches her death of cold. Catherine," he took my arm, "may I present my oldest friend, Tom Grace. Tom, this is my wife, Catherine."

"Your wife!" Tom Grace's eyes went from Halyard's face to mine and back again. He had taken an instant inventory of my bedraggled appearance, my homespun cape, cotton dress, and rope-soled sandals. And I knew that at first glance he had already compared me to Arabella and that I had been found wanting.

"I did not know," Tom Grace said almost inaudibly, "that you had married." He seemed to feel it should still be kept a secret. Halyard smiled.

"I take it that piece of intelligence was not in the Admiralty report." He put his arm about me, holding me to him. "Cat and I met in Spain. We were married in Gibraltar before we sailed. Well, Tom, aren't you going to wish us joy?"

"Yes, of course." Tom Grace reached out his hand for mine and bent to kiss it with the greatest courtesy. His lips were cold to the touch. I felt I had been branded with ice. But when he spoke the words were warm. "Of course, I wish you joy with all my heart."

"And now," Halyard was firm and brusque, "we mustn't keep Cat standing out in our infernal English climate. We were just on our way to the Sailors' Arms where we can all keep dry while I arrange for a coach and horses."

"No need for that," Tom Grace interrupted him. "I have brought your coach."

"You have what?" Halyard was clearly amazed by this turn of events.

"You left your coach with me. You insisted it was mine, as a gift, if you did not return. So like you, Hal, to make a generous gesture. That coach was your pride and joy, modeled after Napoleon's wagon-lit."

"And now I have turned up like a bad penny and you are out your coach."

"Don't talk rot," Tom Grace said stiffly and we turned, the three of us, and walked along the quay toward the dim, flickering lights ahead that burned amber holes into the grey mist.

I found myself between the two of them and felt I had been maneuvered there like some buffer state to prevent further conversation.

Inside the inn there was the welcome warmth of blazing fires. Seated in a cozy private parlor, the constraint between Halyard and Tom Grace seemed to thaw. Brandy warmed me like a flame and brought color back to my cheeks and feeling to my limbs. My cloak lay steaming on the fender before the fire. Halyard stood warming his hands while Tom Grace sat in a wing chair staring up at him.

"You have changed, Hal, I sensed it the first moment I saw you. But that does not explain why you have come back and why all the mystery."

"No mystery, dear fellow." Halyard spoke lightly. "After all, England is my home."

"Home!" Tom Grace made the word sound like a prison

91

sentence. "You swore when you left that you would never set foot in England again. You said that you would prefer to live in hell than here."

"Well." Halyard shrugged. "I have changed. At least I have had a change of heart." He looked at me with such a tender glance that it could not have been lost on Tom Grace. "And now that I am here I cannot wait to be on my way. This coachman you have. Is he yours or mine?"

"Yours," Tom Grace answered stiffly. "I kept old Jeb. I thought he would be better off with me in town than idle down at Longfields. I trust you do not mind?"

"Mind? Not a bit of it. I only wanted to know the coachman's name so that I could speak to him about some fresh horses." He looked at me and smiled, clearly pleased at the manner in which he was handling the meeting with Tom Grace.

"Why are you so anxious to be off?" Tom Grace asked. "To set out at night in this weather would be madness. Surely after all these months away it cannot matter to you whether you get to Longfields tonight or tomorrow?"

"I do not mean to go to Longfields, but straight on to London."

"You must be joking."

"No."

"In God's name, why? Have you forgotten what London was like when you left it?"

"I have business there that cannot wait."

"What business? You cannot mean to go back again as if you had never been away. What business is so important that you would not be better off in the country?"

"I must see my tailor, surely that is reason enough for any man to go to London. Besides, I have promised to show Cat the sights, take her to the galleries and to the theatre. Is Kean still playing Richard? And, of course, I shall want to go to Wattier's. I have missed the dandies. They were always very civil to me as were the ladies at Almack's. I am starved for town company after all those months in Spain."

Tom Grace sat speechless. Halyard, smiling, took that si-

92

lence for success. He was pleased with himself for putting all he had studied to such good use.

"And now," he said, "if you'll be good enough to order us some supper I'll see to old Jeb and the horses."

"We must talk about this first." Grace tried to stop him but Halyard would not listen.

"We'll have time enough for talk in the coach. I have a dozen questions to ask and I want to hear all the news of the town." Before Tom Grace could say any more Halyard was gone, leaving the two of us alone before the blazing hearth.

For a time Tom Grace sat staring at the fire. He pulled nervously at his eyebrow, like a boy in school who has not studied his book and now in the test hopes to pluck the answer from his brow. He was clearly worried and once more I had the impression that he was vulnerable both to Halyard and his own moods.

Not that I thought Tom Grace to be a weak man but rather that he was soft hearted enough to succumb to temptation. Here was the eternal foul-weather friend, always an easy mark one could depend upon perhaps even more in adversity than in those times when luck was in and fortune smiling.

"I see that he is changed." He looked at me suddenly and then away again at the fire. "I sensed that the moment I saw him, but why, oh why, I ask you, has he come back again and to come like this without a word to me? If I had known what he meant to do I could have eased things a bit, prepared the way for him, but to walk into London as if nothing had happened is sheer folly." He stopped briefly and then went on.

"No, we must stay here for the night. I'll talk to him and between us perhaps we can talk some sense into him. You must try to persuade him not to go to London but to Longfields."

"He is determined to go to London," I said quietly. I knew I could not stop Halyard nor was I sure I wanted to. Then Tom Grace gave a sigh and turned to me, leaning in toward me as if he might sink on his knees before me.

93

"Please try to understand. I know you are a stranger, a newcomer to England, but you can have no idea of what it was like for him before he left. He had good reason for going, believe me! The mob jeered him in the street, friends' doors were closed to him, it was a nightmare."

"But why?" I felt a rise of anger. Who were these English that acted like barbarians because a man's wife was dead? "Why would they be so cruel?" I asked. "I know he could never have done anything to warrant such attacks."

Tom Grace closed his eyes. He seemed to be trying to find patience and the right words to win me to his side.

"You are the loyal wife, it does you credit."

"You are his friend," I retorted hotly. "You know what he is like as well as I."

"Yes, I am his friend." He nodded. "And God knows I've stood by him always."

"Then tell me why. Why would they behave so badly toward him, he who deserved their sympathy. It was his grief. It was his wife who had died in a senseless, tragic fire. Why did they not give him support and understanding? What manner of country is this?"

"I hope you may never hear all the cruel things they said of him but at best there were," his hands went out in a helpless gesture of futility, "there were those who felt he had not tried to save Arabella."

"But that's monstrous. Of course he tried to save her. He has the scars to prove it. He loved her."

"He told you that?" It was a sharp question quickly asked.

"He did not have to tell me. I saw the scars and I know he would not marry anyone he did not love." Tom Grace looked away and then settled down into his chair as if he suddenly felt more at ease.

"You must know how much he loved her," I said. I meant to have him tell me I was right. "I have heard that she was very beautiful and greatly loved by all."

"Yes." Tom Grace sighed again. "Arabella was the most beautiful woman I ever saw."

"Then," I said, "if you are honest perhaps you think that I cannot possibly compare to her. That I am such a young and inexperienced girl that in London I would shame him. Is that why you do not want him to go there, because I would embarrass him before his friends?"

I had told him my worst fears of London and of England and he could only stare at me with an expression of great compassion—or was it pity—and then he shook his head.

"Oh no, I think no such thoughts of you. I was Arabella's friend and now I would be yours. No, dear Catherine, it is nothing to do with you and yet," he hesitated, "if Halyard, after all that's passed, now comes back to London with a new bride after such a brief period of mourning there will be more rumors. It will stir up the old muck all over again. He may choose to forget the past. He may laugh it off and make a witty epigram of it, but what of you? They can be very cruel. Halyard should not go to London if he cares anything at all for your feelings."

I looked into his face. I must decide now whether to trust him or not. Whether to tell him the truth and ask his help or brazen it out alone. And I quailed at the thought. I knew nothing of London. I wanted Halyard to be happy there, to have the good time he was so looking forward to. If at every moment he might be set upon I could not protect him from the slings and arrows of that outrageous society. I must have help and Tom Grace was his old and trusted friend.

"He does care for me," I said, "I am as sure of that as I am sure that he has forgotten all that happened before I met him."

Tom Grace stared, caught his breath, and waited for me to go on.

"He does not remember Arabella or the fire or most of the gossip that drove him away."

"Is that the truth?" Tom Grace said slowly, and rose and began to pace the room. I knew that he believed me, but the idea was so new and so unexpected that it had set his mind to racing.

As he walked up and down I told him as briefly as I could how I had found Halyard and what had happened afterward.

"He has forgotten it all, even you, Tom Grace. As far as he remembers he has never laid eyes on you before today."

Tom Grace sat again, nodding in agreement. It seemed that he had accepted my story and now the last piece of a puzzle had just fallen into place.

"Of course, of course, what you have told me explains so many things that had troubled me. Why he did not write. You see, I thought, I imagined all sorts of stupid things." He laughed now as if it were a joke. "I even imagined that he was angry with me, that he thought I too had turned against him or done him some wrong."

"I know," I interrupted him, "that you think he must go to Longfields, but is it not possible that you have exaggerated the reception he will find in London? He must go there on business and he wants to give me pleasure. If these people, all his old false friends and the rabble, are as cruel as you say, they are also fickle by nature. By now they will have had other topics to gossip about."

"Yes." He looked at me with frank admiration and regard. "Yes, that is possible. You are, if I may say so, a most amazing and extraordinary young woman. I envy Halyard his good fortune in finding you."

"Then help me, help him. He is so looking forward to a few days in town. If you were with him constantly as his companion, his friend, you could steer him away from dangerous ground. It is something I could not do for him. I know no one. Surely he deserves a little happiness at last. Does he not?"

Tom Grace studied over what I had said and at last he coughed discreetly.

"Yes, all you say is true, but you must understand that he has not always been a saint. He has often provoked society by doing outrageous things. He was their god, you see, and when they found he had feet of clay they brought him down."

"What did he do that was so outrageous?"

"Oh, in the beginning he made himself notorious because he wanted the attention. He was a lonely chap, not quite from the right drawer. He noticed it, you see, when

96

others didn't. He put a chip on his shoulder and he kept it there like a dare. At one time Lord H. had a limp like Byron but this was cut out and this little bauble remained."

I found what he had just told me curious and contradictory.

"What do you mean, not out of the right drawer? He is a lord, is he not?"

"The family is, how shall I put it, eccentric." Eccentric was the same word Sir Humphrey had used. As for the limp, I had always supposed it to be the result of the accident.

"When we were at Cambridge," Tom Grace went on, intent on giving me a summary of Halyard's crimes, "he kept a bear in his rooms because it caused a stir. When we went on our Grand Tour together he took along a royal retinue and gave it out that we were both M'Lords. It was an embarrassing and vulgar display when what we had really sworn to do was to write our poems.

"We took a trunk of paper and a pail of ink. He, alas, wrote more than I and when he came home again he polished up his pages and found himself famous, although I know for a fact that he made up most of his sins just to shock the ladies."

"And you," I asked him, "are you a famous poet?"

"I am a poet," he replied, "but nothing like as famous as your husband. No, my verse is too fragile, I'm afraid. And as I have no fortune I must make my way by singing for my supper."

"You have been his friend for so long I know that you will not desert him now." I hoped I sounded properly persuasive. "Say that you will come with him to London and that you will stay with him until he decides on going back to Longfields."

"Of course. I will do what I can for him and now that I have met you I am your devoted servant as well."

It was settled then and I hoped that what I had done was right and best and wise.

When Halyard came back we ate our supper. I could see how excited he was, how he was stimulated by the prospect of the days ahead. In the coach he asked a multitude of questions. How was the old King and the Prince Regent? What of Beau Brummell, had the Prince relented? All trivial and meaningless questions, but it seemed to amuse him and Tom Grace, who from time to time sent me a knowing glance as if we were conspirators in this plot to please.

It was all froth and no substance that occupied them, but in a way it was comforting to think that if this was the sort of stuff they said of Halyard it meant nothing and could do no more harm than paper cuts.

The coach that Tom Grace had said was Halyard's pride and joy, a copy of Napoleon's wagon-lit, was as comfortable as the rough roads would allow.

And because it was so comfortable, in time I slept, dozing fitfully as I heard them chattering on of who was up and who was down in the great world; of who had played to win and who had lost all on one turn of the cards.

At dawn, just as we were clattering over Westminster Bridge, Halyard leaned from the windows, pointing out the Abbey and the Parliament. On we sped past the Old Spring Gardens to Piccadilly and Grillon's.

Halyard leapt from the carriage and, without waiting for the footman, dashed inside to secure for us the best rooms available while Tom Grace and I sat staring at each other. Tom said he would not stay with us at the hotel for he had rooms in Albany just around the corner. He promised to come later in the day and then he said a most disturbing thing. He said, and he was smiling, that it was the first time he had ever seen a man drive himself to his own hanging. And I thought it was a queer sort of joke to make.

Chapter Five

Despite Tom Grace's sense of foreboding, Halyard was happy. I had never seen him so gay or full of life. His energy and enthusiasm seemed boundless, as though he were a boy on school holiday. I hoped with all my heart that nothing would mar his present happiness.

From the first, London to me was a bewildering jumble of sights, sounds, and sensations. I could not have imagined such a place. Even at that early hour there was an open market full of people and in the streets tradesmen were busy taking down their shutters. Boys with barrows were making their first deliveries and as far as one could see in all directions street after street flowed out like cobbled streams.

After Tom Grace said goodbye to us we were escorted with much bowing and scraping to our suite of rooms. Even on such short notice fires had been lighted and there were bowls of fresh fruit and flowers; compliments of the management.

Halyard insisted that I must rest before our real day began. He said that he was not the least tired and besides he had a dozen things he must attend to.

I was only too glad for a tub of hot water and a wide, soft bed. As I settled beneath the comforter I felt like a bird that had been migrating forever and at last had found a nest of down. I was warm, safe, and secure, and as long as we were here in the sheltering luxury of the hotel we would not have to face the unknown or the unexpected.

For a time I slept the deep, dreamless sleep of exhaustion; then I woke with a start to hear the babble of excited voices. They sounded sharp and shrill as a flight of starlings. Above all the racket I heard a woman's voice raised to an angry shriek. My first thought was that one of Halyard's female admirers had already found out where he was and had invaded the hotel.

Then Halyard's head appeared peeping around the door. He looked flushed and out of sorts.

"Come, Cat, please do. There's a frightful row going on out here."

I put on his dressing gown and as I entered the sitting room it looked at first glance as if a hurricane had swept through it. There were dresses, coats, gloves, hats, shoes, stockings, and underthings scattered everywhere. They were lying on chairs, draped over sofas, hanging from half-opened boxes. There was a cloud of tissue-thin paper flying in the air and the virago who was responsible for all the confusion was a Madame Michaud, who told me in voluble mixture of French and English that she was, *sans doute*, the best dressmaker in all of London. And she motioned to her two young assistants who nodded in agreement.

She said she had been summoned by M'Lord at this ungodly hour of the morning because he wished her to produce a wardrobe for me in which I would dazzle London. But she insisted she must measure me now before she could proceed with her work.

It seemed a reasonable enough request but hardly worth all the dramatic display of temperament. I quietly allowed her to take my measurements but I refused any fittings until later, saying that I would choose something to wear today from the ample and excellent selection she had

100

brought with her, and, somewhat mollified, she and her staff withdrew, promising to return by teatime with a creation I could wear that evening to the theatre.

When Madame Michaud had gone Halyard heaved a sigh of relief.

"I am sorry, Cat, I wanted all this to be a surprise but when I told her that you were still sleeping and could not be disturbed she had a French fit."

"Never mind," I said. I put my arms around his neck and kissed him tenderly. "I am surprised, truly I am." And I was, for there were enough clothes here to outfit a tribe of wives.

"What a woman," he muttered. "My tailor would never have behaved like that." Then, as I began to kiss him again, he forgot Madame Michaud and her dresses.

From the elegant debris I chose a pelisse, a dress, and bonnet. The pelisse and bonnet were of russet brown and the dress was in moire, the color of rich cream. In London I meant to look my best so as to make him proud of me.

When I was dressed he said that I looked delectable and I was happy that I had pleased him, but all the while I found myself thinking of the extravagance and the thought made me uneasy. If he was in financial difficulties, if his estate was in pawn, he should not be so rash as to spend money on all this unnecessary finery for me. I would have liked to say as much but it would have seemed ungrateful. I knew at this moment he would have put a ribbon around London and given it to me for a present, and I loved him for his open-handed generosity.

Then he kissed me once more, handed me my gloves, and stood back to survey *le toute ensemble.*

"Lady Halyard," he said with undisguised pride and admiration, "you will be the talk of London."

It was the last thing in the world I wanted to be. I wanted no notice taken of him or of me. I wished us to be exceedingly private until he had done with business and then for us to go quietly home to Longfields. What a change that was in my thinking—to call Longfields, a place that I had never seen, my home.

101

As for today I could only hope that Tom Grace's fears had been exaggerated and that all the old rumors had been forgotten in Halyard's absence. Certainly to the hotel staff he seemed like a hero come home.

We were escorted through the foyer by the manager. The door of the waiting carriage was opened by a smartly alert footman. It was not, to my surprise, Halyard's coach that waited for us but a chaise. Halyard said that he had sent old Jeb to rest for the day and hired a light chaise to take us about. Another expense!

To me it seemed that all we did was for show and not worth the price. A hackney coach would surely have done just as well and for a brief moment I could not help remembering other mornings we had shared together standing on the terrace of the little white house, looking at the sea, running along the cliff with the wind behind us.

Here there was no blue, cloudless sky. What little one could see of it was cloudy and grey with only patches of brighter stuff. Everywhere the buildings were crowded so close together and set in such narrow, twisting streets that the small expanses of green were called parks. The streets themselves were filthy with mud and slime. In London the rich rode, the poor walked, and the middle sort of folk dodged out of the way of both. But Halyard seemed as happy as if we had just come to open country.

First we drove along Piccadilly and then into Leicester Fields where there was no field at all. Then down toward a pretty church called St. Martin-in-the-Fields; again no hint of a country field, and past the Old Spring Gardens where to be fair there were a few flowers in a tiny formal garden. Then we turned past Charing Cross and into the Strand.

All along the way he was busy pointing out so many different sights that I would have had to have twenty pairs of eyes to see everything.

"But never mind," he said comfortingly, "on the way back from the City we will take our time and go to the Tower and to Westminster Abbey and drive past Carlton House and down the Mall."

One would have thought to hear him that he had built

the whole of London while I slept, just for my pleasure. And I loved him for it with all my heart; loved him more with every passing day.

He sat there across from me, so handsome and masculine despite his dandy's clothes. I knew that no elaborately tied neckcloth or carefully arranged curls could disguise how hard and lean and tanned he was. Those days in Spain and the voyage home had made him well again and perhaps in better health than he had ever been before.

It would be hard to stay fit and trim in London if one always rode and was made soft by being waited on hand and foot. Here what did one ever have the chance to do for oneself or alone? I, who so loved my solitary rambles, had already been told that in London ladies never walked out alone.

As we came to the end of the Strand he drew my attention back to bricks and mortar. Soon, he said, we would be passing Temple Bar and the Inns of Court, and then in no time I could see the splendid dome of St. Paul's.

"If only there had been more time," he said, "we could have driven past the Monument, which commemorates the great fire of London, but for now that must wait as I have an appointment with my solicitors, Chubb and Dickson, and I don't want to keep them waiting any longer than is necessary."

Just as the Strand became the Fleet we turned up a side street and drew up before a red brick building. There was a polished brass knocker on the door and a brass plate that spelled out the names of Chubb and Dickson in the most discreet of letters.

By this time I had come to expect carriage doors to be opened for us, but I had not expected the clerks all to be standing to attention nor for the oldest of them, stooped and bent with age, to show Halyard and myself into the office of Chubb and Dickson as if it were the greatest honor in all of his long years of faithful service.

There, before a glowing coal grate, stood the two men themselves. Mr. Chubb was as short and round as Mr. Dickson, his partner, was tall and thin. They struck me as comic figures and I was ashamed of myself for the unkind thought. Still, I could not prevent myself from wondering how Mr. Dickson's eyeglasses ever managed to stay on such a long, narrow nose.

They were both clearly moved by the sight of Lord Halyard. Mr. Dickson, the quiet, almost silent partner, said little, but his nose twitched in a most significant way and Mr. Chubb, his eyes pink and moist, was quite overcome.

After much shaking of hands both of them spoke together to say how pleased they were to have his lordship home again, and I was easy in my mind that neither of these men were now or ever had been Halyard's enemies. They were both what they seemed; loyal, interested retainers and no more.

"We could not believe it at first," Mr. Chubb was saying. "We had heard so many dreadful rumors that now to see you here like this is nothing short of miraculous. Though, to be sure, just at first when we received your note this morning asking for an accounting of your assets we did think it might be some imposter. One doesn't know what people will say or do these days. However, we sent to the bank for your strong box though just to be on the safe side we took the precaution of having some stout men from the City Ward walk along with it."

Halyard interrupted this flow of good feeling to present both men to me and they each in turn took my hand with the greatest warmth. If they were shocked or surprised by my presence they were too polite to show it and they wished us the greatest joy.

"Bless me, bless me," said Mr. Chubb. "We've known him since he was a boy and first came into the title and the estate. Well, bless me." Mr. Chubb was temporarily at a loss for words. And so it was Mr. Dickson who opened the door and signaled to a clerk to bring in the chest. From the manner in which it was carried one was sure that whatever the contents they were considered to be of great value.

Mr. Chubb gravely handed the key to Halyard.

"I believe you will find just what you hoped for. The very fact that in your note you asked if certain," he cleared

104

his throat, "certain articles were in the chest made us doubt that the inquiry really came from you."

Halyard smiled knowingly. He obviously understood Mr. Chubb's remark. Without waiting any longer he unlocked the chest. The raised lid prevented me from seeing the contents but from the huge smile on Halyard's face I could see that he was indeed pleased with the contents. With elaborate carelessness he took a handkerchief from his pocket and spread it on my lap. From the chest he lifted out a chamois bag, turned it upside down, and into my lap there fell a shower of diamonds, rubies, emeralds, and pearls. From fitted boxes he added to the pile a tiara, a necklace, bracelets, and rings. It was a treasure trove, a pirate's hoard.

Halyard was smiling but my face was frozen in astonishment, as were Messrs. Chubb's and Dickson's. For a moment there was complete silence, only the fall of ashes in the grate was audible. No one moved, not even when a brooch of diamonds and sapphires fell from my lap and rolled beneath a desk. When we came to life the clerk scrambled to retrieve it and Halyard, who had been waiting for me to make some response, said almost triumphantly, "I promised you, Cat, that I would give you diamonds and rubies, emeralds and pearls and here for good measure there are amethysts and topaz, sapphires and opals as well." And still I could not speak for I did not know what to say.

The first thought that crossed my mind was that surely he did not expect me to wear them all at once. And then came the realization that this was the sort of behavior that had earned him the reputation of being eccentric. What other man would have dumped a fortune in a woman's lap, and how could one explain that it was not odd or a caprice of the moment but something he had thought out beforehand, something he had done from his heart to please me?

"Take the lot of them, Cat. They are all yours now." And as he spoke I heard Mr. Chubb gasp. "You mean to take them all away with you?" Mr. Chubb's eyes were round and frightened by the prospect. "You mean to give them, forgive me, dear lady, to your present wife?"

"Yes." Halyard turned to him, still smiling and pleased with his magnificent gesture. "There can be no objection, I am sure."

"It's not for me to say, of course." Mr. Chubb reddened. "But may I remind you that the jewels are part of the estate. They are entailed and therefore not personal property." He had not been able to keep the shock and disapproval from his voice. "And to take them now, I mean would it be wise, there are so many thieves about these days." Halyard brushed all such cautious and prudent advice aside.

"I'll risk it if Cat will." He seemed to take my willingness for granted. "And now," he said to me, "look over your cache and decide which you wish to wear tonight to the theatre while I have a word or two about business."

I sat staring at the pile of stones upon my lap. They seemed unreal to me, as false as if they had been made of paste. The agate in my pocket had more meaning for me than all these cold, priceless stones set in silver and gold. As I sat staring I wondered what the lifeless things would feel like around my neck. Unfortunately I could not help but overhear the conversation that was taking place.

"Am I to understand correctly that while I was away you two have been trying to find a tenant for Longfields?" Mr. Chubb reddened like a turkey cock.

"It was on your instructions, you may remember, that we were to settle all your debts."

"But surely," Halyard was calm and patient, "surely there cannot have been as many as all that."

"I'm afraid there were." It was Mr. Dickson who was so positive. "There were a great many bills outstanding with the tradesmen. They had gone unpaid for years, and as for the gambling losses, a number of unexpected markers came in to us after you had left England that were, to put it bluntly, staggering. You had asked us most specifically to settle all debts in the best manner that we could. Which left us no choice but to find a tenant." Now it was Halyard's

106

turn to frown and look more serious. The news had come as a blow to him. Mr. Dickson, seeing his distress, tried to soften it.

"If there had been another way, believe me, we would have taken it, but there was none. All the income from yours and the first Lady Halyard's estates was pledged long ago. You must admit your style of living was most imprudent and impractical. We tried to warn you then, you will remember, but you would not listen." Halyard nodded. I knew that he remembered nothing of the kind but could not bring himself to say so. And I wished that I were anywhere else in the world but here so that I would not be hearing any of this.

"Well," Halyard shrugged, "it's no good asking where it's all gone if the money is not available." Mr. Dickson sighed, fearing he had spoken too bluntly.

"I am sorry but even with the sale of the house in London there still was not enough to stem the tide. Which meant that we had to look for a tenant for Longfields as well. Perhaps now that you are home again you'll have some other thoughts."

Halyard stood straight, his smile returned.

"There's nothing for it then but to retrench. I have never been one for cheese paring but now it seems I have no choice."

I knew that at that moment he meant to be sensible but I did not think he knew what the words prudence and economy conveyed to most folk. It had never occurred to me before that he might have played too deep at cards and lost beyond his means to pay. He had never seemed to be the sort who would hazard all on a whim of fate. Yet with all the bad news he had heard he did not seem dismayed, rather he was still remarkably cheerful.

"Please, gentlemen, if you will be so good as to make up a statement for me of what I have in hand and what I owe, noting what must be paid at once and what can wait a while longer, I would be grateful to you both. I have no intention of letting Longfields. I mean to live there myself." With that he bade them both a cordial goodbye and, taking me by the arm as I clung to the bulging kerchief with both hands, he led me out into the street and into the waiting carriage.

Alone with me he was as gay and lighthearted as if he hadn't a care in the world. It did not seem to worry him at all that he was on the edge financially any more than he seemed aware he might always be in danger from his old enemies. He seemed concerned with nothing more than a day's sightseeing and an evening at the theatre.

Perhaps when the moment was right I could tactfully suggest to him that I did not need so many dresses or that we might do without such an ornate coach but now was not the time, he was enjoying himself too much.

He was a splendid guide. He took me first to the Tower to see the beasts. I was suitably impressed by a building of such great antiquity although I did not like to see animals shut up for public view. The poor, caged things went to and fro while people stared and small boys taunted them.

Then on to Westminster and the Abbey where we walked on hallowed stones. It was strange that kings and queens so long dead should have such an influence on my spirits. In the crypt their stone coffins had been preserved with great care. Who was it, I wondered, whose business it was to sort over the royal bones and make sure each lay in the proper vault.

Next we drove across the way past the Houses of Parliament where Halyard sat in the House of Lords. He said he had magnificent robes that he wore on state occasions and he had made a speech, although he could not remember what it was about. Something to do with weavers in the north, he thought.

And then we went up Whitehall past the Banqueting House and the site where once England had beheaded a rightful monarch and afterward repented of it. And down past St. James's Park and the Palace, up St. James's Street past Green Park and around Hyde Park in a circle where we saw some very pretty ladies riding in Rotten Row. I remarked to Halyard that I had never seen such pretty girls and he replied that I most certainly had never seen such expensive ones.

"What do you mean?" I asked him, as innocent as May. He explained that these pretty horsebreakers were whores not out for the love of riding but to display their wares. I asked him how much their favors might be worth for a night but if he knew he would not tell me. I believe that he was shocked that I would want to know such things, and the thought came to my mind that perhaps he might have known one or two of them in a more than casual way.

When at last we finally got back to the hotel Madame Michaud was waiting with a dress worthy of a princess. I stood before a long glass while she made the final adjustments. I knew that the woman reflected back to me was an imposter. I did not know her and I was not sure I wanted to. She might have been any lady of fashion in the town. Certainly her tiara and her necklace were beyond compare. Bright with diamonds and rubies and emeralds, they dimmed the color of her eyes. The dress that was cut low at the neck to show off her shoulders and bosom made her look like an expensive piece of merchandise set on display. I did not much care for this showpiece and I wished that I were by the sea or in a cave or on a cliff, anywhere rather than here.

Madame Michaud, however, was proud of the effect. She promised that there would be other costumes tomorrow; dresses for the morning, the afternoon, and the evening. I must, she insisted, never be seen in the same garment twice. It would be social ruin.

"Surely," I said, looking at Halyard who was admiring me and Madame's creation, or was it the jewels? "Surely, we must try to be a little economical." But he would not hear of it and he swept me off to the theatre where, just as he had wished, we were to see the great Kean play Richard III.

I had never been to a play before and the evening was forever imprinted upon my memory. We arrived at the theatre in Halyard's distinctive coach. We entered not through the public way but via a stage entrance and then up a flight of inner stairs to a landing where we were shown to a private box by the manager. If we had been royalty we could not have been treated with more deference. All arrangements had been made beforehand. As friends of Kean's we were to be his guests both at the play and for supper afterward.

Inside the box Halyard took my cape, then held a chair for me so that I could be seated. I remember how he looked when he turned and took his place beside me. I had never seen him look more handsome nor more at his ease.

The house was already full. The newly installed gas lights were a phenomenon I had never seen before. They gave off a luminous yellow glow, and with the rising heat and the sound of voices swirling all about me, I felt faint; drugged, hot and cold all at once. I was as self-conscious as if I had just come uninvited to a large ball where all the other guests were old acquaintances and I the only stranger. I saw that we were sitting in the center of a horseshoe of boxes, and that a woman in the box next to ours had turned suddenly and seen Halyard. I saw her go pale and nudge the woman next to her and so it went all around the circle; conversation stopped, eyes stared, fingers pointed, heads disappeared behind opened fans.

Beneath us in the pit the reaction was the same. Faces were raised upward, a sea of faces all looking, staring up at him and then at me. A dowager raised her lorgnette, another put her hand to her heart as if she had suffered an attack, one man raised his opera glasses to stare more closely. Mouths were opened, then closed, and where at first there had been stunned silence, then a whisper, now there was a roar of talk and on the top of the wave was his name—Halyard, Halyard.

He did not seem to notice. He looked neither right nor left. Most astonishing of all he pulled from his pocket a small paper twist full of marrons glacés and offered one to me.

"I love eating sweetmeats in the theatre," he said. "It always seems so forbidden and delicious. And just listen to

110

them chattering away. I told you, Cat, that you would take London by storm. Everyone is talking about you and saying how beautiful you look."

I could not believe that he took it all so calmly. I was sure that he must be aware that the stir and uproar was not because of me but because of him. If they looked at me or spoke of me it was only because of my jewels or because I was with him.

I hated being singled out, stared at and remarked upon as if I were public property. I did not want to be conspicuous. Halyard might be used to it but I was not.

For a time I tried to concentrate upon my program, reading over the list of actors and the parts they were to play, but the words began to blur and run together in a meaningless mass. Then, with my eyes still downcast, hoping to avoid those staring neighbors in the nearby boxes, I glanced down into the pit, and there I saw a man who stood out, singular and detached from all the rest of the audience. He was about Halyard's age and very tall and thin. I noticed him first because of the color of his hair, a rich auburn red.

And then I saw the look on his face.

He was standing with his back to the stage, staring up at our box. I knew he saw me too, for our eyes met and I saw him fix my dress and my jewels at a glance. But the real object of his attention was not me but Halyard. He looked up, his features contorted with such hatred as I had never seen in any man's face before. If looks could have killed his glance would have been an act of murder.

I was in a panic. What if he had a gun? It was possible. What should I do? Should I throw myself before Halyard or should I cry out to him to warn him? I could not believe that my husband did not see the man, for he was looking down too.

"The house is full," Halyard said evenly. "Kean always plays to a packed house." I could not believe Halyard did not feel the heat of the man's gaze upon his face, for that look was as corrosive and as scarring as acid.

But still Halyard betrayed no sign of recognition. Did he

111

know him, or was it someone whom he had forgotten, someone who bore him a grudge so deep that he would gladly kill for his satisfaction.

For the first time I fully realized what Tom Grace had tried to tell me. I understood what things had been like for Halyard before he left England. But what could Halyard ever have done to warrant such hatred?

As I sat wondering what I should do the house darkened and there was a hush that spread, settling over the theatre before the rise of the curtain. For the moment the audience forgot Halyard and turned their attention to the stage—all but the auburn-haired man.

He stood where he was, immovable. Not for a moment did his dreadful gaze waiver by so much as a flicker of the eyes. Then, as the curtain began slowly to rise, people in the seats on either side of him began to whisper to him to sit down. Still he did not move, and then at last, as if propelled by some unseen force, he stumbled out of the row.

For another moment he stood in the aisle still looking up and then he rushed from the theatre in such haste that I was afraid he meant to come to our box, open the door, and attack Halyard.

"Who was that man?" I whispered to Halyard.

"I do not know." I continued to watch him nervously. But within a few moments, when no madman had burst in upon us, I found I had transferred my attention and my emotions from the man in the pit to the man upon the stage.

I knew the play, I had read it with my father, but I could not have imagined what power an actor could bring to Shakespeare's lines in a performance. The words were chilling and caught me in a spell.

"Now is the winter of our discontent made glorious summer by this sun of York."

Kean was a magician. He made his Richard a villain one followed step by step toward his inevitable end when upon that last, bloody field of battle he cried out for a horse to deliver him. I found that I wept not for Richard but for all men who despite themselves have done dark and terrible things. Kean made me understand such a man and pity him.

"Poor Richard," Halyard said as the curtain fell. "There are those who think he was innocent of all the crimes that history has charged him with. What do you think, Cat, was Richard a hero or a villain?"

And I did not know how to answer him, for if Halyard himself had been reviled and I knew he was innocent, was it not possible for a king to be innocent as well?

"What does Kean say? Does he think Richard was a hero or a villain?"

"You must ask him, Cat. It would please him." I flushed.

"I will probably be too shy to speak at all. I have never met a genius before."

Halyard threw back his head and laughed and I flushed because I had forgotten that many felt he was a genius.

"A man is never a hero to his wife." He leaned and kissed me on the cheek. "Come on, Cat, we are to meet my friend and undisputed genius at his hotel. He likes to entertain at Hummun's, for it is close to the theatre and just declassé enough so they do not look down on his friends. You will have your first taste of the artistic and sporting life. I wonder what you will make of it and of Kean. I think I must warn you not everyone approves of him."

At the hotel Halyard presented Kean to me, although to do Kean justice I thought it should have been the other way around. I had feared I would be dumbstruck but at once I saw I liked him, and I knew that for some reason I could not fathom he liked me as well.

He was not at all the sort of man I had expected. Gone were all the trappings of the king and with them his height had seemingly diminished.

Kean was a small, short man with dark, sharp, penetrating eyes and an odd rolling gait. Halyard had told me that some said it was because when Kean was young he had had his legs broken, though others said it was because he had been so ill fed as a child.

Kean did not take my hand nor make me a welcome speech nor say he wished us joy but he was Halyard's friend, I was sure of it.

"You saw the performance?" he asked as if he did not already know the answer.

"Yes," I said, "I have never seen a play before and if I were never to see another this evening would have been enough to last me all my life."

Kean set his head on one side, looking at me quizzically, and then he turned to Halyard.

"Your wife," he murmured, "is either a great diplomat or a great liar."

"Cat never lies," Halyard assured him gravely. And Kean turned back to me with a strange, sad expression on his face.

"I am sure that she does not and so I thank you for the compliment."

There were a great many people in the private dining room. They were a mixed bag to be sure. There was Mendoza, the boxer; John Cotman, the painter; a jockey whose name I never caught; and a strikingly handsome girl, Miss Wilson, who looked remarkably like one of the pretty horsebreakers I had seen in the park. All of them made a bid for Kean's attention but he kept me by him even when Halyard was carried off by some old acquaintances.

From across the room he looked over their heads and smiled at me. I did not think he remembered them but it did not seem to matter.

"He has changed," Kean said, glancing at Halyard. "He looks like a happy man."

"Was he never happy before he left England?" I asked. They were almost the same words Tom Grace had used about Halyard, but somehow when Kean said them there was a subtle difference.

Kean shook his head as one might at a naughty child.

"Don't play the fool with me, Lady Halyard, he was miserable and you know it." I felt myself go hot and cold with shame. He had caught me out in a deceit, or so he believed.

"I am glad if he is happier," I said softly. "I love him very much."

"I hope that love will be enough." Kean seemed to doubt even the possibility of hope. "Love alone seldom cures all ills." Then he looked more kindly and began to speak as if he were my friend too and felt he could confide in me.

"We have a great deal in common, you know, your husband and I. Many found our friendship an odd and curious one, for we seemed to come from different worlds. Both of us lived with cruel ridicule and both of us have lived with fame, which is a kind of twisting in itself. One may easily survive obscurity, thousands do it every day, but fame—ah, that is a different matter." He saw that I did not follow him or know what he meant to say. And yet, even without understanding him I knew I trusted him and I blurted out without thinking, "There was a man in the theatre tonight who looked at my husband as if he hated him enough to kill him. Is that part and parcel of fame?"

"No." Kean was thoughtful. "I would say that the man who frightened you so much is simply a man who feels Halyard has done him some imagined wrong. Halyard is a man one either loves or hates."

"All the same, I wish it had not frightened me so much."

"My dear," he took my hand, "you have good reason to fear for Halyard, we are all afraid," and then we joined the crowd at the large supper table and though Kean would not allow me to leave his side he said nothing more that was serious.

Instead, as if he were giving a second performance, he sang songs and posed riddles. He spoke verse and he drank a great deal of wine.

When we took our leave he was slightly drunk and out of focus. He stood unsteadily on his feet but I was sure he still knew what he was saying.

"Will she let you come again, Halyard, this new wife of yours?" He turned, his hand fell heavily on my arm. "Arabella did not like Halyard to keep company with me. She thought I was a bad influence on him."

"And were you?"

115

"Yes," he whispered. The tragic pose was gone now as were the party histrionics. "Yes, I daresay I was."

"My husband does not need my permission to come to see you. He may come any time he likes, and I hope that you will allow me to come as well."

Kean bowed to me and, slightly off balance, staggered so that Halyard had to catch him to keep him from falling. I knew that he was not so drunk as that and wondered if he had pretended to fall so he could avert his head to keep Halyard from seeing the tears in his eyes.

All the way back to the hotel Halyard talked of the wonder and brilliance of Kean's playing and how he wished that some day he would have the skill to write a play, perhaps with a part for Kean. My own fears were beginning to diminish. The day had gone so well. If it had not been for the twisted, angry face of that man in the theatre it would have been a very quiet, peaceful day. Halyard had met with all manner of folk who obviously liked him and wished him well. But there was always before me the memory of that man.

Halyard, seeing how quiet I had become, drew me close. "When we get back to our hotel I'll order us a bottle of champagne and we'll go to bed." He held me, kissing me and driving all my dark and morbid thoughts away.

"It has been a grand day, hasn't it, Cat? I told you that you would like London and you have made a great hit with Kean. He usually does not care for good women."

But there was to be no champagne or an early bed for us. Tom Grace was in our sitting room pacing up and down the carpet like an outraged parent whose children have stayed out too late without permission.

"Where have you been?" he burst out the moment we entered the room. "I have been here twice today and I've looked for you all over town. Can you imagine how worried I have been not hearing from you?" Without waiting for an answer to any of his questions, he asked another. "Has the day gone all right for you? Has there been any trouble?"

I knew what he meant all too well, although Halyard

seemed bemused by Tom Grace's concern. As Tom Grace paused for a moment, I guessed it was because he had at last seen my dress and jewels, and the change in my appearance astonished him.

"Yes," Halyard said, "we've had a splendid day, haven't we, Cat?"

I nodded.

"We've seen the sights and tonight," Halyard continued, "we've been to the theatre, to see Kean play Richard and then we went on to supper with him afterward."

"How could you?" Tom Grace shook his head disapprovingly. "I loathe him. He's nothing but a dirty little toad. How you could introduce him to your wife I do not know, but let that pass. It's all been very awkward not knowing where you were. I promised some of the *ton* that we'd call round at Wattier's. I thought you might like to go there to have a visit and a drink." Halyard frowned.

"I can't, I'm afraid. I'm sorry, Tom, if I've caused you any inconvenience. I do like Wattier's as you know. I want to see my old cronies, but Cat and I had just agreed upon an early night. Another time perhaps."

I could see that though he had said no quickly enough he wanted to go. He had looked forward to dropping into his club to make the rounds of his old acquaintances and it would be better if he did so with Tom Grace than on his own.

"Nonsense," I said. "I'm tired. Besides, by the time I'm out of this gown and have taken down my hair and seen to it and that the champagne is well iced you'll be back."

"Oh, Cat, you're a wonder. What a wife. All right then, I'll order the champagne on my way out. You will wait up for me, won't you?" And I said that I would. He turned to Tom Grace. "What have I done to deserve such a wife?" I saw Tom Grace's eyes. They were clear and wide, but there was something in his look that made me uneasy.

"I admire your gown, Catherine, and of course the woman in it. As for the Halyard jewels, I have seen them often but never before shown to such advantage."

I felt myself flush. In the past Tom Grace must have

117

seen Arabella wearing these jewels. And perhaps everyone who had seen us at the theatre tonight had remembered them as well and compared me to her. The thought made me ill and slightly faint.

When Halyard and Tom Grace had gone I struggled out of my expensive gown and laid it carefully on a chair. Halyard had asked me if I wanted a maid but I had refused. Now I saw that in some near future I would need one. With all those hooks no wonder ladies had to have maids.

I took off the jewels and tied them in the handkerchief and put them into a drawer. Tomorrow we must return them to the bank or put them in a safe. I felt uneasy with them and did not want the responsibility for their safety.

I put on my old shift and his dressing gown, for it was getting chilly. Tomorrow I must ask Madame Michaud for a dressing gown of my own. That, at least, would be one practical and necessary purchase. Then I heard a knock at the door.

There were two men standing outside, one was the waiter with the champagne and the other was the hall porter, who said he was sorry he had not seen us come in, and he had brought up a package that had been delivered earlier. He said the package was for me.

I thanked him. I saw the champagne placed on a low table. When I shut the door after them I remember thinking that I was cold, and wondering if I should light the fire or let it wait until Halyard came back from Wattier's, and I decided to wait.

I sat looking down at the parcel in my hand. It was very thick and official looking. But it must be a mistake. It could not be meant for me. I knew no one in England. Yet there was my name on it, written in a hand I did not recognize.

And because it had my name on it I opened it.

Forever afterward I wished that I had been wise enough to throw it in the fire. But I did not. As I unfolded the paper I saw it was a large cartoon of Halyard. He stood in a boat in his elegant blue coat and polished boots, and on his head was a poet's wreath.

118

Beside him were women, one on each arm, and along-side the boat swam several more, all looking up at him in adoration and wonder. I made myself focus my eyes upon the words in the giant balloon above his head. They were in the form of a poem and they read

> Lord Halyard, Lord Halyard,
> We do thee implore,
>   Since travel's thy fancy,
> Stay with us no more.
>   In England, in England,
> Though it may cause you strife,
>   A wife is no sister,
> Nor sister a wife.
>   Lord Halyard, Lord Halyard,
> We do thee implore,
>   Make not your wife sister,
> Nor sister a whore.

I did not understand what it meant. I knew I did not want to. But I could not help but wonder who had sent it to me and why. Was it a threat or a warning? Who could have hated me enough to wish me to be unhappy? And then I remembered, as vividly as if he were there in the room with me, the face of the man at the theatre.

Chapter Six

I sat before the unlit fire, the packet and drawing upon my lap. From somewhere outside I heard a clock strike the hour but I could not concentrate long enough to count the strokes. At last I lit the fire but it did not warm me.

Who had sent me this wicked, malicious thing and why? Was it to disillusion me, to diminish my confidence in my husband's character? Was it to warn me? If so, of what?

I did not understand the scurrilous verse, and if I were to show it to Halyard when he came back would he understand it any better than I did? Whoever had sent this to me must not be aware that Halyard had no memory or was that only another of my false assumptions.

Once more my mind turned to the hate-filled face of the man in the theatre. Why would I think it was he who had sent this? Was it only because I did not know who else it might have been?

I could be certain of nothing. I was so ignorant of London ways I could not tell friend from foe. It was a chilling thought that I would never really be sure when I met a stranger whether he was Halyard's friend or if he meant him harm.

Round and round my thoughts ran in a meaningless chase around an empty circle. And at last because there was no answer to any of my questions I folded the paper very neatly and carefully put it back into its packet.

I must tell Halyard about the drawing. I had promised to keep no secrets from him and perhaps when I showed it to him there would be some simple explanation. But even as I told myself that sort of fairy tale I knew it was not so. The meaning was something sinister and evil and I was numb with cold, colder than the ice around the champagne that shifted and cracked in the silver bucket.

I sat feeling vulnerable and exposed. The clock struck the hour. One o'clock and the watch in the street cried out that all was well—but it was not so.

It was almost two before Halyard came, and to my surprise he brought Tom Grace with him. Did he think if he brought his friend with him I would not scold? He looked very much the contrite, apologetic husband as he gave me a quick kiss just to test the climate.

"Waiting up all this time? I am sorry, Cat, to be so late but it was unavoidable. There was a great mob at Wattier's. Everyone there wanted to have a word with me. Dan McKinnon was there and Sefton and Alvanley. What a collection of wits and rakes. Alvanley set the tone as usual. He said, 'Ah, Halyard, I haven't seen you in a very long time. Have you been away?'"

Halyard was a good mimic and I could almost see a rotund, myopic man who spoke as if he had marbles in his mouth, but I was in no mood to be amused and when Halyard saw I did not laugh he went on more earnestly.

"It really was remarkable how easily it all went, don't you agree, Tom?" Tom Grace said nothing, not even a greeting to me. He stood staring into the fire as if he did not hear what had been said.

"You must admit they all seemed tolerably glad to see me. No one asked me to resign or cut me in conversation. So much for all Tom's morbid fears." Halyard seemed to be valiantly trying to assure me that the evening had been a great success but still Tom Grace said nothing.

"The only fellow who did not take my hand was Scot-burn, and he is too senile to know his own name let alone mine. Tonight I thought he was as drunk as an old owl." Halyard looked to Tom Grace for agreement but there was to be no help from that quarter and so he made an end of pretense.

"Tom was uneasy about me and he insisted on seeing me home. I thought it only civil to ask him in for a drink. One glass of champagne though and off he goes." Halyard began to open the bottle, easing out the cork with care and skill.

"It's been a long day," he said pointedly, "and I am tired, I don't mind admitting it." There was a hush in the room. Neither Halyard nor Tom Grace spoke. Both stood looking at each other and at last Halyard shrugged in a kind of gesture of defeat. It was obvious he had run out of small talk and now must come to grips with some real issue. Tom Grace spoke first.

"If you don't tell her, Hal, I will." Tom Grace never took his eyes from Halyard.

"I would rather Catherine wasn't told. It would only worry her and what good would that do?"

"Tell me what?" My heart began to race. It had been no accident that Tom Grace had come back with Halyard.

"It was nothing, Cat, a foolish incident, much better forgotten, but Tom is all in a roar. It was nothing, believe me."

"It was something and you know it." Tom Grace's voice was sharp as a slap.

"What happened?" I asked. "One of you tell me, I beg of you."

Tom Grace turned from Halyard to me. His eyes were dark with anxiety. "You will remember that I warned Hal it would be better if he stayed down at Longfields at least until I saw how the wind was blowing, but he would not listen. He is always so sure that he, not I, is right."

"What could have been avoided?" Why could they not say what they had to say instead of all this wrangling over whether it was to be said and who was to say it.

123

"It was nothing of any importance," Halyard interrupted. "We had a nice evening at the club. It all went well, didn't it, Tom?"

"When we came out of the club," Tom Grace said, as if repeating a set of rehearsed facts, "there was a man standing by the steps. Well dressed, a gentleman if clothes mean anything. He was waiting for Hal." My heart turned, stopped, and began to beat again.

"What man?" I asked Halyard. "The man who was at the theatre tonight?"

"Just a man. To my knowledge I never saw him before in my life. Tom didn't know him either, did you, Tom?"

"No," Tom Grace said. He looked at me. Both he and I knew that since Halyard had not remembered his best friend he might have forgotten his worst enemy. "No," Tom Grace went on for my benefit, "I did not know him either. I have never seen him in London. He was not the sort of man Hal would have been acquainted with."

"What happened?" I asked quietly.

"You tell her." Tom Grace looked to Halyard. "If you don't, I shall." Halyard cleared his throat.

"Well, this man, whoever he was, came up to me. He addressed me by name. I saw at once he was not sober. I mean, what gentleman would address a man to whom he had not been properly introduced if he was entirely sober?"

Tom turned in disgust. "You're making light of it. You seem to think you can make a joke of everything."

Halyard sighed. "All right then. I'll be serious enough to suit you. I tried to pass the man but he would not step aside. He took me by the arm and would not let me go. He said a lot of stupid and disagreeable things. I had the devil's own time getting rid of him but now here I am, home, safe and sound. After all, that is what matters."

"No, that's not quite all of it." Tom Grace spoke quietly, finishing off the story in his own way.

"The man claimed Halyard had done him a wrong. He struck Hal in the face and challenged him to a duel."

"A case of mistaken identity," Halyard insisted. "Believe me, I did not know him."

124

"He knew you." Tom Grace would not be put off. "If I hadn't been with you, he meant to fight with you then and there. It is only a short walk to Crown Passage or St. James's Park. Whoever he was, he meant to murder you if he could do it honorably."

"He was drunk, or mad, I tell you, and even if I had had my pistols I would not have fought with him. Why should I? He was a stranger to me."

"What color hair did he have?" I asked and no sooner were the words out of my mouth than I knew how odd they must sound.

"What earthly difference does it make, Cat, what color the man's hair was?" Tom Grace asked. "What matters is that he challenged Hal to a duel and Hal refused the challenge." I felt a great weight had been lifted from me.

"Thank God," I said.

"You still don't understand. When word of this gets around they'll say that Halyard is a coward. In London no man can refuse such a challenge. It will be another scandal. The talk will flare up again." I went to Halyard and took his hand.

"I don't care if they call you coward. It was very brave of you to refuse to fight." He kissed me tenderly. "Thank you, Cat, I knew you would understand."

Tom Grace, at his wits' end, shouted out angrily, "Are you both mad, don't you realize how serious this is? Tomorrow it will be all over town."

"Tom," Halyard tried to soothe his feelings, "I know you are worried about my good name, but I have no intention of fighting a duel with any man, certainly not with a man I have never seen before. In the old days if I had fought with every man who wished to have his name linked with mine I'd have been called out at least once a fortnight. Lord knows I did my best to establish a reputation as a crack shot just to discourage this sort of thing. This poor fool tonight was just some stranger who wanted a touch of notoriety."

"He was no stranger, Hal, he knew you. He said it was an affair of honor."

"I did not know him." Halyard suddenly looked at me

125

beseechingly. "As far as I know I had never seen him before in my life."

"It's possible," I said to Tom Grace, "that it was a man who saw Halyard at the theatre tonight. He looked at him as if he hated him. He was tall, with auburn hair." Tom Grace frowned and shot Halyard a questioning glance, but Halyard remained blank.

"A man with auburn hair—no, this man was fair, I think, and not tall."

"Or," I went on, "it might possibly have been the husband of one of those women who wrote such passionate letters to Halyard even though he has never met them. Any husband reading such a letter would think he had cause to challenge him."

"I'm as sure as I can be that I did not know him." Halyard seemed weary of the subject and I could not blame him for wanting to put an end to this conversation.

"Come on, Tom." Halyard held out the bottle. "Have another glass of wine and then go home. I wish you had never told Cat, it proves nothing, it solves nothing."

"It proves you have enemies," I said.

"It proves you should not go about London alone," Tom Grace said. "What do you plan to do tomorrow?"

"I plan to sleep as late as possible, but come to lunch if you like and then we might all go to an exhibition."

"I'll come, that is if Catherine has no objection."

"No, of course not." I was glad for him to come and pleased Halyard would have his company. Tom set down his glass.

"I am bound to say again that I did warn you London might be dangerous for you."

"So you did, Tom," Halyard said wearily, "and now do go home before it's daylight and we have breakfast together instead of lunch."

When he had gone Halyard turned from the door and held out his arms for me. "I am sorry about all this, Cat, Tom is a nervous old woman."

"He is your friend."

"I know, but still it's late and our evening, yours and mine, has been wasted."

126

"You must be tired," I said.

"Not that tired." He gave me a longing look and I sent him off to prepare for bed while I turned down the lamps.

I had meant to tell him about the cartoon. Now it was too late and in some larger way it no longer seemed so important. What had mattered to me was that he knew he had enemies and that he must take care. I had hoped that when he did know he would consider going down to Longfields.

Now this terrible thing had happened he must realize someone hated him enough to wish him dead. Surely now, even if there was no talk or scandal, he should behave with caution, and soon we would leave London for the country and the peace of home.

I took the packet from my pocket and threw it on the fire. I watched it curl and blacken at the edges and then turn to ash. With Tom Grace for his friend and companion I hoped nothing worse would happen to Halyard.

When I went to bed he drew me to him. As he touched me the coldness that had been around me all the evening began to thaw and melt away. My desire for him was as undeniable as his for me and I was quick to respond to his caresses.

I knew that if I lived with him for a lifetime I would never grow weary of making love. Our love would never pall or grow stale and ordinary, yet if I were to spend a thousand nights in his arms I was equally sure that there would never be another as passionate or intense as this one.

From the moment he touched me I was sure that this night was different from other nights we had spent together, and then suddenly I knew why. For I had been seized with an unshakable premonition, a vision of some future time when he would no longer be with me. And I knew that in this one night while he was still mine I must store away enough warmth and passion to last me through an age of ice. Whatever was to happen, whatever nameless thing it was that I feared, this love would endure when all else had vanished from the earth.

In the morning he woke refreshed while I was hollow eyed and weary. He drank cup after cup of coffee and ordered a breakfast of the size that only the English can contemplate at that hour of the day.

"Cat," he asked casually, "is Madame Michaud coming here for a fitting this morning?"

"I am not sure." I hedged. "Why?" I had learned to be wary here in England of even the simplest questions.

"I must go out for a little."

He was being too offhand and casual. I did not like the direction of the conversation.

"I wanted to be sure you had something to do, something to occupy you."

"Where are you going?" I asked him. I knew it was direct and perhaps too blunt, but I wanted a plain answer.

"I must see my publisher this morning. I have some matters to settle with him."

"Is Tom Grace going with you?" I did not want Halyard wandering off alone, surely he must know that.

"No," he said, suddenly becoming very busy with his bacon and eggs. "Tom's coming for luncheon. I think that was the way we left it."

"Then I'll go with you." I saw he did not want me to go, he meant to put me off, but I was not to be so easily dismissed.

"I shouldn't if I were you, Cat. It will be all business; very dull and tedious for you. Besides, it may become downright unpleasant. Fanner wants to bring out a cheap abridged edition and I won't have it, no matter what his arguments." I saw his face flush and knew that even the idea of such a thing made him angry.

"I won't be bored," I said, "and I won't come in with you if you don't want me to. I'll wait in the coach."

"I am not taking the coach," he countered. "Fanner's offices are here in Albemarle Street."

"Then I'll walk up and down and look in shop windows."

"I've told you, Cat, no lady of fashion walks alone in London." I could see his patience was wearing thin.

"Then I'll wait for you in the outer offices and later you can walk with me as chaperone." I found I could be as determined when I set my mind to it as he and I suppose it was, in fact, our first domestic quarrel.

But I meant to go with him because I remembered how angry he had been when he read his publisher's letter on the ship. It had been the first time I had ever seen him in a temper, and now I feared if he were provoked too far he might be goaded into a duel.

Within the hour we set out together arm in arm toward Fanner's. The day was brisk and the sky the color of dull slate.

He was not expected at his publisher's. He wanted his arrival to be a surprise and it was. Nor did he wait to be announced, but strode purposefully across the hall and into the offices of the senior partner while I dutifully stayed outside to wait for him and to think my own thoughts.

No explanation had been given for my presence. I saw a clerk and an errand boy eyeing me speculatively from behind a partition. I had never been a woman of mystery before and it was a rather unsettling sensation. Then someone higher in rank than the clerk appeared around the corner and disappeared as quickly, and I was left alone.

From within I heard voices raised in anger. He had been right to warn me that this was not going to be a pleasant meeting. Then, after a few more moments the door was opened and Halyard came out again, his cane clasped tightly in his hand as if he wished it were a club and he was free to use it.

Behind him there was a dignified-looking man I took to be the senior Fanner, but Halyard made no move to introduce us, and when the man held out his hand Halyard did not return the courtesy or the bow that was made him.

He walked quickly past me then stopped, turning back as if he had just remembered I was there. Roughly he reached out his hand, raised me up, and propelled me out into the busy street.

If he remembered that we had intended to walk a while he gave no sign of it. Instead he hailed a passing hackney cab and growled at the driver, "Drive around the park and don't stop until I tell you to."

129

He sank back against the seat pale as death, the vein at his temple throbbing as if it would surely burst. We were halfway around the park for the second time before he spoke, and then it was more to the air than to me.

"It's incredible," he said, "unbelievable." And I saw that for the present it was all that he was going to say on the subject. Whatever had happened behind those closed doors, it had affected him so deeply that he was still too angry to speak.

Like any other London couple of fashion we came in from our morning drive in plenty of time to attend to my dressmaker and his tailor. Today Madame had brought me her finest creation yet. It was of rich rose and mauve silk as light as spring and as exquisite as a dawn. It was so lovely because it was so simply made, a work of art and skill. Halyard admired it extravagantly and once again when Madame had gone I mentioned the price of all these new clothes. When I had done with my prudent counsel he said, "I've been thinking, Cat, that you must have a maid. No lady in London society can do without one." I did not agree, but neither did I mention that I had done without one all my life.

Promptly as the clock struck the hour Tom Grace arrived. He was in high good spirits and when he had inquired how we were we all began to speak of the weather, which seemed much improved. Showers were not likely in the afternoon. We drank some sherry and made snippets of small talk, though all the while Tom Grace must have noticed Halyard was abstracted and not himself. At last, because Tom Grace could no longer ignore him, he asked, "What is it, Hal? What has put you in such a state this morning?"

"I went to see Fanner." Halyard gave him a darting glance but it might as well have been a blow.

Tom Grace's hand as he set down his sherry was unsteady. A drop of amber liquid spilled upon the polished table and quivered like mercury. Again that look of vulnerability came back into his eyes.

"I see," Tom Grace said quietly.

What was it Tom Grace saw that I was blind to? Clearly the news had some particular meaning for him. I thought for a moment that it was because Halyard had led him to believe he would not go out alone. But I was wrong. Halyard soon said all that he had kept to himself in our ride around the park.

"I went to see him this morning because he had written to me in Spain that he wanted to abridge *The Nomad*. He wanted to cut what he called the more controversial passages so that he could bring out a cheap edition. I went to tell him face to face that that was absolutely out of the question and what did I find?" He waited for a moment but Tom Grace did not reply.

"I found," Halyard continued angrily, "the type set and the galleys pulled not only on an abridged, but a posthumous edition. Fanner said that he had thought that I was dead, and therefore would not mind the cuts, and to top all his impertinence he said he had persuaded you to write an introduction, a memorial to a dearly loved but very dead friend.

"The idiot had the nerve to say that he had expected the profit from the sale to be substantial. He was not a little put out to see me alive. It seems I am worth more dead than alive!"

"Be fair to him, Hal." Tom Grace was pale and shaken by this outburst. "Everyone in London thought that you were dead. All the rumors were the same. There seemed to be no hope that you could still be found alive. I too thought it must be true. I was your oldest friend and I had heard nothing from you, not a word in months. Well, I ask you, what else was I to think?

"When I heard they were bringing out a cheap edition and Fanner asked me to write an introduction as a tribute to an old friend I reasoned that you would rather I took on the task than some stranger."

"I am not blaming you, Tom." Halyard seemed surprised that Tom Grace could so have misinterpreted his outburst. "It is the firm that I am blaming. They looked for a quick profit. A dead poet is a much easier commodity

131

to sell than a live one, especially if more scandal can be told of him when he is no longer there to defend himself."

"Don't think," Tom Grace protested, "that I did not try to hold off publication. If only you had written me one letter, just one."

"Well." Halyard threw up his hands in resignation to the inevitable. "It's too late now to worry over what I might have done. At least you benefit from this. You'll get to keep the money Fanner paid you for the introduction." Tom Grace went red with embarrassment, which Halyard ignored. "One of the benefits of being dead is not having to read your own last reviews."

And carelessly, as if to indicate that for him the subject was closed, he picked up a pile of letters that had come for him while we were out and opened one.

"Look here," he cried, his face flushed with sudden pleasure, "it's a voucher from Lady Jersey, an invitation to Almack's. Well, what do you know about that?" He looked up, his eyes so bright and his smile so genuine and happy that I knew I should share his enthusiasm.

"You can wear your new dress, Cat, the one that Madame brought today. A Wednesday night at Almack's means the cream of London society, or so they will tell you. It will be far more elegant than supper with an actor after the play."

"My God!" Tom Grace stepped forward in great agitation. "You don't mean to accept."

"But I do." Halyard was puzzled and annoyed.

"You mean to keep company with the very sort who shut their doors in your face?"

"Sending me an invitation is hardly shutting the door in my face, Tom."

"The voucher," Tom Grace said patiently, "is from Lady Jersey, not the others. She was always partial to you, but if you remember the ball she gave before you left, you will admit that it was far from a pleasant evening."

"I think you are exaggerating all this, Tom. I was well enough received last night at the club."

"That was different and you know it. There it was all

men; they were without their wives. That formidable tribe of dames at Almack's are the arbiters of fortune. They make a reputation and they can break it as well."

"Oh." Halyard raised an eyebrow. "I thought it was *The Nomad* that had made my reputation. Perhaps I was mistaken."

"You know very well that I mean. Those women were the first to repeat gossip about you, to spread it and enlarge upon it until every morsel became a feast of scandal."

"My dear Tom, if all they said of me was true I was not fit for England and if not, then England was not fit for me."

"Damn it, Hal, you think you can change the world with one of your epigrams." Tom Grace turned away, trying to regain control of his emotions.

"I am sorry you should think so. Please come with us tonight and you'll see that all your fears are nothing but shadows."

"I won't go." Tom was resolute. "I won't watch you walk into the lion's den. Besides, they seldom ask me. If you go to Almack's, you must go alone."

"As you like, Tom. Now let's have our lunch."

Afterward, when Halyard and Tom Grace had smoked their cheroots, we set off in the coach for an exhibition at the Royal Academy. Despite the forecast for good weather a mizzling rain had begun to fall. There were small puddles gathering in the shiny crevices between the cobblestones.

The Academy was not crowded that early in the afternoon and we were free to wander unhampered by a jostling mob. Tom Grace and Halyard appraised the merits of each painting. They spoke of Constable and Turner and Crome in knowledgeable terms. All of the canvases were of English scenes. There were fields and streams, castles and cottages.

Superimposed upon the canvases I saw my own private visions of other scenes and landscapes. I could see the sea and the sand and the jagged rocks at the far end of the beach where I had found him. I saw, clear as day, the little white house on the cliff set on an expanse of hard, red, rocky soil. I saw the terra cotta pots dotting the terrace filled with hardy flowers; and I remembered him as he had been that first day, sitting on the terrace staring at the sky.

When Halyard and Tom Grace had looked their fill at the pictures we went back again to Grillon's for our tea. All was very easy between them. They laughed at each other's jokes and agreed with each other's opinions, but when Tom Grace rose to leave I knew that Halyard was still not satisfied.

"Change your mind, Tom, say you'll come with us to Almack's; I'm going on afterward to the House of Lords, I have not been there yet. We want you to come, don't we, Cat?"

"Yes, of course," I murmured, but Tom Grace had a stubborn streak that matched Halyard's own and he would not be moved from his decision.

"No, Hal, I'm sorry, but you already know that I think you are tempting fate. You should go down to Longfields until this business of yours is finished, and then why not travel? You have the means." He left before he could be forced to change his mind.

When it was time we dressed with elaborate care. I was surprised to see Halyard in a different evening costume from the one he had worn to the theatre. Tonight he was in black knee breeches. He said it was the rule at Almack's that only breeches, not trousers, were allowed to the gentlemen. There could be no break or deviation from the rules set down by the women who had formed the club, though the ladies might wear what they chose, within the fashion, naturally.

"Naturally," I said and asked him to fasten up my new gown. I could not manage all the hooks on my own. Once more he remarked that I must have a maid. He made it seem a reasonable thing, for as he pointed out, he might not always be there when I was dressing. And so I agreed to think about it, but I refused to wear all the jewels he had chosen for me. After the stares and comments we had caused in the theatre I thought a little modesty and re-

134

straint might be better suited to this occasion. A necklace and a pair of earrings were all that I would allow.

As he placed the cloak of rich silk around my shoulders I knew he was confident that I would make a good showing, and I was sure I would be admired for my dress and jewels if nothing else.

Almack's was in King Street off St. James's. When we arrived there was already a great crush of coaches and carriages. The street was well lighted with the new gas lamps, but even in this well-guarded area around St. James's Palace the wise and prudent insisted on carrying a second postillion and hiring a link boy to run ahead with a torch, just to stay on the safe side. A man's purse full of gold or a lady's diamonds would see a pickpocket through a long winter.

As our coach stopped at the door I could not see that the entrance to Almack's was any more astounding than lesser portals. Even the stairs were not any wider nor any better covered than those of Drury Lane. And the upper hall, as we entered it, seemed plain.

A maid took my cape, a footman Halyard's coat, our card was given to the Master of Ceremonies, and in his face I saw nothing that was not polite and civil. For that card, that voucher, was our passport to this exclusive and elite society.

If I expected to see a more splendid sight once we were inside the rooms themselves, again I was doomed to disappointment. Here it was not decoration, nor dress, nor wealth, nor beauty that gave one the entree, it was solely the permission and the sanction of the patronesses.

The lady from whom he had received our voucher, as a subject receives a royal fief, was Lady Jersey. As we entered the middle room she stepped forward to greet us. She was a handsome, florid woman, and with her expansive declamatory manner she would have been at home upon the stage, but this assembly was her theatre. She fell upon Halyard and though she acknowledged me it was in such a way that I felt as if I had been slighted.

"She's charming, Halyard. Very young, of course, but

charming." I was, it seemed, to be discussed and dissected as if I were not there.

"And you look well too, Halyard," Lady Jersey continued without allowing for contradiction or dispute. "Although I must admit that I was surprised to hear you were back in England. After all, it has not been very long since Arabella died. Was it wise, do you think, to come back again so soon? And then one would have scarcely thought London the place for a honeymoon. But you know my feelings for you are always of the warmest, and as you're here we must make the best of the situation. I am sure you must have had good reason to ask me for a voucher, though when I received your note asking for an invitation I was bowled over. At first I thought it might be better if I did not send it, but I never could refuse you anything, any more than being wise was ever your long suit. I hope this evening is happier for you than the last time you were here. That was a fiasco."

Through all of this aria she was smiling as if she were paying him a long-winded compliment.

"My note?" Halyard asked. He could not disguise his astonishment.

"Yes, you wrote and asked if I would, for old times sake, send you a voucher for this evening when you very well know I should have called on Lady Halyard or she on me before I could issue one. That is the rule, dear boy, but then when did you ever live by the rules?"

"I thank you then for excepting me." He bowed.

"After your reception at the theatre last night and at Wattier's, I suppose you had your own reasons for wanting to come here as well. A troika of triumphs to put you in the swim again." She was unremitting. Were all English women of place and position like this one or was she as he had told me, the best of the breed?

I felt myself sinking with fright. This evening had not begun well and now it was going entirely in the wrong direction. I remembered Halyard's face as he had opened the invitation. He had been so pleased, so happy to receive it, and now that happiness had been extinguished and taken from him.

The room was better than half-full of the *haute monde*. There was no hush as there had been last night at the theatre. There was no babble of talk. It would have seemed to a naked and unpracticed eye that our entrance had not caused a ripple but it was not so. We had been noticed and the reaction when it came was a more savage, a more cruel and rending one than if they had been a den of hungry lions. Even lions never killed merely for the sport of it.

These beasts killed with a thousand little paper cuts of cold exclusion. Very simply, they ignored him. As Lady Jersey tried to introduce him to a couple standing alone they nodded to her politely and then quietly and firmly moved away. It was as great a cut as if the Lord High Executioner had severed a head.

Undaunted, Lady Jersey then tried to approach another larger group where by the merest rustle of a gown or a closing of a fan the ladies signaled to their friends and partners that it was the moment to withdraw, and they flew away as birds do when by mischance another species settles on the same branch.

There was nothing overt; it was all done with little looks and in muted whispers, but the results were plain. There was no one to whom he might be introduced, there was no conversation he might join, no circle open to him, even in the large room where a general gathering managed to part themselves away from us as if they were the Red Sea and we the fleeing Israelites.

We passed through, and at the entrance to a little alcove next to the central room Halyard, pale as death, thanked Lady Jersey for her kindness but said he preferred not to trouble her further that evening as he was sure she had other guests to greet. She, as if she were more puzzled by his desire to remain here than by the treatment he had received, went, leaving us mercifully alone. We could look out upon the central room and they could look at us as well. Now they had closed their ranks behind us, they had left us no way out. We were trapped on exhibition like the animals in the Tower; caught, held in a cage so all might stare and judge.

Their pleasure, it seemed, was to ignore us. If they looked at us it was as if we did not exist, or they stared fixedly at a point beyond our heads.

It would have been kinder if they had struck him in the face. From the refreshment room I heard sounds of laughter and such was my present mood that I was sure they were laughing at Halyard. He had been exiled. He was the outcast, the unforgiven. He stood, unrepentent, as stiff and unbending as a rod of steel. His eyes were bright and the jaw was clenched as tight as his fists. I prayed that he would not lose his temper and cause a scene. He held a chair for me and motioned me to sit. I did as I was bid, as if I had no will of my own.

From somewhere in the next room the music began to play for others—the dancing was about to begin. Surely then, when they were occupied with their own company, we could slip away unnoticed.

I felt his hand fall on my shoulder and I turned to look up at him, a thing I had not trusted myself to do before.

"I did not ask for the invitation," he said.

He did not have to tell me that.

"There has been a hideous joke played on me. Someone else wrote to Lady Jersey in my name, but why?" He looked at me as if I had the answer. All this he had said *sotto voce*. As far as anyone who might have been observing us could have told, we were merely making pleasant, meaningless conversation, and as he spoke he smiled so they would not see how wounded and humiliated he had been.

It was as if suddenly all my old fears had been realized. Here I sat in London on a little gilt chair, dressed in strange foreign clothes. In the next room dancing had begun and it seemed I could see animated pages from my father's periodicals. Men and women, hand in hand, skipping like sheep down a shambles. Only it was he and I who were the lambs to the slaughter.

138

Beside me Halyard remained impassive, betraying nothing of what he must be feeling; in fact he was ominously calm.

"Please," I said, trying to keep my face as expressionless as his and failing in the attempt. "Please, let us go home now."

"We'll go in our own time, Cat, and not in theirs." He had made that decision final.

I hoped that if we stayed I would not disgrace him. I hoped against hope that I would carry it all off in a manner that would do him credit but I felt my resolve crumbling. I was angry and I was hurt. It took all my effort to keep my eyes, like the dancers, on a neutral point.

But to my shame I felt the tears begin to rise. Oh, I thought, I must not cry, I must not be seen to be so affected and so I looked down, staring into the safety of my lap. It was then, sitting there, head bowed and in danger of making a display of myself, that I saw the figure of a man approach. I could only see his knee breeches and the fine silk of his stockings. Then I heard his voice as he spoke to Halyard.

"Lord Halyard, will you allow me to welcome you home again?" The voice was loud enough to reverberate through the rooms and to be heard by all. It was a voice of great authority and I looked up to see a face even more familiar than Halyard's. It was the face of a hero whose profile, with its aquiline nose, might have been lifted from a medallion.

The face and the presence were unmistakably those of Wellington, and my heart began to beat like a regimental drum.

"May I have the honor of being presented to your wife, Lord Halyard?" Again the voice might have been in command of the troops upon the battlefield. "My congratulations. You are a fortunate man to have married the daughter of a gallant soldier like Major Rainey." There was a pause. I saw Halyard's eyes open wide with wonder. Every head in the adjoining room had turned and all eyes were fastened upon the scene now taking place before them.

"Catherine," Halyard said in a clear but softer voice than Wellington's, "His Grace, the Duke of Wellington." Wellington bowed politely.

"My dear, you were a pretty child and now you are a lovely woman." His eyes were piercing and the look he gave me might have put the French to route, but I gained strength from it, and felt a thrill of courage flow like some warm current in my veins.

"May I have this waltz?" It was more of a command than a request, but he looked to Halyard all the same. "Unless, of course, you have already claimed her for it."

"No," Halyard said stiffly, "I do not dance in this company. The reason, I believe, is obvious."

I wanted to say no to Wellington, but before I could refuse him his hand reached out for mine, and in a daze I followed him to the ballroom as others followed him into battle. He marched me to the center of the floor. By now the music had stopped and all around was silence. Then he gave a signal and the music began again and we began to circle around the room. I felt as if I might faint from the dizzying spiral that we traced, and from my nerves, which were near the breaking point. He must have felt my hand trembling in his for he said, "You are a soldier's daughter, Catherine. Let them look and be damned."

For my part I was more than willing to see them all in hell. My head lifted, my eyes met his, and I found myself making conversation, smiling and laughing with him as if he had been my friend all my life. When he saw that I was myself again he told me how sorry he was that my father was dead.

"We grew up together in Ireland," he said sadly, as if he could see the Celtic green even now and remember what he had been like all those long years ago.

"I have always felt responsible for his going out to Spain."

"It was his duty, so he said."

"Did he?" He looked at me hopefully. "Well, we all thought of duty then." Oddly enough it seemed that it was he, not I, who was in need of sympathy.

140

"We had a good life together in Spain," I said. "My father wrote a history of the campaign and a reminiscence of what your friendship meant to him."

"Did he?" He looked up gratefully and we danced on in an even faster whirl. "I would like to read it if I may."

I agreed and said that I would send a copy to him.

"Was it in Spain," he asked, "that you met and married Halyard?"

"Yes." I told him a little about our meeting and what had followed.

"Are you happy? I only know him by reputation, which can sometimes be deceiving."

"Yes," I said, "I am very happy." He gave me a hard look.

"Have you seen your grandmother since you have been in England?"

"No, and I do not intend to." I held myself back from him for a moment. I hoped he was not going to tell me that I should see her, but his views were like my own.

"It would be wise to avoid her. If you are happy she will only meddle. She can be a damn wicked woman; your mother found that out to her sorrow." He seemed very sure of his opinion and I knew I was a little in awe of him after all. His force, his reputation were undeniable, but I was most impressed with the manner in which he had taken Halyard's part before all these people. Was it only for my father's sake, or did he admire and respect Halyard as well? I looked at him, searching for some answer in his face, and saw he returned my gaze, but it was a question that must be asked if it was to be answered.

"I hope," he said, "that if you should ever be in need of a friend or a champion, Catherine, you will come to me. I am, I believe, not without some influence in the world. Promise me you will let me help you." His hand held mine like a pledge.

"Yes," I said, "I promise," and we began to circle in a final spiral of music. I did not think that I would ever forget that waltz or my partner. He had drawn me to him and absorbed me into his sphere of admirers. No wonder he could carry a multitude with him. He was far from a common man and I knew if he came to me as he had come to my father I would have followed the drum and gladly. He was someone I could trust implicitly. He, of all men, would never lie. If I asked him a question surely he would give me a straight answer.

"Why," I asked him abruptly, "why have they cut my husband like this?" I felt my lips were stiff and the words formed themselves with difficulty. He looked perplexed more than annoyed, as if he too sought an answer or the right words to say.

"He has not lived by their rules." Did he blame Halyard or the company, I could not tell. "They won't allow that, you see. I came here to Almack's once without my knee breeches. I had come, I believe, straight from the palace, but I was turned away because no one may break their rules."

"But what rule did Halyard break? What has he done that they find so unforgiveable?" He looked uncomfortable.

"Has he told you nothing then?" I felt his eyes piercing mine.

"No." He sighed and I thought he looked suddenly drawn, as if my answer had been a heavy burden to him.

"It's not for me to say, Catherine. You must ask him. But I am bound to say I do not see how he could bring you here tonight. How could any man, let alone a gentleman, deliberately expose his wife to this sort of thing?"

"He's not to blame, you must believe me. He would never deliberately do anything to harm me." I felt I could not tell him any more, it would be a betrayal. He shrugged as if he doubted my statement.

"You are a bride, Catherine, and obviously very much in love. That does not always make for sound judgment." Then there was a change in his mood, as if it were a signal he meant to change the subject.

"Well, Lady Halyard, now we've shown the enemy our artillery, shall we retreat and regroup our forces?" He danced me out of the ballroom and back to Halyard.

"I believe, sir," Wellington said in a most commanding voice, "that I've had all I can stomach of this assembly. I'm for home and I suggest that your wife has seen enough of London society for one night, so why not leave with me? We can walk down the stairs together." As if it were the most ordinary thing in the world he took my arm and we walked out with him to get our wraps and then down the stairs into the cleansing night air. All the while he had been correct and formal and gave no hint to Halyard of our private conversation. He was the supreme general and had commanded us as if we were in his personal convoy.

"What direction are you going, Lord Halyard? May I take you in my coach?"

To which Halyard replied in just as polite and detached a tone of voice, "No, thank you, your Grace, our own is waiting." Wellington disappeared into his coach and we into ours, which was the next in line. At once, when we were alone, Halyard took my hand.

"I am sorry, Cat, this hideous evening is all my fault. What I have put you through. Tom Grace tried to warn me but because of my pride, my pigheaded arrogance, I would not listen and I have made you suffer."

"Please don't let's talk of it. I know it wasn't your fault. And you held yourself so marvelously well that I was proud of you."

"Proud of what? It took a Wellington to rescue you." His eyes were dark and full of pain. "What have I done, Cat, or not done that they would treat me like that? What imagined outrage against them could provoke such deliberate insults? I don't care for myself, but for your sake I must have an answer and some satisfaction."

I saw that as we had turned out of King Street he went not in the direction of Piccadilly but down St. James's Street toward the palace.

"Aren't we going back to the hotel?" I asked him. All I wanted at this moment was to close the door, draw the blinds, and have a little privacy in which I might deal with my feelings.

"No," he said shortly, "I won't hide in some hotel room.

I won't bow my head in shame as if I had committed some crime."

"Where are we going?" I asked, alarmed by the tone of his voice.

"I am going to the House of Lords. I understand that they are sitting tonight. The say the Lords is the last refuge of fools and scoundrels. It seems the world may think me both. Perhaps there I will be able to find some charitable soul who will tell me what the charge is against me. If I am to be accused let it at least be by my peers." His voice was rising. I had never seen him so out of control.

"Please," I said, "let's go back to our hotel."

"No." I saw his jaw tighten.

"Then let me go with you. I'll wait for you as I did this morning."

"No."

"I want to be with you," I pleaded. "I don't want to go to the hotel alone." He turned and rapping with his stick against the driver's box, he said, "Don't argue with me, Cat. I'll walk the rest of the way. Don't you understand, I don't want your company. I want to be alone." He got out of the coach and gave directions to Old Jeb. He was to drive on the last few feet to the bottom of St. James's, where he could circle round and then drive back to Grillon's.

And without another word, or even so much as a good-night, Halyard was gone.

I was hurt to think he did not want me. I tried to believe it was because he did not want me to see his pain and disappointment, but I was not sure of that excuse at all.

The coach rolled on to the bottom of the road. At the Palace Yard it began to turn. It was a heavy, ill-sprung thing. Its great weight made it awkward to maneuver and the axles creaked as we came about.

It was a dark night. There was still a thick cover of clouds although the rain had almost stopped. As we started up the street it was so dark I could see no sign of Halyard. He seemed to have disappeared. But suddenly, across the road, I saw a man standing against a wall. He was almost submerged in the shadows, his face hidden by the tilt of his hat and the collar of his coat. Surely that was not Halyard, he could not have crossed over without my seeing him. But all the same I did not feel easy. I rapped at the driver's box and asked Old Jeb if there was another way that Halyard could have gone without my seeing him.

He thought for a moment, scratching at his head. "Perhaps," he said, "M'Lord has gone down Pall Mall or into the Palace Yard toward St. James's Park and over, then to Horse Guards Parade."

But I knew Halyard could not have gotten that far already. Then Jeb remembered Crown Passage, a way through to Pall Mall between the buildings off St. James's Street. It was, he said, a place where London gentlemen sometimes went to settle their differences, and before he could say more I heard a cry for help. It was Halyard's voice, I was sure of it.

I opened the door of the coach while it was still in motion, and I began to run, calling back to Jeb to bring the postillion and link boy and to hurry.

At the entrance to Crown Passage there was a gas lamp that had been extinguished. The hollow way between the two buildings was dark and damp. Even so I did not need the light to hear the sound of fists beating against flesh and the thud as they struck bone. The damp stones made an eerie background for the outline of three men, not fair odds even for this sort of business. As I came closer I heard a scream and knew it was my own voice. When they saw me backed by the coachman, postillion, and the link boy with a torch they gave one more series of savage kicks to the heap lying on the stones and ran.

I knew it was Halyard lying there. He had been badly beaten, and when he had fallen his head had hit the stones with such force that he had been knocked unconscious. As I bent down beside him I felt the blood. It was on his forehead; the blows had reopened his old wound. Then I realized that there was too much blood on my hand to come from just that one source. Dimly, by the light of the torch, I saw a gaping tear in his coat and there was a flow of blood so warm and fresh it smelled sickly sweet.

"Carry him to the coach," I said. "Don't stand there staring." The postillion and the link boy wanted to give chase to the ruffians but I held them back. What good would it have done, they were already long gone.

In the coach I was relieved to find the cut on his shoulder was only a gash, a flesh wound. The knife had not hit the bone. But though it was easy to staunch the flow of blood with his handkerchief, I was worried that Halyard had not regained consciousness. The head wound had not seemed that severe.

Even though I was occupied with Halyard, as we passed on I looked out of the window of the coach for an instant, and I saw the man still standing by the wall. He had not moved, had not come to our aid. Who was he? If I had not been so concerned with getting Halyard back to the hotel I would have stopped and demanded some explanation. But even by the time I had thought of what I might have done we were past him and into Piccadilly.

In the coach with Halyard lying unconscious, his head upon my lap, I felt a sense of *déjà vu*. Twice I had found him. Twice I had rescued him from danger, only this time the danger was of a different kind. The threat to his life came not from nature but from man. Someone had planned this attack. What had been the orders—to rob him, to kill him? Once more I must decide what was best for him. I did not choose to stay in London a moment more than was necessary; not here where I did not know who might be his enemy. I could protect him better at Longfields. There we could draw in upon ourselves; fill the moat, raise the drawbridge, set a watch on the battlements, and if that was too fanciful, at least he would be in his own house, which they said was an Englishman's castle.

Halyard stirred and his eyes opened. He seemed unsure of where he was and unsure of who I might be.

"It's all right," I said. "We're going to the hotel to collect our baggage, and then we are going to Longfields. You are

146

going home." I did not know if he had heard me before he lapsed once again into oblivion.

At Grillon's it was all quickly done. I sent Jeb in to fetch the manager. I said that Halyard had suffered a sudden indisposition. I saw the manager thought Halyard was merely in a drunken stupor, but I did not care to make any further explanation. I ordered him to have our trunks packed and loaded as we meant to get away at once. And I asked to have a small dressing case put inside the coach. I knew Halyard kept brandy in it. Then I wrote a hasty note to be left for Tom Grace, telling him we had gone down to Longfields and asking him to join us there as soon as it was convenient.

Within the hour we were on the Great West Road driving smartly away from London. I had managed to put some fresh handkerchiefs on Halyard's shoulder and to coax him to drink some brandy. He was conscious for a brief moment as he drank and he looked at me with eyes I felt I had never seen before. They were cold and hard, a stranger's eyes. The blow to his head had transformed him not to the man I had rescued once before nor to the man I had married, but to a stranger, and I knew then that those eyes belonged to a man I had never met. They belonged to the notorious Lord Halyard, the man he had been when he left England.

Chapter Seven

As the coach swayed heavily across Hounslow Heath the chilling enormity of my discovery exploded in my mind. Halyard was not the same man that I had known, I was sure of it. I knew I no longer feared the long journey or the danger of highwaymen in this wild, desolate place as much as I feared the look that I had seen in his eyes.

In this one terrible night it seemed as if the words he had spoken that day in Gibraltar had now become a prophecy fulfilled. There in a labyrinthian London passageway he had met a hydra-headed monster in the form of his assailants, and although he had survived the attack, something within him—my friend and companion, the lover I had known—had been destroyed.

He had said that he had not recognized any of his attackers and I believed him, but if robbery had not been their motive, and he still had his purse and ring and watch, then what had been their real intent? Was it murder?

And what was his crime? What had he done that had made at least one man wish him dead and all the great London world turn their back upon him? What was the charge that was so unspeakable no one would tell it to me?

149

Tom Grace had refused to repeat the slander, Kean had wept when he considered what love could not hope to cure, even the great Wellington had not had the courage to tell me. But to tell me what?

I wished now that I had saved the anonymously sent cartoon instead of throwing it on the fire. It might have offered me some clue. If I had shown it to Halyard he might have been able to explain it to me. I could not remember the rhyme exactly; I had read it hastily and wanted to forget it, but I recalled the words *wife, sister*, and the ugly word, *whore*.

I glanced at him as he lay sleeping beside me. He had drunk a quantity of brandy, which acted as a blessed anesthetic. This extravagant coach designed for sleeping had paid its keep tonight. The interior was so cleverly fashioned that the back rests could be drawn up on hinges. Behind them there were compartments in which fur robes and pillows were stored. The space between the two seats was bridged by a raised and fastened flap and all made up into a bed, which, though narrow, was long enough for him to stretch out in comfort.

I doubted that he was entirely without pain but he was no longer aware of the cuts and bruises, and I was grateful for that. I had no notion of sleeping myself. As I looked out at the passing night I heard the faint chimes of the traveling clock as it struck the hour. By this time tomorrow Jeb had said we would be at Longfields, and I meant to stay awake for the moment when Halyard opened his eyes. I wanted to see in them what he remembered of me and of the past.

In that long night we changed horses for the third time somewhere on the Marlborough Downs, and it was there we left the Bath Road and turned south toward Longfields. Beside me Halyard stirred and moaned softly but still he did not wake. As we took the southern way I saw dawn begin to break and despite my intentions I dozed off for a while. When I woke Halyard was sitting upright, the box of pistols was on his lap, and he was looking out the window at the passing landscape. I could not see his eyes

150

nor guess at what they held. I was stiff with cramp and wished that we were already at home, for I longed to get out of this London finery and into something sensible. I was hungry too, but I did not like to say so, it seemed so useless a complaint.

He did not seem to notice that I was awake, but sat holding the pistols with one hand, the other over his wounded shoulder. Outside the passing hedgerows and fields made it seem that we were submerged in a rural sea of English green.

"How are you?" I asked him.

"How should I be?" He answered my question with one of his own, but still he did not look at me.

"Are you in much pain?"

"It is not a deep wound but it will serve." He answered with a wry smile as if he enjoyed his use of the quotation. Then he turned, and the coldness of his gaze was like a winter gale. I saw he recognized me, but he was so indifferent to my presence I might have been a chance passenger with whom, for manners' sake, he was obliged to make conversation, a person who was to share his journey but nothing more.

"What were you thinking of just then?" I asked him.

"I was not thinking so much as remembering," he said slowly and deliberately. "It seems that I have a multitude of memories this morning."

My world turned upside down, just as his must have done the night before. The blow on his head had indeed jarred his consciousness, and from the deep dungeons of his mind those memories now arose to the surface one after the other, memories that did not include me. Today he would remember Arabella and compare the two of us.

"We'll be coming into Longton soon. The village is part of my estate. If you look quickly you'll see an old stone bridge. There is a mill on the stream and a weir. It's quite a pretty little village. Built of the native stone." His eyes now were not cold as much as indifferent to me, and I did not know if he saw me or only the scenes of the past.

"I remember coming here for the first time. I was nine,

151

and I had just inherited the title and the estates. We had come from Wales—my mother, Amelia, an old maidservant, and me. Wales had been the only home that I had known. We were traveling in a hired coach, a shabby thing but more than we could afford. When we came over that stone bridge into the village my mother insisted that we stop at the inn, the Halyard Arms. She wanted to be the first to announce the arrival of the new little lord and to bask in the reflected glory of the reception she was sure that they would give to me.

"What a sight we must have presented to the villagers. A fat, tipsy Welsh woman who had to be held up by her maid to keep her from stumbling on the steps; a little girl of eleven and a shy, small boy.

"She ordered a round of drinks and then another. I can see her face now, her cheeks flushed with gin and pride. She was never a great beauty, my mother, but she must have been quite pretty when she was young; the high color, a flawless complexion and a full figure, 'generous' I believe it is called these days.

"When she had drunk my health several times she bawled out loudly in her slurred Welsh accent, 'Who do you think this is then?' There was no answer from anyone. Either they were deaf or struck dumb by her manner. She reached down and, her hands beneath my arms, lifted me up onto the table top.

"'Well, I'll tell you who he is, you country clods. This is the sixth Baron Halyard, the new lord of Longfields, that's who. What do you think of him? He's a pretty boy, isn't he, even if he is like his father.' And she began to cry, the tears rolling down her rouged cheeks, always a sure sign she was about to recite the sad story of her wretched life. It was a performance she repeated at least once a fortnight in pubs and parks or on any street corner. She was going to tell them how, as a Welsh heiress of good family, who had gone down to Bath to take the cure, she had met there a dashing ex-captain, late of His Majesty's forces. How Mad Jack Halyard had wooed and seduced her, had married her for her fortune and when he had spent it, fled to

France to escape going to prison for his debts. How she, with only a tiny annuity left, something he had not been able to touch, had been abandoned, left with two children to care for.

"Poor, duped thing, she had gone back to Wales thinking her family would help her but they did not want to know her or her brats. She had been left to cope alone, defenseless, so was it any wonder she learned to hate her former lover; that even when he died a pauper's death in France she had not shed a tear.

"It was a story as familiar as it was embarrassing to me. I stood with my head down, staring at the table top, wishing the earth would open and swallow me.

"I saw Amelia's small, pale face below and heard her whisper, 'Don't mind her, Hal, please don't. She can't take this day away from you.' And it was true, she could not take the day nor my inheritance. This was the day that I had waited for, and I did as I had always done when she was drunk and loud, I pretended I was somewhere else and another person entirely.

"In my short life I had done quite a lot of pretending, one way and another. We had lived in a grubby back street in Cardiff. It should be made an eleventh commandment, that those who live in Cardiff should be born rich. We lived in near poverty, just enough for bread and cheese and gin in three rooms up a dingy flight of stairs. How she pitied herself there, away from gaiety and any hope of love or youth returning. Somehow the sharpest prick of all her woes was my likeness to my father, it seemed the final indignity. If people failed to notice or remark she pointed it out to them as if I resembled him on purpose, just to spite her.

"'He's not bad looking,' she'd say, 'look at those eyes and his curls, pity he's a Halyard. There's bad blood there.'

"I felt there was some taint in me and I could not bear the reality of my life, not even with Amelia for company. So I made myself a kingdom of the mind and of the imagination. I was a knight of old, a parfait, gentil knight who would keep myself pure and good so that I would be able

153

to sit at Arthur's round table and some day seek and see the grail. I would dedicate myself to the slaying of dragons, all but Welsh ones, and the salvation of damsels in distress. Can you imagine what I felt when I discovered that I actually was heir to a title and a great estate?

"I felt vindicated, as if all along I had known I was a prince, a changeling who had been held captive in Wales for his own safety until it was time for him to return and claim his rightful kingdom.

"But even this marvelous revelation of my true birth did not come in an ordinary manner. No letter arrived, no solicitor called. It was in the morning paper wrapped around the fish. There, on a back page, was the notice of my father's death and the announcement at the end that at my great-uncle's death I, Mad Jack's son, would be heir to Longfields.

"It was two more years before the old lord died and still no solicitor called. A neighbor told my mother she had heard that the old baron was gone."

Halyard looked at me and though he smiled and gave a short, hard laugh there was no warmth or gaiety in either. In the night his focus had changed, his point of view had altered. Today he saw life from a different prospect. As if before his vision had been distorted by seeing the world through rose-hued glass, while now the glass was broken and he was his realistic, cynical self once again.

"What a family you have married into, Catherine. If I had known I would have warned you. No wonder that day at the inn when my mother made such a spectacle of herself no one noticed. To the villagers and tenants all the Halyards were laughing stocks.

"My great-uncle from whom I inherited the property was known as 'the wicked lord.' I know every family has its black sheep but he excelled in mindless villainy. I say mindless, for his most celebrated crime was to kill his cousin Rupert Halyard in a ludicrous duel over game preservation in their mutually owned wood. He had not meant to kill him. He said so at his trial in the House of Lords and so they let him go home again.

"His brother, my grandfather, was an Admiral of the Blue. He was called Foul Weather Halyard by his men since he had only to take ship and set out to sea for there to be some great disaster, a hurricane, a typhoon, an earthquake in the Caribbean. In one such disaster he nearly ran the fleet aground and they posted him to the Admiralty where he could do as little harm as possible.

"Still, many felt his greatest blow against a defenseless nation was to leave it his son, my father.

"The navy would not have him; at least in the navy one must have some skill or aptitude, even if only for disaster. So my father bought himself a commission in the army where they will take anyone for a price. By several clever exchanges he finally seceded himself from the service. Mind you, it was never proved he seduced the colonel's lady or pilfered the mess accounts, never proved he cheated at cards, but still and all they were not sorry to see him go.

"And at Bath, where he had gone to find an heiress to keep him, he met my mother, who I understand fell in love with him at first sight. Ah, there's no accounting for taste, is there?

"But always, no matter what the Halyards were like, the house at Longfields remained a glory and a monument to what the human mind and spirit were capable of building. I found a picture of Longfields in a printshop and pasted it in my copy book. When my mother drank and raged and cursed, and Amelia cried, and there was not enough for supper I looked at Longfields, which one day would be mine; the Tudor front, the shell of broken abbey window next to it and on the other side a church, the living of which would be mine to give.

"When at last we heard the old lord had died we set out for England. I was in such a high state of excitement and elation that not even the stop at the inn could damp my spirits, and as we left to make our triumphal drive up to the house I felt as if I were about to enter paradise.

"I was totally unprepared for the sight that met my eyes. It was a scene of total desolation, looking as if there had been a war and this lunar wasteland were a pillaged battlefield. I could not imagine what had happened, and even when I knew, it was past my comprehension that the childless old baron had hated me enough to spoil his own land; that just to spite me he had sold off the timber and had laid the estate to waste so that I could not have the benefit of it.

"The stumps of those noble trees that had stood there outlasting Celt, Dane, Saxon, and Norman had fallen before his hatred and greed. One stand of timber alone remained, one which he had held jointly with the cousin he had murdered.

"In the park he had drained the lake, let it go to slime and the fish die. Their bones showed white like spiny runes cast all about by some mad sorcerer.

"The garden had gone to weed and bramble, not one flower bloomed, but it was in his wanton destruction of the house itself that he had excelled himself. The leads had been sold or ripped away. The drains hung loose and were stopped by the leaves of a dozen autumns. Above, in the facing of the castellated walks, stones were loose and some had fallen, smashing onto the courtyard below. The windows made me weep. The panes had been all smashed out and the space bricked up so he would not have to pay the glass tax. The great doors of this ancestral home hung sagging on their hinges. Inside, the wreck and carnage of his dislocated mind were unbelievable.

"He had lived in the kitchens with a wench by the name of Bess he'd brought from the village. The rest of the rooms were bare, the furniture sold, the silver and the china and the plate. In the attic, stored away, molding from the damp and gnawed by the rats, were the portraits, the paintings, and furniture he could not dispose of.

"From that house, as we opened the door, there came such a cackling and a stench that we ran and hid behind the coach. For his amusement or profit or perverse pleasure he had kept chickens in the great hall. They roosted on the hammer beams in the minstrels' gallery, on the stairs, or where they pleased, and everywhere they had left their feathers and droppings. Some had died, others had run mad without food or water.

"There was nowhere in that house for us to sleep, no food or no fuel. So on that day I came into the inheritance of chicken droppings and dry rot of mold and mildew, of rats and rain and ruin.

"There was nothing for it, we had to turn back and spend the first night at the inn.

"My mother tried to set the house right. She called in workmen—gardeners, stonemasons, plasterers, the lot. She signed the bills with my name and promised to pay but there was no money. At last the court appointed a guardian, a kind and sober man who proposed that the house be let to tenants for a time until my majority. They would be bound by the terms of the lease to make repairs. He bundled Amelia and my mother off to lodgings in London, and I was sent to school.

"I hated it from the first day. I was not strong and did not know how to defend myself. The boys bullied me and made fun of my Welsh accent. I was a lord of the realm, and I had no home, no friends, not even pocket money. If it had not been for Amelia's letters I would have died of unhappiness. She wrote me, sent me parcels, the pudding full of sixpences. Her letters were a lifeline to sanity, to hope, to the future."

He stopped then for a while, his head upon the glass, cooling his forehead, looking at the fields and woods along the narrow road. And he sighed; tired, bone weary, a man going home again. If I had been wiser I would have reached out to him then, taken him in my arms and held him like a disappointed child, but I was afraid that he would push me away. After a time he went on again, as if he had never stopped at all, the memories bombarding him relentlessly.

"I did better at Harrow. I fought the bullies, beat them bloody, and won prizes for my Greek and Latin. And when I went from there to Cambridge I even had a circle of congenial acquaintances. I made a friend in Tom Grace.

What times we had. Once I brought a trained bear into hall. I had found it in a traveling show and I bought it and made it a pet, a mascot. When it died, poor thing, we had it stuffed and presented to the college.

"Yet all the time I was a world away from Longfields where I longed to be. It was a testing, to wait until I was twenty-one to go home again. Oh, and what a summer that was. I brought my mother and Amelia from London. I engaged a proper housekeeper, Mrs. Griffin, to take care of them. I invited Tom Grace to spend the summer with us. I had a house and money and tenants who had made repairs. The windows had glass again. The tree stumps had been pulled, the chickens banished, the lake stocked with fish, the garden neat and green, bursting with flowers. From the attics the furniture and paintings had been brought down and repaired. The place was fit for a lord and his lady."

For a moment he paused and then continued.

"It was that summer that I met my cousins, Arabella and Rupert Halyard. They lived not too far away, at Halyard Hall. We still shared the wood over which my great-uncle had killed their great-grandfather. It was a romantic tale by then. Time had passed, blurred, given a sheen to bloody deeds.

"From the moment I set eyes on Arabella I was in love with her. There was never anyone like her, not then or now. No one could touch or match her beauty. From that first day I was her slave, her knight, her servant. I would have died for her if she had asked me."

When he said her name I had felt my heart stop. It was this moment I had dreaded; the hour when he remembered her and compared me to her. He looked at me then and it was a gaze without pity, a cold, hard stare, no quarter given. If he meant to wound me his aim was flawless, an arrow had just found and pierced my heart.

"You wanted the truth," he went on mercilessly, "and you shall have it, or what I know of it. We'll see then if there is any remedy in truth or if, like all other highblown words, it is hollow and false.

"Arabella was, quite simply, the most beautiful creature I had ever seen. Her hair was bright like a halo made of a summer sun and her eyes—I have never then or since seen eyes like hers. They were cat's eyes, first green, then amber flecked with gold and brown. They changed color as the fire does when one looked into them.

"But it was more than her astonishing beauty that appealed to me. With her the knight errant in me had found his cause, his crusade. I set myself to be her champion, felt it to be my right, my duty, my pleasure all in one because, you see, if it had not been for me Arabella and Rupert would have inherited Longfields. The two properties, Longfields and Halyard Hall, would have been theirs.

"If I had not been born she would have been living in that house, not I. And so the idea came to me that by marrying her, by making her my wife, we could both share in the splendor of the inheritance."

He smiled, remembering his boyish fancy, smiled because he remembered her and a summer I could never see or share. I felt naked and cold, all my feelings as exposed as a rock in a winter rain.

"That summer," he went on, "I couldn't see enough of Arabella. We were always together—Arabella, Rupert, Amelia, and I. It was a glorious, enchanted summer. The house was full of company. We dined and danced and rode out into the park and when Tom Grace came down he too became a part of that enchantment. Even my mother was no longer a burden or a termagant. For the last months of her life she too joined in our good spirits.

"And I was glad of that. Perhaps it was because she felt noticed and admired. Tom and Rupert always included her in our conversations and our rambles. They were the perfect, devoted sons she might have had instead of me. Whatever her reasons she drank less and seldom gave way to rages.

"I knew that in time I would ask Arabella to marry me. I waited for the perfect instant, a day when the garden would be at its best, and the roses all in bloom." His mouth twisted in a grimace of pain.

"When I finally got around to it, most sensibly, of course, she refused me. She said I was too young; that I did not know what love was.

"Strange, of all the things that I have forgotten in these recent months, I never would have thought it possible that I would forget that summer day. The garden, the heat, the scent of roses, and a bee buzzing in the hedge. And Arabella sitting, looking at me incredulously, as if before I spoke such a thing as marrying me had never entered her head.

"'Marry you, poor Hal. I have never thought of you in that way. No, it would be impossible.' And without giving my proposal a second thought she rose and left me there.

"I sat I do not know how long. Long enough so that she must have been sure I had gone away, for I heard her talking to someone behind the hedge.

"'Guess what? The most amusing thing has happened, you won't believe it when I tell you. Hal has just asked me to marry him. Poor Hal, he must be mad to think I could love him.' I heard her laugh as if it were some absurd joke. 'Why I could never marry that Welsh nobody.'

"For me, the summer was over then but not the pain of loving her or the cure. I was enchanted, bewitched, possessed by love for her, and she was forbidden to me. I wished myself dead or in hell and felt that I was both.

"And, as if she had caught my mood, my mother, her spirits long buoyed up beyond her usual melancholy, began to drink again. It spoiled our outings and parties. There were no more picnics in the park. She drank herself into a coma from which she did not rally. It is not a pretty death the drunkard makes. When it was finished I wanted to get away from the memory of those last days, from Longfields and from Arabella too, and so Tom Grace and I decided to go upon a grand tour together.

"I did not like to leave Amelia, but Arabella and Rupert promised they would look after her while I was gone. So with our bags packed and a retinue of servants large enough to wait upon a regiment, Tom Grace and I set out to see the world.

"Already in my mind a poem had begun to form; a poem about a wanderer who fled from a secret love, a passion he could not forget.

"It was moonstruck stuff, full of self-pity and a sense of sin, a boy's howling in the night, a baying at the moon.

"I wrote reams of words on quires of paper. Tom must have thought me mad. Both of us had tried our hand at poetry at Cambridge and both had been published in a small way, but he said I worked too quickly, that the thing could not be any good, for he wrote only a line or two a week and the choosing of a word would keep him frowning the better part of a morning. I wrote cantos while he wrote next to nothing. I might be facile but it was shallow, surface verse compared with his. He was the finer poet, we both agreed on that.

"When we sailed home after our year's travels were at an end we put in at Plymouth and I, holding a portmanteau containing a finished poem that I hoped only needed a bit of polishing to make me famous, was eager to get down to Longfields again, to see how the house was and to see Amelia. I had missed her greatly. I had not heard from her in months, which was worrying but not unduly so, for the post had been forwarded so often many letters had gone astray. I was also eager to see Arabella, for I already knew that somehow in the very writing of that poem I had made a medicine that effected at least a partial cure from the worst of my love sickness. I felt oddly relieved, as if a burden had been lifted from my soul; so much so that I was surprised to find Arabella had come to Plymouth. She was waiting at the dock to meet Tom and me. Rupert had not come with her, which was somehow mysterious and singular.

"Soon enough I was to know the reason she had come alone. She said Rupert could not bring himself to face me when I heard what she had come to tell me." Halyard stopped struggling for self-possession and then continued.

"Arabella had come to tell me that my sister Amelia was dead. Shortly after my departure Amelia had gone away from Longfields. She had died and had been buried in

Wales. I was stunned. At first I could not believe it was true. It seemed incomprehensible and completely out of character. Why would Amelia have left Longfields? Why would she have gone to Wales? No matter how I pressed Arabella for some explanation she was unable or unwilling to give me a satisfactory answer. She would only say that Rupert had been shattered by Amelia's death. She said that Rupert had been in love with Amelia and she with him, and that Amelia's death was so painful to him he could not bear to see me again, for it would only remind him of Amelia."

For a time Halyard sat motionless and I did not know what to say to him. At last he had tried to tell me what he remembered after all those months we had been together, but it seemed his losses were beyond any I had reckoned on. My love, my darling, how I wanted to reach out to him, but I felt I had no right to intrude upon his grief. I was a witness to a death in the family and could offer nothing to take the place of the departed. Slowly he forced himself to go on.

"I had no heart for Longfields without Amelia. She had been more than a sister to me, she had been mother, father, friend, companion, and confidante, and yet I know I was surprised that Rupert had been in love with Amelia and she with him. I had known that he was fond of Amelia, of course, but I had been too blinded by my passion for Arabella to notice they were in love. But it was too late for regret, and in the chill of first shock I found I was able to sit with Arabella calmly, to make small talk, and I knew that I could manage to make some kind of life now without her.

"Instead of going back to Longfields Tom suggested I go up to London for a while and I agreed. I took rooms in the Albany and I began to rewrite and to polish. I kept at it day and night. Work was my new obsession. In a few months I was finished and when it was published I woke up one morning to find myself famous."

He rubbed at his eyes as if to wipe away the past and his present fatigue. He looked tired now, but there was more and he meant to tell it all.

"It was amusing at first to be famous. I had a mantelpiece covered with invitations, more than I could have accepted if I had been twenty men. I don't know if I can explain the exhilaration of having been obscure one week, ignored, scarcely spoken to in the street, and the next week having the whole world know my name.

"Ladies I had never met sent me locks of their hair and you've already seen the sort of letters that they wrote to me. Suddenly I was irresistible—I, who had been too shy, too inept to win the one woman I had wanted.

"Several put it out that they were having love affairs with me. One rode naked past my window to attract my attention. I had to laugh, it was all so absurd. I think," his eyes darted to mine and then, flushing, he looked quickly away again, "I think it would have been impossible to escape them all. And to be honest I am not sure I would have tried. I had my love affairs. I will not deny it. I slept too often in beds that were not my own. I cuckolded husbands who had done me no harm and I was not always discreet. More than one of those jealous husbands swore to challenge me to a duel, but I cannot say I blame any of them. I don't know if the fellow who stopped me outside my club the other evening was one of them but I imagine that he was. In the old days I used to advertise myself as a famous shot. I took great care to show my skill at Manton's. Most wronged husbands thought twice about going to the field of honor with me.

"Nor were women the sum total of all my follies. I had made a reputation as a sinner with *The Nomad* and I meant to live up to it. In those days I drank too much and I played too deep at cards. I owed more than I care to tell you and I ran up accounts that I was not prepared to pay.

"I was the dissolute rake, the fop in the blue coat, the dandy full of disdain for my fellow man. I was not, in short, someone I would have cared to meet or to take by the hand and call friend. Sick of myself, I was ready to go home to Longfields and to hide myself away.

"It was about this time that Arabella came up to London. She said that she had come to marry me. She had thought it over and now she meant to save me from myself. I couldn't believe that I had heard her right. I must have showed my shock and surprise. It was ungallant of me and I saw that I had hurt her.

"I can see her eyes now as they filled with tears; green amber brimming over with semiprecious drops. She asked me if I had forgotten I had once asked her to be my wife and that if I now repented of it she would release me, and so I had my moment, you see, when I could have turned back tragedy. But I did not because she made me feel so guilty.

"It was all done so subtly I felt I should have been constant and true. Once I had wanted her more than my own life. I had written a poem that had given me fame just to prove that love, and now I did not want her.

"I should have told her so. I should have said that both she and I had changed, that I knew she did not love me as a wife should love her husband. But I was a coward, I was stubborn, I was a fool, call me what you will. I agreed to marry her. It was with me a matter of some wild, stupid pride.

"You thought that I loved her," he said.

He reached out his hand for mine and took it. "You thought I fled away from England out of grief and when you found me you feared if I remembered that I would not ever love you as I had loved her. I never really loved her, Catherine. It went wrong from the beginning. Not one day went as married life is supposed to go. There was no *lune de miel* for us.

"At first we stayed in London, Arabella insisted on it. She wanted to have the season, to buy a house, to become a great hostess. She wanted gowns and jewels, carriages and servants.

"It was beyond our means. Even with her settlement there was not that much money to be spent. We could not afford that house nor the style of living required to keep it up. Arabella proved to be more extravagant than my mother and myself rolled into one.

"In the end I found the bailiffs in the hall. They camped there day and night; there was no evicting them unless we

164

paid. And I could not pay. There was nothing then but to retreat to the country.

"We got out of town through the back garden and set out for Longfields in the dead of night, fled as we have fled tonight, only then it was only my pride that was wounded. I had only been set upon by bailiffs, not by ruffians.

"It was that night in the coach, driving down to Long-fields, that she told me just what it was that she had done, just why it was that she had married me. She told me she had done a thing so terrible that I, even I . . . " Suddenly he went pale and began to retch, leaning forward, holding at himself as if he had just suffered a seizure.

"Stop the coach," he gasped. "Stop." I beat at the roof, pounding at the driver's box until the coach drew to a halt and Halyard sprang out, his head bent over the ditch. He was sick, the spasms wracking him as if he had been poisoned. It was a long time before he came back and now he was more pale than ever.

He signaled that we should go on. He said nothing, sat head turned, sick and ashamed, and at last he whispered hoarsely, "I was sick then too, sick to my very soul at what Arabella told me."

"What did she tell you?" My lips felt numb.

"I don't know."

"But you must know. Tell me now and have done with it, have done with her."

"I don't know, I swear it, but if I did I would not tell you."

"Why?"

"Because it would be too dangerous for you to know. What she told me was unspeakable. The things that she had done, they were beyond human comprehension, things so dreadful and terrible that any hope of happiness for the two of us was gone forever.

"When we came to Longfields Arabella and I each went to different parts of the house to live in isolation from each other and from the memory of what she had told me.

"We lived with a barrier of silence between us, for how long I cannot remember, but something broke the silence like a dam that has cracked and floods the world. For some reason we quarreled; a bitter, violent quarrel. I know that I struck her and in revenge she led me down the corridors to the west wing of the house. It was all a blur, a maze of horror. I followed her, saw her fling open a door, and then there was a struggle and a candle fell and a fire blazed up. The flames were leaping everywhere. I tried to save her, I know I did. I beat at the flames with my hands, with anything I could find. It is not true, the cruel gossip that I let her die, that I did not try to save her. I would not have let a dog die like that. I have the scars still on my hands and arms to prove it.

"No matter how I hated her I would not have let her die in that fire.

"So I went away from England, planning never to return. And now, here I am, I have come back again full circle."

As the coach clattered into Longton, I saw, as he had promised I would, the little stone bridge, the mill, and the pretty weir. The houses and the shops were all made of native stone; small and compact, they lay along a narrow high street. The largest was the inn, the Halyard Arms.

"I am sorry, Catherine," he said as we entered the driveway to the estate, "we ought never to have come back here. I should never have brought you to this house and its dark dreams. I wish with all my heart, for your sake, that you had never found me on the shore. I wish that I had never married you only to bring you to this place."

"Don't say such a thing."

"It is true, I should not have married you. I should not have married anyone. I am not fit to be any woman's husband; Arabella told me so often enough. You remember that I said that one day I would make you unhappy." I could not believe that he was saying these words to me.

"But I love you, I am not unhappy."

"Ah, Cat, but you will be," he said sadly. "The ghosts at Longfields will see to that."

Chapter Eight

And so it was that we came home to Longfields and its ghosts. I sat, stunned by all that Halyard had just said. Could he really believe that it would have been better if we had never met? From the first I had feared the time when he would remember Arabella because I had been certain that he loved her. Now he had remembered, he had said that he had hated her with all his being and I was more afraid than ever, for now I knew that the bond between them had been a more potent and powerful force than any I had imagined.

Whatever the revelation Arabella had made to him in that coach coming down to Longfields, whatever the secret, I felt sure the answer to the riddle lay ahead in that house that was now to be my home.

In the weeks that followed I was to discover that I had come to live in a nightmare that merely gave the illusion of reality, and that the memory of the lovers we had once been would come to seem but a distortion of the truth. For at Longfields nothing was to be what it seemed and the eyes as well as the heart were to be deceived.

At the gatehouse a sturdy countrywoman, surrounded

by a cluster of flaxen-haired children, had watched us pass. The largest of the boys had waved and I had waved back at him, but Halyard had sat silent and unnoticing, occupied with his own dark thoughts.

On either side of the drive stood a line of young trees. Beyond were fields where the stumps of that lunar waste Halyard had described to me had been pulled and in their place the land had been sown in winter rye and vetch.

I was surprised that the village was so near. The driveway was only an extension of the high street, and I had looked curiously at the winding stretch of low stone wall that separated the village from the park.

Then suddenly, at the top of the rise, I saw the house. The sun, which had been trying to break through the dull, grey clouds all the morning, won out for a moment and its rays caught the mass of windows that filled the impressive Tudor south front. The reflected streamers of light were blinding, but almost as quickly as it had appeared, the sun vanished behind the clouds and later I was to think that it had been an omen. But at the moment I only considered what it must have cost to replace the panes of glass in the windows and the fortune that must have been spent to restore the place to its former glory. Now, with the roof repaired, the leads in order, and the missing stones of the castellated walk that ran from tower to tower above the south front replaced, I knew I had seen the house as it must have looked when it was built.

Yet, for me, the true splendor of Longfields was not its size nor its antiquity, but the one remaining fragment of a window wall of the ancient abbey church. It stood at the east end of the house. The gothic outline was pure beauty shaped in stone and mortar. Long ago, tendrils of ivy had climbed the shell and covered it lovingly in an embrace of deepest green.

The wall was not joined to the house proper but stood so close to the tower of the east wing that it almost seemed to be a part of it, and beyond, at the west end of the house, was a small Norman church that gave balance and symmetry to the whole.

168

"Longfields is really lovely," I said. "How wise of the first baron to leave the abbey wall and to set the church in that location." Halyard gave a short, unpleasant laugh.

"What a hopeless romantic you are, Catherine. The first baron left the wall because it masked the stable block he had built behind it, and as for his neo-Norman church, it is so close to the house because he disliked going into the village to worship. In fact, he had a tunnel dug from the house beneath the terrace to the church so that in bad weather not a drop of rain would fall upon his head on his way to his prayers."

As the coach pulled into the circular drive and drew up in the court before the ornately carved doors that bore the Halyard crest, I felt as if Halyard had ridiculed not only his ancestor but me.

I wondered if any of the other Halyards had ever brought a bride home to Longfields in such a fashion. For us there was no prospect that Halyard would carry me across the threshold or that the servants would be lined up in the hall waiting to make us welcome.

Through the doors came a young footman hastily buttoning up his liveried jacket. Then, seeing that this was no casual visitor who could be turned away, he stopped short, turned, and ran back into the house to fetch someone above his lowly station.

In a few moments an elderly manservant appeared, and recognizing the coach, forgot his dignity and age and rushed down the steps toward us. He stood at the window of the coach peering in, his face betraying his astonishment. There could be no doubt that he was amazed by the sight of his master.

"M'lord," he gasped, "m'lord."

"Don't stand there gaping, Rule," Halyard said. "Open the door and help me into the house." Rule did as he was bid and I followed behind them like a stranger who has no right of entry.

Just at the door Halyard stopped and turned to look behind him. A low, anguished cry escaped him. He might have been a prisoner who had come to the place of his execution. I had thought he would be happy to come home to Longfields but in that I had clearly been wrong. And I sensed that he had remembered something about the house itself, something he had forgotten until this moment.

Inside the entry hall was dim, the shutters closed against unwelcome light. Overhead the chandelier was bagged in muslin and all around us was the musty odor of airless rooms and dusty hangings. A damp, creeping chill that overlaid the pervasive smell of wood smoke was the legacy from that tragic fire.

Halyard's introductions were brief. If either Arthur, the young footman, or Rule wondered at my appearance or our unheralded arrival, they gave no sign.

"Where is Mrs. Griffin?" Halyard demanded, and in answer to the question, from the top of the wide stairs I heard a woman's voice.

"Here, m'lord." As she descended through the gloom and advanced toward us, I saw a short, middle-aged woman dressed in prim, dark grey. From her waist there hung a chatelaine. Mrs. Griffin was the director of this household and she managed to convey the impression of both great efficiency and disapproval. "We did not know you were in England. You should have sent word that you were coming home."

"I am sorry, Mrs. Griffin," Halyard said drily, "there was no time to give you warning."

"Sorry never mends." Mrs. Griffin spoke as if by custom she was allowed a freedom of speech forbidden to others. "Look at the house," she said severely. "Nothing ready. The rooms not aired, the fires not laid. Since you've been away I've kept only a small staff. We are not prepared to entertain visitors." She did not look at me directly, but I knew the remark was meant for my ears.

"I do not expect to entertain, Mrs. Griffin," Halyard said shortly. "I am sorry to have come without giving you warning, but I am sure that, as always, you will do your best."

She seemed mollified, but I thought it strange that he

should feel it necessary to apologize to his housekeeper for coming to his own house.

"You know the difficulties as well as I do." Mrs. Griffin went on as if she could not let the subject rest. "It is not easy to manage here at the best of times. However, as you say, I will do my best." Then her manner softened. "I am pleased to see you, m'lord. Never for an instant did we believe the rumors that you were lost at sea. When did you return to England?"

"Only a few days ago," Halyard replied. "We stopped in London where last night I was set upon by ruffians."

"M'lord!" Her hand went to her heart and she gave me a reproving glance as if she suspected that I was in some way responsible for the incident.

"Catherine rescued me," Halyard continued. "It was her decision that we leave London at once, or I would have sent word to you of our arrival."

For the first time Mrs. Griffin saw the tear in his coat and the bloodstains on his shirt.

"Oh, m'lord, you have been wounded. It must be seen to at once."

"My wife," Halyard replied, "has already attended to it. Catherine and I were married in Spain. I know that I can rely on you, Mrs. Griffin, to do what you can to make your new mistress comfortable."

There was a silence in the hall. Mrs. Griffin, taken by surprise, could only stare at Halyard and then at me. "Your wife?" She seemed unsure at first whether he was telling her the truth or not. Had he, I wondered, often brought home his partners of the London evening, still dressed in last night's rumpled finery? Then Mrs. Griffin, deciding that she had heard him right and that she must make the best of the situation, turned and gave me a long, encompassing look before she dropped me a civil curtsy.

"Lady Halyard, I would have arranged a far different reception for you had I known that you were coming," and I heard myself mumble that it could not matter less.

"Please, enough apologies," Halyard interrupted. "I am very tired and I wish to go to my bed."

"You'll be wanting your old rooms, I imagine," Mrs. Griffin said. "I will have them prepared at once for you and . . . " she hesitated before she said my name, "Lady Halyard."

"No, Mrs. Griffin," Halyard interrupted sharply, "I am sure Lady Halyard will be more comfortable in my mother's old apartments." I was so unprepared for his suggestion that without thinking I blurted out, "But I would rather be with you."

"I am sure you would, Catherine," Halyard said coldly, "but I must insist that you take my mother's suite. If my wound makes me feverish I would not want to disturb your rest."

No one looked at him or me. I had been rejected, rebuffed, set aside. I felt as if he had divorced himself from me publicly, shamed me in front of the servants. I knew that my place at Longfields had been defined. I was to be isolated. He had made it painfully clear he did not want me with him, and I was too proud to beg him to change his mind. A thought came to me that he had decided on this separation when we were in the coach, even before we had come into the house.

I followed him up the stairs. Rule was at Halyard's side and Mrs. Griffin was by mine. I could not understand what I had done to make him so unhappy with me, so unwilling to have me near him.

At the top of the landing Rule turned down the corridor to the right while Mrs. Griffin motioned me toward the left.

"Shall I come and dress the wound for you?" I asked. Halyard stopped and looked mockingly back at me.

"No need to play the nurse again, Cat. I would think you had had enough of that in Spain." It was a second rebuff. I would not give him the opportunity for a third. "Whatever you want, Cat," Halyard said brusquely, "Mrs. Griffin will see to it."

His eyes were cold and his manner distant. He had

meant to turn me away and he wanted the servants to know it. It would have been impossible for Rule or Mrs. Griffin to guess that only yesterday we had been lovers who had shared one bed, lovers who had lain in each other's arms and been swept by passion. I watched him walk away from me along the corridor, waiting until I saw which door he turned in at, for I would have been too proud to ask where in the house my own husband was. I felt a tightening in my throat that brought the tears to my eyes.

"The house is very large," I said. "I don't think I will ever find my way in it."

"Of course you will," Mrs. Griffin reassured me. "It is quite large but the plan is a simple one. The house was laid out in the shape of an E to honor Queen Elizabeth. See, here we are in the very center. The glass gallery on the north is the middle bar of the E."

And I saw behind me an open gallery bordered on three sides by glass, like the stern of an old-fashioned ship of the line.

"It's pleasant to walk there on rainy days and in fine weather the glass catches the sun. Lord Halyard's rooms are to the east of the gallery and yours to the west." I was suddenly riveted by her words.

"Am I to be in the west wing, then?"

"Oh no." Mrs. Griffin seemed shocked that I should ask such a question. "The west wing is closed. It was badly damaged by a fire." She looked at me quickly, wondering how much Halyard might have told me. "No one lives there, or could. The floors were burnt through, the timbers charred. It's not safe to go there now. No, Lady Halyard, your apartments are in the west corridor, but not the west wing. Your suite is in the same location as Lord Halyard's is in the east corridor. I am sure that you will find it comfortable. Lord Halyard's late mother was particularly fond of it. It was designed to be the royal suite. They say Queen Anne once slept there." Mrs. Griffin opened the door and stood aside, waiting for me to enter.

I could not deny the room was large. The fireplace was

wide enough to roast an ox, but as the sofas, chairs, and even the bed hangings were covered in dustcloths it looked as if it had been draped in shrouds.

"You see," Mrs. Griffin said, as she pulled at a bell rope beside the door, "there is a dressing room and a water closet, and you have a fine view of the gardens." She led me quickly past the white wasteland of chairs and tables to the windows and drew back the curtains. Through the diamond panes I saw a knot garden bordered by hedges and flowerbeds. To the right of my window I could see the outline of the glass gallery, to the left the long line of the west wing and in the distance, a thick stand of trees, the lucky survivors of the wicked lord's reign of destruction.

"Of course," I heard Mrs. Griffin say, "the gardens are not at their best at this time of the year. But in spring they can be quite lovely," and I almost said, I will not be here in the spring. For a moment I wondered if it were true, a presentiment of what the future held.

"I've rung for Megan and Rose. They will put the rooms in order for you. I regret your seeing Longfields like this. You must have a sorry first impression of the house. As for the staff, you must make allowances. Both Megan and Rose are only country girls from the village. I have done my best to train them, but the most that can be said for them is that they are willing. It has been difficult these last months with m'lord away. Of course, cook stayed on. She is an excellent woman."

Two fresh-faced girls appeared at the door with mops and dusters, pails and brooms. Their eyes were round with curiosity; they were unable to keep from staring at their new mistress. They made their nervous, awkward curtsies and set about removing dust sheets while Arthur and another footman, Robert, brought in huge canisters of hot water and the trunks. I tried to keep out of their way by standing at the windows.

"Would you like one of the girls to unpack for you," Mrs. Griffin asked, "and to wait on you until your maid arrives?"

174

"I have no maid," I said.

"Ah." Mrs. Griffin nodded, as if she had suspected as much. "Perhaps Megan can be of help? You will have to tell her what you expect of her, but she will try to please."

"Indeed, I will m'lady." Megan looked delighted, which was more than I could say for Rose, whose face went dark and sullen.

"Rose already has other duties," Mrs. Griffin said. Rose made a face. Whatever her other duties were, she did not care for them. Both girls set about the cleaning with such vigor that the dust they raised caused me to sneeze and to sneeze again.

"Lady Halyard," Mrs. Griffin said gravely, "if you would not think it forward of me, while your rooms are being prepared, would you like to wait in my parlor? It's just up one flight of stairs in the west tower. There's a fire there and I could offer you a cup of tea."

She meant to be polite, but there was something more in the invitation, an element of mystery that made me accept her offer.

In the corridor Mrs. Griffin again took the lead, and once more began a running description of the house. "You see," she said, "the west corridor ends at these doors." She opened a pair of double doors to reveal a square hall landing. "This landing," she went on, "gives onto the west stairs. There is another flight of stairs on the east side of the house. By these stairs you can go down to the reception rooms or up to the second floor and the tower. The two towers, east and west, are connected by an outdoor walk along the battlement. On a fine day you can see for miles. It really is a magnificent sight."

"I am sure it is," I said. Mrs. Griffin had paused on the west landing and now pointed to some doors behind me.

"Those are the doors," she said, "that lead to the west wing. As I explained, the rooms are closed. Those doors are always locked and I have the only key." She held it out for my inspection. "It would not be safe for the servants to go prowling about. The flooring might give way. The wing was quite ruined and as there are so many other rooms available that are not in use, I am sure Lord Halyard feels repairs are unnecessary."

I felt sure Mrs. Griffin had told me all this for a reason but why she had wanted to be so explicit was a mystery.

"And now, if you will follow me up the stairs I will show you where my rooms are. I moved into them after m'lord left England. I hope you will not think I have chosen an apartment above my station, but the rooms are most convenient and as the staff is small I put the maids on the same floor so I could keep an eye on them. Of course, you may want to make other arrangements. If so you have only to tell me."

"No," I said. "I am sure that whatever you have done in the past will suit me well enough." I could not say how little I cared where she or the maids slept, nor did I understand why it was of such importance to Mrs. Griffin.

Her parlor was cozy and warm. The fire burned brightly in the grate and the kettle was singing on the hob. Again I wondered why Mrs. Griffin would think I might want her to change her rooms.

"I've always tried to please the ladies of the house," she said, her voice shaking with emotion. "First Lord Halyard's mother; then his sister, Amelia; and then the Lady Arabella." She cast me another quick look, trying to guess what I might know of Halyard's first wife.

"Have you been in the house long?" I asked.

"Yes," she said proudly. "Since m'lord came of age and took up residence at Longfields. I've seen many changes here." She looked away, her cheeks flushed with two bright spots of color. "It's a remarkable house," she said, "full of beautiful, valuable things. I have made an accurate inventory." Did she imagine I wished to count the spoons and inspect the linen?

"Mrs. Griffin," I began tentatively, "I must tell you I am not used to such a large house as this. I grew up in a small house by the sea. My father was a retired officer who stayed in Spain after the Peninsular Campaign had ended. We lived simply." I did not mean to make Mrs. Griffin my confidante, but I thought it better to get our lines straight at the beginning. "I do not want to usurp your place in the household. I know nothing about running an establishment."

"I see." It seemed as if what I had told her was an unexpected revelation. At length she said, "I had a nephew, Ned, who was killed at Badajoz."

Whatever Mrs. Griffin had concluded about me, apparently her attitude had changed for the better. Not that I had made a friend or an ally, in England one did not make friends of servants. But now at least I felt that she was not an enemy and that she would not take an active part against me.

"Ned used to write what a different sort of country Spain was from England. He said he had actually seen dates growing on trees."

"Yes," I said, "Spain is a very different sort of country."

As we drank our tea we sat in silence, each occupied with her own thoughts; I, dreaming of the warm sun and the sea, of Paco on the terrace among the pots of geraniums, and of Maria Luz busy in the kitchen.

"Well," Mrs. Griffin said at last, stirring herself, "I imagine your suite is ready for you. I will take you down again."

"No need for that. Your directions were so clear I can find my way back on my own."

"But I should go with you."

"No," I protested, "really, it's all right."

"Well then," she agreed reluctantly. "But I meant to ask before, would you prefer to dine off a tray in your room or alone in the dining room?" It was her way of telling me I need not expect Halyard to come down to dinner, and I was grateful to her for asking, for now I would not have to sit alone, staring across a wide expanse of polished oak, trying to appear cheerful.

"I will have my dinner on a tray," I said. "And thank you for the tea."

I easily found my way back to the stairs and then down to the hall below and here again I had an odd sensation as I looked at the doors of the west wing. Mrs. Griffin had

177

made a great point of telling me they were locked and only she had the key. Why, I wondered, had she made such a show of informing me that the west wing was dangerous and forbidden territory? Whatever her reasons, she had made her message clear.

I walked on down the west corridor to my own door and into the magnificent apartment I was to occupy alone. There I found Megan in the dressing room hanging up the last of the expensive gowns Halyard had had made for me.

"Oh," she said, her face shining with pleasure, "what beautiful dresses and so many of them. I've never seen anything so fine."

"They are pretty," I said. And I thought how useless they would be. I could hardly wear them to sit alone in my room or walk along the corridors.

I bathed and dressed, and I allowed Megan to do my hair in a fashion I had never tried before and she declared it most becoming. I saw that Megan would need little training, for to be a lady's maid was the pinnacle of her ambitions. Later she carried up a tray of delicious food for which I had no appetite. Afterward, when she came back to turn down the bed, she started to draw the curtains.

"Leave them open, Megan," I said.

"But m'lady, there's nothing to see in the dark."

"Leave them open anyway," I said.

"As you like, m'lady," and she left me to my solitude.

It was a dark night. Clouds hid the moon and stars. I wanted to see Halyard, but if that was to be accomplished I knew that I must make the first move. For some reason he would not come to me. I rose and, taking a candle, walked across the vast expanse of floor to the door.

I went slowly down the dark corridor, pausing at the entrance to the glass gallery. There, for an instant, the moon slipped out from behind the clouds and the room seemed a ghostly galleon tossed on cloudy seas. I walked on uncertainly toward his door where I hesitated for a moment, then knocked and entered.

I was met by a blast of desert heat. In the fireplace the

178

logs had been piled high and the flames were licking up the chimney like a blazing inferno. Yet Halyard sat in bed beneath a heavy pile of covers.

"What do you want?" he asked sharply.

"I came to see how you were," I said.

"I am well enough." But he was not. I could see that for myself. His eyes were overbright and his speech was slurred. Beside him, on the night table, I saw a half-empty bottle of brandy and a small, dark vial of laudanum, and my heart sank. He must be in worse pain than he had let me know. He must surely have insisted upon separate rooms so that I would not suspect how ill he was. He had done it only so he would not worry me.

"Do you have a fever?" I asked and reached out to put my hand upon his forehead, but he drew back as if he thought I meant him some harm.

"No," he answered quickly.

"Shall I change the dressing on your wound?"

"No," he said again. "I want to sleep."

"Do you want me to stay with you?"

"No, it is best you do not stay." I was sure now he did not want me to worry on his account. It was so like him to be generous, to think of me before himself. Surely I had misread his earlier mood.

"Very well," I said, "I'll say goodnight." I kissed him on the forehead and out of habit I smoothed at his pillows, straightening them behind his head, and as I did so I felt something beneath them; something cold, hard, and metallic. For the first time I suspected that not only was he in pain but that he was also frightened.

The pistols were there, at the ready. I sensed that there was something in this house he would rather die than face. Was it something real or something imagined? Whichever it was, it would do no good to question him about it now, not in his present frame of mind.

That night, alone in my bed, I could not sleep. I remembered the nights he had lain beside me, the nights that had been made of love, and I longed to feel his arms about me, his lips on mine. Those nights of fire had made it impossi-

179

ble for me to live without his love. I could not believe that now he had remembered so much else he no longer wanted me or the life we had shared. As I lay unable to sleep, I heard the wind blow, howling like a trapped animal at the window panes.

When I slept I heard a child crying—a child, frightened, alone in the dark, and when I awoke I found there were tears on my cheeks, and it seemed then that the child I had heard must have been myself.

Chapter Nine

In the morning I awoke to a sense of unreality. When I had dressed and breakfasted, I sat before the fire trying to make sense of Halyard's behavior. I was determined to see him, to talk it out with him.

I walked down the hall to his room and raised my hand to knock. As I did so the door opened, but it was not Halyard who answered, it was Rule. He put his finger to his lips and whispered to me, "M'lord is still asleep. He had rather an uneasy night, I am afraid. Can I give him some message?"

"Tell him I was here and that I will come again."

"Very well." He looked uncomfortable. "But I believe m'lord prefers to be alone today."

"I see," I said, but I was uneasy. I wondered if Halyard was truly asleep or if he had sent Rule to make his excuses. I was at once ashamed of such a thought. This house seemed to infect the mind with doubts as if it were a carrier of a disease that afflicted all those who dwelt here.

I went to my room again and dressed in my oldest dress, put on my stoutest shoes, and, carrying my cloak, I walked down the main stairs past the dim, damp hall and out into the day.

In the forecourt I stood looking back at the house. From here it was easy enough to say it was only a pile of stones and mortar, yet somehow I had the feeling the house was alive and that it meant to crush me in its embrace. Those walls were a prison of the memory and the mind.

I walked hurriedly on toward the window wall of the ancient abbey and put my hands upon it, as if by that gesture I could draw some strength from it. Then, to give myself some excuse for being out of doors, I decided I would walk down to the stables to see how Old Jeb was. He deserved some praise and reward for having brought us home safe and sound. Overhead the sky was dark and lowering. A brisk wind blew from the east. I walked along the brick path, wishing that on my first day at Longfields the sun had shone to give me a feeling of welcome.

One of the stableboys, a shy, rawboned country lad, said Old Jeb had gone to the village, and slyly, with a wink, he mentioned the Halyard Arms, where Jeb always went for his morning ale. As I left I heard them whispering behind my back. A new mistress was worth the time for speculation. What were they saying? What did they think of me? Were they comparing me to Arabella?

I walked away from the stables on toward the garden and looked up at the south front of the house. From here it seemed as if all was order and reason, as carefully planned and laid out as the knot garden. But I knew that the symmetry of those walls was deceiving.

I turned to stroll along the borders and between the hedges. There were yew and clipped privet all lined by lime walks and beyond, in the distance, was the wood, conifer, oak and wild thorn and holly. As I turned in the path I suddenly came upon an elderly gardener kneeling down by a border, lifting out the last of the summer bulbs and piling them in a basket.

"Good morning," I said. He had not heard me approach and my unexpected presence startled him. He looked at me, his eyes dark beneath beetling brows. "The garden must be lovely in spring," I heard myself say nervously. He made no reply but gave a guarded growl of agreement. Again I had the feeling that I would not be here in the spring, that the flowers would bloom but that I would not see them. The sky seemed to be descending like a weight. A gust of wind tore the hood from my head and whipped at my cloak. With the bitter wind came the first large, heavy drops of rain, which fell on my face. The gardener looked up reproachfully.

"It be rain," he said glumly, as if the weather were all my doing, and he began to gather up his tools and basket. Regretfully, I knew I would have to go in again. I looked up toward the house, wishing there were some porch beneath which I might take shelter. As I looked, in the window of the glass gallery, pressed against one of the panes, I saw a face.

It was blurred but it was unmistakably the face of a child, and the drops of rain seemed to be streams of tears falling down her cheeks and, as I stared up at her, she suddenly disappeared. I knew it was not a vision; I had seen a child's face just as I had heard a child crying in the night. I turned to the gardener, who was rising to his feet, his basket on his arm.

"Who was that?" I asked.

He looked at me but did not answer.

"Who was that in the window? I saw a child's face; up there, looking out from the glass gallery." He hesitated, as if he had not understood my question, then at last he mumbled, "I didn't see no one."

"I did," I said, "she was there."

"I didn't see no one," he repeated. He started away down the path.

"Who is she?" He turned back.

"You'll catch your death standing out in the rain," and he was gone.

He must have thought me a madwoman and perhaps I was, a woman who did not have the sense to get in out of the rain. I ran along the path and around the house toward the front door, then into the hall and up the wide

183

stairs to the landing. There was no one in the glass gallery, but on one window pane there was the small print of a child's hand.

I went to my room and took off my cloak and stood at the window, looking down at the rain falling on the garden. I knew I must see Halyard. I had some questions he must answer. If he were asleep I would wake him; if indifferent, I would plague him. There were things about Longfields that I must know. Megan had come with my luncheon tray but that could wait. I had no appetite.

I went to Halyard's room, half-expecting Rule to bar the way, but Halyard was alone, sitting in his dressing gown in a wing chair before a roaring fire. Behind him the curtains were drawn and once more the heat in the room was overpowering. Beside him, on a small table, was a tray of untouched food. It seemed Halyard had no more appetite than I.

"How are you feeling?" I asked him. "Did you sleep well?" He shrugged, as if his health were a matter of indifference to him. I was not sure he even knew I was in the room. He looked dull and listless. His eyes were clouded and his face bore an unhealthy pallor.

"Are you all right?" I asked again. For a time he did not answer and then he roused himself.

"Yes," he nodded, "quite all right, thank you."

"Does your wound pain you?"

"No." He turned away from me so I could not see his eyes. His speech seemed thick and slurred, and I wondered how much of the laudanum he had taken.

"I came to see you earlier," I said, "but Rule told me you were still asleep."

"What did you want?" he asked coldly, as if I might have had some ulterior motive for wanting to see him.

"I came to see how you were," I said, "and because I missed you. Last night was the first time we have been apart since we have been married. I was lonely without you." I waited for him to tell me that he had missed me too but he was silent, and I went on hurriedly to cover the gulf that now lay and widened between us.

"I was going for a walk in the garden and I thought you might have liked to come with me." Again I waited for some response but there was none. He sat in a state of total apathy, seemingly indifferent both to me and to his surroundings.

I had come to ask him about the child whose face I had seen in the window, but now I was here I was only concerned about his condition. He was ill. I was sure of it.

"It's too hot in here." I walked quickly to the windows and drew the curtains and flung open the windows before he could protest. Then, crossing back to him, I said, "I insist on having a look at your wound." I held aside the collar of his dressing gown and lifted the bandage from his shoulder. I fully expected to find the wound inflamed, but it was clean and already beginning to heal. Now I was truly puzzled. If it was not his wound that had caused him to behave so strangely toward me, then what was it that troubled him?

"If you are feeling up to it, why not come out for a walk with me now? This room is suffocating. You need some fresh air and exercise."

"It is raining," he said dully and withdrew his hand from mine.

"The rain has stopped. We can walk in the gardens or you could show me the house. Mrs. Griffin says the view from the castellated walk is magnificent."

"Then let Mrs. Griffin show you the house," he said angrily. "It is her domain." But I would not be put off.

"Would you prefer a walk in the woods?" I was determined to get him out of that room.

"Perhaps tomorrow." He turned back to the fire as if he considered the matter closed.

"I want you to come," I said. "I want us to be together. Besides, there are some things I have to talk to you about. There are some questions I must ask you."

"Won't they wait?"

"No," I said firmly. "There are some things about you and Longfields I must know."

He sighed and for a moment I thought that he was in

185

pain, but then he looked at me searchingly, and I saw the cloud had lifted from his eyes. I knew that he had heard the urgency in my voice.

"Yes," he said, "you are right. We must talk." Again there was a change in him. It was as if he were quicksilver. In the space of five minutes he had gone from seeming indifference to anger and then to something approaching resignation.

"Yes," he said again heavily. "We'll go out for a walk in the garden. I can see you'll leave me no peace until I do." The last was a sharp, unexpected barb, hardly the reply that I had hoped for.

"Well," he said suddenly, "do you want to stay and watch me dress? Is that why you are hanging about?" I shook my head. I felt the tears start up in my eyes, but I was determined not to let him know how he had hurt me with his sarcastic manner.

"No," I said evenly, "not if you can manage on your own. I'll get my cloak and wait for you in the glass gallery." I left him, unsure of what to think of his behavior. I was dealing with a man who had looked at me as if I were a stranger, or even worse, an enemy.

When he came for me I was shocked by the sight of him. I had never seen him dressed with so little regard for his appearance. Not even in those early days in Spain had he put himself together with so little care, and it seemed to reflect some inner chaos and confusion.

He motioned me to join him but he did not offer me his arm. He walked briskly ahead of me and down the wide stairs without even waiting for me to catch up with him.

Once out of doors he walked at a more sensible rate, and I was able to take a better look at him. He appeared to be drained and altogether wretched. His color was still poor and somehow we were oddly out of step. I became acutely aware that Halyard was making an effort not to touch or even brush against me. Suddenly I found myself praying that he would take me in his arms, then surely everything would be all right again. But he did not stop or turn to me, and I knew he felt the strain as well as I.

Once we had spent our days gazing at each other. Now

he would not look at me. I could not fathom what had changed him so. He seemed to be suffering from some deep, invisible hurt.

"You said you wanted to talk to me," he said abruptly, "and now that we are alone you are silent. Is that to punish me?"

"Punish you for what?" I gasped. He turned to me for a moment, frowning as if he could not make out if I were testing him or telling him the truth. Then he walked swiftly on and I followed after him, bewildered by his words.

"I wanted to talk to you," I said, "because this morning as I was walking in the garden I happened to look up at the house and I saw a face in the window of the glass gallery." He said nothing but I saw him pale beneath his present pallor. There was a silence between us as ominous and unrelenting as the sky. "It was a child's face," I said quietly, and waited.

For a long time Halyard said nothing. There was anguish in his eyes. Why was this so difficult for him to talk about? I knew now that if the child was so important to him I must have an answer to my question.

"You had not told me there was a child at Longfields," I said, but still he hesitated before replying.

"There is a great deal about Longfields that you do not know."

"Who is the child?"

"She is my ward," he said stiffly.

"Your ward?"

"Yes, my ward." He was angry now, though why I could not guess. "A child for whom I am responsible." He had grown rigid, and when his eyes met mine they were cold. A chill wind caught at my cloak and worried at it like a terrier. "She need be no concern of yours, Catherine. Mrs. Griffin is well paid to look after her."

"But who is she?" I felt myself shivering. "Who were her mother and father?" He frowned. I saw I had displeased him.

"They were people I knew long ago. Now leave it alone, Cat, don't badger me." But I had to know more.

"Why did they leave her in your care? Are they dead?"

187

"There was no one else to look after her," he said sharply, annoyed that I would pursue the topic.

"At least you can tell me her name." He turned to face me then and his eyes, like the basilisk, froze me to stone.

"Her name is Amelle," he said flatly. I felt the ground give way beneath me. I had come to believe that Amelle was no more than a figure in a poem and now I found she was a child who was Halyard's ward, a child whose parents were a mysterious part of his past. The greatest shock of all was in knowing that he did not mean to tell me more than that. He stood aloof, unyielding as granite. I had made him angrier than ever with my questioning.

He walked on down the path toward an arbor. "I've told you the child need not concern you," he said, grinding out the words.

"Everything to do with you concerns me."

"Not this, Cat. I warn you—do not ask any more questions about the child."

"Why not?"

"Because you would not like the answers. Hers is a sad story. You know nothing of such tragedy."

"I know what it is to lose a mother and a father," I said. "Perhaps I could be some help to her. And why should I not ask questions? You yourself said that there should be no secrets between us."

"Ah." A great sigh escaped him. "But that was in a different time. Everything has changed since then." To Halyard, Spain might have been a world away from here.

"I am still the same," I said. "I have not changed." I wanted some denial from him, but it did not come.

"No, you have not changed," he said sadly, "but I have. I know now what sort of man I was. I am myself again."

"You are the same to me," I protested.

"Am I?" His eyes probed mine. Then unexpectedly he took my hand and held it as if it were a fragile flower or a treasure he was afraid to hold too close. "Do not think me harsh or unfeeling if I do not tell you any more. Believe me, it is to spare you, Cat, that I am silent. I do not mean to be cruel or unresponsive. If I am, it is circumstances that make me so." I was more bewildered than ever by his sudden change of tone.

"I do not understand you."

"If it were possible, if things were different, I would always be open and sincere with you. I would hold nothing back. But that is impossible now." He looked at the lowering sky as if to find some explanation that would satisfy me. "There have been deeds done by others . . ." he paused again, fighting for self-control as his voice shook and his hand trembled over mine. "There have been deeds done both by others and by me that will color and affect all the rest of our days. The memory of those deeds has altered your life and mine. Things can never be the same again between us." My heart turned to stone. I did not know what he meant. To me he was an enigma, a riddle to which I could find no answer.

"But why?" I pleaded, "tell me what you mean. I am your wife and I will take the good with the bad."

"There are some things I still do not remember about the past," he hedged. "I cannot tell you what I do not remember."

"No," I said, "but you can tell me all you do know. I think it is my right to hear about your past."

He looked at me then with undisguised scorn and let fall my hand. "And do you think you know right from wrong? Do you mean to judge my past?" He was shouting now, too angry to notice his manner.

"I did not say I meant to judge you, I think you know me better than that. But I want to know everything about you. You are a part of me now. Does that seem so very strange to you?" He shook his head and his anger diminished, but all the same a high wall had gone up between us.

"You do not want to know me, Cat. There are things that happened in my life before we met, dreadful things. To think of them fills me with remorse and loathing. I despise myself because of them, but that will change nothing."

"But," I protested, "if those things happened in the past

189

they are done and over with. If you are sorry for them can you not forget them and let them go?"

"No, Catherine, the deeds were done and the blot, the stain, remains forever. The memory of them is a burden that I will have to bear for the rest of my life."

"Whatever you have done," I pleaded with him now, seeing that he was in earnest, "whatever it was, you can tell me. If you will share it with me it will make the burden lighter."

"No, that I will never do." His jaw was set. His mind was made up. "If I told you what I know of myself and of my true nature you would never want to see me again. I cannot take the chance of that. Let me at least keep the memory of the happiness I had with you."

"We have been happy," I said. "And we will be happy again."

"Bless you for that, Catherine. Until I met you I had always believed happiness was for others, not for me. It was a mirage that always vanished, and then you found me and you changed my life. I cannot risk losing the memory of that."

"No matter what you have done," I said, "I would always love you. I swear it." He put his fingers gently to my lips.

"Don't swear, Cat, don't make a vow you could not keep. If you knew my nature, my sins, but then you could not imagine such things." He stood back from me and held me away from him as if he feared that he had come too close and that he might infect me with some sickness of the soul. "If I told you," he said, sadly, "you would leave me."

"I would never leave you," I protested, but he did not hear me.

"If you knew what I have done you could never forgive me."

"There is nothing you could have done in the past or could do now," I said, "that I would not forgive." But again he went on, unmindful of my protests.

"It's no use, Cat, don't you see it is too late? If I told you even a part I would have to see your face. First there would be the doubt, then the despair, and I would have to watch as you learned to loathe and despise me as I do my-self. I could not bear to see what would take the place of the love I see now in your eyes. If I tell you nothing then at least you will have the memory of the man you believed I was."

We had come to the arbor where there was a single stone bench and I knew that this was where, once long ago on a summer's day, he had sat with Arabella. It was here he had told her that he loved her and wanted to marry her. I knew that even now when he said and believed that he had hated her, there was still a bond between them; a bond more terrible and enduring than any I could imagine.

If Arabella were alive now and here at this moment, I would have fought for him. Now she was dead I still must fight her ghost, her shade, for his very life was in danger and mine as well, for without Halyard no true life was pos-sible for me.

"It would not be possible for me to stop loving you," I whispered. "It would not be possible for me ever to hate you."

"It is not possible," he said, wooden, cold, and unrelent-ing, "for us to be as we once were." He was calm now, as if resigned to some ordained fate. "All that is over between us. I have sat up half the night trying to think of what is best to do and I think that it would be better for you to leave me now, to go before it is too late."

"Too late for what? Tell me what you mean. What is it you are afraid of?"

"I am afraid that you will come too close, that you will see me as I really am."

"I will never leave you." I was amazed that he would think such a thing possible. "You cannot make me go." I saw him change expression. He made a sort of grimace that told me nothing.

"If you stay," he said, "it must be on my terms." I felt re-lief flood over me, but it was short lived when I heard those terms. "If you stay it must be understood that we will not live as we did. I cannot be the husband I was. You must _accept that."

"Yes," I said, but I did not understand in what way he meant us to be different.

"I love you," I said, "nothing will ever change that."

"You say that," he said bitterly, "because you believe in the power of love. You are so good you know nothing of evil. If you stay one day you may come face to face with that evil. What will you do then? What weapon will you have for your defense against the power of such a force? I have enough to carry on my conscience without that."

"I will never leave you. I promise that. And I promise you that there is nothing you have done or could do that I would not forgive. I already know what sort of man you are. You have proved it to me every day we have been married." But as I spoke I saw that I was wrong, for here beneath these autumn trees there sat not one man but two. There was my lover, my husband, my friend and there was a stranger. There were two natures in one, both chained to each other by some common guilt. Both were in torment, tortured by a shared memory, and I must fight one or both of them against all odds, and in the end I must win for his sake and for mine.

"I will stay," I said, "whatever your terms. I will not leave you."

"Then let us go in, Catherine. There is a cold wind blowing and it is almost dusk."

That night, at my suggestion, I dined with Halyard in his suite. We sat before the fire. We talked and laughed; it was almost like old times. I felt sure I knew how the evening would end. I would stay and in that great canopied bed of his all fears and phantoms would vanish.

Then the clock struck ten and Halyard rose and held out his hands to me and pulled me to my feet. I expected him to put his arms around me, to embrace me, but he did not.

"Ten o'clock, Catherine. It is late." I held my face up to his and waited to be kissed.

"Can you find your way back again to your own door?" He drew away from me and stood just out of my reach. I felt ill, betrayed.

192

"You don't want me to stay? Is that what you are saying?" He yawned.

"At Longfields," he said, "I make a habit of early nights. My routine is set. In the morning I work at writing and in the afternoons I see to estate business."

"And in the evenings?" I asked. "What of the evenings?"

"In the evenings I am tired. I usually dine alone. I told you, Catherine, I could not be the husband you had known."

"You do not mean me to share your bed?" I saw him wince. I had struck home.

"Since you put it so baldly, no." I could not believe he meant it. I still felt sure I had misunderstood his meaning.

"Not ever?" His jaw tightened.

"Surely, Catherine, you did not think the honeymoon would last forever. I told you my terms. Take them or leave them. It is up to you. But if you stay on at Longfields you must honor my wishes and I do not wish to be disturbed." I was suddenly angry; at least anger dulled the pain and hurt.

"You do not have to worry," I said. "I will not disturb you. You will not have to bolt your door against me." I walked swiftly away from him. But at the door I faltered and turned back.

"What am I to do here alone all day?" I did not ask what I must do with my nights.

"Amelia was always busy," he said. "She always found things that needed doing about the house." But, I thought bitterly, Amelia was a sister and I was a wife. What a world of difference in our expectations of life at Longfields.

"I shall be so lonely without you." It burst out. I could not help saying the words that were in my heart.

"One grows used to loneliness," Halyard said, and when I had gone into the corridor he shut the door behind me.

193

Chapter Ten

Halyard had said that I would grow used to loneliness but it was not so. I felt I had been exiled, banished to some Siberia of the heart. I did not sleep till dawn. When I awoke it was to find Megan by my bed with my morning coffee. It seemed as if even the weather had conspired against me to make me feel low in spirit. The sky beyond my window was dark and ominous. The rain fell steadily in torrents.

I was determined to weep no more but to live each day as it came and to do all in my power to make him mine again. Yet even with this noble and fine resolve the time weighed like lead. Every second and hour was a millennium and there was nothing to fill in the long, lonely void.

For the first time in my life I wished I had some skill with a needle, then at least I could have spent the hours stitching ladylike embroidery. When I could sit still no longer I moved the furniture about to rearrange the room. I pushed the chairs from here to there and back again and in the end it looked the same.

At noon Megan came with my luncheon on a tray. It was excellently cooked and served but I had no appetite. In the afternoon it was still not possible to go out of doors. The rain beat at the windows and the wind lashed at the house. I could not bear to sit idle, doing nothing, and I decided that at least I could explore the house.

I looked in at the long gallery, which ran the length of the south front. It was hung with ornate mirrors and large, somber portraits of long dead Halyards. Unused for so long, the gallery was as cold and desolate as the moors. I shut the doors behind me and walked on to the glass gallery, where the rain was flowing in a river down the window panes. Once more I had the feeling I was on board a ship. Then, above the storm, I heard a sound no louder than if it had been made by a mouse in the wainscot. The sound came from behind a large Jacobean chest and, turning slowly, I caught sight of one small eye peeping out at me.

"I can't see you," I said, "but I know you are there. Your name is Amelle, isn't it?" There was not a sound from behind the chest. "I won't bite you," I said. Still there was no response. "If you come out I'll tell you my name, is that a bargain?" Slowly the child began to emerge. She was very small, about four or five, dressed in a clean pinafore, but her hair was not combed properly and she was so painfully thin that her arms and legs looked like sticks. She seemed half-starved, and it was clear that she was frightened nearly out of her wits. When I saw her I thought of Halyard and that there was not one, but two people in this house who lived in fear.

Her hair was chestnut, like Halyard's. Her eyes were dark and so large that they dominated her face. She stood before me trembling. She made me think of one of the wounded sea birds I used to find upon the shore. But why on earth was she so afraid of me?

"My name is Catherine," I said. I knelt down beside her. "Why are you afraid? You have no need to be." She only stood staring. Her terror twisted at my heart. "Were you not supposed to be here?" I asked. "Are you afraid someone will punish you? I won't tell," I said, "I promise you."

196

She shook her head but I doubted that she had even heard what I had said to her.

"What is it, can't you tell me?" Her great eyes turned on mine.

"I thought she had come back," she whispered.

"Who? Who did you think I was?"

"The other one." She stood shaking; she could not stop the trembling, like a puppy that has been beaten and does not know the reason why.

"You're cold," I said. I took off my shawl and started to put it around her, but she drew back as if I might strike her. "I'm only going to put this shawl around your shoulders," I said gently, "so you'll be a little warmer." She thought a long time before she made up her mind to take that first step toward me. "I'm Catherine," I said. "You thought I was someone else, didn't you?"

She nodded.

"Who did you think I was?"

"The other one," she whispered again, as if even the words were forbidden. Her eyes were dark and troubled. She hesitated; it seemed to be all she could remember. Then she began again. "Once there were two ladies." Her eyes went past me, searching out the shadows. "One was kind to me, I sat on her lap and she sang and told me stories, and there was the other one . . . " I saw tears form in her eyes and her shoulders shook with soundless sobs. I had not meant to upset her with questions. By two ladies, did she mean Arabella and Amelia?

"You saw me this morning from the window and you thought she had come back again."

She nodded.

"She hasn't come back," I said. I thought of Arabella dead in the fire and of Amelia dead long before. Neither of them would ever return. "There's nothing for you to be afraid of here," I said. "There are only Mrs. Griffin and Megan and Rose." As I spoke Rose's name Amelle came closer to me and she was trembling again. She was hiding here from Rose, I was sure of it. Amelle must be the extra

197

duty Rose disliked and I could not say I blamed Amelle for hiding away from her. Nor was it true there was nothing to be afraid of in this house. There were dark shadows in the corridors and in every room that held Halyard as a prison.

"Would you like to come with me to my room? There's fire there and you could get warm." I held out my hand. "We could have some hot chocolate and cake. It's almost time for tea." I thought Amelle would never answer. Then at last she put her hand in mine. It felt small and fragile, like a new leaf, not yet wholly formed.

At the door to my suite she hesitated; listening, waiting, reluctant to enter. Did she remember being there before? I could not tell. At last she went in and stood before the fire but even when she was warmed through she would not take off the shawl.

I rang for Megan. "Would you like some chocolate?" I asked. "Some cake? What about some biscuits or some sandwiches?" She stood fidgeting, trying to think of an answer. "Never mind, we'll have them all," I said. The answer seemed to take the weight of decision from her shoulders and she was almost at ease until Megan came, and then Amelle quickly hid her face in my lap as Megan began to scold.

"Well, Miss, there you are. Rose has been looking everywhere for you." Megan turned to me. "I'm sorry, m'lady, she shouldn't have bothered you. She's a naughty, wicked girl, that's what; wandering off like that, the goblins will get her yet, you mark my words."

I felt Amelle go tense; her thin shoulder blades were sharp even through the thick wool covering of the shawl.

"That will be enough, Megan," I said. "You should not frighten Amelle with such stories. Tell Rose that she is with me. We are going to have a tea party here by the fire. We want hot chocolate and cakes and sandwiches, lots of sandwiches." Megan shook her head.

"There's no need for you to order all that for her, she eats like a bird."

"We'll see," I said, "but now, do as I say."

198

"Are you sure, m'lady?" Megan was still uncertain. "It's no trouble for me to take her back upstairs to Rose again."

"I'm quite sure. Amelle is my guest." I felt her little hand clutching at my knee. "When we've had our tea," I said, "I'll take Amelle back upstairs myself so Rose needn't come down to fetch her."

On the whole the party was not a great success. We did not make much tea table conversation, but Amelle drank two cups of chocolate and I lost track of the cakes and sandwiches she consumed. She ate as if she had been starving all her life and she would not leave my knee. She seemed as attached to it as lichen to rock. I knew she had not really been starved. Mrs. Griffin seemed a kindly woman and even the sullen Rose did not look like a cruel keeper. But all the same Amelle was hungry for attention and affection and that need had been ignored.

As I looked at her large eyes and felt her hand upon my knee I knew she was a child who needed me almost as much as I needed her.

When at last I took her upstairs and reluctantly left her with Rose, I made a point of asking that Amelle come down next morning for a visit. I said I would be waiting for her, that I wanted her to come if she would like to do so, and she eagerly agreed.

Then I went down the corridor to Mrs. Griffin's door and knocked. Mrs. Griffin was surprised to see me there. "You should have rung for me," she said. "I should have come down to you."

"I was passing by your door," I said. "I had brought Amelle up to Rose." Again Mrs. Griffin was surprised, her mouth set in a straight line of annoyance. "I want to ask you some questions about Amelle. I understand from Lord Halyard that Amelle is his ward." It seemed to be a relief to her that I knew even that much. She nodded. "Did you know her parents?"

"They are both dead, I believe." She had answered quickly, as if the answer had been rehearsed.

"I see. Then Amelle's upbringing is entirely Lord Halyard's responsibility?"

"I suppose so," she answered uneasily, not sure of where I was going with that line of questioning.

"Should she not have a governess?" I said.

"She did have a governess but she went away. Longfields is a lonely house. It's difficult to find someone suitable who will stay," she said.

"And so Rose takes care of Amelle?" I asked.

"Yes. Rose is not a governess, of course, but she does her best."

"I'm sure she does, I meant no criticism of Rose. But I was thinking, as I have my mornings free, I would be able to spend them with Amelle."

"I wouldn't want to trouble you," Mrs. Griffin said stiffly.

"It would be no trouble," I said calmly. "I am not used to being idle. My husband is so busy that I would like to have Amelle's company. It would help me pass the time and it would leave Rose free for other duties." I saw Mrs. Griffin flush. I knew she disapproved of the idea.

"Just as you like, m'lady. It is too bad really that this house should have been so long in mourning; first Lord Halyard's mother, then Miss Amelia, and," she hesitated a moment, "and Lady Halyard. Perhaps now you are here you will open up the house again. In the old days when I first came to Longfields the house was always full of company. There were balls and picnics, and Lord Halyard particularly liked to go out riding in the park." I supposed she meant to be kind but the decision to entertain was not mine to make.

"We'll see," I said. "Whether we entertain or not depends upon my husband. For the present, please have Rose bring Amelle down to me in the morning." I turned to go, and as if it were an afterthought, I said, "Amelle might even like to stay for luncheon. Tell cook to send up two trays instead of one."

It was true I wanted to see Amelle was taken care of properly and to teach her her lessons, but her company also helped give some form to the long days. I knew

Amelle began to look forward to the mornings when I was with her as much as I did, and the time with her flew by like the wind. And because we were both busy our appetites improved. I found I always regretted it when Rose took Amelle off for her nap. In the afternoons if the weather was fine, we walked out in the gardens and came in, our color high, our spirits improved by the fresh air, in time for tea.

Yet even with part of my days accounted for there was still an empty space without Halyard. Without him the heart had gone out of me. I was more lonely than I had been before I met him, for at least then I had had my dream to keep me company.

It seemed that he set himself to avoid me. When I went to his room he found some excuse to get rid of me and when I met him in the halls I never knew if he would acknowledge my presence or not. If I managed to speak to him his reply was short, sharp, and sarcastic.

He would have preferred to have ignored me altogether, as he ignored Amelle. She might as well have been invisible for all the attention he paid to her.

Once when she had done her lessons particularly well I asked Halyard if he would like to see her copy book and to have her recite for him.

"Recite?" he drawled. "How boring, how tedious. I do not care for the prattle of children." Nor, I thought, did he care for the company of a wife, and, because I was hurt and angry, I was unable to stop myself from lashing back at him.

"If you are so bored would it not be better to have some other company than mine? Mrs. Griffin says the house was once full of amusing people. Why not ask friends, relations, a house full of guests to relieve the tedium?"

"Who are we to ask?" he countered. "What friends have I? I am an outcast, remember, a pariah. Who would accept our invitation? The Vicar? Shall we ask him in to tea? Or would you prefer to command the tenants to a ball? No, my dear, none of the gentry would be seen passing through my gates. Certainly we cannot ask Rupert Halyard though he is our next neighbor. I have not seen him since Amelia died. The only soul in the entire county of our sort who would condescend to visit us would be Lord Stavion."

"Then by all means let us ask him."

"And he would come," Halyard continued, "because he would not lose his reputation by being seen here for he has no reputation or good name left to lose." We parted then in enmity. Each day it seemed our relationship grew more strained and bitter, and yet, at times when I caught him unaware, I thought I saw a look of longing and desire flood out toward me, only to have it replaced almost at once by a dark, cold stare. I felt he was deliberately hiding his love for me and that there was a contest of wills between us, that I felt I must employ every cunning if I was to get him to betray his true feelings for me. Once, by chance, he touched my hand but then, as if to punish himself, his mood changed again and his words were brutally sharp. I knew in my heart that he was afraid to be alone with me for fear he would take me in his arms, and then he could not hide his love. But in this house there was always the means to avoid me.

As the weather worsened so did our tempers. We had come to November and the first black frost, which was replaced by a belated Indian summer. The days were unnaturally warm and a sick wind blew. I stood out on the castellated walk that overlooked the south court. I had taken refuge there and a sort of comfort in thinking of how I hated this house that had robbed me of the man I loved so dearly. In his place the house had left me a cold, scornful stranger who drank too much.

I knew, for I had heard him stumbling on the stairs when he had come in from a night at the Halyard Arms. I did not know if he worked at all, or if that were only pretense. He kept to himself behind closed doors. But as for work, I doubted it.

In the long nights he sometimes walked up and down the glass gallery as if he were walking round and round the decks of a ghost ship. Once he had come down the hall to my door. I had heard the footsteps outside. I thought that I had seen the handle of the door move but then he went away again and when I ran after him meaning to ask him in, despite the bruises to my fragile pride, I saw that he had gone, not back toward his own room but on toward the west wing. He stood there looking at the locked and bolted door, staring like a man possessed or a man who had drunk more than was good for him.

The house and its memories were the evil, not Halyard. At night alone I heard the patter of mice in the wainscot, the squeaking of rats in the ceiling, and a sighing that was more than the cold north wind. It was more than my imagination. I was sure of it, and I became so obsessed with the house and its hold on Halyard that I, in turn, infected Amelle with my mood.

In a few short days she had come to care for me and I for her. She had given me all the affection she had stored away. Until now her world had been peopled by Mrs. Griffin, Rose, and Megan. All of them took care of her for wages but I gave her my time and my affection because I wanted to; because I liked her. She became dearer to me every day; her small face and her enormous eyes made her look so fragile that it seemed she might blow away in a strong breeze. Yet even when the weather was sharp she was ready to go out with me.

On a brisk, bleak afternoon, as we were walking in the knot garden, Amelle's hand in mine, I looked up at Halyard's suite. I had not seen him that day or the day before. I wondered when he was alone if he ever thought of Spain or the sea or our magic cave, if he remembered the lovers we had been. It was then, as I was lost in my reverie, that I heard Amelle cry out. I felt her hand tighten in mine and I looked down at her but she was not looking at me, rather up at the windows of the west wing. Quickly I followed her glance. I could see nothing but shuttered windows and a bit of glass covered with soot and grime.

"What is it?" I knelt down beside her, but her eyes were hypnotized by those windows. "What is it?" I demanded again, this time more insistently. I saw her eyelids flutter and I felt her revive and come back to me as clearly as I felt the chill wind on my back. "What did you see?" I asked.

"I saw her. I saw the other one. She was there in the window." I felt relief flow through me. It had only been Amelle's imagination, a trick of the eye, nothing more. She had caught my fears but it was nothing.

"No," I said, "you didn't see her. She hasn't come back. You couldn't have seen her. There is no one in the west wing, no one lives there now."

"I saw her. She's there."

All I could do for her was to hold her close to me and wish that I could give her a portion of my strength, for no matter how far fetched it was, I knew that she believed she had seen someone in the window, someone of whom she was deathly afraid.

"We must go in," I said, "it's time for tea."

But even hot tea and a blazing fire did not thaw Amelle or warm me. We were both like statues carved in ice. When Rose came for Amelle she took her off, muttering crossly that we had stayed out too long and that I had let Amelle catch a chill.

That night when Megan came to turn down my bed and brush my hair, a nightly ritual she enjoyed and took pride in, I sat thinking of Amelle's face and tried to shake it from my mind, but the memory clung and I found that I was still shivering.

"Are you cold?" Megan asked.

"No," I said, "only a little tired. Amelle and I went for a long walk today; Rose says we stayed out too long and I am sure she is right. Amelle was overtired. She even imagined that she had seen a woman's face in one of the windows of the west wing. I told her that it was impossible." Megan stopped her brushing in midair.

"Maybe she did see someone."

"How could she?"

"Because someone could be there." Megan's face was still and tight.

"But Mrs. Griffin said the west wing was locked, that no one lived there."

"Oh well, she would, wouldn't she? But we've heard things, Rose and me. If there was any other work nearby we'd have gone long ago."

"What did you hear?"

"Voices," Megan said solemnly, "and sometimes crying in the night, and once or twice there have been trays left outside. Now why would they be there if no one had put them there or took them away?" Megan flushed. Proud of her own importance, she had taken me into her confidence and made me a fellow conspirator.

"Who takes the trays?" I asked.

"Not Rose or me, nor none of the footmen, neither. It must be cook, or Rule, or Mrs. Griffin herself."

"Didn't you ever ask Mrs. Griffin about the trays or the sounds that you heard?"

"Oh yes, in the beginning, but Mrs. Griffin said we was to mind our own business or go. She's always polite when you're about but when it's just Rose or me, that's something else again, isn't it?"

I should have taken it as a piece of servants' gossip, but I could not let it rest. I had become so sure the house was somehow the conductor of my unhappiness that in a mood of vulgar curiosity I went up to see Mrs. Griffin. I felt perhaps she might be willing to shed some light on the night sounds. As always, she seemed amazed that I should come to her or be able to find my own way up a flight of stairs.

"Mrs. Griffin," I said, "today, while Amelle and I were walking in the garden, she said she saw a woman's face in a window of the west wing."

"Did she?" Mrs. Griffin shot me a sharp, penetrating glance. "Well, Amelle's a fanciful child; always imagining she's seeing something."

"She half-convinced me."

"She has a way with her."

"So," I went on boldly, "I asked Megan and it seems that both she and Rose claim they have heard voices coming from the west wing."

"They're simple country girls," Mrs. Griffin answered scornfully. "They often claim to hear things in the night.

It's easy in a house this old and large to imagine almost anything. That's one of the reasons I keep them near me, so if they are frightened they can tell me instead of inventing stories. No doubt it's Rose and Megan who put such nonsense into Amelle's head."

"But Megan said she and Rose have seen trays of food outside the door." I saw Mrs. Griffin's eyes flicker and her jaw went tight.

"They are right. Sometimes I leave my tray there so Rule will not have to walk up another flight of stairs. As I've told you, the west wing is dangerous. The flooring was burnt through and there are rats," she said. "That's likely what Rose and Megan hear at night. Is there anything else, Lady Halyard?" Mrs. Griffin had dismissed me as surely as if I had been a servant girl.

"No," I said. "Goodnight." I went back to my room feeling foolish and inept. I knew I had handled the affair badly. I sat trying to think how to make an opportunity to talk to Halyard. I had to find a way to make him listen to me.

After a few minutes there was a knock at the door. It was Megan. As she crossed the room she hung back, staying in the shadows. It was almost as if she were hiding something.

"What is it, Megan?" I asked.

"I came to say I'm sorry, m'lady," she mumbled. "It was wrong of me to gossip. It's only rats that Rose and me hear in the night, the rest was just a story I made up, and now goodnight, m'lady." She turned to go.

"Wait, Megan." I rose and walked toward her. I meant to ask her if Mrs. Griffin had told her to come, and then I saw that Megan had been crying and there was a red mark on her cheek, and I had my answer. "I'm sorry, Megan." Because of my stupid curiosity about this house someone else had paid a price.

"This is my fault, Megan," I said. I did not have to tell her what I meant, both she and I knew. "I wish it had not happened and I would like to make it up to you. Please, tomorrow, take the cherry silk dress that you so admired and

206

choose another for Rose. You can take them home with you on your half-day off." It was little more than a bribe, a salve to my guilty conscience.

"Thank you, m'lady."

"No need to thank me. And again, I'm sorry."

When she had gone I sat for a long time before the fire. This house affected all of us; it ran like a chain, from one link to another—from me to Halyard, to Amelle, onto Rose and Megan, and now to Mrs. Griffin. I knew that she was at heart a kindly woman. Yet she had struck Megan. And all for what?

When at last I slept it seemed that I could hear a whispering in the walls and the pattering of mice in the wainscot. From somewhere in the cold, dark rooms and galleries laughter broke like crystal and echoed in my dreams.

Then suddenly I was awake; thinking, as my skin went cold and prickly and my heart began to beat, that this was no dream, no fancy. Someone had been in my room, someone who had stood by the bed and watched me in my troubled sleep. Had I seen the door handle move, turn? Had it been Halyard who had been there and who had said nothing?

I put on my dressing gown and, lighting a candle, went out into the corridor. I could see no one, but then I had hardly expected whoever had been in my room would wait to be discovered, or if it was Halyard would want me to know he had been there. I had the feeling that whoever it was had gone on toward the east corridor.

I walked haltingly toward the glass gallery, half-fearing that at any moment something, someone would fly out to attack me. But as I passed the darkened opening I heard nothing but the magnified sound of the wind beating at the panes. Beyond I saw a glimmer of light. Halyard must be still awake for his door was ajar, and then I heard him cry out, a strangled cry of terror.

Without waiting to knock I opened his door full and was so startled by the sight that greeted me I nearly let the candle fall from my hands.

Halyard was sitting upright in his bed, his back pressed

against the headboard. His eyes were wide with fright. In each hand he held a pistol aimed straight at my heart, and for one dreadful moment I thought he meant to fire. For although he was looking straight at me it seemed his eyes beheld a strange, more horrifying image.

I called out his name as softly as I could so as not to startle him, and his eyes flickered. He seemed to waver, undecided as to whether I was friend or foe.

"What is it?" I asked, "what has frightened you? What did you see?"

"Nothing," he said, but his eyes went once more to a point behind my head. I was about to start toward him to ask him more when I heard a noise as loud and sharp as gunfire and I thought Halyard might have pulled the triggers after all. But it was only the door that had slammed behind me, and then I had the sure feeling that there had been someone standing there behind the door, someone whom Halyard had seen, a person who had frightened him.

"Who was it?" I asked. "Who was there?" I thought at first he had not heard me, for he continued to stare blankly into space.

"Someone was there, I know it." But he only shook his head from side to side.

"But there was, there must have been," I persisted. "Someone has just been in my room and then they came here, I heard you cry out. Who was it? Tell me."

"No one was here." The pistols dropped from his hands onto the coverlet and his eyes met mine in a stony cold stare. He was lying, I knew it, but why?

"What do you want? What are you doing here?" He was trembling. Was it with fear or rage?

"I heard you cry out."

"A dream, a nightmare, nothing more. You should not have come. I told you I did not want to be disturbed. Those were my terms."

"But there was someone in my room and in yours. I am sure of it."

"Are you mad? Have you let your imagination run away

with you or is it an excuse to do as you please?" He threw back the covers and came toward me. I saw a vein standing out throbbing in his forehead. "I could have shot you. I could have killed you. Tell me, if I had, who would have believed it was an accident? Now go and don't come back again." It seemed he cared more for being obeyed than he did for my feelings.

"No," I said, "not until we talk."

"I have nothing to say to you."

"But I have some things to say to you." I knew if I were to make him mine again, to break through to the man I had loved and who had loved me, I would have to get him out of this house. We would have to be somewhere we could not be spied upon, and suddenly I remembered Mrs. Griffin saying that Halyard had liked to ride. "I will not go until you say you will come riding with me."

"What sort of whim is that? What put that into your head?" I had taken him off guard.

"Will you come? Yes or no. I'll tell the stables to send up two horses at noon tomorrow. I wouldn't want to be responsible for interrupting your work."

"Yes, I'll come." It cost him dear to agree.

"You promise? You won't forget?"

"Yes, I promise, only leave me alone." It seemed he could not wait to be rid of me.

Chapter Eleven

I was elated to think that Halyard had consented to
come out riding with me and when Megan came with my
breakfast she found me amid a pile of dresses, jackets, and
skirts. I was standing before a pier glass holding up one
and then another for inspection.

"What's all this?" Megan asked.

"I am going riding this afternoon with my husband, but
I have no riding habit. Megan, can you sew?"

"Yes," she said uncertainly. "Mama taught all of us to do
plain work."

"Then do you think if I asked you, you could alter this
skirt?" She looked doubtfully at the garment.

"Yes, I suppose so, but there's no need to go to all that
trouble."

"Why not?"

"Because," Megan said, still looking uncertain, "I know
where there's a riding costume at Longfields."

"Where?" I hoped that Megan was right.

"It's in a trunk, in the box room." Megan flushed. "I saw
it when me and Rose was sent to tidy up in there." I was
sure the flush and the uncertain manner were because Me-

gan had opened the trunk and she knew very well that Mrs. Griffin would not like to have her prying into what did not concern her.

"Do you think you could find it again?" I looked at Megan hopefully.

"I don't know," she mumbled.

"I won't tell anyone that you told me where to find the riding costume," I said. "It will be our secret. All right?" Again she hesitated.

"Do you think you could find it for me now?" Megan nodded and in a few minutes she was back again bearing a beautifully tailored black riding habit.

It had been made for a woman taller than I, but with the hem turned up and a tuck here and there it was a perfect fit. I had to admit viewing the severity of line that I could find no fault with my reflection. Even the hat and veil became me. From the cloth there rose the fragrance of verbena—sharp, pungent, and evocative.

Before breakfast I had ordered the horses curried and exercised. They were to be brought to the front of the house at noon. The groom had said he would send Halyard one of his favorites, Dickon, and that I was to have Daisy; not as fine a piece of horseflesh, but as I had explained I was not an expert rider. He assured me Daisy was spirited but safe.

Now, a few minutes before the hour, I was ready and waiting. I had decided I would let Halyard go down first. Then when I appeared he would get the full benefit of a new and different-looking Catherine.

As the clock struck twelve I heard his boots in the corridor. I waited until I thought he was safely down the stairs and through the hall before I ventured out This day was so important to me because it was my chance to have him to myself.

When I opened the door and stepped out onto the terrace Halyard was already mounted on Dickon, a large black hunter. He held the reins tight as the horse reared up. Halyard's back was to me and when he wheeled about I saw he was smiling. The expression on his face was joy to

212

my heart but the instant he saw me the smile vanished. He took one long, enveloping look at me and suddenly went white with shock and rage. He raised his crop. If I had been closer I think he would have struck me. Instead he let it fall on Dickon's flank and, digging his heels against the horse's side, he rode around the side of the house without a backward glance.

The groom helped me to mount and I followed after Halyard. He was well ahead of me, galloping past the gardens and the woods toward the great park beyond.

Daisy was no match for Dickon and by the time that I had caught up, Halyard was in a clearing by the river bank at the far end of the park. He had dismounted, letting Dickon wander, his reins loose, nibbling at the sparse grass.

Halyard had heard me ride up but he stood with his back to me, his fists clenched, and when he turned he was shaking with uncontrollable rage.

"What is this game of yours?" he shouted. "What do you hope to accomplish by it? Is it to torment me?"

"I don't know what you mean."

"I think you do. I think you know very well that was Arabella's horse, Arabella's habit. What did you hope to gain?" His nostrils flared as if he, not the horse, had been running. I could only stare at him, dumbstruck.

"You planned this!" He was still shouting. "You planned it all very carefully. What I want to know is why?" He strode toward Daisy and pulled me roughly from the saddle. His hands on my shoulders were biting at my flesh as he shook me savagely, until the hat fell from my head and the pins from my hair.

"I planned it because I wanted to get you away from the house. I wanted to be alone with you." I gasped out the words, afraid that I would begin to cry.

Then, as suddenly as he had begun his attack, he let me go, thrusting me back roughly against a tree.

"Well, now are you pleased with yourself and the reaction you have got from me? I warn you, do not play games with me or I might do something we would both be sorry for." He was still breathing heavily, but the anger seemed to have been drained from him.

"You already have." I tried to catch up my hair and to straighten my coat. I too was angry now, how dare he behave so? "You have left me alone ever since we came to Longfields. You have treated me like a stranger, or worse, some unwanted guest in the house. Yes, I planned to get you away from the house so you might be yourself again."

"I am myself, Catherine."

"No, you were a different man before we came to Longfields. I remember if you do not. I hoped if we were alone things between us would be as they once were."

"That is not possible."

"I think it is."

"It is too late."

"I don't believe you."

"You must believe me, accept it, you have no other choice." He was adamant but the fury was gone and it seemed, though he denied it, that he too wished for the past.

"No, I won't accept it," I said, "I want the man you were, not this stranger you have become. I want my companion, my friend, my lover. I want my husband."

"You find fault with me as a husband?" Again the old sarcasm returned and the sneer of scorn. "I think that I have done my duty. What do you want that you lack? I have given you dresses and jewels. I leave you undisturbed. Many women would be happy to be so little troubled." As he spoke his insolence and arrogance increased.

"I am not one of them. I ache with missing you. What are jewels and dresses when I do not have you? What am I to do? How am I to fill my days?"

"If the house is not enough for you," he drawled, "then take up good works and charity."

"Why won't you make love to me? You haven't touched me, not once, since we came here." I felt ashamed, as if I were a beggar.

"If that is all that troubles you, then take a lover." I

214

struck out at him then, my nails raking at his face until he caught my wrists and held them.

"A Cat with claws? I did not know you were such a tiger." He had bent me close to him, so close I could almost touch him.

"I can't live like this," I heard myself sob. "I can't endure it." He looked at me and the line around his mouth hardened.

"Then leave me." I wrenched free of him and stood back, but I did not let my gaze waver from those cold eyes of his.

"I have told you I will not do that, ever."

"Why not, if I am cruel, unkind, not a proper husband to you?" We stood so, eye to eye, each waiting for the other to speak. At last a cry escaped him, half-anger, half-torment.

"What is it you want me to do, Catherine? Tell me."

"I want you to take me in your arms and hold me."

"And then what, Cat, pretend to a love that's past? Shall I tell you a pack of honeymoon lies?"

"I don't believe it's over. We made love grow once, we can again. I think you are afraid to touch me." I saw I had caught him on the raw. "I think you know that I am right, for if you touched me, kissed me, you could not keep up the pretense of indifference." He was silent now, wary, but I knew he was at least listening to me. "You say you have changed, that you are a different man." He put up a hand of warning.

"I have changed, you can see that for yourself."

"Yes, you have changed, but the man I see now is not the true man, he is a counterfeit. I remember the other Halyard even if you do not. I remember the days by the sea and lying beside him on the warm sands. I remember trust and understanding, and a time when there was nothing that could not be said. I remember too that there were days when we never stopped talking. I remember nights when you never stopped making love to me. That was my life and yours, and I cannot bear the present without that

215

man. He was my whole life." I saw him struggling for control. He lowered his eyes and then raised them back to mine.

"Have you finished?"

"Not yet." I had to make one last effort. "You know it is true. You were such a man—tender, gentle, loving. I want you to touch me now and then tell me you are not that man." I reached out to him.

"No."

"Then at least admit that there are two men, two forces within you. One who wants me and another who turns away and runs from me. But for pity's sake tell me why. Why do you turn away? Why won't you hold me, make love to me?" I waited for an answer, as if for the repeal of a sentence or the remission of an illness. At last he said, "Don't ask me that. Just believe me, you must get away from me while you still can."

"You want me to go? Is that the truth?" He nodded.

"I have told you I will not leave you and that there is nothing you have done or could do that I would not forgive."

He shrugged. "Then I must find a way to make you go before it is too late."

"Too late for what?" There was the mystery again, the words that only made me more confused.

"Before you get close to that past. I warn you, Cat, I will stop at nothing, for you are right, I *am* afraid."

"Afraid of what?"

"Afraid of what may happen if you stay. My nature is not what you think. I am far from kind and gentle. I can be more cruel than you know, and I warn you—do not try to guess at the past. You've already come too close. Now it's late and too much has been said. The next time you take a notion to go out riding get one of the grooms to go with you. Come, I'll help you mount." This was perhaps my last moment with him, my last chance.

"No." I stood my ground. "I am not going back until you take me in your arms. Not until you kiss me. If you are not a coward then I dare you to take me in your arms and then to tell me I have come too close." I waited until at last, almost as if spellbound, he reached out for me and drew me to him.

His arms enfolded me. I felt the hard outline of his body, felt him rising up toward me as he bent to kiss my lips. It was a long, hungry, lingering kiss. I would gladly have been lost in those arms, held in that embrace forever. I felt myself trembling, the old magic of flame and desire beginning. I clung to him, my arms clasped around his neck. If I was moved by his nearness I knew he was more shaken than I, and then his hands, that had begun to caress my breast, seized at my arms and pulled them from him. With a cry of anguish or disgust he pushed me away.

"Now," he said hoarsely, "you can see what I have told you is true. The past is over. I no longer desire you as I did. I no longer care for you as a husband should." Each word was spat out at me like a stone, but I knew that despite his protests I had won a kind of victory, for he was lying.

"Now, will you go?" he demanded heavily. "Have you found out what you wanted to know?" I nodded and, as if in a great hurry, he found Daisy's reins and helped me to mount. Even his hand beneath my foot was unsteady. Then I waited while he gathered Dickon and drew himself up in the saddle. We both sat our mounts as if we were opposing generals on a field of battle, the horses facing in opposite directions.

"I have learned," I said coolly, almost triumphantly, "that if you had followed your desire you would have taken me here and now on the hard winter ground." I saw him flush. He was angry again. I had meant to make him so. But there was more than anger in his face. There was the fear again. "Why," I pleaded with him, "why are you afraid?"

"It is you who should be afraid now." His tone was steely. "Not I."

"Of what?"

"Of me." I shook my head. I was so sure I had the upper hand.

"No, I know now that I was right. There are two men within you, one who wants me and loves me and one who does not. I mean to fight for you. I will never let you rest. I mean to fight until I have won you back as you once were. There, that is my challenge. I will not give up what is mine."

"It is you who should be afraid," he repeated.

"Afraid of a man who is in love?"

"That I might treat you as I have the others. In the end, you see, it was my nature that destroyed them. I am responsible for their deaths." I knew he meant what he said and that he believed what he said was true. But Arabella's death had been an accident. Once he had believed that.

"You would never willingly hurt me in any way," I said. "I know you and I know how good you are and how kind."

"Are you so sure?" His eyes were cold again and dulled by his inner pain.

"I would stake my life on it."

"Careful of what you say."

"I know you as I know myself." He seemed astonished, as if he could not believe in my constancy.

"You still trust me after all that I have done to you?"

"Yes."

"You are not wise."

"When was love ever wise?" Daisy was fretful and uneasy, eager to be off. We had kept the horses standing far too long.

"Remember," Halyard said slowly, "I have warned you. The goodness you see in me is yours, not mine. If you looked at me with a clear eye without the distortion of romantic love you would see a far different man. And now we must go back." I felt myself grow weak with a sense of failure and dejection. I had tried and this was all my gain. When would I ever have the chance to be alone with him again? I only half-listened to what he was saying.

"Did you hear me, Catherine? We'll go back by the way of the east farm. That is, if you think you can manage it. There are five fences to jump."

"I can manage it."

218

"Are you sure? The first four are low enough but the last is high and a double width. You'll want to come in to the left and jump wide."

"I told you I can manage." I lifted my chin in defiance.

"Are you sure you want to go that way?" I turned away, jerking at the reins and hurting Daisy's mouth.

"I have told you. I am not afraid of fences or of you."

I set off ahead of Halyard but in no time he had caught me up and passed me. Daisy was no contestant for Dickon, he was by far the better animal, but Daisy cleared the early fences as if they had been nothing more than branches in the road.

I had taken the first and the second easily and smoothly. Daisy was a darling horse. I was not all that experienced in the field and she gave me extra confidence.

By the third and fourth fences I had become exhilarated, partly because I was riding well and partly because, watching Halyard there ahead of me, I had come to believe that one day soon, despite all he had said, the pain would be gone from him, and by some miracle he would shed this veil from his soul. Then the memory of the past would vanish, and we would be free to spend all our days together like this. I clutched at this scrap of hope and comfort because I knew that he still wanted and desired me whether he would admit it or not.

I was so preoccupied with this dream of a happy future that for a moment I did not hear him calling me and when I did it was already too late. I saw him turned in the saddle shouting words at me that were lost in the wind. He was waving wildly at the stone fence ahead.

I did not understand what he wanted me to do. I could see no danger. Then I saw him rein Dickon in and the horse rear back on his haunches, his eyes rolling wide with fright and pain as the bit ate into his mouth. As I passed, coming in wide to the left as Halyard had told me to do, I saw, too late, where the wall had crumbled.

The stones were lying loose, scattered in all directions. As we rose, horse and rider arching high into the air, I also saw the deep ditch that lay beyond.

In that brief moment I knew that Daisy, out of instinct, had tried to refuse the jump but that I had urged her on. Then in midair I heard a scream, mine or Daisy's, or both, I was not sure, and I felt the impact as we hit the hard, rough ground. I felt the searing pain as Daisy rolled over me. I thought that I would never be free of that crushing weight but then she scrambled to her feet and I thought, thank God, her leg is not broken, before the sky went black and I lost consciousness.

Halyard got me back to Longfields in a farmer's cart. I was not badly hurt, only a sprain and a few bruises, nothing more, but he would not believe that. He stayed by me in the cart, cradling me in his lap. There was fear in his eyes and love, a love he made no attempt to disguise any more than he tried to hide his tears of relief when I was able to hobble up the steps to the door of the house. Then he insisted on carrying me the rest of the way to my room.

After I had bathed he came and sat by my bedside and held my hand as if he never meant to let it go again.

"I'm sorry, Cat, it was my fault. We should not have come that way. I should have known better than to chance it."

"It's not your fault."

"But it is. Twice you could have been killed because of me. I will see to it that there is not a third time."

He would not listen to anything I said. He blamed himself for not remembering that the workmen had been sent only a day or two before to repair the wall. And later he made me drink a sleeping draught, though I did not need it and took it only to please him.

As I slipped off to the whirling pool of unconsciousness I heard him say again, "You will be safe now. I promise you I will see to it that you will leave me." And I whispered through numbed lips, "I will never leave you," but I did not know if he heard me or not.

Chapter Twelve

The next morning I expected Halyard would come to see how I was. Instead it was Megan who came with a note he had left for me. When I opened it I saw that it was brief, one line that read,

> If you will not leave me, then I must leave you.
>
> H

It was like a saber cut, a far more painful blow than my bruises. In time they would fade away but not this. I did not understand. Why had Halyard gone, and where? Had he left because he held himself responsible for my accident? Megan did. She kept muttering that it was a wonder he had let me ride by way of the farm when he must have known the wall was not safe. While I could not help but wonder if she had deliberately suggested I wear Arabella's riding habit to pay me back for having spoken about her to Mrs. Griffin. Yet that did not make sense. Megan had not been at Longfields when Arabella was alive. How could she have known it was Arabella's habit? It might have belonged to anyone.

No matter what the reason, the fact was Halyard had gone and I did not know if he would return. Without him I was more desolate and bereft than I had been before. It had been one sort of loneliness to know he was here in the house at the other end of the corridor and quite another to realize that now there was no hope that I might at least meet him by chance.

I tried to concentrate on Amelle and her lessons, but my mind was ever on Halyard. I began to think that everyone who saw me must pity me. I even imagined that I could hear Arabella laughing at me, poor Catherine, the abandoned wife.

He had been gone over a week when I came out into the hall one morning to find the house in the throes of activity. The windows were open and the rooms were being aired. The dust sheets had been removed and everywhere floors were being waxed and the brass polished. Mrs. Griffin was giving orders to a bevy of new maids and then I saw her deep in conversation with a strange woman. At first I thought they were arguing but then Mrs. Griffin looked up and saw me. She looked a trifle guilty, as if I had caught her doing something forbidden.

She spoke again to the strange woman, dismissing her. Her words now were loud enough so that I could hear them. "We'll discuss the matter later. Please wait for me in my sitting room." The woman looked cross at being put off, but she shrugged and went off in the direction of the west wing.

"I am sorry to have kept you, Lady Halyard," Mrs. Griffin said, advancing toward me. "I hope all this bustle has not disturbed you." Then she smiled. "I've just had a message from his lordship. He's coming home and bringing a houseful of company with him. We haven't much time to make everything ready."

"Oh." It was all that I could say. She must know that I had had no word from him. Then, to mask my hurt and disappointment, I asked, "Who was that woman you were talking to?" I thought that Mrs. Griffin looked unsettled, but she replied, "Just a sewing woman. She has come to look over the linen. We've not had the sheets out of the presses in some time and there will be mending to be seen to. And now if there is nothing else I have a great deal to attend to. Lord Halyard wishes the house ready by tomorrow."

I resented the fact that Mrs. Griffin had been told that Halyard was returning and that I should have heard nothing from him. Still, I had some shred of pride. I had made up my mind that I would not rush down the stairs to meet him. I would wait for him to come to me. When I heard his steps on the stairs I held my breath, waiting to see if he would turn to the left or the right. Then suddenly he flung open the door without bothering to knock and stood in the doorway. His manner was something overbright. It was as if he had forgotten the accident or had never been away.

"Well, Catherine, still here I see. And how have you been keeping?"

"Well enough."

I had never seen him so brittle. "You said you wanted company and so I have brought you a houseful. We dine in the great hall tonight. I want you to wear your best, the rose silk, I think, and all your jewels. And now I must go and change. It has been a dusty journey." He bowed and was gone as quickly as he had come; no real greeting, no kiss, no embrace. He had returned more of a stranger than when he had left.

He had said he wished to show me off and I did my best to make myself presentable. I could not wear the rose silk, it had gone to Megan, but I settled for a watered silk of palest green. I chose it for it seemed to detract from the shadows beneath my eyes, the legacy of all my sleepless nights, and in the end I thought I looked well enough to do Halyard honor.

When he did not come I went down alone a little after the hour. From below I could hear the sound of voices. As I descended the stairs I was dazzled by the blaze of lights and the masses of flowers that had been brought in from the greenhouse. In the great hall the table had been laid for twenty. It was set with the finest silver and the most delicate and rare of china. Footmen under Rule's watchful eye were scurrying about in swarms, making sure that everything was perfection.

From the drawing room I could hear the sound of laughter and a babble of voices. The company was larger than I had expected. Certainly they were unlike any gathering that I had ever seen. I supposed that I had thought they would be like the good-natured folk that I had met at Kean's hotel, artistic, sporting types and actors, but these people came from some other sphere than Kean's or those I had met at Almack's.

They might all have been in fancy dress, each costume an exaggerated copy of the current fashion. I stood, uncertain of what I should do until Halyard spied me from across the room and came forward, bringing with him a man with whom he had been in earnest conversation.

"Ah, there you are at last, Catherine," he said in a voice loud enough to be heard by all. "We have been waiting for you. May I present Lord Stavion, with whom I have been spending the past weeks. I have persuaded him to change his venue and, as you were alone, to bring his house party over to Longfields to keep you company." So this then was Lord Stavion, who had no reputation to lose by being seen at Longfields.

As Lord Stavion drew nearer his carefully arranged illusion of youth vanished. It was possible that once he had been handsome, but now he had fallen into ruin. With each step he assumed the character of some painted player king. His elaborately dressed and powdered wig was a relict of some past age. His face was as white as if it had been enameled and then the brows painted in, the cheeks rouged and the mouth stained a cherry red.

His knee breeches were satin and his coat a mouse velvet stitched in silver. At his neck and wrists was ruffled lace and his high buckled shoes had heels of lacquered red.

He walked with little mincing steps and, affecting an elaborate court bow, he looked up at me, his eyes searching up and down to fasten on the first flaw. His smile was not a leer but something far more chilling. The small black

224

eyes were cold, small, glittering like the adder's, yet it was his mouth that was his worst feature—the lips, slack and moist, revolted me.

He took my hand, which I had not meant to offer him, and bent to kiss it. The touch of his lips was damp and loathsome.

"A charming bride," he said to Halyard. "It is wicked of you to have kept her to yourself for so long. She is so young and such an innocent." I felt myself blush and I heard the whispering and the laughter as all the company looked on, a witness to this scene.

"When Hal described you to me he did not do your beauty justice." I felt myself go hot with shame. To think of Halyard's speaking of me to this horrid man was abhorrent.

"My dear." Lord Stavion smiled. "You are blushing. How amusing of you." He took another cold reckoning of me. And Halyard stood by without a word.

"No wonder Halyard would not allow you to come to my house. He did not want to share you with his friends, but now that we are here I am sure he will allow me the honor to take you round and introduce you to the company." Again he held out his hand and I was forced to take it, hoping that I did not betray how reluctant I was to have him touch me. I looked to Halyard to rescue me, but he waved us on as if I could wish for nothing better than to be handed round a room by Lord Stavion.

"I see that you are shy." Lord Stavion whispered close to my ear. "I find that alluring and most becoming if it is not a pose. It is indeed refreshing to find such virtue still exists. There is something so challenging about the uncorrupted." I would have drawn away from him but he kept my hand in his.

"No need to be bashful with us. We are all old friends here. I hope Halyard will allow me to initiate you to our circle. What better way to begin than to introduce you to our mother superior. Long of her order, she was once a mistress of novices, were you not?" He had addressed this last to a figure in a nun's habit. It was the habit of an order

I had never seen in Spain. "Mother Waller gives sanction to our revels," Lord Stavion said. The woman smiled a smile as hard and insincere as his.

"Many have taken orders under Mother Waller." Lord Stavion smirked as if he had made some joke I did not understand. "Well," he addressed the woman. "And what do you make of Halyard's bride?"

"Don't pay any attention to this old fool. You, my dear, would do well in any company. If you ever get bored with the country you must visit me in town. I promise you would never be bored there and it would be to your profit. Ask for me in Covent Garden. Everyone knows of me, Molly Waller." I saw she had annoyed Lord Stavion with her suggestion.

"You are not bored are you, my dear, not yet? Mother Waller always prides herself on being a judge of character, but in this I am sure she is wrong."

"No," I said, puzzled by the conversation. "I am not bored." I was as greatly puzzled by the woman's attire as I was by her words. She too wore paint and there was a line of red hair that showed around the rim of her coif. It seemed no more holy than the rest of her behavior.

"If you ever were to find life at Longfields tiresome," Lord Stavion gave my hand a squeeze, "I hope you would first come to me as a neighbor and a friend before you went rushing off to town." The woman's eyes narrowed. She seemed to view him as a rival or an adversary.

"I fancy," she said sharply, "that I know the market as well as anyone. What," she turned to me, "what do you make of that lot?" She pointed at a group of young women who stood giggling in a corner. Their dresses were cut startlingly low and their hair was piled up on their heads in an exaggerated style. "He never got them from me, I tell you that. I take pride in what I send into the world." Then she nodded in the direction of two handsome young men who were preening themselves like peacocks. "That's more your taste," she said spitefully to Lord Stavion. "Those boys look as if they'd give full value and would be more to your liking." She turned abruptly and left us alone.

"Poor Mother Waller," Lord Stavion sighed. "She has many vexations and I am afraid that I am one of them." He had not taken his eyes from the young men. "Yes," he said smiling, "Those two are rather special pets of mine. I do find them more to my liking than the ladies, I don't deny that. In fact, I make it a rule never to deny anything that is said of me."

I suddenly felt out of my depth. I wished that I were any place rather than here. At least, in part, I took his meaning, and I could think of no way of replying to him.

"In the country," he was rambling on, "they talk every sort of nonsense about me. They say I keep a company of devil worshippers. What rot! Nothing could be further from the truth. I keep an altogether different kind of congregation. But I encourage the gossip and the scandal, it keeps out the curious and the vulgar. In town, of course, everything is so much easier. No one pays any notice there and I can go about my business."

"What is your business?" I blurted it out without thinking of what his answer might be. His eyes met mine for a moment. He frowned.

"You're serious, aren't you? You're not making a joke at my expense?"

"No."

"Innocence is such a rare commodity, one forgets. But as to my business . . ." He tapped his chin with his quizzing glass. "Let us say that my business is the pursuit of pleasure. I bring people together. I am a, how shall we call it, a matchmaker by Royal appointment. Oh, do not look so surprised. The Royal dukes know me well. But now I heard the cry for dinner. I am to take you in, Halyard says. I know he wants us to be special friends."

I could not believe that Halyard wished such a thing. I could not understand why he had invited these strange people here or why he had delivered me into the hands of this unsavory man.

Formally, as if we were at court, Lord Stavion offered me his hand, and Halyard bowed to Mother Waller. We four led the guests into dinner and behind, in order of some precedence they all seemed to know and to comprehend, the motley congregation of guests followed after us.

Once at the table I looked around me and once again I had the feeling that they were all dressed to play a part. None here seemed to enjoy the easy manners of rank or fortune. They talked too loudly. They drank too much. Their laughter was too shrill. Someone made a ribald remark and it passed from mouth to mouth. I tried not to show my displeasure; they were, after all, Halyard's guests, but I could not disguise my distaste.

"You disapprove," Lord Stavion said in a low voice. "Surely you are not a prude. That would be no way to hold Halyard. Or is the honeymoon over already? Is that why he came to me?" He had made a sharp, shrewd thrust and he had hit home.

"Believe me, I understand." He put his hand on mine. "I sympathize. It cannot be easy for you to be married to a man like Halyard. I know, for I have loved him far longer than you." I was dumbstruck and turned to him so sharply that he saw the shock in my face.

"You look surprised, but it is true. He is the most fascinating man I have ever met. He is an Adonis, a Greek god. Look at him, have you ever seen any man more handsome?" I followed his glance. At the other end of the table Halyard was seated between Mother Waller and a young, pretty, vapid-looking girl who was making a display of her ample bosom. A pang of jealousy struck at me. I could not help it.

"Yes," I said, "he is handsome."

"Surely it does not come as a surprise to you that Halyard is susceptible to pretty women. That one is young and highly available." And I wondered—how many more such available young women had he met in the past week?

"I don't know if you are aware of it," Lord Stavion drawled, "but I was one of the first guests Halyard invited to Longfields when he came of age. To be sure he asked the county in, but I was one of the first to accept. We established an instant rapport. He was such a pretty boy that I hoped we would be great friends. We seemed to have a great deal in common—love of beauty and the arts—but I soon learned that what I had taken for a natural affinity was nothing more than diffidence. To my chagrin my hopes were dashed. So," he shrugged, "I gave up the field. You see, contrary to popular opinion, it is almost impossible to seduce or to corrupt the truly innocent.

"That summer I stayed as close as possible to him, content with the crumbs from his table. He was in love with Arabella, not with me. It was hopeless, of course, that passion of his, I could have told him but it would have done no good. He would not have believed me. Love is blind, they say, but it is also deaf to good advice. Still I stayed. I had hopes that one day . . ." He did not finish that thought. "Ah, but then old men are ever fools.

"Then Halyard went on his travels and when he turned up again in London he had changed. The death of his precious sister was a great blow to him. Personally, I never knew what he saw in her but I do know this, if ever he loved anyone it was her."

"Naturally I offered him my sympathy. Again I tried to bend him to my persuasion but he would not be lured. He still preferred the ladies. With the coming of his fame it was even harder to keep his attention. All I had to offer him was a never ending variety of women and I set myself to offer him variety. As you see," Lord Stavion pointed to Halyard, who was whispering in the young woman's ear as his hand caressed her shoulder. "As you see, he likes variety. Halyard tires of everyone eventually. He even tired of Arabella. Certainly he soon sickens of anything that comes to him too easily. You must not worry if he strays, he will always come back in time. But he wants excitement, change. He is always thinking not of the present but the next love affair. He is not suited to married life. I was curious to meet you." He turned to me and smiled. "I thought you must be remarkable to have kept him even this long."

It seemed to me that I saw Halyard smile too, as if he had overheard.

"If you mean to try to keep him," Lord Stavion said, his eyes sweeping me like the buyer of some faulty piece of merchandise, "then you must learn a multitude of tricks to hold him. You must make yourself into a dozen women if you are to suit all his moods. His palette is jaded. No good, faithful wife, no mere love and devotion will do. I know his needs, believe me, and you must learn new tricks if you are to keep him. Sad to say, but I do not think you have studied in such a schoolroom." I thought that he would never end his speech and that if he did not stop now I would be ill here before them all.

Lord Stavion leaned back, assaying the effect of his words.

"Perhaps what you should do, after all, is to take instruction from Mother Waller." Then he stopped at last and fell silent.

We were on an island of silence in the midst of the laughing and jeering company. I might have been set down at table with apes and baboons, naked in a jungle of less than human creatures. These were animals feeding at a zoo, an exhibit of the self-exposed.

"I wonder," Lord Stavion said, "if you have taken my meaning?"

"Oh yes," I said, "I understand you well enough. You have made yourself plain. Fortunately I am not such a fool as you took me for. I am untutored, it is true. I am also ignorant of the arts that you have mentioned but I am not altogether stupid, merely inexperienced." He made a small bow toward me with his head, as if I had won a point at court tennis and he had conceded the point.

"Then you accept my offer?" he asked.

"What do you offer besides the dubious instruction of Mother Waller?"

"Oh!" He arched one painted eyebrow. "I could offer you anything in this room, any last that suited you, satisfaction guaranteed. One is always wise to learn new ways. How do you know what would suit your taste until you have tried a number of dishes? If you love Halyard and hope to hold him you must apply yourself to learning."

"Thank you for your advice," I said, "but I must depend upon my own natural charms to keep him. I must have faith in his good taste rather than some worldly pose or attitude." I knew it sounded high flown, but I meant to set him straight so he would not pursue the subject further. I saw he knew better than to argue with me. He smiled and bowed again. He had lost the game and meant to lose with grace. He rose and tapped at his wine glass.

"Silence please. Lord Halyard, I ask your permission to toast your wife." Halyard looked up from his own conversation and nodded his assent. Then Lord Stavion said, "Ladies and gentlemen, I propose a toast to innocence, which, like ignorance, is bliss." There was a murmur of laughter and then in answer Lord Halyard rose and, looking first at Lord Stavion and then at me, raised his glass.

"I too wish to toast that paragon of virtue, my wife. She is very loyal and true. I can find no fault with her." I saw some drink and others stare as he went on with his hateful attention to me.

"Yes." Halyard smiled. "Catherine is the perfect wife while I, alas," he shrugged, "am not what she had hoped for in a husband. She has every reason to find fault with me. I have failed her in the most important way a man can fail a woman, I have failed to plough my own field." At first there was stunned, shocked silence and then a roar of nervous laughter. Glasses were raised again and filled. All around me I heard their laughter; wild, sharp, and shrill as it rolled on and on, sweeping over me like the sea and I wished I had been drowned and dead in it rather than to feel such pain.

"And now," Halyard roared over the laughter, "let the serious drinking begin. As you know at Longfields we do not suffer the ladies to leave the table, we know it is to our interest to keep them with us." He had let his hand slip down upon the shoulder of the young, the willing, girl beside him. I saw it fall ever lower toward her bare breast.

I rose and started toward the door. I could not stay here any longer to be witness to such shame, such a grave and cruel death of the heart. But he was too quick for me. Halyard caught me by the arm and led me unwillingly into the center of the hall. He gave a signal to the minstrels' gallery

231

and the musicians began to play as he took me in his arms and began the dance, a spiralling, dizzying waltz. A few couples joined in while the table in the great hall was cleared away. Then more and more couples began to circle round and round. Near the windows tubs of iced wine had been brought in. No guest's glass was empty for long.

"Smile, Catherine." Halyard spoke close to my ear. "You seem displeased and I know you do not want to make our guests uncomfortable." I drew back from him. I would have run from the room then but he would not let go of me.

"What of me? You have made me uncomfortable."

"Have I indeed? I only spoke the truth." He was mocking me now, making fun of me again. "Was that not what you wanted, Catherine, the truth?"

Before I could answer him someone else had stepped up to claim me. He was a pale and sallow youth and without asking my permission Halyard handed me to the boy. As we danced away into the circling spiral of dancers I saw Halyard go to join Lord Stavion, and it seemed as if both were watching me and laughing at my discomfort. All around the room there were shouts of drunken laughter. Some were singing a set of obscene catches and glees.

Again and again I was claimed by a new partner. Halyard watched me being passed from hand to hand and he did nothing to rescue me from what he must know was distasteful company.

He continued talking to Stavion, one arm about a girl who had joined them. I saw Lord Stavion offer Halyard a box of what I thought was snuff, but when he took it the stuff was white and crystalline. He inhaled it from his hand, first one nostril and then another, and his smile became a burst of laughter. As if this rush of laughter and high spirits had suddenly reminded him of me he came toward me, his arms outstretched, to claim me for another dance. I had never seen an expression of such cruelty in his face before. This man was not my friend nor my lover, nor my husband. This man was more cruel than a Caliban would have ever dared to be.

232

I broke away and ran from the hall, up the stairs and into my room. I shut my door and leaned against it, weak with shame and rage and a hurt that ran through me like a sword.

When Megan had undressed me and I had sent her off to bed I sat listening to the noise from below: the shouts and the laughter, the music and the shattering of glass. I sat waiting for something else to happen. I did not know what, and when it came it was not what I had expected. I heard horses in the forecourt, and carriages. I ran across the hall into the long gallery and looked out of the windows onto the terrace below. All of the ladies of the company were being put into carriages and coaches. Some of the men were on horseback. The party was over and the company was leaving, but why?

As the last of them disappeared down the drive I hurried back to my room, wondering if Halyard had gone with them.

Then the door opened and Halyard was standing there in his dressing gown.

"Still awake?" He came in and shut the door behind him as if he always came to me at the end of an evening.

"I thought you must be tired or have a headache. I thought that must be why you left so hurriedly. Well, answer me, Catherine."

"No," I said softly. I could not find my voice. I seemed to have lost the power of speech.

"No? Then you must have left because the company displeased you, so I have sent them away again and now we are alone, just the two of us at home." His eyes were overbright. He seemed tense and highstrung. "If their company was not pleasing to you, Catherine, then I am afraid we will always be alone here at Longfields, for no one else would visit us." He looked at me for a careful moment and then he said, "Well, aren't you pleased to be alone with me?"

I turned and looked into the fire. I saw a log break and fall into the showering embers. I did not answer him because I did not know how.

233

"Why so cold, Catherine? Is it because you were offended by my toast?" I looked up at him then with all my wounded pride showing in my eyes.

"How could you, before all those strangers?"

"A true confession is good for the soul. It was true what I said, I have neglected you. I have not done my duty as a husband should, and now I mean to make up for it." He came nearer to me, stopped, and then took another step and drew me close to him. "I know you were hurt, Catherine, but you will forgive me I know because you have promised to forgive me everything." He held me now in an iron embrace and began to kiss me.

I knew he had been drinking but there was something more, something I had not known in him before. His kisses were hard, urgent, and he was holding me too tightly.

"Why so cold, Cat, I thought that this was what you wanted, for us to be as we once were. I thought you would be pleased that I have come to you tonight." He reached down and undid the ties of my robe.

"No," I said, drawing back. "This is wrong."

"What could be wrong between us, Catherine?" He did not stop, instead his hand went to my breast. "Has it been so long that you need some persuasion?"

With one sharp wrench he had torn away my nightgown and now his mouth found and covered mine, so that I could not cry out. I fought against him but he was too strong for me. This was not Halyard, this was not my lover, but a ruthless, brutal stranger who meant to take me against my will. I fought, I beat at his back and clawed at his shoulders but the struggle was unequal. He forced me to the floor; for one moment I saw him poised over me, his face cold and impassive.

"You mean to fight me," he said, "that will make it all the more interesting for me." His hands caught and pinioned mine above my head. He thrust a knee between my thighs and spread me open before him. "I mean to take you all the same, Catherine. That is my right and it is your duty to submit. You are my wife, my property."

I heard myself moan and cry out in anguish but he seemed not to hear.

"Once you liked me to kiss you so and so. You liked me to touch you here and here. Why are you so cold to me now?" He poised over me once more and then he drove into me with harsh, brutal thrusts.

I was not ready for him, nor was I willing to receive him. I was dry, unyielding, and the pain was sharper and more piercing than if I had been a virgin. He who had once been so gentle with me, so sensitive to my wants and desires, was now coarse and brutal. Each driving thrust was a shattering violation of the sweet and tender love that there had been between us. This was an animal coupling, a base sundering of flesh. Where now was the glorious union, the joining of two to make a whole? This was a travesty, which left me sick with loathing.

With one last shuddering, driving thrust he spent himself, and I lay beneath him, paralyzed by my shame. He had used me with less consideration than he would have a woman he had found in the streets, a woman he had bought for an hour's amusement.

I drew myself from beneath his weight and tried to cover myself with what was left of my nightgown. In his arms that night, for the first time, I had become ashamed of my naked body.

"What is it, Cat?" he asked. "Have I hurt you?"

I could not answer.

"Well, what are a few bruises, they will mend. Or have I left you unsatisfied, is that it?"

I looked at him then, unable to believe the words he was saying to me. This mask, this man, was he the reality, not merely a part he was playing? Was this man to be my husband for the rest of my days?

"Have I hurt you?" He repeated the question.

"You know you have." I closed my eyes so he would not have to see the pain.

"Sometimes," he said slowly, "pleasure wears different faces. Each are different sides of the same coin. If I have not given you satisfaction then, if you like, I will stay with you tonight and in time perhaps I may be able to accommodate you again and to give a service more acceptable to your need."

Again I could not believe the words that he had spoken. My body was raw and tender, my spirit was sick with shame. I was shattered with hurt. My dreams and illusions were broken like a child's dearest toys. Was that why he had behaved so, was it to destroy my love for him? If so, he could not have chosen a more sure or telling way.

"Do you want me to stay? If so you have only to say so."

I shook my head. I knew I was going to be sick and I wanted him to go. He rose and tied the sash to his robe.

"As you like, Catherine, but before I go can you tell me now that you love me? Can you now say that there is nothing you would not forgive me? Are you sure that you will not want to leave Longfields and me?"

And as suddenly as he had come he was gone again.

I tried to be calm but I could not stop shaking. Why, why would he have taken by force what I would have given him so freely? Was it because he was drunk or in torment? I had known that I must fight for him and for the life that we had once had but was it possible that such a life between us could still exist?

Chapter Thirteen

When dawn came I was still awake, unable to believe such an ugly, brutal act had really taken place between us. It might have been a nightmare or a bad dream; only it was not a dream, I bore the bruises, and the memory of Halyard's hard, cruel words still echoed in my mind.

He wanted me to leave him, to go away from Longfields, and if I did as he asked where was I to go? And if I loved him how could I abandon him to such inner torment? For despite his savage violation of that love, I still believed that if only I could get him free of this evil that possessed him he would once again become the man I had known.

Yet I could not face him, not just yet. I needed time to think, to forget. I wanted, if only for a few hours, to get away from that house and everyone in it, to find a hiding place where I might think more clearly and decide what must be done.

I went quickly down the stairs. Everywhere around me were the mute reminders of that dreadful party, the wilted flowers, stale wine, a shattered glass, a tawdry ribbon, and a soiled satin shoe without a heel.

The debris could be cleared away, the house could be set

to rights, but what of our marriage? Could we put love together again and mend the break between us?

I let myself out the front door and walked across the flagstone courtyard toward the church, but even as I walked toward it I knew it was useless for me to look for help there. The living of the parish was Halyard's to give. I could not expect the Vicar to listen to my suspicions or my fears. At Longfields Halyard held the power, right or wrong.

No, the church would offer no refuge for me. I drew up my cloak around me and walked on toward the woods. The day was bright and clear, the sky a pale but piercing blue. In the fields a band of rooks took flight, cawing out their dark cries to the cloudless heavens. I went on blindly, knowing I must escape even if only for a short while. I could not bear such unhappiness much longer. I could not endure Halyard's indifference. It demanded more courage than I possessed to watch him suffer such torment and not be able to help him. Why would he not let me near him? Whenever he was with me he was like some wild, tortured beast caught in a trap, trying to evade its captor. But I was not his enemy, I was his friend and though he had remembered most of his past, it seemed that in the process he had forgotten me and the love that we had shared.

Whether he admitted it or not, I believed that he still wanted me and I knew that while that possibility existed I could not leave him. I must stay on until the end, whatever it might be.

But how was I to help him when I could not guess what held him in such a vise of fear? I wished I had someone in whom I could confide, someone whose advice I could ask, and the only person I could think of who knew both Halyard and me was Tom Grace.

Why had Tom Grace not come down to Longfields before this? Perhaps he had not got my note. Surely he would have come by now if he had known how badly off we were. I decided that I would write to him at once to ask him to come. And because at last I had made some sort of decision, I felt a lightening of my spirits.

I walked on more swiftly and then I began to run, as

long before I had run down the path from the terrace to the sea. But the mood did not last and I feared that never again would things be as they had been between us. When I came to the dark wood I found a narrow path between the ivy-laden oaks and followed it, twisting, turning, on and on, until at last the path ended, the way blocked by a fallen tree.

I sat on the tree and covered my face with my hands, not weeping—I was past tears—but I hoped to blot out the vision of Halyard's terror from my mind. The silence of the forest was disturbed only by the rustling of the squirrels in the trees or a rabbit in the undergrowth. Somewhere a bird sang and then stopped as abruptly as it had begun.

I could not say how long I sat there trying to avoid the memory of what Halyard had said to me before I realized that I was not alone. I was being watched, observed; not by some woodland creature but by a human. My heart began to beat wildly. I peered through my fingers but I could see nothing except the trees. I wanted to take flight, to scream for help but some instinct warned me not to give away the knowledge that I knew there was someone else in the woods, for that knowledge was my only advantage.

I rose slowly, trying not to betray my alarm, looking for the path by which I had come, but in my wandering I had lost all sense of direction.

As I walked deliberately away from the fallen tree, I was unsure of whether I should turn right or left. I could hear soft footsteps behind me. When I went quickly so did he. When I stopped he stopped and then as I stood still, holding my breath, I heard a twig snap behind me and my nerve broke. I began to run wildly, blindly through the underbrush, the brambles catching at my cloak, the limbs of trees cutting at my face. I ran until I tripped over a twisted root and lay like a fallen quarry, heart pounding, eyes wide, searching for some sign of my pursuer. And, when I could see no one, I stood ready to run once more. When suddenly from behind a wide oak tree, a man stepped out to bar my way. At the sight of him all sense of caution left me and I screamed.

If he had been the devil himself I could not have been

more surprised. For here before me was the man I had seen in the theatre, the man who had stood looking up at Halyard with hatred in his eyes, the man with auburn hair.

"What are you doing here?" I gasped.

"I might well ask the same of you." He was dressed in a hunting costume and carried a rifle in the crook of his arm.

"You have no right to be here," I said. "These are Lord Halyard's woods and you are trespassing."

"I have more right to be here than you to wear my sister's jewels."

"Your sister's jewels?" I repeated like a parrot.

"I am Rupert Halyard. My sister, Arabella, was once married to Lord Halyard. Those were her jewels I saw you wearing at the theatre."

"There must be some mistake."

"Yes." His eyes narrowed, his hand clenched into a fist, and I thought he meant to strike me. "It was a mistake for Halyard to come back to England and a mistake for him to give Arabella's jewels to a London whore and then bring her to Longfields to sleep in Arabella's bed. But he has done as much and worse before."

"You're wrong," I said.

"Am I?" He stepped toward me. Rage distorted his features and made him look as if no crime were too great or terrible for him to commit. "I saw you there with Halyard, sitting beside him in his box at Drury Lane and you saw me, you can't deny it. While all the time Halyard pretended not to know who I was."

"He did not recognize you, you do not understand," I said, trying to find the words to explain the truth of what had happened.

"I understand more than you think. I understand Halyard is as wicked as he is dangerous, but he is mad if he thinks I will let him go free this time. I should have had it out with him long ago."

"My husband," I said, "has done nothing wrong."

"Your husband." He laughed derisively, as if I had made a monstrous joke. "You can't expect me to believe that."

240

"As his wife," I continued, "I am entitled to wear the family jewels."

"Halyard married you?" Rupert Halyard was still laughing, although the laughter was without mirth. "What do you take me for?"

"A misguided man," I said quietly. "If you had made any inquiry you would know I am his wife."

"Marry you, I don't believe it."

"Because," I said, "you don't want to believe it. You want to go on thinking the worst of him. Like all the rest you are unwilling to give him a fair chance to explain. You all want to see him humiliated and disgraced, though not one of you has had the courage to tell me why." His eyes looked me up and down and the laughter stopped. He seemed to be taking his own time to assess my words and to reach a conclusion to all I had just told him.

"You are his wife." He was still disbelieving. The fact seemed to be too incredible for him to accept. "You would swear to it?"

"If that would satisfy you," I said.

"I am sorry." He bowed to me. "If what you say is true I owe you an apology."

"I do not ask for one. But now will you let me pass?"

"I am sorry," he said again.

"It does not matter, let me pass."

"Oh, it does matter, for if you really are his wife than I pity you with all my heart."

"I have no need for your pity." His words had stung deep.

"Now," he said, "it is you who are wrong. How could you marry Halyard, a man with his reputation?"

"I married Halyard because I loved him." It was true even after all that had passed. I loved him.

"You could not love him if you knew him. Oh, I know that he is handsome and that he has a way with words. They are his stock in trade and he is clever enough to convince any young girl that he loves her, but it will not last, I promise you. I know him. He is both dangerous and mad. He made his sister's life and mine a living hell, as he will yours if you stay at Longfields."

241

"Let me go," I said. "I don't want to listen."

"But you must hear me out. Your life may depend upon it."

He began then and I listened, unwilling but spellbound.

"From the moment he met Arabella," Rupert said, "he pursued her. He said he loved her. He begged her to marry him. He swore that he would kill himself if she would not have him and when she had the courage to refuse him, he went off like some lovesick boy to travel about the world. He played up his departure as if he were some prince going into exile, all the while keeping the real reason for his going hidden from everyone." Rupert paused, his lips trembling. To continue speaking seemed to be a great effort for him.

"While he was gone we promised to look after his sister Amelia, and God knows Arabella did her best." He stopped again and then went on. "But by then the damage was done. While he was gone, because of him, because of his . . ." He did not seem to be able to find the proper words, "Because of his neglect Amelia died.

"When Arabella went to Plymouth to tell Halyard the news she would not let me go with her. She was afraid of what I might do to him because he had so cruelly abandoned Amelia. You see, I loved Amelia. I don't know if Halyard has spoken of her to you but I tell you this, Amelia was unlike her brother in every way. She was gentle and good; she was sweet and pure. How could he have used her so vilely? How could he have made her of all people his victim?" He looked away and then back again, his gaze steady once again.

"I loved Amelia. I had asked her to marry me. Even after she went away I should have followed her to Wales but I did not. I could not then because I could not understand after all that he had done to her that she, like you, found something in him to love. I did not follow her and now I will regret it always to the end of my life." He broke off, unable to finish.

I remembered her face from the miniature and it seemed Amelia had been more truly loved for her goodness than Arabella for all her beauty.

"When Arabella told Halyard that Amelia was dead," Rupert went on with some of the old anger, "he did not even have the courage, the decency to come down to Longfields. Instead he went off to London where he wrote that damnable poem. When it was published his name was spoken everywhere. Overnight he became notorious and he had the gall, the impertinence to say that Arabella had been the inspiration for the thing. It was terrible that my sister should be so singled out for attention. She was determined to stop his folly if she could and so she went up to London to face him, to have it out with him. Again she would not let me go with her for fear of what I might do. She said that she could deal with him, but somehow he got round her and with that black magic of his persuaded her that if she would marry him she could reclaim him. He made her believe his salvation depended upon it.

"She was a fool to have listened to him or to have married him. Later I discovered that almost from their wedding day he had made her life a torment with his coldness and his unkindness. He was jealous of her for no reason and he subjected her to outbursts of his insane temper both in company and in private. She never knew what to expect." I knew I should not listen to Rupert Halyard's accusations but I was mesmerized, held silent in a state of thrall.

"He had sworn that he loved her, that he could not live without her and then, when he had won her, when he had married her, he treated Arabella worse by far than if she had been some woman of the town. He humiliated her in public. He drank and drugged. He gambled, and not content with ruining himself with his extravagance, he spent Arabella's fortune as well. At last, when there were bailiffs in the house, he forced her to steal out the back way with him like some common criminal and run for the country and for Longfields.

"At Longfields Halyard kept Arabella a virtual prisoner. He would allow no callers to come to the house. At first he said that he was working on another poem. I never went there. I could not, for if I had seen him face to face, I would have killed him, and what good would that have done save to make Arabella a widow and create a scandal. It would not have brought Amelia back again."

As I listened to him I thought I was going mad. It was the same story in substance that Halyard had told me, but a different version entirely. Which was true and which was false? Not noticing my confusion, Rupert Halyard continued.

"One day Arabella sent me a note by her maid asking me to meet her in the woods. She said she had something to tell me that she did not want anyone to overhear. I thought it strange but I wanted to see her. It had been weeks since I had had any word from her at all.

"We met here. You see on the tree are the initials, AH. That summer, when we all had been so happy, it had been a joke between us that no one would confess who had carved the initials or whether they stood for Amelia or Arabella Halyard. That day when Arabella came I was shocked by what I saw. She, who had always been so proud and beautiful, looked drawn and old, as if her spirit had been broken. I begged her to tell me what was going on in that house. It was then she told me such terrible things about her life with Halyard that I have never repeated them to a living soul. I will only tell you part of it now because although it is too late to save Arabella or Amelia it may not be too late to save you."

All Rupert had said still seemed to be a distorted repetition of Halyard's words. Each of them, Halyard and Rupert, seemed to be sure he alone knew the truth about Arabella, while I felt more mystified than ever.

"Arabella said that she had discovered a secret in that house, something so terrible that she was afraid to tell me what it was. I could see that she was truly frightened, afraid for her very life. I pleaded with her to come home with me then, to leave Halyard and come back to Halyard Hall, but she refused. She said Halyard was her husband, that she must stay for better or for worse. She said that from that day on, she could not even trust the servants to deliver messages but that she would leave letters for me here in the hollow of this lovers' tree as she knew a secret way to slip out of the house.

"And so every day I came here to the woods to see if there was some word from her. She wrote often, nothing of any great importance, mostly memories of the old days when we had been young and carefree. And then I found that last note." He stopped abruptly and raised his hand to touch the tree, as if he were reliving the moment when he had got that last message.

"Arabella must have had a premonition of what was going to happen. She wrote a long letter and in it she told me the real reason why Halyard would not allow visitors to come to the house, why he would not see even me. She wrote all that she had been afraid to tell me before." He turned away from me for a moment and then, resolved to spare me nothing, he turned back and said almost tonelessly, "She wrote that Halyard had threatened to kill her if she told anyone what she knew. She told me he kept his mistress in the house and their child as well."

For a moment I could feel nothing but shock and then, little by little, the pain began; the pain of my own rejection, the hurt Halyard's words had caused me, the humiliation I had suffered before the servants. I saw Amelle's small face in the window, the rain streaming down like tears upon the glass panes, and I remembered Halyard's face white with rage as he had shouted at me that I must ask no questions, that Amelle was his ward, his responsibility and no concern of mine. And yet, out of the memory of the love we had once shared, I heard myself defending him.

"I don't believe you," I said. "Surely, Arabella was mistaken. She must have confused the child in the house with the story of the wicked lord. They say he kept a mistress in the house, a wench from the village."

"No." Rupert shook his head. "Arabella made no mistake. I know the story of the wicked lord, I'd heard it often enough, and so had Arabella. It was the wicked lord who killed our grandfather. Besides," he said, as if he were sorry to take away my last illusions, "the child who lived at Longfields is too young to have been the old lord's brat. She is just the right age to have been born the year Halyard was away on his grand tour. Halyard never really cared for Arabella, that was all a pose, like the rest of his life. I think this mistress is the reason why he did not want to bring Arabella home to be married, why he insisted they stay up in town. He did not want Arabella to learn the truth. Not that he had not done the same and worse before. Perhaps he still had some conscience then, felt some sense of guilt for what he had done. Or perhaps in London he hoped to hide his true nature from the world and his wife. It was only when he was in debt and forced back to Longfields that inevitably Arabella found out about the woman and the child. And when she threatened to expose him, he killed her." I gasped in horror.

"No," I said, "that's not true. It can't be. The fire was an accident." Rupert looked at me pityingly.

"That is what you have been told, but this is what I think happened. Arabella confronted Halyard with what she knew. They quarreled, and as a result of that quarrel, Halyard's insane temper got the better of him. He killed Arabella and set the fire to destroy the evidence of the murder. Somehow the fire got out of hand and his mistress perished in the flames."

I felt as if the earth had opened up and I was falling into a dark and endless void. I had wanted to know the reason for the change in Halyard but I could not accept this explanation.

"No," I said, "no," repeating the word again and again, like some charm that would erase what had been said, but now Rupert had begun he would not stop until he had come to the end of his story.

"The next day, after the fire, two women were buried in the church at Longfields, both in the Halyard crypt. Two women from the same house, surely even you must see that is more than coincidence."

I began to shake uncontrollably and Rupert, thinking that I was cold, pulled up my cloak around my shoulders while I could only stand mute, looking wordlessly into his face. Each of his features was an exaggeration of Halyard's—his face longer, his eyes larger, his nose more prominent. At first sight I had not guessed Rupert was related to Halyard but now I knew that they were cousins I saw how alike they were and wondered if Arabella and Amelia had resembled each other in such a mirrored way.

Then I suddenly thought of Amelle, whose eyes were the same color as Halyard's, her face the same shape as his, and I pushed that picture from my mind as forcefully as I could. I could not, would not, believe what Rupert Halyard had told me. I would not accept it. No one could be expected to take Rupert's word as proof. Arabella had been his sister. He must take her part and in his heart he still held a grudge against Halyard, for he blamed him for his loss of Amelia.

"If you loved your sister and felt she was in danger why didn't you go to Longfields and take her away?"

He shrugged, not a gesture of indifference but one of infinite sadness. "You're right, of course. I shall never be able to forgive myself. If I had thought Arabella was in any real danger I would have gone. I have no excuse. I can only offer this in explanation. I had warned her to leave him, begged her to come home, and she had refused because I think in her heart Arabella did not believe he was wicked, any more than you believe me now, and by the time I had found her last letter and had read it, Arabella was dead."

Still unwilling to believe Rupert had any proof of what he had told me, I lashed out at him, wanting to wound him as he had me.

"So for your revenge," I said, "you spread those damnable rumors about Halyard all over London. You told them and told them until he was publicly disgraced, until you saw him driven away from Longfields and from England."

"No. You must believe me. I never said one word about Halyard after Arabella died." Rupert seemed genuinely shocked. "Why would I? Of course I heard those rumors, they ran like wildfire, but not because of me. I would not have wanted such gossip spread about my sister. I would not have wanted to drag her name through the mud. She was dead, it would not bring her back." He sounded sincere but I could not allow myself to believe him.

247

"That night at the theatre," I said, "I saw you standing there looking up at the box. You hated Halyard and you hated me because you thought I was some whore wearing Arabella's jewels."

"Yes," he said, "but now we have met I know how wrong I was to think such a thing of you. I have said I am sorry."

"But that night," I went on relentlessly, "you hated me enough to send me a cartoon of Halyard and you were coward enough to send it anonymously."

"What cartoon?" he asked.

"The cartoon was a caricature of Halyard standing in a boat. There were women swimming all about him in the sea. There was a terrible verse on it. I can't remember it all but there were the words *wife* and *sister* and *whore*." Rupert shook his head.

"No, again you are wrong. I did not send it. How could I have done? I did not know who you were. I have not seen that particular cartoon but there were many like it. They were printed by the score. Halyard was jeered at in the streets. The mob threw stones and mud at him. The rabble booed and hissed him at the theatre and at Lady Jersey's ball all London society cut him dead."

Again I felt cold. I knew by my own experience what London society could do.

"Believe me, I did not send the cartoon to you. I never started any rumors. Even if I had not loved Arabella I have too much pride in the Halyard name to see it blackened any more than it has been in the past. The name is mine as well as his."

All his arguments sounded plausible but still I had to try once more to discredit him, for the alternative was to believe him and that prospect was too terrible to accept.

"Then perhaps," I said, "because you wanted to avoid further scandal, you hated Halyard enough to hire some men to kill him while you stood in the shadows and watched." I saw Rupert Halyard flush.

"I hate him, that is true, and I wish him dead, but I would not send others to do my work for me. If I meant to kill him I would do it myself."

We stood staring at each other. It was only his word against my word, his will against my will. Despite myself, I had believed a great deal of what Rupert Halyard had told me. I no longer believed he had sent me the cartoon. Why would he deny it? Nor did I believe he had hired assassins to murder Halyard. If he wanted Halyard dead Rupert would kill him himself and count the murder as his pleasure.

"I want to go back to Longfields," I said at last, "but I do not know the way."

"Then I will walk along with you," Rupert said, not unkindly.

He took me to the clearing and before he turned to walk back the way that we had come, he caught at my arm and held it as he looked intently into my eyes. We stood in silence until a sudden gust of wind caught the leaves and rained them down on our heads like a sudden shower of lost hopes.

"I am sorry," he said. "I have caused you pain but if you have believed anything I have told you, you will know it was for your own good. I ask you to be careful. I know you must have loved him when you married him but I think you've already seen him change, become a different man than the husband you had dreamed of. Remember this, if he treated Arabella badly because of what she found out about him in that house, then you too may be in danger. If he did kill my sister he might well now try to harm you. I think you are in danger.

"I know you do not think it possible, but before it is too late you can put what I have told you to the test. Go to the church at Longfields. Look at the burial records. You can see for yourself that two women were buried in the Halyard crypt on the same day. One was my sister, Arabella, the other was Halyard's mistress. He was responsible for the death of both of them. If I do not hear from you I will come to Longfields to see that you are safe."

Rupert stood looking at me for one moment more, then he turned and disappeared into the woods. I felt rooted to the spot. Finally I broke the spell and ran as if all the fiends of hell were behind me, ran until I was back again at Longfields. I ran past the church, where, if Rupert Halyard was telling me the truth two women had been buried, two women from Longfields, whose spirits were restless specters, who stood looking at the living, filling Halyard with a terror of the past and its bloody deeds.

When I went in I saw the house had been put straight. The rooms had been cleaned of all traces of the party. Once more the blinds were drawn and dust sheets shrouded the furniture.

Last night might never have happened. Halyard's act of cruel force might never have taken place, but it had been real. He had been cruel, unfeeling, and now I had a possible reason for his behavior. I felt numb and sick with shock.

I did not go in to see him. I did not want to ask him how he was or to see the bottles of brandy and laudanum by his bed. I did not want to smooth at his pillows and feel the pistols he kept beneath them. I did not want to reach out only to have him draw away, repelled by my love, which he could no longer return. I did not want to see his face or to read the fear in it, the terror that perhaps sprang from his conscience and his sense of guilt.

For the first time I realized why Halyard might have said I must ask no questions, for the answers could be dangerous; why he might have had such a necessity to forget his past life, a past so terrifying that for his sanity's sake even now he was unwilling to remember what terrible secret Arabella had told him. And I saw at last why he might want me to leave him and this house before I learned any more.

But much as I wanted to avoid Halyard I could not refuse to see Amelle. Megan said that Amelle had been waiting for me all day and would not be put off now she knew I was back in the house. I told myself I let Amelle come down to my rooms because she would not go to sleep until she had given me a kiss goodnight, but if I had been honest it was because I wanted to dispel in part the ugly suspicions Rupert Halyard had put into my mind.

250

As I studied Amelle's face by the firelight, the shadows of the flames made her seem a different child. She changed before my eyes. Why had I refused to admit the striking likeness between Halyard and Amelle? Was it because I had preferred to remain blind to the obvious? Her eyes, her smile, the curve of her brow, and her hair with its chestnut sheen were almost identical to his.

But if she was his child, how could he neglect her so? He hardly ever saw or spoke to her. Did she remind him of someone or something he wanted to forget? Amelle was of an age to have been born while Halyard was away on his grand tour, but even if I allowed myself to believe that Halyard might be Amelle's father and that he might have kept a mistress here at Longfields even before he left England, I still did not know who her mother had been. Amelle had said that once there had been two women here at Longfields, one who had been kind to her, sung to her and held her on her lap, and another who had been cruel, a woman Amelle still feared.

I held Amelle to me and caressed her hair as I whispered, half to myself, "Amelle, were there really two women here long ago?"

"Yes." Her answer was so soft it was almost inaudible.

"Who were they?"

"One was kind to me," she said. "She let me sit in her lap and she sang to me. And the other one . . ." She stopped.

"The other one?" I prompted her.

"The other one was mean and cruel."

"What did she do?" I asked.

"She locked me in a room. I was all alone and it was dark."

"Why?" I asked, "why would she do such a thing?" But try as I would I could not coax her to tell me any more.

If Rupert had told me the truth, there had once been two women in the house, two women who had died in the fire and had been buried in the Halyard crypt on the same day—Arabella and Halyard's mistress. Was what he had told me true? The answer lay in the church records if I dared to look at them.

Chapter Fourteen

Next day, as I set out for the church, I knew I had taken the first step on a path from which there was to be no turning back. I wanted to know the truth both for Halyard and myself. One way or the other I must know what it was that possessed him. We could not go on living as we were.

Inside the church was small and plainly decorated but over the years the Halyards had been generous in their gifts. The stained-glass window above the altar glowed red, blue, and yellow, becoming more brilliant as it caught the sun. The communion plate was silver and the lectern, in the shape of a great bronze eagle, bore an inscription commemorating the restoration of Charles II. Somewhere within me a small, mean voice said that the Halyards of that day must have turned their coats to suit every political wind that blew. But perhaps their perfidy had been worth it, for the house still stood and was in Halyard hands.

The family pew, as I had expected, was the largest and most ornate. The crest carved on the door was illuminated in Halyard colors—red, black, and gold. The seats were cushioned in velvet, the kneelers were thick and handsomely embroidered. In the corner of the pew was a small brazier to insure no Halyard would suffer from the cold during the service. Later Halyards had insisted on comfort just as the first baron had built a tunnel beneath the courtyard so he could walk from house to church without getting wet.

I opened the door to the pew and sat with hands folded as if waiting for some miracle, some sign that all would yet be well. Beside me on the cushioned seat lay a Book of Common Prayer, but where was there a prayer for a desperate young wife or a haunted husband? Where was there a prayer that would exorcise the evil and the terror from that house? Day by day I could see some force destroying him and I must find out what it was. I must find the truth.

But what then? What if I found that Halyard had done some dreadful deed, then would I want the truth? What had brought me here to this church? Was it to pray for the truth or was it merely vulgar curiosity that made me want to know if what Rupert Halyard had told me was true? Had two women from Longfields been buried in the crypt of this church on the same day and, if so, who had the other woman been? Had she been his mistress, the mother of Amelle? Even if such a woman had existed, died, been buried, and left a child, it did not prove that Halyard had murdered Arabella.

Halyard had never tried to hide from me that there had been many women in his life before he had met me. He had never denied that he had once loved Arabella; a wild, impetuous calf love that had burned itself out in a poem just as he had been candid and told me he had not loved her when they had married.

What I really wanted to know then was—had Halyard murdered Arabella? Had he stood by and let her die and his mistress as well, or had their deaths been an accident? Was he the notorious Lord Halyard the world spoke of and thought it knew? My Halyard was another man from theirs. He smiled in the summer sunshine and wrote out my name on the sands. My Halyard believed in magic and could not wait to share the moonlight and the dawn.

This Halyard who kept to himself at Longfields was a stranger who was destroying himself a little more each day. Who was there then to tell me what manner of man Halyard really was? Perhaps only facts could bear valid witness. If I wanted to know him I must begin with the facts that were a matter of record in this church.

I reached out to open the door of the pew. Just as I felt the handle in my hand I heard a voice say, "Good morning," and I was so startled that I jumped as if I had been burnt. I turned to see a young man in clerical garb. He was not much older than I, with a ruddy, open face. His eyes were steady and clear though now he seemed to be dismayed by my reaction to his greeting.

"I'm sorry," he said, "I didn't mean to frighten you. May I be of help? I'm Mr. Nichols, the curate."

"I was just admiring the church," I said, and he flushed as if I had paid him a personal compliment.

"Yes," he said, "it is quite lovely but we don't get many visitors."

"I am not a visitor," I interrupted, "I am Lady Halyard." He flushed as if caught out, his thoughts an open book.

"Yes, of course, I see," he said, "I should have known." I wondered what he had heard about me. It clearly differed from the woman he now saw.

"I should have recognized you," he said.

"We only arrived from London a few days ago."

"Yes, I heard you and his lordship had returned. I called but they told me he was indisposed. I hope he will be better soon."

"So do I." I hesitated, trying to find some tactful way to begin my search. "I've never been to Longfields before," I said. "We've only been married a short time," and thinking he might wonder why we had not chosen the parish church for our wedding, I went on hastily. "We married in Spain before we sailed to England." He nodded and I saw him flush again. He had been too shy and polite to ask and my answer had satisfied him. Warming to my story, I went on.

"I am trying to learn all I can about the family history.

Some of it is very confusing. There were a great many Halyards."

"Yes," he said. "I too found them confusing when I came to the parish. This church was built by the first baron, of stones from the abbey ruins. The family was always generous to the church, with the exception of the last lord." I saw him color again. "I understand that he was . . ." he said, as he cast about, clearly at a loss for some suitable word.

"An eccentric?" I asked innocently, and he nodded gratefully.

"What confused me in the beginning," he said, "was that there are two branches of the family."

"Indeed."

"Yes. There's Rupert Halyard's branch who lives at Halyard Hall and your husband's people, the barons of Longfields. When I first came here I was interested in the history of both the families. Perhaps it would make things clearer if you keep in mind that the Longfields memorials are in the right aisle or wall, while the Rupert Halyard connection favors the left. Of course that is not always so, for from time to time the two houses intermarried and in the case of Rupert's grandfather, took the Halyard name."

"Yes," I said, "my husband's first wife was Rupert's sister, Arabella." I saw relief written on his face. He had been wondering how to mention a painful topic so that it might be easier to explain the ins and outs of all the Halyards and their connections. He was eager to show me up and down the church, chattering all the while about the Halyards. There were memorials to a host of them, even those who had been buried elsewhere; to Halyard's grandfather, the admiral, who had been lost at sea, and to his father who had died in debt in France, but I saw none to Amelia, who had been buried in far-off Wales, and I thought it odd.

"It's all very interesting," I said. "I am sure you must keep a church register. Perhaps if I could have a look at it, it would put all the Halyards in some clearer perspective. There are church records, aren't there?"

"Oh yes," he said. "The record is kept most accurately.

The bishop would be vexed if the records were not exact," and he led me into the vestry where he unlocked a wooden cabinet from which he took a large leatherbound book. "Here it is, you see. All the marriages and deaths, christenings, any event of importance has been written down from the beginning of this church."

"May I look at it?"

"Of course." He seemed delighted that I was interested. I turned the pages, trying not to appear too anxious or curious.

"I am sure," he said, "that you will find all the Halyards listed there."

"Not quite all," I said. "Amelia, Lord Halyard's sister, was buried in Wales."

"Wales?" he said. I might as well have told him that Amelia had been buried on the moon. As I turned the pages, looking at all the entries, I let my finger slide down the page, noting all the occasions of joy, sorrow, grief, and rejoicing. I wondered if my name might be added to this book one day or if I would lie far from Longfields. I turned on, page after page, until I found the record of Arabella's burial and there, upon the line beneath it, was another entry on the same date. It was the name of a woman: Agnes Hill.

I felt my throat tighten and my stomach turn. What Rupert had said was true then, another woman had been buried on that day and her residence, like Arabella's, was Longfields.

"It's strange," I said, "to think that two women from Longfields were buried on the same day. Did you know Agnes Hill?"

"No," he said, "I'm afraid I did not know either Lady Halyard or Agnes Hill. I have only been in the parish three months and so you see I was not here at the time of the fire."

"I see," I said. I had come this far and I could not leave it now. I must pursue it. "I wonder how I could find out more about this Agnes Hill. I am going to make calls upon all the village families. I would not want to call upon her

257

relations and not mention her, especially if she died at Longfields." He looked perplexed.

"It's a pity the Vicar is not here, he knows everything of that sort. When he returns I am sure he will be able to tell you all you want to know."

"When will that be?"

"Hard to say, he's at Cheltenham for the waters."

"I must begin my calls soon," I said. "Do you know of any way I could find out about this Agnes Hill?"

"Yes." He smiled. "I know someone who can tell you. Will Green. He was sexton here for many years. He would remember. He's old, of course. He retired before I came but he knows everyone. When they were born, who they married, and when they were buried. He knows, if you can get him to tell you."

"Why do you say that?" I asked quickly.

"Will's turned into a recluse. These days he keeps himself to himself."

"Thank you, you've been very kind."

"I am sorry not to have been of any more help. Lady Halyard," he said nervously, "will we see you and Lord Halyard on Sunday?"

"If my husband is feeling better."

"Of course, only you see," and he flushed again, "I take the sermon myself this Sunday."

"We'll try to come then." Poor young man. So much depended upon Halyard's praise and favor. It was easy to forget what a power he was in the neighborhood. He had the living of the church to give as he pleased. His tenants did well or ill because of his management. He was powerful enough to say what should be written or what left out of a church register. It was for him to say who was buried in the crypt.

As I walked across the courtyard to the house it was only a short distance, but the house seemed to be a thousand miles away. I felt I was walking with weights upon my limbs. I was seized by terror as if I had an ague of fear. It seemed I had come close to at least some part of the secret of this house, stepped to the brink of the forbidden. I could, as the young curate had suggested, go to see Will Green, but I wanted Halyard to tell me who Agnes Hill had been, why she had been here in this house, and how she had come to be buried in the crypt the same day as Arabella. I wanted to ask him but I was afraid that if I questioned him he would be even angrier than when I had seen him last. So instead I went to Mrs. Griffin. She had been in the house since Halyard had come of age. Whoever had lived here since she would have known of it.

I walked along the corridor past the locked doors of the west wing, then up the tower steps to the next floor where I knocked upon her sitting room door. As I entered Mrs. Griffin was at her table busy with her needlework, a piece of old-fashioned knotting. She seemed surprised that I should have come.

"You should have rung for me, m'lady."

"I wanted to talk to you in private," I said. "It is something I would not want to discuss with Megan or Rose." I had hit my mark. She knew I had found out she had punished Megan for gossiping.

"How can I help you?" she asked stiffly. I wished that I were clever or cunning at asking questions but I was not, so I went directly to the point.

"I was in the church today," I said. "I met the curate and he showed me around. I saw in the church register that on the same day the Lady Arabella Halyard was buried, a woman named Agnes Hill was also buried in the family crypt."

"Yes," Mrs. Griffin replied. She sat very still. She meant to give nothing away, to volunteer no information.

"I could not help but wonder about her," I went on, "as the register gave her residence as Longfields."

"Yes." Mrs. Griffin rose and busied herself with the fire while she decided on how she would reply. "Yes," she said at length, "Agnes was a servant here at Longfields."

"Is it usual for servants to be buried in the family crypt?"

"The circumstances were unusual. Agnes Hill died in the fire with Lady Halyard and so she was buried with her."

"Why not in the churchyard?"

"There's nothing mysterious about it," Mrs. Griffin said quickly, "she had no family here or elsewhere, for all we knew, and she had been very loyal and devoted. She'd been engaged when Miss Amelia was ill and when Miss Amelia died, Agnes Hill stayed on in the house."

"You say she had no family here?"

"No."

"Where did she come from?"

"London, I believe."

"Why would you send to London for a nurse?" I asked her and, as if she had been expecting this question, Mrs. Griffin had a ready answer.

"Miss Amelia's doctor recommended her."

"What was wrong with Amelia? Why did she die?"

"She had consumption. Her doctor felt that she should have a nurse experienced in such cases." It was neatly done. Mrs. Griffin had provided a reasonable explanation, but I felt that if it were not an outright lie it was something very short of the whole truth.

"Yes," Mrs. Griffin sighed, "it was a very sad time indeed. The house seemed to be always in mourning. First Lord Halyard's mother, then his sister and his wife." She looked up at me speculatively. "I hope you will not think me impertinent but it is best not to talk of the past too much, it only brings back painful memories." I knew that she had told me all that she intended to. The interview was at an end.

I thanked Mrs. Griffin and I left her at work once more on her knotting. I too hoped things would be different but the prospect seemed bleak. As long as Halyard was tormented by the past he would continue to shut himself away, to make himself a prisoner in a fortress from which he shut me off.

But now, at last, I thought I knew why he was punishing himself. Rupert Halyard had told me part of the reason. Halyard had had a mistress. She had borne him a child and in the fire at Longfields, Halyard's wife and the woman he had loved had died. In some mistaken way he still

260

blamed himself for the accident. I knew the fire had been an accident, for I would never believe that Halyard was a murderer.

If the climate of our lives was going to change I must tell him of my suspicions and then perhaps, at last, we could begin to build a bridge between us.

He sat in a wing chair, staring at the door. Beside him, on the table, were his pistols, ready to shoot at any unwelcome apparition. What did he so fear that he would see? Whom did he expect? I knew it was not me. He barely acknowledged my presence. I went to him and knelt down beside him and looked up into his face, once so beautiful. It now showed all the traces of his misery. I pitied him with all my heart. I wondered if he had been aware of what he had seen that night or if his vision had been so blurred by drugs and drink that he believed his visitor to be only a delusion of a tormented mind.

He looked older now and gaunt. There was more grey in his hair.

"Still here?" he asked. His eyes avoided mine.

"Yes."

"I thought that you had gone."

"No."

"You had every reason to leave me."

"I stayed because I love you." He turned then; the look of helpless anguish vanished and I felt his cold fury.

"Do you expect me to apologize? Have you come to hear me say that I am sorry for what happened?"

"I came because at last I think I know why you are so afraid for me to ask questions."

"Do you?" His eyes were still cold but there was fear in them now as well as anger. "What do you think you know?"

"I went to the church today," I said. "While I was in the church I..." I could not go on, I felt my stomach turn again. It was painful to ask what might result in an even more painful answer.

"While I was there," I said at last, "I looked at the church register."

"Did you?"

"I saw Arabella's name in it," I said, "and on the line below was the name of a woman, Agnes Hill." I waited but he only looked at me blankly.

"Do you remember her?" I asked softly. He did not answer and I did not know if he was trying to remember or to forget her name.

"Mrs. Griffin says she was Amelia's nurse."

"Ah," he said, as if I had told him something new. "I was not here at Longfields when Amelia was ill or when she died."

"Agnes Hill stayed on afterward," I said. "She stayed in the house." I felt that I was cast in lead. "You must remember her."

"No." He shook his head. Was he telling me the truth? Had he forgotten or was he a better actor than any the stage had ever seen?

"You must remember," I said, "she died in the fire, the fire that killed Arabella. I know you remember the fire."

"I remember the fire." He caught his breath in a short, sharp gasp. "But I do not remember everything that happened that night. I have told you not to ask questions and again you disregard my wishes. Do not," he said heavily, "ask me any more." But I could not stop.

"Did you know Agnes Hill?"

"Let it alone, Cat, let it alone. It is dangerous to ask questions to which you may not want the answers."

"I think I know why you do not want me to ask questions," I said. "Not because it is dangerous to me but to you. You think I will find out what torments you so."

He sat staring at me.

"You are afraid that I will find out that Agnes Hill was your mistress; that she lived here in this house with you, and that Arabella found out about her and you quarreled so violently that somehow a fire broke out. I believe that Amelle is your child, yours and Agnes Hill's. That is why you will not see her or have her near you. You feel guilty and that sense of guilt will not let you rest. But my darling, don't you see I don't care that you loved others before me.

262

I don't care if Amelle is your child; I have come to love her. Do not push her away, do not ignore her; she is innocent, she must have love and affection if she is to grow. She must have your love if she is not to wither just as I must." He stared at me incredulously.

"You think I had a mistress named Agnes Hill and that Amelle is my bastard?"

"Is it true?" I asked. "Is it true, please answer me." He looked at me then, his eyes cold, hard, and unyielding.

"If you knew the truth, Catherine, you would find it far more terrible than that."

I did not know what Halyard remembered or did not remember, but I knew the next step that I must take on the path to discovery was to see Will Green.

Chapter Fifteen

When I left Halyard I was no closer to the truth than before. The only fact I had to hold was that two women had died here at Longfields. Both had been buried on the same day.

I let myself out of the house and walked past the church, through the churchyard to a little gate in the stone wall that separated holy ground from the village. This was the path that the villagers used to come to church instead of entering through the main gate. It was a small back door to heaven, an entrance for the common folk who were obliged to travel to paradise second class.

The gate opened onto a short, narrow, cobbled street, which led down to the center of the village. Near the Halyard Arms and the market cross were two or three small shops flanked on either side by little cottages. Near the watering trough a small boy was throwing stones at a tethered horse, not so much out of any real animosity as out of boredom. I recognized him as the son of the gatekeeper, the flaxen-haired boy who had waved at me on my way to Longfields.

"Hello," I said to him, "can you please tell me the way to

Will Green's cottage?" It seemed a simple enough question but he stood and stared, mouth agape, as if I were an alien creature. "I'm Lady Halyard, I saw you at the gatehouse when I arrived. You waved at me and I waved back at you." He nodded, wiping at his nose. I thought surely he must remember the coach if not me. Still he uttered not a word and though his eyes looked alert and he seemed quick enough I began to wonder if he were mute. Then he came and planted himself in front of me.

"What do you want to know?" he demanded in a rough country accent.

"I want to know the way to Will Green's cottage. Does he live here in the village?" He shook his head in scorn.

"No, he don't live here, not in the village. Will Green lives over yonder in the little wood."

"Then will you show me the way?"

"I can't go there, me mam won't let me."

"Why?"

"Will Green's a loony one. Me mam won't let me go to his house."

"Then just show me the way to the wood."

"Well." At first he seemed doubtful. "That's all right, I reckon." We set off, he walking backward, facing me, just to be sure he kept sight of me.

"What's your name?" I asked him.

"Alf," he said gruffly, as if I should have known that all along.

"Alf, why do you say Will Green is a loony?"

"Because he is, that's why." There was logic, clear and simple, and as I had asked him a question he seemed to feel it was now his turn. "What do you want to see him for?" he demanded. "Nobody ever goes to see Will Green."

"I am going to call on all the cottagers," I said, "and I thought I'd start with him because he's old."

"Biddy Gillis is older than him," he declared, and having said all he intended to he wheeled around to walk beside me. He took me to the end of the village, then along a path over a rise to the edge of a thicket.

"He's in there," Alf said. "You can't miss his cottage,"

and remembering his mother's warning, he turned and ran back the way that we had come.

The path continued but was so overgrown with weeds and vines that for a time I thought perhaps Alf had played a prank on me, but at the end of this twisting trail I saw a small derelict cottage made of local stone. The roof was a sort of thatch that caved and sagged ominously. Some of the walls were crumbling and even with a tendril of smoke wisping out of the crooked chimney, it looked more like some animal's byre than a human's dwelling.

The door, made of split planks, hung crooked on its hinges. Between the boards were holes that had been stopped with old rags. Surely, I thought, the parish could have done better by their sexton than to let him burrow away in this shed. I took courage and knocked. The door gave beneath my fist. There was no answer and so I knocked again. Still no answer, but I saw in one of the holes the rag withdrawn and one eye looking out at me through the chink. Then I heard a rough voice, so low the words were barely audible. "What do yer want?"

"To come in," I said. "I am Lady Halyard and I must speak with you." The door opened a crack and then wider. The man before me was old, yet age alone could not account for his appearance. He was gnarled, bent, and twisted by rheumatics. His skin was pasty white as one is who never gets the sun. His beard was all matted with droplets of caked food, and from behind him the stench that came from the cottage was overpowering. No sun or fresh air, no soap and water, had been inside those walls for months. He stood staring at me blankly. There was a film over one of his eyes and he seemed so nearly blind that I was not sure if he knew what I looked like.

"Who be you then?" he asked, his voice querulous and uncertain.

"Lady Halyard." At that he began to bow and scrape, trembling as if a fever had struck him.

"Come in then, lady, come in." The whining tone was as servile as a cowering dog. He motioned me to a chair and stood bowing as I sat. On the table beside me was a heap of unwashed dishes and scraps of molding food. His bed in the corner was nothing more than a pile of rags but the sight of his craven attitude was even more distressing to me than the surroundings.

"I knew you'd come back," he said, "I knew it. You've come to take poor old Will Green away. That's it, isn't it? Now Will's old and dying you've come to put him in prison or see him hanged for what the devil made him do." He began to weep then, snuffling like a child that has lost its pocket handkerchief, not bothering to wipe at his eyes or his nose. "They'll hang me for what I done, won't they?" He was so grotesque a sight that it made me draw back from him. It made me ill to see such revolting behavior. I was already queasy from the smell of this foul hut, yet most horrible of all to me was the knowledge that I felt so little charity or sympathy for him or his condition.

"No," I said stiffly, "I don't know what it is you've done and I have not come to take you to prison. I've only come to ask you some questions about the day the last Lady Halyard was buried." He stopped sniveling then, his eyes trying to focus and he raised one thin, dirt-grimed hand to them, peering at me as if a light had blinded him.

"If you ain't her, then, be you the other one?" I felt my skin crawl. They were almost the words that Amelle had used, but when he spoke them they contained a meaning wicked and sinister beyond my fathoming.

"No," I said, "I'm not the other one. I am Lady Halyard, Lord Halyard's second wife." I felt a cold wave of nausea sweep over me. I was afraid for a moment I was going to be ill. Little beads of clammy, cold perspiration stood out on my upper lip and forehead. I knew exactly how Halyard had felt in the coach as we were coming nearer and nearer to Longfields, how ill he had been at the instant he remembered what Arabella had told him. It had been something he did not want to hear or to remember again as long as he lived. For him, as for me now, it was a moment when something momentous had happened, after which nothing could ever be the same again. Like one possessed, I went on with my questioning.

"I want to ask you about a woman who was buried on the

same day as the first Lady Halyard, a woman named Agnes Hill." For a moment he was still as an animal who thinks that by being so it is invisible to the hunter, and then he went on, his voice high pitched.

"Aye, and that be what I was telling you about. It's because of what happened to the lady and the other one that I be going to prison or to hang."

"What happened?" I asked sharply. "What happened to Lady Halyard and to Agnes Hill?"

"There she was, you see. She and the other one. Two ladies from the big house to be buried on the same day. Both of them laid out in their coffins in the crypt." He put his hand before his eyes to hide what he had seen so long ago from his present sight.

"I never seen such before or since. God is my witness, I wish I'd been blind so I'd have never seen neither of them. They was all burned like, their faces too." He stopped as if I could see them both as well and would not want him to go on with the rest of it, but I would give him no escape.

"It was my job, you see. It was because I was sexton at the church, it was because it was my job to put the lids on both their coffins that I seen it."

"See what? What did you see?"

"A ring," he whispered. "A ring with a red stone, a stone that looked like blood. I knew it must be worth a deal of money, a stone like that, and so I says to myself, what good would a ring like that do her and she being like she was. I meant to give some money to the poor." He looked to me but I could offer him no hope that I either could believe or condone what he had done.

"I meant to give some money to the poor," he repeated, "and to keep a bit beside for me. And why not, I got nothing, you see; no kin, no proper home. There's no one to do for Will Green. What harm could it do her for me to have the ring, tell me that if you can?" But I could tell him nothing. Indeed, what harm would it have done to anyone if this nearly blind old man had had a ring instead of its going into a tomb with a dead woman to remain there till the last trump sounded.

"I did not mean to keep it, not all the money." Now he

was sniveling again. "I swear it. " For one terrible moment I thought he meant to kneel and beg my forgiveness. Instead he gave a cry of anguish. "I done it." The cry had burst from him like a confession. "I took the ring from her finger. It must have been the devil made me do it." His voice now fell almost to a whisper while he recounted what he remembered of his crime.

"I had to work to get it from her hand and I held it up to a candle so I could see it. It's dark down there, you see. So I held the ring up to the candle and that was when it happened." He began to tremble again, shaking so hard his teeth chattered, his eyes growing large in their sunken sockets.

"What happened?" I demanded. "Tell me, you've come too far to stop now." He stood, mute with shock.

"Tell me."

"She moved. One of them moved. One of them was alive. I was scared half out of my wits thinking it was the one I took the ring from and that it was the devil's way of punishing me. I was afraid she would rise up from the dead and put her hands on me. And then I thought I heard someone coming along the passageway, the passage from the big house, and I ran up the stairs and through the church and ran away. I ran and hid. I sent them word I was sick and couldn't come again." Even now I saw he was trembling as if a fever had seized him.

"I stayed away that day and the next and when I came back both of them was shut in their tombs. They're buried now in the crypt, so they are. Only in the night I think I hear one of them. I see one of them moving. I hear her cry out and I know one of them wasn't dead when they buried her." He began to cry, rocking back and forth, mourning for what was done and could not now or forever more be undone.

"But you can't be sure," I said, trying to let him go free, for no creature should be held in such a grip of guilt. "You can't be sure she was alive."

"Oh yes," he said defiantly, "I'm sure. I know. Old Will knows one of them was alive."

I could not deal with the horror of what he had done or

what he had told me. I, like Will Green, wanted to shut it away, for such knowledge would surely drive one mad. But I heard myself cry out, "Which one was alive? Which one, tell me for the love of God, which one?" And as I said the words I remembered Halyard's cry from the hellish depth of his delirium, felt his hands upon my throat, holding me as if he meant to kill me, and I understood at last what those words might have meant.

"I don't know," Will Green moaned, "which one was alive. I don't know, I tell you. They both been so burned in the fire they hadn't no faces. The hands was so raw and twisted you couldn't have told one lady from the other."

Oh my God, I thought, let this be over, let me get away now. What good would it do me now to know whether it had been Agnes Hill or Arabella who had been buried alive in her coffin. It no longer mattered what either had done in life or what either of them might have meant to Halyard. Neither of them had deserved such a death and yet, at last, there was some tangible piece of evidence from all the dark dreams and shadows, something more than mere imagining, however horribly it had been come by. The ring Will Green had taken from a woman's hand was something real at last, something one could see and use as evidence.

Even if the old man was mad and making up half of it, whoever had worn the ring, whoever it had belonged to, someone would be sure to recognize it and I would know if Halyard had given the ring as a love token to his mistress or if had been a part of the inheritance and had belonged to Arabella.

"Where is the ring?" I asked. "Do you still have it?" He nodded, his head turning up and down as if on a hinge.

"I hid it," he said, as if he were proud of his cunning. "I didn't want it no more, you see, not after what had happened. I would have given it back to her but how can you give a ring to a woman in her tomb."

"Then I want it," I said. "If you will give me the ring I will pay you for it. If you don't have the ring you won't have to worry about it anymore."

"But," he said, "what if they come for me? What if they

271

put me in prison? If I give you the ring you'll send them to get me."

"No," I said, "no one will come, I promise you. If you give me the ring I won't say anything, you may depend upon it. I won't say anything to anyone, it will be our secret, yours and mine. If I have it then you won't be responsible for it. You won't have to think about the ring anymore." I saw him sigh, the burden of his guilt lifting from his shoulders. "I'll give you money," I said. "You'll be able to have some comforts, some good food and warm clothes. You can have one of the women in the village come in to clean and cook your supper for you. You'll be looked after and taken care of. You won't have to worry about prison or hanging anymore." He began to cry again with great, wracking sobs as if a dam had broken and at last the terror of death behind bars or upon the gallows was gone.

He went to the heap of ragged quilts that covered the bare frame of his bed and began to dig at the earth beneath it like a terrier who has at last remembered where he has hidden his bone.

"I hid it," he said. "I hid it." At last he turned up a battered box and, prying it open, groped inside and then stood triumphantly and handed me the ring. With it he gave me all the guilt for his crime and in return I gave him some gold and silver. As he held the coins, turning them over one by one, I edged toward the door. I could not find it in my heart to say goodbye to him. I now had proof in my hand, though proof of what I was not yet sure. But someone at Longfields would remember to whom the ring had belonged. I held it like a passport, a talisman that would carry me to the truth.

Chapter Sixteen

I had gone to Will Green to ask him what he knew of the two women who had been buried at Longfields church on the same day. I had meant to ask Will Green how old Agnes Hill had been and what sort of woman she was, pretty or plain. But what he had told me was so horrible I still had difficulty in accepting it, let alone coming to terms with it.

Was Will Green telling the truth or had his conscience played him tricks? Had he only imagined that he had seen one of them move her hand and reach out toward him? He was old and a little mad. Perhaps he had been addled on that day too or perhaps the events, real or imagined, had driven him to hallucinate, just as Halyard had fled from the reality of that fire. He had sworn that he had tried to save Arabella from the flames and he had the scars on his hands. But had he really been trying to save Arabella or to save Agnes Hill?

If he had hated Arabella would he have tried to save her? He had told me they had had a bitter quarrel and that she had led him down the corridor to a room that was the scene of her own immolation.

It was dusk. The village was quiet and lighted lamps began to show in the windows of the cottages. Farmers had
come in from the fields, shopkeepers home for the evening meal. Inside those humble houses there were happy
families, wives who loved their husbands, parents who
loved their children. Tonight I would go back to the great
splendor of Longfields where ghosts cried in the night,
where specters walked the halls, where memory must be
drugged or drunk away, a house where a husband and
wife lived separated from each other and a child went un-
loved.

Once past the high street and inside the gates I began to
run. There were no villagers to see me now and I ran,
arms outstretched, as if I hoped to take flight and leave the
world behind. As I came up the rise toward the house,
there in the forecourt I saw a large, ornate, old-fashioned
coach and four.

I thought Tom Grace had come at last. We knew no one
else who would call. I had hoped that he would come to
keep Halyard company, and me, for Tom Grace was the
only person we could both talk to. Yet now with the ruby
ring in my pocket I was not sure this was the hour I would
have chosen for him to arrive.

Yet perhaps it was for the best. What Halyard could not
remember, Tom Grace might help him to recall. He had
been there the summer Rupert and Arabella and Halyard
had first met. He had known them and Amelia too. They
had all joked together about that trysting tree with the initials *AH* carved on it, initials which might have stood for
Arabella or Amelia Halyard or, as I now realized, for
Agnes Hill. Tom Grace knew them all better than anyone
else and that must be of some help both to Halyard and to
me. I rushed up the steps and inside, expecting to greet
him, but it was not Tom Grace I found in the hall, it was
Mrs. Griffin.

She was so upset that she was near tears. I never could
have imagined that there was anything or anyone on earth
that could have upset her equilibrium to this degree.

"Oh, thank goodness you've come back. I've been look-

274

ing for you everywhere. She's here in the drawing room. She insisted she would wait for you. She refused to see Lord Halyard although I have told him she is here. I've done my best, Lady Halyard. I've lighted the fires and served the tea, but now she will not let me come in the drawing room. She has sent me out like a scullery maid."

"It's all right, Mrs. Griffin," I said, trying to calm her. "I am sure you've done your best." But Mrs. Griffin was too agitated to listen.

"She wanted to see the child." Mrs. Griffin wrung her hands. "So I sent for Amelle. It took only a moment to fetch her. She was walking in the garden with Rose. When Rose brought Amelle in she set upon her, accused Rose of having kept her waiting and of being rude and ill mannered to her."

"Never mind," I said, "please calm yourself and tell me who is here. Who is causing all this fuss?" Her eyes went wide. She stood taken aback, as if she were amazed I had not already guessed.

"It is your grandmother, Lady Blessing, or so she claims. She says she's come to see you. I could not very well turn her away."

"No," I said drily, "I'm sure you've done the best you could under the circumstances. Now go and tell Rose I apologize for my grandmother's behavior."

I was sure Mrs. Griffin could not have turned my grandmother away at the door but I wished she had not come. I did not ever want to see my grandmother and especially not here tonight. I took off my cloak and smoothed my hair and went into the drawing room.

She stood very straight, carrying herself like a queen instead of a mere countess in her own right. She wore a dress of rich material and a headdress that had been fashionable in the last century. In her hand she carried a walking stick, which she was now using to poke at the dust covers or at furniture that stood in her path. When she heard me open the door she wheeled about sharply, expecting, I suppose, to find some servant she could bully but there I stood instead.

"Catherine?" she asked. She seemed not to believe her own eyes. Then she said, in a voice as imperious as it was demanding, "Well don't stand there gawking, gel, come let me have a look at you." I went to her and allowed her to stare me up and down. "You look like your father, more's the pity."

As I could think of no civil reply I kept silent, knowing she would have more to say, and she did. Proud and cruel as some tartar queen she began a tirade in a ringing tone that allowed no disagreement.

"I am very angry," she said, "very angry indeed to think that you have come to England and have been here all this time without informing me of the fact. I only heard you were here by chance," she said. "Someone sent me a clipping from the *Morning Post,* an account of Lord Halyard's return and with it a note asking if Lady Halyard was not the late Major Rainey's daughter." She stopped, her eyes wide with fury. "Think of it, my granddaughter actually married to that man.

"Well, I'll say this for you, you are an even bigger fool than your mother. At least she was married for love. Your father was unsuitable in every way but even I never doubted that he loved her. For them it was all for love and the world well lost. But he never took a penny of her money. Your situation is worse by a hundredfold. Now I have seen you it is obvious why he married you. I suspected it, of course, but now I am sure." She became so agitated by her suspicions that she paused long enough to dig her cane into the carpet, giving it a few punishing blows before she could continue.

"He married you because he knew about your fortune. There can be no other reason. He ran through his own long ago. I daresay he found out you were my heiress and couldn't wait to woo you."

I remembered our journey to Gibraltar and Halyard's refusal to ask me to marry him until he knew his identity. Was it possible he had not asked me to marry him until he had learned of my grandmother's fortune from Sir Hum-

phrey? It was in Gibraltar he had found out I was no poor
soldier's daughter but heiress to Lady Blessing's fortune.

"Well, he won't have it," she said firmly, "not a penny.
I've come here at some peril to take you home with me, to
get you away from his unsavory influence. Not that you
deserve such kindness but it is my duty to rescue you. I
would never rest in my grave if I thought I had left you
here to end up like poor Arabella Halyard. Arabella was
everything you are not. She had wit and brains and beauty
and look what happened to her."

"Madame," I tried to interrupt, but she would not be put
off.

"Be quiet, let me finish. You may think you know what
you are doing, he may have gulled you into believing he
wanted you for his wife but I know he cannot have told
you the truth about himself or you would never have married him."

What was it she thought she knew of Arabella or Halyard that would have made me refuse to marry him?

"What makes you feel you know the truth?" I asked.

"It was common gossip here in England. All the world
knew that he kept Arabella a prisoner at Longfields and
when she found out he kept his mistress in the same house
and threatened to expose him, he killed her." She seemed
to relish her revelation. I put my hand into my pocket and
held onto the ruby ring.

"I know nothing of the great world," I said, "but surely
keeping a mistress cannot be a reason for murder. Surely
this was not the first time a man of fashion kept a mistress
or a child in the house with his wife. They say that in England it is done everywhere by the best people."

"You know nothing," she said sharply. "Don't try to pretend to wisdom you don't possess. Yes, men have had their
mistresses and women their lovers but always the forms,
the rules of discreet conduct were maintained. Even the
Duchess of Devonshire and that menage never caused an
open scandal. No, my dear, this was quite different. This
was a situation Arabella could not be expected to counte-

277

nance and he killed her for it. If he had let her go, if she had separated from him legally, it would have cost him what was left of her fortune and what little he had left of his reputation, though why any right-minded person ever received him in decent society in the first place I will never know. It is all true, all they ever said of him. I know it for a fact. Not an hour ago I saw that child with my own eyes. One look was all that was needed to know who she is. It is no good denying that that child is a Halyard."

Now I had nothing to say in Halyard's defense. Amelle was a Halyard, I had seen that for myself, but I tried one last time to find some excuse for him.

"And what if she is his child?" I said. "That may be true. Other men have had children out of wedlock. Perhaps he did keep his daughter here and her mother too, but as for murder, I don't believe he killed Arabella any more than I believe he was responsible for the death of Agnes Hill. The fire was an accident. For all you know Agnes Hill might have been a servant who came to Longfields when Amelia was ill. What proof is there that Agnes Hill was his mistress or Amelle's mother?" She stood staring at me in amazement.

"Are you completely simple?" she demanded incredulously. "Why would you mention anyone named Agnes Hill? Who, pray, is Agnes Hill? I've never heard of an Agnes Hill in all of my life. Why bring a servant into this conversation?"

"But," I stammered, my confidence falling like a feather on the wind. "But I thought you meant that the woman who lived here and died in the fire with Arabella was Halyard's mistress. Her name was Agnes Hill."

"Oh, Lord give me strength, he's made a fool of you for fair. No one ever said anyone named Agnes Hill was his mistress for the very good reason that everyone knew all along that Halyard's mistress was his own sister, Amelia Halyard."

I know she said more but I did not hear it. I was struck deaf as my father said soldiers often were from too much cannon fire. What the world had said and the mob had ridiculed, what no friend would tell me was that Halyard and his sister were lovers. The scandal that had followed the fire was not merely because they considered him a murderer but because he had indeed broken the rule by which society, and all people everywhere, lived, a taboo as ancient as it was unspeakable. This then was what they had said of him, what they had whispered behind his back, had written in verse and printed in cartoons. For this the mob had jeered and called him everything that was monstrous and vile, and when he could not deny it any longer, he had left England meaning never to return. It was more terrible than anything I had imagined. It could not, must not be true.

"It is not true," I said. I felt as if my lips were made of ice. "It is not true." It was wicked and spiteful of her to say such awful things to me.

"How can you be sure it is not true?"

"He loved Amelia," I said, "yes, that is true. But Amelia was dead long before Arabella came to Longfields as a bride." She pitied me, I could see it in her face.

"Oh, you poor deluded child. It was what he wanted the world to believe, that Amelia was dead. But it was obvious to me she was here all the time, and after the child was born he kept them both hidden here in this house. They had always been lovers. It was for his sister, not Arabella, that he wrote that vile, disgusting poem. Anyone with half an eye could read between the lines and see it was his sister he loved. She was the forbidden love he wrote about. Any sensible soul would have known then what a monster he was. Have you read *The Nomad*?"

I nodded dumbly.

"But surely you saw it was all about an unholy love whose name he was forbidden to speak. What did you think he meant? And the child. Amelle was the name of the child born out of that unholy love while he was away."

"Amelle is his ward," I said, and I thought of how much she looked like him and of the way he refused to see her.

"No," she went on, savoring every moment, "Amelia was his mistress and Amelle is their child. Only a ninny of a girl

279

like you, raised in some outlandish place like Spain by a malcontent father like yours, could possibly believe otherwise. Only a fool like you could believe what Halyard told you. Oh, he is a master of wickedness and seduction. He was not even true to his own sister, why should he be true to you? I suppose he told you he loved you, and that he needed you, but all he wanted was your fortune."

It could not be true what she was saying. He had wanted me. At first he had refused me, would not say he loved me until he had something he could offer me. It could not be true that all those days were sham and show. I had not imagined the passion we had shared. I had not invented the nights we lay in each other's arms, and as if to echo my thoughts, a voice came from the shadows by the door.

"I did love Catherine, I loved her from the first and I love her now." It was Halyard's voice. He stood, dressed in his blue coat, his neckcloth tied in a perfect cascade of white linen. For the first time in weeks he had taken great care with his appearance and though the lines of fatigue and strain were still visible in his face I knew I had never seen him more handsome nor had I ever felt more drawn to him. How much had he heard of our conversation, how long had he been standing there listening to all the horrible things my grandmother had said of him?

"I will love Catherine all my life," he said quietly, looking at my grandmother but not at me.

"Those are pretty words but they won't wash with me," she said. "The less we say to each other the better. I've come to take Catherine home with me."

"She is free to go when she pleases, Lady Blessing. Catherine is not my prisoner. In fact, if any of what you have been telling her is true, she should go away from Longfields and from me. I have already asked her to go."

"No," I said, stepping toward him, "I don't believe what she has said. I don't believe her. You knew one day she would try to take me away. Just because she says such wicked things does not make them true. Tell her she is wrong. Tell her what you told me, that your sister Amelia died the year you were away, that Arabella took care of her and was with her when she died. You said that Arabella came to Plymouth to tell you the news that Amelia was dead."

"Yes, that is what I told you and I believed Amelia was dead because Arabella told me so, just as I believed Amelia had been buried in Wales."

"I cannot stay here to listen to this." My grandmother pointed her cane at him. "He twists everything to his advantage. There's not a word of truth in him. If you want to know what I believe, I believe Amelia is here now, in this house. I believe they're still lovers. I think Arabella died in that fire but not his precious sister." Halyard stared at her.

"Then who was buried that day with Arabella?" he demanded. "Who was Agnes Hill?"

"I'll tell you who she was, just another of your tricks. You used a servant's name because you did not want the truth to come out. When that deception did not work, when the rumors began to spread all over London, you had to get away and so you left England saying you would not return. You went out of the country only to bide your time, building up sympathy for yourself by pretending to have been lost at sea and now you're back you're still pretending, giving it out all over London that you have lost your memory, as if by that you could absolve yourself from all your guilt. Well, I'm not such a gudgeon as to take that bait. I see through you even if Catherine does not."

There was a silence in the room as she rested her case from which he seemed unable to defend himself. The fire began to flicker and die and with it all my hopes. Halyard looked at me with infinite sadness.

"I loved you, Catherine, but I should not have married you. I would not have done so if I had known I would bring you to this. I am sorry for the way I have treated you but I thought you would be safer if you stayed away from me. I felt I was cursed and that by being with me you would be in danger. I hope that one day you will forgive me the hurt I have caused you but there is something in me and something in this house that is evil. Whatever you have sensed or seen in this house let it remain a secret of these walls. And now I think it would be better for you to do as your grandmother asks and to go with her."

I wanted to believe he loved me just as I wanted to believe Agnes Hill was a servant who had died in the fire and was now buried with Arabella. I would even rather believe that he had been capable of murdering Arabella than believe he was guilty of . . . and there my mind stopped. I found that like Tom Grace and Kean and Wellington, I could not speak the name of the crime the world had accused him of.

"You must know," he said, "that I loved you there by the sea in our magic cave, loved you more than anything else in this life or the next."

Again there was a silence in the room until I felt I was drowning. I put my hand in my pocket and drew out the ruby ring I had got from Will Green. I kept it hidden in my palm.

"If you loved me then answer me one question, even if the truth is painful."

"If I can," he said.

"Look," I said to Halyard, "look at this and tell me who it belongs to." I held out my hand and opened it. The ring lay in the hollow of my palm like a drop of blood and without a moment's hesitation he said, "Why, it's Amelia's ring. Wherever did you find it?"

"I got it from Will Green," I said, "just this afternoon. He took it from the hand of one of the women who was buried at Longfields." The cold of the grave was not as killing as the cold in my heart. "Was it Amelia?" I asked him. "Was it Amelia who was buried with Arabella?" I watched his face and I thought soon he will answer and if he tells me it was true, that it was Amelia who was buried that day, then all the rest I had heard was true as well. He had had a mistress and she had been his sister Amelia and Amelle was their child, the child of incest.

Lady Blessing frowned and pointed her stick in his direction like an instrument of accusation.

"Well," she said, "why don't you answer? What have you

282

to say for yourself now, Lord Halyard?" He looked at her but not at me. Could he not face me, was that it?

"I cannot deny," he said to her, "what I cannot remember. All I can do is to try to find the truth. I will go to London and see the doctor who recommended Agnes Hill as a nurse for Amelia during her last illness. It has been a long time ago but I will make enquiries, it is all that I can do."

Then he turned to me, his eyes no longer cold, but warm, full of an expression of such tenderness that it broke my heart in two. "Catherine, on the chance your grandmother is right about me I think you must go with her, you should not stay here. Whatever I find, no matter what lies hidden in the past, you must know that I will always love you. I promised your father no harm would come to you, that I would always be your friend." He held out his hand and took mine. He bowed and kissed it as formally as if he were taking his final leave of court. Before I could ask him to stay he was gone. I called out to him but he did not hear and as I started to follow him my grandmother held up her cane like a barrier to bar my way.

"Let him go and good riddance. You can count yourself lucky that I came in time. Now pack your things. I wouldn't spend a night under that man's roof for all the tea in India. You must have some clothes, surely he has provided you with something better than that dress you are wearing."

I remembered how eager Halyard had been to shower me with dresses and jewels, to take me out in London to the theatre and to dine. He had been so happy then and he had wanted to make me happy too.

"Hurry, Catherine, I'm not used to being kept waiting." I turned and faced her.

"There is no need for you to wait. I did not ask you to come and I do not ask you to stay. I am not going with you." She seemed unable to believe what she had heard.

"Why, but why? You can't believe him after what I have told you." I tried to think of some argument that would convince her that I was never going with her.

"You said that you came for me because you felt it was your duty. I too have a duty. Mine is to my husband."

"It is madness for you to make such a rash decision. Do you wish to die here like Arabella?"

"No, but I will stay no matter what he finds out about the past. Not just because I love him and once he loved me, but he needs me and you do not. You need no one but yourself." Our eyes met like swords and I thought how different my mother's life and mine would have been had this woman been kind and loving.

"Very well," she said icily. She knew that she was beaten but she wished to have the last word. "You are as stubborn as your mother was before you but remember this was your chance to come with me, to have wealth and position, to live under my protection. I came for you but only this one time. From tonight on you need never look to me for sympathy or help. As for the fortune that will come to you when I die, if I could I would leave it to dogs or cats or to the nation before I would see it come to you," and she swept past me, her pride carrying her like a wind.

She was a sad, old woman who would live out her life alone. She had lost my mother and now she had lost me. Yet I could not feel sorry for her, my thoughts were all for Halyard. He had gone and I did not know if he would ever return.

That night, for the first time, I was alone at Longfields.

Chapter Seventeen

Without Halyard the heart had gone out of the house and out of me. It hurt me to think he would have let me go so easily. He had said he loved me but he had not tried to keep me. Instead he had been willing to send me away from Longfields and from him to live with my grandmother. It was one more contradiction in his character and behavior to say on the one hand that he loved me, and then to send me to the one woman from whom he had promised to protect me. Yet now it seemed I had reason for new hope. If he had not been able to remember Agnes Hill then perhaps, locked in his memory, was an explanation that would clear him of all the rumors and the gossip.

In the days that followed his departure I tried to keep up my spirits and to pretend for Amelle's sake that everything was going to be all right. I did not want Amelle to guess how worried and anxious I was when I heard nothing from Halyard and he did not return. Waiting for him seemed an endless, barren waste of days and yet even in those dark times there was some light. The bond between Amelle and me grew stronger and I came to love her more than I would have thought possible. Her face became as dear to me as his had been and when I looked into her eyes it made me feel closer to him. Whoever her parents had been, whatever they had done, she deserved to be happy; to laugh and play and to live in the sun.

I tried to make a little island for her when we were together, full of warmth and affection, where she could grow into the happy woman I knew was possible. I taught her songs and games and read to her, and in those hours we spent together I sometimes almost forgot the heavy weight of my own heart.

But always, when she had gone back to her nursery, there were the long, lonely nights that no lamp could light nor fire could warm. All around me the house seemed filled with despair. I wondered if the spring would ever come to Longfields as the wind blew and the hard rain fell against the windows, and it seemed the world outside was weeping for all that I had lost. On those nights I slept badly, tossing and turning, and as I heard the floors creak and the wind in the chimneys, I imagined I heard the sounds of rats in the wainscoting and the moaning of ghosts walking up and down the galleries. I became so accustomed to my fancy that when in the night I did hear the door to my room opening and the sound of footsteps on the floor I thought it was only my imagination once more till I felt a cold, small hand laid on mine. But it was no ghost who stood by me, it was Amelle. Her eyes were wide and filled with fear.

"What is it?" I said. She stood in her thin white nightgown shivering in the dark but she did not speak. She seemed to be in a state of shock.

"What are you doing out of bed? Where is your robe, you are freezing." I lifted her up into the bed beside me. Her little feet were bare and cold as lumps of ice. As I wrapped her in the comforter she seemed no larger than a little sparrow, her little arms and legs no more than twigs. "What is it?" I asked again. "Did something wake you?" She buried her face in my neck and I felt her breath come and go.

286

"She has come back," she said. I held her, cradling her, rocking her in my arms.

"Oh no," I said, "it's only a bad dream. Go back to sleep." She shook her head and burrowed closer to me.

"She's there, I saw her. The other one has come back again." My heart began to pound and now I wished I could believe it was a dream.

"Where was she?" I asked. "Where did you see her?"

"She came to my room and stood by my bed. When she left I followed her. I saw her on the stairs but then she disappeared and I came to you. You won't let her take me away, will you?"

"No," I said, "I won't let her take you away. You can stay here tonight and sleep with me, and when you wake up everything will be all right, I promise you." I pulled the covers up around her and I waited for a time, thinking Amelle was asleep before I got out of bed, but she was still awake.

"Where are you going?" she asked. Her hand clutched at my sleeve.

"I am going to build up the fire," I said, "and then I'll get you some hot milk. You stay in the warm bed and close your eyes." As I brushed the ringlets from her forehead I saw the furrows in her brow. They did not belong in childhood. It was not right she should be so frightened. I sang to her softly and her eyes grew heavy and her breathing more regular.

"I can stay here all night?" she said, half-asleep.

"Yes."

"You promise?"

"Yes, I promise." I bent and kissed her. I loosed her fingers from my sleeve and slipped away from the bed. "I'll leave the light while I am gone." She sighed and fell asleep.

Had Amelle seen someone in her room? Had she followed her down the stairs? Much as I would have liked to believe it had been a dream I knew in my heart it had not. Amelle had seen someone and as there were no ghosts in

287

this house there was a woman who walked in the night, someone who wept, who once had come to my room and to Halyard's. He too had seen her but who was she, this woman in the night? If Amelia and Arabella and Agnes Hill were all dead, who was here now?

I was worn out with wondering, tired of asking questions to which there were no answers, tired of the power this unseen woman had over this house, over Halyard's life and mine.

I could no longer live in fear and dread of what I might discover if I looked for her, found her, confronted this specter. Before my courage could fail me I lit a candle and tiptoed to the door.

In the corridor I turned toward the west wing. It was dark and cold as I walked toward the doors to the west hall. I felt a growing determination to see for myself if there was anyone there or not. I had no key but Mrs. Griffin did. No matter what the hour I would ask her for it, let her say or think what she liked.

The day I had come to Longfields she had said I must think it odd she lived in the tower apartments and kept the maids so close to her. She had told me it was because Rose and Megan imagined they heard things in the night, but I knew now there was more than their imagining. Mrs. Griffin had chosen to live in that apartment because she would be close to the west wing, because she knew there was someone there. If there were trays of food left by the door it would be almost impossible for Mrs. Griffin not to know who they were for.

As I walked down the corridor my eyes became accustomed to the dark and I saw there would be no need to ask Mrs. Griffin for the key to the west wing. Someone had left the door open, like an invitation.

I knew that I was taking a risk as I opened the door wider and crossed the threshold into the west wing. A draft of cold, damp air caught at the candle flame and blew it out. All around me in the dark was the acrid smell of charred wood. I could no longer see clearly and I put out my hand only to find that I touched rough, cold plaster.

288

I could not see much in the dim light but I had the impression of fallen timbers and gaping holes. I remembered Mrs. Griffin's warning that the flooring was unsafe and then, as I made my way along, step by step, I saw a thin yellow line of light, a mere splinter of gold beneath a door. Someone was here.

I stood outside that door looking at the little line of light, undecided as to what I would do and then, without waiting to knock or give warning, I went in.

It was a large room plainly furnished. There was a coal fire burning in the grate. On a table beneath a lamp was some sewing and a pair of spectacles. To the right was a recessed wall bed with the curtains closed and on the left was an open door through which I saw another room almost as large as this with a bed, a dressing table, and a clothes press.

As I glanced back at the room it all seemed so homely and domestic a scene it might have been the subject for a still life. If I had seen it in a picture gallery I would have thought the mistress had just stepped out for a moment. There was nothing sinister or evil here, yet there was something wrong, something not quite right that I could not put my finger on, and then I saw the polished paneling on the far wall, paneling that had been left untouched in the fire. I knew it must be the original wood, for nothing about it was in keeping with the rest of the room. And then I saw what it was that had caught my attention. I felt stupid not to have noticed it before. It was an opening in the panel, a space large enough for me to pass through. I went to it to put my hand out, wanting to be sure it was no trick of the eye, but it was a space with nothing beyond, it seemed, but dark and air. I touched it, as one touches at a mirror to be sure of a reflection, and I saw that past it was a set of stone stairs that led down into an even deeper darkness.

I felt as if I had been mesmerized. I had come this far and now I could not turn back. I went through the open panel and down the stone steps. The courage that had fortified me when I had started deserted me before I was halfway. I knew I should go back but I was too proud or stubborn to turn and run away. So I went on, step by step, until I came to the bottom and the entrance to a tunnel.

In the dark I could not tell how long the tunnel was but I heard the drip of water and felt the slime beneath my feet. The place had long been shut up and unused. I knew that if I lived to be a hundred I would not forget that passageway. It was a place of pure horror; damp and foul, there was the smell of death in it, and even with that morbid thought in mind I did not dream that it would end in the crypt of Longfields' church with another door standing open, waiting for me to enter.

With a sickening shock I realized that the smell of death had not been in my imagination, it was real. The seeping decay, the conversion of matter, had made this place a hell that went before any hope of heaven and I realized that this tunnel must have been the first baron's passage, the tunnel he had had built so that he would not have to walk outside to church in bad weather. He had only to come down from his sitting room, walk beneath the courtyard through the crypt, and up to his pew to hear a sermon preached to please his ears. I wanted to laugh hysterically as one sometimes does at horror, laugh to lessen the fear or pain, but the laughter caught in my throat when I stood in the crypt and the full nature of that place was borne in on me. The pillars that supported the church floor were twisted like crippled branches of stone. The yawning arches beyond led to the walls in which the dead were sealed away and in the center of this cavern was a table, its top a slab of stone where bodies had been laid out awaiting burial, a place where two women, burned beyond recognition, had lain and where from the hand of one of them a greedy old man had taken a ruby ring.

It was here that Will Green believed one of those women had quickened and moved, a woman who had still been alive when the lid had been fixed on her coffin, and it seemed to me, alone in this horrible place, that I shared the full horror of her fate. Had she been conscious? Had she known at the end as the lid came down, what was happening? I felt as if I too was choking, stifled, clawing up at the coffin lid for want of air to breathe. I closed my eyes, gasping, trying to overcome my panic and when at last I felt a breath of air in my lungs I opened my eyes, and it was then I saw her.

A shadow, a specter, shrouded in white, slipped from behind one of the vaulted arches. The figure was draped from head to toe in a flowing robe of white. The head was veiled. It stood in silence as still as a carved effigy. I knew I saw this creature as surely as Amelle and Halyard had seen her for this was no ghost, this figure was real. I had only to take a step toward her to reach out and touch her to prove it. I felt panic change to icy dread. I felt my face turn to a mask of fear just as Halyard's face had done when he sat in his bed with his pistols pointed at my heart. It was this he must have seen behind me, this phantom dressed in white, like a bride, a specter he might well have believed was the result of laudanum or a nightmare, something that appears from the depths of delirium, and I heard myself cry out as he had long ago in Spain, cry out and echo Halyard's first words to me, "Which one are you, for the love of God, which one?" As I stood, rooted to the stones with horror, the figure moved slowly toward me, brushed past me, and disappeared into the tunnel from which I had come. I felt defiled, as if I had been infected by a leper's touch.

If I had been brave I would have followed after that phantom but though I knew it was made of real flesh and blood the idea of being confined, shut up in that dark tunnel with the unknown was beyond my courage. I ran after the vanishing figure only to shut the door and bar it. And then I stood leaning against the wood and found I was trembling uncontrollably. I do not know how long it was before my knees were strong enough to bear my weight again. I walked across the crypt and up the stairs into the vestry. Then I ran quickly down the center aisle of the church and out into the fresh night air. It seemed impossible that the outer world should still be here. Down in the village the lights showed pinpricks of silver here and there in the inky darkness. There were people at home in their houses, people in their beds, people who lived free of fear. As I walked toward the house I realized I had never thought I would be eager to be inside those walls. Since the day I had come to Longfields I had tried to get away from that house, which had seemed a prison to me, and now in the courtyard I saw a coach before the door. It was like some miracle. It was Halyard's coach. The front door was open and I heard his voice calling me.

As I entered the house Halyard was halfway up the stairs and Tom Grace was beside him. At first Halyard did not see me. I heard him as he called my name again. When I answered him from the hall below he turned, saw me, and ran to me and took me in his arms.

They were warm, sheltering arms. He held me close to him as he had not done in weeks. I clung to him, my head upon his shoulder and I felt weak. I must tell him what I had seen in the crypt but not just yet, not for a few precious moments. I had been so afraid that I would never see him again that I began to weep tears of relief, wept great wracking sobs that I could not control. Now he was here everything would be all right.

"Cat, what's the matter?" He kissed my hair, my face, and my lips; warm tender kisses and still I could not stop crying. I had been close to hysteria in the crypt and I had not given way, but now the dam had broken and the tears flowed like a pent-up river.

"I thought you were not coming back," I sobbed. "I thought I would never see you again."

"Oh Cat, no. No."

"You said I was to leave you and Longfields. You said I should go with my grandmother."

"And I thought you had." He held me closer to him but still the sobs continued. "When I came in and you did not answer I thought you had gone. I wouldn't blame you if you had, Cat, but never think that I would leave you, not ever. Now dry your eyes and come upstairs by the fire. You're trembling with the cold. What on earth have you been doing out of doors?" Again I clung to him, unable to tell him that at last I had seen the specter, the ghost who haunted Longfields.

He led me up the stairs into his apartment and even when I stood before the fire I would not let him go. When he sat in his familiar wing chair I sat on the floor beside him and held my arms about his knees, my head resting in his lap. I sat looking at the blazing, warming fire through tears that would not stop, clung to him as he caressed my hair. Tom Grace had turned aside, embarrassed, not wanting to be a witness to Halyard's hysterical wife, and now sensibly he poured out some brandy for us all. I still could not believe Halyard was here no matter how close I was to him.

"I thought I would never see you again," I said once more.

"Oh Catherine, my dear, I am sorry, but when I came into that drawing room and found your grandmother there with you, when I overheard what she was saying about me, it was the first time I had known what it was the world had accused me of and I confess it was a cruel shock.

"I had forgotten the charge against me and with good reason. To think that anyone could believe that I had been Amelia's lover, kept her as my mistress and that she had borne my child—what kind of mind invents such a story? Oh God, who could be so low?" I felt his fingers hard upon my shoulder. "Who could hate her and me enough to harm her memory in such a way?" Then he turned my face up to look at him. "When your grandmother said Amelia might still be alive, that I was still keeping her here as my mistress, I told you you should go. I had to have some time to think, to try to disprove what had been said to you and I wanted you out of this house because I was afraid for you. I have been afraid of what might happen to you ever since we came to Longfields. I knew there was something here, I felt it as I came to the door, something evil and terrible. If you thought it was weak of me to try to escape that evil by drugs and drink I tell you now it was my way of keeping you safe, in making someone in this house believe

293

I was too drunk to know what was going on. I felt I saw shadows everywhere; and when I was faced with your grandmother's monstrous story I fled in horror from the possibility any of it might be true. I think I was not myself again until I found I was in the coach on the London road."

His eyes left mine and looked into the fire. It seemed as if he hoped that there in the flames he would see some vision that would make all the past clear to him. I sat by his side and across the room Tom Grace leaned against a writing table, listening to Halyard as if he were a spectator at a play.

"It was a long journey," Halyard said, "and I had time to think, to try to put certain events in sequence, and by the time I came to London I had begun to make some small sense out of the chaos. If the charge against me was that I had always been Amelia's lover and had been even before I wrote *The Nomad*, if, as your grandmother claimed, it was about our guilty, sinful love, then it did not stand to reason that when the poem was published, anyone would have received me. If everyone knew of this forbidden liaison, knew it all the time, then why did the fashionable world accept me, make me the hero of their drawing rooms only to turn me out and revile me later for that same crime? It did not make sense. Something was very wrong, something out of order. In London I went straight to Tom Grace in the Albany. He had known me, had been my friend the summer I had met Arabella, the summer Arabella refused to marry me. Tom had gone with me on my travels. He was with me when I returned and Arabella came down to Plymouth to tell me Amelia was dead. If Amelia was alive why would Arabella have told me she was dead? If Amelia was alive Arabella would have known of it."

Yes, of course, I thought. It's true. If Rupert had thought Amelia was alive he would have married her. Arabella would not have married Halyard if she knew that Amelia was alive and she had suspected that they were lovers. If there had been a child surely Arabella would have known of it, and at last it seemed I had something left to hope for, some prospect of our old happiness.

"I never went back to Longfields," Halyard said, "after I was told Amelia was dead. I went on to London. If I had thought she was alive would I have done that? I love Amelia and you know it. No one was ever so dear to me in my life but you, Catherine, and that love was as pure as it is possible for love to be. Amelia was the one constant in my life until I met you.

"You know too when Arabella came to London saying she had changed her mind and was willing to marry me at last, I no longer cared for her in that way. I would not have married her, I think, if I had not been grateful to her for all I thought she had done for Amelia. Tom Grace knows that is true. He was my best man. He stood up with me. He knew how I felt about Arabella. He remembers how I felt then." Halyard paused and looked at Tom Grace to confirm what he had said.

"It is true," Tom Grace said. "Halyard's feelings toward Arabella had changed, he said as much to me at the time, but I thought it a passing mood. I should have taken him more seriously, I see that now. But then I thought it only a case of wounded pride because Arabella had refused him once before."

"No, I did not love Arabella when I married her. I was grateful to her but that was all. But while we were talking, Tom and I, I suddenly remembered the name of the doctor that Arabella said she had called in to examine Amelia. I remembered the doctor's name because it is the same as a cousin of Tom, a Dr. Morland. I thought if I could find him he could tell me when Amelia had died.

"At last I located him in Hampstead and Tom and I went to call upon him. At first Dr. Morland was reluctant to discuss the case. He had been called to see Amelia by Arabella, who had asked him to treat the matter with the greatest secrecy. But when I told him who I was and pressed him to tell me all he knew he broke down and confessed at last that he had gone down to Longfields to examine Amelia and he had found that she . . ." Halyard bent his head and put his hands before his eyes. "Tom must tell you the rest that Dr. Morland said for I cannot."

Tom Grace stood and walked about the room. He looked ill at ease, unsure of how to begin. From the first I had noticed that he looked more tired than Halyard. The time away from Longfields had improved Halyard's appearance. He was no longer as gaunt and haggard as he had been before he went away, although he must be weary from the journey, while Tom Grace looked as if he were under a great strain.

"As Halyard has told you we went out to Hampstead where we met this Dr. Morland. He told us that at Arabella's request he had gone down to Longfields where he found Amelia was suffering from delusions. She believed she had had a lover and that when she found out she was going to have a child her lover had abandoned her. She believed that she had been delivered of this child, which had later died. But she said she could still hear the child crying in the night, crying out for her. She was not violent unless she heard, or thought she heard..." Tom Grace corrected himself, "the child. But then she had to be restrained or she would walk about the house day and night, searching for her baby. She even went out upon the walk between the towers calling out for someone to help her find her lost child. If anyone tried to speak reason to her, to say that she had had no lover, no child, that it was all in her imagination, she became unmanageable and force had to be used to restrain her from doing herself and others harm."

I could not look at Halyard. My hand went out to him. What he had suffered by all this I could not guess.

"Dr. Morland suggested to Arabella that Amelia be put into a hospital but this Arabella refused, saying that she was sure Lord Halyard would not want the facts known to the world and that Amelia would receive better care at home. It was then Dr. Morland recommended a nurse for Amelia who had had great experience with such cases. Her name was . . ." He looked at Halyard.

"Her name was Agnes Hill." Halyard finished for him.

"I asked Dr. Morland when Amelia had died but he did not know. He had never seen Amelia again. He suggested that if Amelia was dead Arabella must have called in a local man instead of sending up to London for him. Dr. Morland then asked me how Agnes Hill was keeping. He did not know that she was supposed to be dead. In fact, he believed she was still alive."

"But," I gasped, "why would he think that?"

"Because," Halyard said quietly, "Dr. Morland still sends her wages to Longfields every quarter. That was the arrangement Arabella had made with him, that he should pay Agnes Hill's wages. The money comes to him from an account at Coutts' Bank."

Halyard and I looked at each other.

"Yes," Halyard said, "I know what you are thinking. You think perhaps the money comes from me, but that was our next stop, the bank. The money did not come from me. Arabella had arranged a special account that did not stop at her death."

"But if Agnes Hill is still alive, who was buried in the crypt?"

"Your grandmother claimed that I had only used Agnes Hill's name. She believed Amelia was still alive."

"But it was Amelia's ring that Will Green found," I said.

"It was then Halyard insisted we come down to Longfields at once." Tom Grace looked at Halyard, who nodded. "Halyard was afraid for you. On the way down he talked of nothing but getting here in time to see that you were safe. Just before Longton, he remembered something, something that affected him greatly. What it was he refused to tell me until he knew that you were safe. Believe me, I had never seen him so ill."

I too remembered that curve in the road and how Halyard had reacted.

"Thank God you are safe, Catherine. But what were you doing out in the night?"

"Not yet," I said. "First please tell me what it was you remembered." He sighed a long, sad sigh.

"I remembered at last what Arabella had told me. I re-

297

membered all that I had so wanted to forget. That night we had left London, flying down to the country because there were bailiffs in the hall, Arabella had been very quiet all the way until we came to that turn in the road. Then she said, 'Now we are almost at Longfields there is something I should tell you. It may come as a shock, but I lied to you.'

"'What about?' I asked, knowing how often she had already lied in our life together.

"'I lied to you when I said that Amelia was dead. She is still alive.' At first I did not understand her. 'Did you hear me?' she said. 'Amelia is alive at Longfields.' I was dumbfounded.

"'It can't be true,' I said to her. 'You told me she was dead. You came to Plymouth to tell me she was dead. You told me so and Rupert too.'

"'Oh, Rupert believed it was true,' she said and she was smiling. 'He believed all I told him. Rupert was almost as big a fool as Amelia or you.' She smiled again. I had never seen her more beautiful. Her green eyes were like emerald fire. There was an ivory fan in her lap and she began to play with it idly, as a cat does with a mouse.

"'When you went away,' she said, 'you left Amelia in my care. Not long after you had gone she asked me to come to Longfields. We walked in the knot garden and then into the hedgeway. We stood beneath the lime tree near the bench where you once asked me to marry you. Amelia said she was going to have a child. She was very happy at the prospect though it meant marrying Rupert before your return. She wanted to tell me first, she said, even before she told Rupert, because now we were going to be more than friends, we were going to be sisters. Poor Amelia, what a fool she was. She thought I cared for her when, in reality, I hated her.'

"'But why?' I asked her. 'What had she ever done to you?'

"'I hated Amelia,' Arabella said, 'just as I hated you.' She looked at me then, her green eyes cold. 'You have no right to be lord of Longfields. You are not fit to be master of that house any more than your sister is fit to marry Rupert. That house should have belonged to Rupert and to me. How I loathed you, with your drunken mother and your stupid sister. How I hated you all. Amelia was such a fool she made it easy for me to stop her marrying Rupert. 'Let me tell him about the child,' I said to her. 'Now that we are nearly sisters I have the right to ask,' and she agreed."

It seemed as Halyard spoke that I could hear Arabella's voice and see her face. I felt that she was with us here, now, in that room.

"When Arabella came back to Amelia the next day she told her that Rupert no longer cared for her, that he would not marry her and refused to recognize the child, but as her friend, her sister, Arabella agreed to stay with Amelia until the child was born. Mrs. Griffin arranged for rooms for them in the west wing. She dismissed any servants who were likely to gossip. No one was to know about Amelia's condition. There was not to be a breath of scandal. Through those months Arabella stayed with Amelia.

"When the child was born the labor was long and the delivery difficult. Arabella took the child and told Amelia that it had died but Amelia would not believe her. When she thought she heard the baby crying she went wild trying to find her child. It was then Arabella called in Dr. Morland who, when he saw Amelia's state of mind, said she must be confined and Agnes Hill came to act as Amelia's keeper. I could not believe," Halyard said, "in the sense of anything she told me. 'Why?' I asked Arabella. 'Why did you come to Plymouth to tell me Amelia was dead?'

"'Why,' she said, as if surprised that I should ask, 'I could not have Rupert think she was alive. I had told Rupert quite a different tale, and I thought, what a great surprise, what a homecoming it would be for you, to find her like that. But you did not go to Longfields,' she said, 'you went to London. In no time you were famous. Everybody knew your name and I decided it would be more amusing if I were to marry you. If I were your wife I could do whatever I pleased, live whatever sort of life I liked. You could never stop me for I could always threaten to tell the world about your precious sister. I could have all the dresses and the jewels that I liked, sign my name to any amount of gambling chits because I would threaten to tell the world about your mad sister and her child born out of wedlock. That's why I married you and I enjoyed it while it lasted. It is a pity I overplayed my hand. And now we're here on the road to Longfields I find I don't want to stay in the country, mewed up with nothing but dull county folk coming in to call. You'll have to find some money for me somewhere. You will have to sell Longfields.'

" 'I would never do that,' I said and she smiled again and said, 'We'll see, we'll see.'

"And that was how we came home to Longfields, Arabella and I. Perhaps I was a coward, but I could not bear to see Amelia or her child. I could not bear to think of her being wretched. I would see no one. I shut myself in my room. I was like a fox who had gone to ground. I drank too much but there was not enough brandy in the world to keep me from remembering what it was Arabella had told me. It was then I discovered that she had a lover. I had put up with all the rest. I had even suspected she had a lover in London but had not cared. But now she had brought him here into this house. It was a situation I could not endure. I went to her rooms, meaning to have it out with her.

"I said we could not go on as we were. One of us must go away and that I meant her to leave Longfields. She laughed at me as if I had made a joke. 'No,' she said, 'I'm your wife; your loyal, loving, devoted wife. You won't turn me out of doors. For all the world knows I am a paragon of virtue.'

"At last she said that if I turned her out she would make sure the world would know about Amelia and I knew she meant it. I was in an insane rage and I struck her and she smiled, her eyes were little narrow green slits. 'It was wrong of you to do that,' she said. 'Now I will make sure the world sees what I want it to.' She ran ahead of me down the corridor toward the west wing. I followed her, afraid of what she meant to do. She flung open the door to Amelia's room.

"Agnes Hill was there, I remember, but Arabella sent

300

her away, told her to get out. She dragged Amelia from the curtained bed. She was so old. Her hair was nearly white. Her eyes were vacant, dulled by all the pain that she had suffered. Arabella stood there, holding Amelia by the arm. If Amelia heard what Arabella was saying or knew what was happening she gave no sign of it.

"'Here,' Arabella said, 'here is my triumph.' She held onto Amelia as if she were a high card that she meant to play for great stakes. 'Who would the world believe?' she said, 'me or this mad creature? If you try to turn me out I will tell the world that you were your sister's lover. That the child is yours and that she went mad because of your use of her. Think what a scandal that will make.'

"'They will not believe you,' I said, but she only smiled.

"'They will believe me just as Rupert did when I told him Amelia had gone away to have your child. Rupert believed me, that is why he never came to Longfields to find her, that is why he never followed her. Look at her, Halyard, look at her. If you put me in the dock who will they believe, me or this mad thing? I have made her just as you see her now. She is my doing. I took the child she never knew had lived. I told her it was born dead. She does not even know the child exists. And when you die, Halyard, and I hope that it may be soon, then I will have Longfields. It will be Rupert's and mine.'

"As she spoke those words about the child I saw Amelia step forward and I saw Amelia's face. For that instant she had become clear in her mind. Her confusion had vanished and she knew what Arabella had done and she understood all the misery and torment it had meant to her.

"Amelia struck out at Arabella. It took her by surprise and she fell back against the table. The lamp went down in a crash. The fire leapt up, spreading across the tablecloth. It caught Arabella's dress. Suddenly she was in flames, Amelia still struggling with her. I tried to part them, to put out the fire. I called out for help, for Agnes Hill or Mrs. Griffin, but no one came. The two of them, Amelia and Arabella, were gripped in a struggle for life and death. I could not part them and out of their agony they struck at me and I fell with my head against the stone hearth. The last thing I remember before I lost consciousness was seeing them together in the flames and being horribly aware that I too had been burnt.

"When I regained consciousness I was told they were dead, both Arabella and Amelia. Mrs. Griffin and Agnes Hill had laid out the bodies for burial. They were already shrouded and in their coffins in the crypt. I think I knew what was on Mrs. Griffin's mind even before she spoke. She had loved Amelia and as everyone believed Amelia to be already dead, and to have been buried in Wales, why not let her memory rest? Why let the world know that she had borne a child and died mad in a tragic accident? Far better for there to be a little harmless deception. Why not have it thought that Agnes Hill had been buried with Arabella and not Amelia? I could pay Agnes Hill. She agreed to that. As she had no family and no home it did not matter to her how it was arranged.

"My hands were bandaged and very painful. I took some more laudanum and at last I fell asleep again. When I awoke I was not sure whether what I saw was from the opium or a delirium. The door opened, and there was someone in my room. I held up the lamp and then I saw her, a woman in a shroud, her face burned beyond recognition. I cried out for Mrs. Griffin, for Agnes Hill. I screamed out in the night, for one of the women they had sent to the crypt was alive. One had come back, crept up through the tunnel to the ruins of the west wing. She was there, now, standing before me, and I cried out, 'Which one are you, for the love of God, which one?' There was no way of knowing whether it was Arabella or Amelia. The ruby ring that had been on Amelia's hand was gone. One of them had lived, one had come back like a ghost to haunt this house and me.

"The day of the funeral, prayers were said for two women but one coffin was empty and at Longfields there was a woman who was alive but could not speak to tell me who she was.

"I could not stay in that house any longer knowing that

302

at night she might walk, might come to me again. I went to London, leaving Mrs. Griffin to see to the house and Agnes Hill to nurse the creature, only to find that in the town the story that Arabella had threatened to tell was already spread everywhere. By whom I did not know. I suspected Rupert but I had no proof and if not he, who would have hated me enough to tell it, that I had been my sister's lover, that she had borne me a child, and that when I had found out I had killed her for it, or at the very least had let her die in the fire rather than save her. If all the people whom I had counted as my friends believed such malicious slander, if all they said of me was true, I was not fit for England, and if they were wrong, England was not fit for me. I was determined to get away.

"I went to Dover and Tom Grace went with me to say goodbye."

"And you left me your coach as a present, you said, in case you did not return," Tom Grace said softly.

"I did not mean to return," Halyard said. "I wished to be dead. It was no accident that I went out in the storm. I meant for them to find the boat but not me. But in that storm, over the sound of the sea and the wind, I heard a voice calling me, a voice crying out to me to come and be her love. As I was drowning Catherine called out to me. You did, didn't you, Catherine?"

"Yes," I said, "I called to you. I knew that you would come to me one day."

"You willed me there, you willed me to live. With you my life began again. Everything was new, the pain was washed away. Yet even then I began to remember. I knew something kept me from you though I did not know what. I sometimes had brief flashes when I almost knew who I was. At last, when I knew my name, I thought I had the right to ask you to marry me. I only wanted to give you joy. It was not until the attack in London that I knew I had no right to have married you at all. I had no right to be any woman's husband. Arabella had told me that often enough. And when we came to Longfields, I could not bear to go in for I knew that in that house there was some-

303

thing evil; a specter, a ghost, a horror I did not want you to see."

"But I have seen her," I said. His face went ashen.

"When?"

"Tonight."

"Oh God."

"She'd been in Amelle's room. Amelle was frightened and came to me. When I got Amelle back to sleep I went to look for her. I wanted to find out who it was who terrorized this house. I was on my way to Mrs. Griffin's room when I saw the door to the west wing was open. I found the room where she lives."

"You saw her?" he asked.

I told them then about the open panel, the tunnel that ended in the crypt; of the figure in white and how I had run away from her and that when I had got back to the house I had heard him calling me.

"You should have told me then," he said.

"I couldn't," I said, "not then with your arms around me."

"She must still be in the house," Halyard said. "We must find her before she does more harm."

We went, the three of us, down the corridor to the west hall and through the dim passage toward that hidden room. The door was still open, nothing had been touched or disturbed. The only alteration was that the panel in the wall was closed. Halyard stood, undecided as to what we should do next, when suddenly we heard a stirring behind the curtains of the wall bed. Halyard flung them roughly aside to reveal, not our specter, but a stout, middle-aged woman who had obviously been asleep. She was even more surprised to see us than we her.

"Oh, m'lord," she said, "forgive me." She scrambled clumsily from the bed and looked about the room. I knew without being told that this was Agnes Hill.

"Where is she?" Halyard demanded.

"Gone," she said, her face crumpled in dismay. "Oh, it's my fault. I lay down for a moment and I must have dropped off. I must not have locked the door. I am sorry,

304

m'lord, but I get very tired. The days are so long, all alone with her."

"Where do you think she might be?" he asked. Agnes Hill considered for a moment.

"It's hard to say. She doesn't know where she is half the time. She could be in Amelle's room, or Lady Halyard's. She sometimes goes out onto the tower walk."

"Come on then," Halyard said. We followed him, Tom Grace and I. In the west hall, as we were about to start up the stairs to the tower, Tom Grace hesitated and hung back.

"She may be dangerous," Tom Grace said. Halyard nodded. "Shall I fetch your pistols, Halyard?"

"Yes," Halyard said. "They are in the coach." Tom Grace disappeared down the corridor, running toward the stairs, and we began to climb up toward the tower. Together we climbed to the door that led out onto the battlements. As we opened it we were met by a rush of cold, brisk wind.

She was there, as I had known she would be, looking out at the world beyond this house. She turned toward us, a woman veiled in white. He held my hand in his, held it tight. She had made his life a torment, a despair. We stood in silence, not knowing what to say, until the wind caught at her veil and blew it, wafting out into the dark night. What the flimsy covering had hidden and what was now sickeningly revealed was not a face but a blended mass, like melted wax; the nose and eyes and cheeks all twisted, the wisp of hair, the mouth that looked like nothing human. And yet she was alive, staring at us. She made a sound, not speech, not coherent, but something blurred and gutteral.

"Oh, my God." I knew I had said nothing, nor had Halyard. It was Tom Grace who had spoken. At the sound of his voice she held out her hands to him. They were twisted, deformed, webbed together like claws, catching at the air. She made a noise again that was beyond human comprehension. Not a name, but a sound, repeated over and over, which might have been his name. She was calling not to Halyard but to Tom Grace. She might not be recognizable either to Halyard or to Tom Grace but it was Tom Grace she knew, Tom Grace she was begging to embrace her as she came toward him.

He cried out again, "Oh God, how could you let her live like that? She was so beautiful. She would be better off dead than as she is. Why did you let her live no better than an animal?" The figure stopped. The head turned. There was no way to hide that deformity. She tried to put her hands up like a mask before her face, but they were an even more terrible reminder of what lay behind them.

"Why?" Tom Grace said, staring at her, and then he turned to Halyard. "Was it to punish Arabella and me?"

"What are you saying? Why would I want to punish you?"

Tom Grace's face was white, white as her dress. "You must have known. You must have suspected that Arabella and I were lovers for a long time." Halyard did not reply and then he said, "No, I suspected nothing." Tom Grace looked back then at what had been the beauty of Arabella Halyard.

"That summer we all met, we were attracted to each other. That summer, when I had come down to Longfields because I had no better place to go, she and I laughed at you from the very first. We both thought you were ridiculous with your pretensions of playing the great lord. We laughed at you behind your back, made fun of your lovesick moonings over her but you never even noticed.

"When you asked her to marry you she ran to tell me what a lark it had been. It was Arabella and I behind the hedge that you heard laughing. She thought it was a marvelous joke. 'Why,' she shrieked with laughter, 'why would he think I would marry him? He is nothing but a crippled boy.'"

"But you were my friend, I trusted you."

"Your friend? I despised you. When you asked me to go abroad with you I agreed because you were to pay the expenses. I became a paid companion because with your fortune you could afford to travel and to write. You could afford to go or stay as you pleased. It meant nothing to you to take me along as if you were my condescending patron on your grand tour. You paid and paid as though you could pay for friendship but I hated you far more than Arabella ever did."

"But why?"

"Because you wrote the poem. You won the fame. You took the place in the sun that should have, by rights, been mine. I was a better poet than you but the success, the laurel, went to you. You were the darling of Almack's, I was only invited when I went with you. You moved in all societies. Ah yes, you took the laurel, you took the prize and so, in exchange, when you married Arabella, I decided to take your wife. I made a cuckold of you, Halyard, even in London. I slept with your wife in your own house and you were too stupid to know it. Almost as stupid as Rupert Halyard, who believed all Arabella had told him about you and Amelia. He never once suspected that Amelia might be alive or that the child had been his. How Arabella and I laughed at the pair of you. Even here at Longfields, when you came down to escape your creditors, I came here as well and again you never suspected until the end. And then because she let you know of it.

"I know she played a dangerous game but then that was what she liked; loved more than me, to play deep, to go against the wind. She gambled away your fortune and signed the chits in your name. Perhaps she wanted to find out just how far she could go before you would kill her. That last night she sent me back to town and then she taunted you into provoking a scene. When the fire broke out I thought she was dead. It was I who spread the stories in London, her stories about you and Amelia being lovers, and about the child Amelle being yours. Arabella had shown me what to do. She left me revenge, like a legacy.

"I meant to drive you from England, from Longfields, to make it impossible for you ever to show your face. When I heard you were lost at sea and there was no word of you I rejoiced. As your friend, the last person to see you in England, at last I gained a sort of fame of my own. I was asked everywhere. Your publisher persuaded me to write an introduction to the posthumous edition of *The Nomad*. I lived in a reflected glory of your untimely death.

"No one could have been more shocked or surprised than I to hear that you had been seen in Gibraltar, that Calford's yacht had been sighted in the channel and that you were aboard on the way to Dover. I was afraid that you had come back because at last you had put two and two together and knew what I had done. I feared you were coming back to even the score, that's why I came to Dover, not out of friendship but out of fear and self-interest. And then like some supreme joke, you remembered nothing, you had come back to make a clean, bright new beginning. For you it was as if nothing had happened. To crown it all you were even happily married.

"It was Catherine who told me you could not remember anything and for that I thank her. It gave me time to make new plans, to think of some way I might get rid of you before you remembered the past. That night in London, outside your club, a stranger challenged you to a duel. If you had accepted it, it would have saved me a great deal of trouble, but you refused and I was obliged to hire assassins to attack you. It was Catherine who suspected something when she saw me in the shadows and saved you from being killed. Perhaps if I had not sent her that cartoon of you she would have been less wary."

"But why?" Halyard asked. "Why would you want me dead? You had taken my reputation, why would you want my life as well?"

"Oh, a dozen reasons, Halyard. But let us just say I could not bear your arrogance. Never once did you consider that that fee to write the introduction to *The Nomad* could be of any importance to me. All through the years that we have known each other you were so rich in money and in talent you never knew or considered what it meant to me to be your poor friend. With you dead I became important for the first time in my life. And you were so sure, so arrogant, you never once suspected that your enemy was I.

"I mean to kill you, Halyard, as I should have done long ago." He raised Halyard's pistols. "It is a pity Catherine must die too but that's fair, don't you think? Your life for the one you cost me and hers for Arabella's." He raised the pistols and took careful aim. In that instant Halyard stepped before me. Arabella's grotesque hands beckoned to Tom Grace. Was it because she wanted him to fire or did she mean him to stop? I would never know, for it was then that the first shot rang out, followed by a second.

Chapter Eighteen

For an instant we all stood like statues sculptured in stone. Then I saw Arabella's twisted face, her head thrown back, and her clawlike hands catching at her bosom where the blood, red as roses, was running down her white dress. I saw her sway and it seemed that she was taken by surprise. She looked at the blood on her hands and then up at Tom Grace. He too had a look of complete amazement, as if he had hoped yet to be able to undo what he had done, to recall the shot that had struck his accomplice, his confederate, his partner in evil. He stumbled toward her, his arms outstretched, and he held her for a moment in a macabre embrace, as Halyard turned to hold me. Just as they fell over the parapet together, I saw the bullet hole in Tom Grace's back.

Halyard and I stood until we heard the sound of their bodies hit the flagstone courtyard below. The night around us was so silent we dared not break the spell. We stood waiting, not wanting to look down at the two who had caused us such unhappiness, scarcely able to hope that the tragedy was ended, not understanding how it had happened that we were alive. It was then that we heard Rupert

Halyard's voice and turned together to face him. Rupert stood at the head of the tower stairs, his hunting gun in his hand.

"I came because I thought you were in danger, Catherine," Rupert said. "The curate came to Halyard Hall to tell me someone had broken into the crypt. I thought you were alone but when I arrived I saw Halyard's coach and the lights and I was afraid for you. When I came in I met Mrs. Griffin on the stairs. She said that you were here on the parapet. I came in time to hear what Tom Grace said.

"He was right, I was a fool. If I had not been I would have come to find Amelia, I would have followed her no matter what Arabella had told me. Then I might still have Amelia and our child. Arabella lied to me as she did to you, Halyard. When I saw what Tom Grace meant to do I fired. I have killed him. I am not sorry for that, but I am sorry to have shot him in the back. I would have preferred to see his face as he died.

"We must now add another murder to the Halyard name. I, who was so proud, so eager to keep that name untarnished, and who blamed you for bringing it to dishonor, I am a murderer."

In my mind if I had been judge and jury I would have acquitted Rupert Halyard for the murder of Tom Grace, but I was not judge nor jury; I could not pass sentence and let Rupert go free.

That night, or what was left of it, we three became conspirators. We made up a story to give to the world. Rupert's fiction was to be that he had seen Tom Grace about to shoot Arabella and had shot him in her defense. Tom's shot had struck Arabella by accident, at least that much was true. It was something to be told at the inquest that must surely follow.

To protect Rupert, Halyard would tell the same story though it meant opening up a past that he would have liked to have kept secret from the world. There would be no escape now from sordid gossip, for he was the notorious Lord Halyard. Every rumor would be twisted, bent, told, and retold about him as long as he lived and perhaps even afterward. Halyard, calm, sure of what he was asking, was adamant that before the Sheriff was called, or the inquiry begun, he wanted me to go away from Longfields and to take Amelle with me. He would not listen to my protests or allow me to refuse. He would not hear any of my arguments for he did not want me involved in the affair. Arabella had still been alive when we were married, our marriage was not binding, he had committed bigamy, and I was not his wife.

Halyard wanted me to take Amelle with me, for she must not live all her life branded as Rupert's bastard or Halyard's child of incest. I must take her away. Halyard knew I would not go without her. Amelle had become as dear to me as if she were my own. So in the end Halyard's arguments prevailed. I let him send Amelle and me to safety, for all that I could do for him was to leave him.

The trunks were hastily packed. Amelle was taken from my bed and carried down the stairs in Rupert's arms. It was the only time he had ever held his child and his expression as he handed her into the coach and gave her to my care was one of such tenderness that it made me weep. Then Halyard put the leather jewel pouch on the seat beside me. "They're yours," he said. "Once I promised you emeralds and diamonds, rubies and pearls. I have given you nothing but heartache and despair."

"No," I said. I felt the ache in my throat. "I don't want jewels, I want you. I want us to be as we were. I want us to be together." But he would not give me hope.

"Take them," he said, "if not for you, then for Amelle. I don't know if I can ever come to you. I don't know what I can salvage of this house or of my fortune." Then he closed the coach door and gave the signal to Old Jeb, who whipped up the horses, and by the time I could turn and look back again I could no longer see Halyard's face.

This time we took the road, not to London and to Dover, but south to Plymouth where I engaged passage on the packet to Gibraltar. I used my own name, the only name I was now entitled to. No one paid Amelle or me any special notice. We might have been any ordinary soldier's wife and child going out to join the garrison. No one took any interest in us. There were no whispers or hint of scandal. At Gibraltar I hired a cart and driver to take us up the coast upon the road of Hercules to Los Molinas. There, at the end of the journey, was the small white house upon the cliff. And on the terrace to meet us, as I had known they would be, were Maria Luz and Paco, who had kept everything with as much care as if it had been their own.

They were overjoyed to see me, to accept my story that Lord Halyard had been detained in England upon business. As for Amelle, she became their delight. Maria Luz took her into her arms and held Amelle, this motherless child, as she had taken me in and embraced me long ago.

There, in Spain, the winter was almost passed. In a few short weeks it was April. The spring weather was warm, the sky sunny, the sea inviting us to the shore. In those few weeks Amelle had changed. Her eyes were no longer frightened. Her palate was tempted by all the dishes Maria Luz prepared especially for her. Amelle grew in the warmth of all our attention and love. Each day I heard her chattering away on the terrace or singing in the kitchen with Maria Luz.

As we walked down the cliff path to the beach she held my hand firmly, without fear, with absolute trust. I showed her the beach hut. We made castles in the sand. I began to teach her to swim her first few strokes in the shallows of the sea, and all the while Amelle bloomed, I moved like one in a dream, remembering how, because I had willed it, he had come to me from that sea.

And in the night when I awoke from the depths of the old, dark and haunted nightmare, when sleep would not come again, I lit a candle and I began to write. Not to remember the past, for I would not forget what had been, but because it brought him closer to me to relive all the days we had spent together, and I would gladly have given as ransom all the jewels he had given me for one agate that then was mine; given every golden guinea of my present fortune to see his face again.

In the mornings, as we walked along the shore, Amelle

and I, gathering shells, the water lapping at the sands, I could almost see myself as I had been, that young, wild, carefree girl who once was me. It seemed sometimes I could see him walking toward us and I ran to meet him but it was only a mirage, a dream and nothing real.

The summer came, the sun was burning hot. At noon I lay beneath the thatch of the beach hut, Amelle drowsy beside me. I was thinking of how once he had lain there and I had heard the sea pulling at the sand.

"Listen," I said to her, "listen. You can hear the sands singing in the sea." But she was asleep and did not hear me or the voice behind me that said, "It is not the sands you hear, Catherine, but mermaids singing in the sea," and that day he was not an illusion or a mirage. He was there, standing with his arms stretched out to me. He was wearing an old shirt, open at the neck, rough corduroys, and a wide hat he had bought from the muleteer who had brought him up the coast. And I ran into his waiting arms as the sea bird flies home.

The End